SKYSEEKER PRINCESS

SI'EMPRA: THE STORYTELLER AND THE WEBCLEANER

SKYSEEKER

SI'EMPRA: THE STORYTELLER AND THE WEBCLEANER (BOOK 1)

PRINCESS

MIRIAM VERBEEK

Copyright © Miriam Verbeek

Published by Miriam Verbeek, 2017
www.miriamverbeek.com.au

This work is copyright. Apart from any use permitted under the Copyright Act 1968 (Commonwealth of Australia), no part may be reproduced by any process, nor may any other exclusive right be exercised, without the permission of Miriam Verbeek, Urunga, NSW, 2455.

This is a work of fiction. Names, characters, places and incidents are either the product of the author's imagination or used fictitiously. Any resemblance to actual persons, living or dead, events or locales is entirely coincidental.

Cover design by Andrew Brown

ISBN 978-0-6480245-0-7 Trade paperback
ISBN 978-0-6480245-1-4 ePub edition
ISBN 978-0-6480245-2-1 Kindle edition

*For my father,
who taught me to love books, imagination
and the word "why"*

Author's Note

THIS BOOK FITS INTO the fantasy genre but don't expect magic, giants, goblins, fairies, parallel universes, or other such trappings of the usual fantasy genre. There are certainly a few fantastical creatures in this story but they are not what drives the story. The people you'll meet don't have powers beyond what you and I possess. They form relationships, love and hate, appreciate beauty and fear being hurt; they struggle with life's issues in the same way you and I might, and they search for meaning in their lives.

The island of Si'Empra, like any country, has a complicated history. You'll get the drift of the history as you read through the novel but, if you want to alleviate confusion early, click into my website (www.miriamverbeek/about-siempra/) and have Si'Empra history (background) explained to you. On the website you'll also find a map of Si'Empra and a spoiler free glossary to help with keeping track of all the characters and the foreign terms you'll come across.

CONTENTS

Author's Note	vii
Part One: Rape	1
1. Ellen	3
2. Joosthin	22
3. Cheng Yi, Greçia, Phan, Müther	33
4. Webcleaning	52
5. The Journey Begins	71
6. The Hunt	92
7. Rescue	109
8. Redel's Betrayal	121
9. Reality	133
10. Finding Religion	142
11. Fadil	148
12. Norm Tucker	165
13. Ellen's Hide	175
14. Webcloth	191
15. Lian Achton	197
16. Lian Isoldé, Redel, Mary	204
17. The Guild Masters	221
18. Striking a Bargain	237
19. Promised Deliveries	245
20. Tharnie's Questions	252
Part Two: Song and Dance	263
21. Winter Begins	265
22. Schathem	280
23. Father Augustine, Chocolate Pudding	295
24. Pedro's Room	312
25. The Telling	324
26. The Oldest Dance	341
27. Acknowledgements	351
About the Author	352
Glossary	353

PART ONE

RAPE

CHAPTER 1
Ellen

Occasionally, as she moved from one table of exhibits to another, Ellen picked up an item and gently blew it clean of dust before carefully replacing it. No one disturbed her slow appraisal of the small museum and its evidence of the interwoven history of Skyseekers, Crystalmakers and Cryptals.

She stopped at an open-topped cabinet, reached in and stroked her fingers over a space, reading the label of what should have been on display:

> *Virigin: Replica of the Guild Sceptre.*
> *The original is said to repeat more than ten words of authority.*

One rumour had it that her former English tutor had stolen the replica; another rumour had it that Redel had sold the replica to finance one of his extravagant hobbies.

Fingers still lingering over the replica's space, Ellen turned her head to look out of the library's picture window. Clouds swirled and swooped before the sun, causing patches of early spring snow on Si'Empra's rocky, steep, treeless landscape to glow and fade. In the distance, the white tops of mountains ducked in and out of the same cloud-dance. Ellen dropped her gaze to a more immediate scene far below: a large, green SUV, almost as wide as the bridge that spanned the frothing, ice-laden, surging waters of the Si'Em River, was forcing its way slowly through a crowd of pedestrians and goats. Goats were bucking and rearing in panic, tipping the carts they pulled; some people were dashing around picking up spilled goods, others were trying to calm the goats, and others again were trying to push a passage to one or other side of the bridge and out of the way of the motor vehicle.

The SUV belonged to her half-brother, Ülrügh Redel. It and a yellow convertible sports car had arrived a few days ago on the first cargo ship to make it through the melting Antarctic Sea ice. Elbows leaning on top of the wall enclosing her private garden high up on Si'Em Bluff and overlooking the harbour, Ellen had watched the vehicles being offloaded. Her childhood nursemaid, Katherina, had been standing next to her, sunglasses over her pale eyes and wide-brimmed hat pulled low on her forehead. "The colour of the big one is called titanium green," Katherina had said enthusiastically. "It has an Arizona-beige interior, a three-litre engine, ABS brakes and four-wheel drive. It can make the journey from Baltha to Sinthén much faster than the bus!"

Amused, Ellen had not been able to resist a little teasing. She knew that her devoted carer had little understanding of why any such details were significant; doubtless she had heard them from others. "Why do you think it's necessary to get to Sinthén more quickly?"

Katherina, who barely ever left the confines of Si'Em City and had certainly never been to Sinthén, frowned. "I'm told Sinthén is smelly," she murmured.

Ellen had almost added: "And Sinthén Road is too badly rutted for the low chassis of a sports car," but then Katherina would have puzzled over the words "chassis" and "ruts".

Ellen turned her attention from the growing chaos on the bridge back to the museum. She had seen a similar scene an hour ago when the car had forced its way across in the other direction. It was likely that Redel was driving the car. Ellen had fallen into the habit of limiting her movements around the Serai when there was a chance she might meet her half-brother. Sure of his absence now, she had taken the opportunity to visit the museum to do as Pedro asked.

She picked up a slim book with a plain leather cover embossed in child-like lettering: "The Book of Rhymes".

"Could you please substitute this book for the one that looks like it," Pedro had said in his quiet way. "I will copy its contents and then you can return it to the museum. I have been asked by the Crystalmakers to make a copy."

She had not asked Pedro why the Crystalmakers wanted the book. She knew that her mother and Pedro had a clandestine association with the belowground peoples. In secret, they had even taught her the Crystalmakers' language. They promised – "one day when it is safe" – to share the details of their bond with Crystalmakers. Doubtless it had to do with the fact that her mother's pale features signified a certain amount of Crystalmaker blood.

As Ellen held the copy of the book in her hands, her curiosity about the association piqued in a way it had not for some years. In fact, in these last three years, very little had stirred her usually enquiring nature; she sometimes felt like a disembodied avatar of herself, tracking through the motions of being first lady among Skyseekers while her thoughts and emotions battled to find some meaning to her life.

She bent her head to blow dust from the book cover. From the corner of her eye she saw an adjutant saunter past a gap between two aisles of bookshelves. He paused when he saw her and retreated. She wrinkled her nose with distaste. The adjutants were Redel's special group of young men. They were all equally arrogant and the complaints about their offensive behaviour were increasing. But Redel laughed away the complaints and most lians, whose families the adjutants were careful never to offend, did not challenge his dismissals.

Ellen straightened, making as if to settle the folds of her loose blouse, and her thieves' hands made the swap: Pedro's copy, which had been nestled in the wide folds of her waistband, lay on the display table and the original book had taken its place. The same tutor who was suspected of stealing the replica of the Guild sceptre had taught her the craft of a thief. She had enjoyed the learning and used the skill often. *Probably more often than I should.* Ellen's lips twitched with a mischievous smile.

She left the museum, threading her way through several aisles of books and into the large open foyer of the library. Once she had been a frequent visitor there, making full use of its comfortable lounges, tables, chairs and computers. She had her own computer, of course, but the screens were bigger in the library. "I'm getting lots of ideas for writing the best stories!" she had announced to her tutors and librarians as she borrowed yet more books to read. Only her father, the Ülrügh Briani, had opposed her plan to become a storyteller. He would ruffle her red curls affectionately and say: "Attend instead to the lessons that will ready you as Ülrügh". "Father!" she would giggle – when he was in one of his gentler moods – "Ülrügh is your job and then it will be Redel's job." Sometimes, when her father' moods had been more severe, he would thunder at her flippant rebuff: "There is duty!" And for a while she would pretend to attend to his ambition – until she charmed him out of his surliness. Nevertheless, she had never harboured an ambition to be Ülrügh.

Now her dream of being Si'Empra's storyteller seemed the only worthwhile part of her. In the past two years, she had spent most of the summer months travelling from one isolated summer village to another, entertaining people with news, music and stories – some of the stories were ones she had created, others were ones she read out or recalled. The villagers always welcomed her and, in their company, it was easy to smother thoughts of her troubled existence in the Serai.

That troubled existence had some roots in her father's ambition for her. Some of the more powerful lians, such as Lians Chithra, Julian and Dane, treated her with suspicion because of it. Any submission Ellen made on behalf of the increasingly disadvantaged majority of Si'Emprans was dismissed as a self-serving bid for more influence. Nowadays, there were few lians who did not pretend other duties and hurry away when she neared them. Only protocol and, incredibly (and distastefully to Ellen), Redel's apparent high regard of her, ensured that she was accorded the respect due to a member of the Ülrügh's family.

Ellen could bring herself to ignore the lians, but the threat of more abuse at the hands of Redel gnawed at her constantly. She and Redel used to be the best of friends. They were both fearless and active. Sixteen years her senior, Redel had taught her how to climb and to dance. Since her tenth year she had partnered him in the winter ceiling game, schathem. She had shared her most intimate secrets with him, thinking he entrusted her with his. When her father had died unexpectedly almost four years ago, she had enthusiastically supported Redel's election as Ülrügh, and been astonished at rumours that some people thought that she, at barely fourteen, should be leader instead.

She realised now that Redel had many secrets he had not shared with her and that his friendship was actually jealous possession. This translated, nowadays, into excuses that he wanted to help her, even "heal her" –

Ellen's thoughts came to an abrupt halt.

The adjutant she had seen earlier stood in the library doorway.

Nervousness fluttered against her diaphragm, though she was careful not to show it.

A librarian was the only other person in the library. As Ellen walked past her desk, she smiled her thanks at the elderly woman, who rose and bowed her head respectfully. "Warmth and light, Lian Ellen", she said.

"Warmth and light," responded Ellen.

Like the librarian, the adjutant bent slightly into a bow, but the movement was mocking, causing their bodies to touch as she stepped past – his "Lian" was a jeer.

Ellen entered the roofed, spacious forecourt of the Serai. Sunlight slanted in through the wide, arched gateway and spilt on to colourful garden beds. In the middle of the forecourt stood a raised pond bathed in light from a crystal dome above. A fountain – a clear tube that jutted out from the centre of the pond – sprayed out an umbrella of rainbow drops that tinkled as they landed. Golden fish swam lazily in the clear water, occasionally plucking at the stems of water lilies, causing the wide, round leaves and open, pink blooms to sway.

The forecourt was the hub of the Serai. At the furthest point from the entrance was a café with tables and chairs out front. Spaced evenly around the forecourt were the openings to eight passages that radiated into the Serai: one passage led to the administration offices; another downstairs into Si'Em City; a third led past the library and down into the storage and shopping precinct of the city; a fourth to horse stables and dog enclosures; a fifth to the helicopter pad, garages, hangars and fuel storage areas; a sixth to the Ülrügh's private quarters; the seventh to rooms occupied by the rest of the Ülrügh's family and attendants; and the eighth to a wide balcony edged with a stone balustrade that looked out over the Antarctic Ocean. The Serai itself sat atop an enormous bluff separated from the rest of the island of Si'Empra by the Shotover and Si'Em River gorges. Into the bluff seamed the labyrinth of Si'Em City, permanent home to some six thousand Si'Emprans in summer and more than twenty thousand in winter.

When Ellen had entered the Serai's forecourt half an hour ago it was filled with people. Now it was empty; not a person in sight, not even those who usually served in the café.

Adrenaline pricked at Ellen's fingers and trickled over her scalp.

She had been trapped into this pattern before. The adjutants would stay just out of sight. They would make sure she did not escape into a passageway. They would make sure no one saw.

Ellen quickened her step, adjusting the riding harness she still wore. The car must be closer than she'd anticipated – but not yet in sight from the archway. *I've got time. I can get back on to Rosa and go*, she told herself. Straining her hearing to pick up the sound of an engine labouring up the hill towards the Serai, Ellen pulled a strap up between her legs and was in the act of attaching it to the belt buckle when his voice –.

"Sister, how nice to see you!"

Ellen stumbled, catching her breath and pressing a hand against the stolen book behind her waistband.

Redel is not driving the car!

She spun around. Redel was coming towards her, arms outstretched in welcome. She backed away.

"I came as soon as I heard you had come to visit me." He smiled warmly, teeth white, dark eyes appraising her. His richly embroidered shirt – open at the neck and tight enough around chest and waist to define his muscles – glowed with the sheen of silk. His arms reached more eagerly.

She continued to retreat, feeling for one of the many stone benches set into the forecourt walls. Even as the panic rose and clouded her thoughts, she retained enough presence of mind to know that Redel must not find the book on her. Drawing her lips tightly over her teeth, she turned her face towards the forecourt entrance and gave a piercing whistle.

Redel's smile broadened. He paused his step and turned his attention to the forecourt entrance. "Is your Rosa waiting for you? Are you asking her to join us?"

The instant he looked away, Ellen feigned another stumble. Her hands reached out – one hand gliding past her waistband – to steady herself; she slipped the book out and into a crack behind the seat of the bench.

"Aah. Here she is," Redel purred. "Here is your bird."

Rosa pranced nervously into sight under the arch. The glasaur had heard Redel's voice from outside and was reluctant to come closer.

"She seems somewhat hesitant," Redel observed, turning back to Ellen. His eyes appraised her. "Your beauty surpasses your mother's loveliness."

Ellen sprang forward, away from the wall, towards the exit. He was quick – too quick. In a few strides he had blocked her path. The smile was gone; his eyes hard with desire.

Ellen backed again. She could hear Rosa emitting small, unhappy, hissing sounds, her calloused feet scraping noisily over the flagstones as she shuffled with indecision. Rosa was afraid of Redel. He had treated her cruelly when she was a chick and, even now, when in reality she could knock him senseless with talon or beak, she kept her distance.

Redel's hand shot forward, closing around Ellen's wrist. She struggled against his grip but he pulled her towards him. With practiced moves, he unhitched the strap between her legs and dragged her loose trousers down from her waist. With a flick of his wrists she lay helpless under him.

She gave a sob as he mounted her, his own pants opening with the release of a clip. "I've missed you. I've missed you," he whispered. He let out a gasp of pleasure as he thrust into her – thrusting again and again, deaf to her whimpers of pain. "Oo-aah," he sighed at last, leaning forward in a suffocating embrace. He let out another long breath. "Ellen. My beautiful Ellen. You make this so difficult. All I want is to help you. This could be so wonderful. Why make it seem so unseemly?" He said the words softly and sadly. "I miss you." He still held her wrist, his grip so agonising she could barely move. With his free hand, he stroked her cheek gently.

She averted her gaze, disgust forming bile in her mouth. As he leaned forward to give her another kiss, she spat in his face.

Redel did not pull back, though his eyes narrowed with the swift anger that was one of his defining characteristics. The hand on her cheek travelled slowly up over her temple to her forehead where it paused, the palm settling flat over her brow. His fingers stroked into her curls, gripped her hair and dragged her head up. With a sudden push, Redel smashed Ellen's head back against the flagstones.

"Don't you ever do that again," he whispered, putting his lips very close to her ear. He gave her a light kiss and stood, adjusting his clothes. Eyes still examining her, he drew a lace handkerchief from his trousers pocket, carefully removed the spit on his cheek and dropped the cloth on to her face. "Thank you, sister," he said pleasantly. "I do hope that the next time we come together you are more reasonable." He turned and began walking casually away.

Rosa advanced, keeping a wary eye on Redel. She nudged Ellen with the top of her hooked beak, chirping urgently to encourage her to rise. Ellen responded sluggishly. Supporting herself on Rosa's neck, she pulled herself up. She was dimly aware that Redel had stopped and was watching. Rosa's nervousness increased. It took several attempts before Ellen's shaking hands could attach her harness – still buckled around her waist, though the securing strap between her legs dangled free – to the dolphin clip on the pulley cord on Rosa's saddle. She placed her foot in a stirrup that also hung from the pulley, and gave a small tug to activate the mechanism. As soon as the pulley started to lift her, Redel darted back towards her. Rosa bolted, running awkwardly with Ellen bouncing at her side. The pulley continued to lift while Ellen groped for a hold to steady herself; unsecured by the strap between her legs, the harness rode up past her waist and pinched under her arms. Behind her, she heard Redel burst into laughter. The pulley mechanism locked and Ellen lifted her legs as high as she could, giving Rosa's wings room to spread. Rosa used each wing downbeat to increase her speed.

Ellen clung to the saddle – eyelids squeezed closed – slipping and jolting from side to side as Rosa ran. Only the locked pulley cord kept her from falling. She had no idea where Rosa was heading. Everything but the pain in her head and between her legs seemed unreal. Rosa swerved suddenly. A car horn sounded loudly and there was a shout of alarm. Ellen forced open her eyes but could only see grass and stones race past the bird's outstretched neck. The ground disappeared and below them gaped the depths of the Shotover gorge.

Dazed though she was, Ellen knew not to move. Rosa was a clumsy flier. At best she could use her wings to direct a glide. If Ellen encouraged her, Rosa could usually extend the glide and land smoothly, but Ellen was badly mounted and incapable of giving directions or shifting her weight.

The floor of the gorge raced towards them. Dark, jagged rocks leered up. Rosa banked and flapped her huge black wings, managing a scrabbling landing between the rocks.

Distressed, the bird sat where it landed, beak open, wings unfolded, chest heaving.

Ellen retched. Water rushed and plunged through the bottom of the gorge, the roar a palpable beating on Ellen's already-overtaxed senses. She retched again and vomited, barely managing to avoid soiling Rosa. Roused by her mount's movements, the glasaur stood, whistling sharply, demanding directions. Slowly, Ellen pulled herself properly over Rosa's back, clicking four loops sewn to the saddle – two at the front and two at the back – to clips on her harness. She eased the hold of the pulley cord, trying to focus her thoughts, but the effort was too great. She laid her head on her mount's soft feathers. Tucking her hands into the chest straps that were part of Rosa's saddle fastenings, Ellen drifted into semi-consciousness.

Still whistling and chirping anxiously, and occasionally twisting her long neck to nudge her rider, Rosa picked her way along the bottom of the gorge towards the wider Si'Em River gorge. At the junction with the river, she followed a barely-discernible path further away from Si'Em City. By dusk, she had come to a river flat where much of the sedge-like vegetation had partially submerged in the snowmelt-swollen river. Rosa stopped at the point where the flat was at its driest and made another attempt to rouse her mistress.

Ellen pushed herself up to sit, wincing as pain stabbed inside her body. She released her harness, activating the pulley to lower herself to the ground. Once off Rosa's back, she laid on her side and curled into a foetal position.

Rosa nudged and chirruped.

"Let me be," Ellen muttered.

Tweeting unhappily, Rosa turned her attention to the thick vegetation and tore out a whole plant. Using her talons to hold the morsel steady, she began to eat it piece by piece, her gaze focused on Ellen.

Rosa's hiss stirred Ellen hours later. *Redel again!* Panicked, Ellen opened her eyes. Daylight was gone. Rosa had covered her with a wing, a shield against the cold. The bird was staring intently into the gloom.

Ellen tried to sit, but again the twin pain of her head and abdomen stopped her.

Still hissing, Rosa lunged to her feet to stand over Ellen.

Not Redel, Ellen thought. Rosa never stood her ground against Redel.

Shadowy figures moved over the sedge. They made soft, moaning sounds. Rosa's hiss calmed. She swayed her head back and forth enquiringly.

The figures stopped.

Even from a distance they smelled bad.

Cryptals, Ellen thought, relaxing a little. She had no fear of Cryptals, though she had never seen one in the flesh. Pedro and her mother had often spoken of them. They were Si'Empra's most ancient inhabitants. Arguably, they were responsible for the island's very existence and for the continued survival of the two types of people who lived on Si'Empra: the Crystalmakers and Skyseekers.

But what were they doing here and what did they want? They seemed to be motioning to her and then, when she did not move, to confer. One of them gave a commanding bark and Rosa sank to the ground. Their apparent control over Rosa startled Ellen. She came to her knees. The stars in the sky exploded in her head. She slipped against the soft breast feathers of her mount, gulping for breath.

The shadowy figures moved quickly, bringing with them their choking odour. Long-fingered hands pushed a wad of moss into Ellen's mouth and over her nose, and lifted her by her wrists and ankles, racing her away from the river's edge.

It was Ellen's last memory of the evening.

THE SUN WAS AT noon in the sky by the time Ellen felt strong enough to crawl to the river for a wash. The odour of the Cryptals was faint but present. She could just make them out, watching her from the shady recesses of an overhanging rock. They, or Rosa, had placed twigs full of berries within arm's reach. She was not at all hungry, but the Cryptals had earlier prodded her with a long switch until she had eaten.

The ancient creatures were careful to keep their distance. Ellen's skin was red and blistered where they had touched her the previous evening, and her throat and face felt burnt from the fumes she had inhaled despite the moss they had placed over her mouth. Why the Cryptals had bothered to take her away from the edge of the river and its vicious horde of midges – in fact, why the Cryptals bothered with her at all – Ellen could not fathom.

Rosa seemed to be totally unaffected by the Cryptal fumes and touch. The bird even seemed to like the beasts. All morning, she had paused her endless search for food to visit them in their recess. As far as Ellen knew, Rosa had never before met a Cryptal, but, then, Rosa was, after all, a Cryptal creature. Legend had it that there had been many glasaurs when the original Crystalmakers came to Si'Empra. No one quite understood why the Cryptals had stopped creating them. Pedro suspected it was because the Cryptals found humans better served their needs.

A strong breeze blew down the river valley. Ellen figured that it would calm the midges long enough to allow her to clean herself up. Rosa followed her to the water's edge.

Ellen plunged her hands into the cold river water to try and soothe the sting of blisters, then peeled off her clothes. They were filthy with blood, dirt and the reek of Redel's body. She dropped the clothes into an eddying pool to soak and curled herself up again on the ground to ease her headache and nausea.

Redel had given her a decent blow. She put her hand up carefully to touch the back of her skull. Her hair was matted with crusty, dry blood. She supposed she should soak her head clean, but made no move to do so.

Anxious moaning and barking, and Rosa's beak roused her again. Midges rose off her body when she moved. In her misery, she had ignored the drop in wind that brought the insects out of their shelters, but she could not ignore Rosa's constant prodding – and now the Cryptals had come closer, urging her away from the river's edge.

Ellen swished her clothes in the water, scrubbing out as much dirt as she could. After the previous – now five – times Redel had abused her, she had thrown away the clothes she had been wearing. *As if that would get him out of me!* she thought bitterly.

I'm not going back! I'm never going to go back to the Serai! I'm never going to go anywhere near him again.

Using a sash bundled in her hand, she mopped her body. The water was too icy for a bath, but at least she could remove some filth from her skin.

She moved slowly, her muscles reluctant in spite of the continued assault from the tiny insects and the unrelenting Cryptal calls. Finally, she dragged her clothes from the water, squeezed them and spread them out to dry on rocks. Shivering, she crawled back over the broken ground to where Rosa's saddlebags lay. She found clean underclothes in one bag, pulled them on and tugged a sleepsack out of another saddlebag. She slid into the sack and laid her pounding head on the crook of one arm.

Despondently, she whispered her dead mother's name: "Constance". She was only vaguely surprised, on this day that seemed unreal anyway, when the Cryptals began a soft, crooning hum: a melody to the lullaby her mother used to sing to her. Ellen listened, staring unseeing at rounded, smooth river stones before her eyes, words from the song playing in her mind:

> *The sky is wide*
> *My little child*
> *I hold you tight*
> *My little child*
> *I love you so*
> *My little child*
> *I'll keep you safe*
> *My little child*
> *I love you so*

ELLEN

Warmth and light I'll bring to you
Never fear the dark and cold
Colour is all around
I am here to care for you

Night spread its shadows again. A Cryptal shuffled closer, its smell touching her nostrils. It was a terrible smell, making her gag, but, strangely, it also seemed to clear her head and make her feel a little better.

The Cryptal pushed another twig full of berries towards her with its switch. "Eat!" it urged with its gesture, then retreated again. She put a few berries into her mouth. Rosa settled against her back, providing warmth and soft support. It would be another cold night.

Ellen studied the Cryptals as they watched her. The beasts had been hunted mercilessly by her grandfather, her father, and now Redel – Redel was especially murderous, offering a bounty to those who came forward with information about Cryptal sightings.

Cryptal fur, which quickly lost its toxicity when the beast died, had a high value. The hide could be tanned. The fur could be spun, woven and, even more incredibly, Crystalmakers could turn it into hard crystal that could be fashioned into ornaments, delicate optical instruments and – its major use for Crystalmakers and Skyseekers alike – to harness light. Every country on Earth was prepared to pay a fortune for Cryptal crystal.

Nowadays it was difficult to find Cryptal crystal. Crystalmakers were hunted as brutally as Cryptals. A very few, such as Katherina, were captured young enough to turn into workers at the Serai. Most were simply murdered.

The berries tasted sour. Ellen sipped water from the canteen stored in a holster on Rosa's saddle, and laid on her side again. The ground was hard, jagged and cold. Somewhere in the saddlebags was a sleeping mat, but Ellen didn't have the energy to find it. She closed her eyes.

Sometime during the night she woke from a feverish doze to the caress of a hand. She stared into the pale eyes of an elderly woman, hardly reacting to the new presence, wondering vaguely if she was dreaming.

"Let's see if I can make you more comfortable," the woman said. Her voice was soft and deep, and she spoke in the gentle melody of the Crystalmakers' language. "Can you sit up?"

Supported by the woman's strong arms, Ellen sat up, breath expelling with a soft gasp at the sharpened pain the movement caused. The Cryptal who had pushed food at her was still in the same position, its powerful digging claws wedged into the ground, long, slender arms stretched forward for balance over thick, bent knees. Two other Cryptals, smaller and darker, had joined it.

"I came as soon as the WhiteŌne told me about you. The Cryptals are not quite sure what is wrong with you. Perhaps you could tell me. I have a mat for you to lie on, and a coverall which should be more comfortable to wear than what you have on."

The woman spread a mat as she spoke. She helped Ellen shift her body on to it, dressed her in a soft garment, spread the sleepsack over her again and placed a pillow beneath her head. She didn't seem to expect Ellen to speak.

"There. That's better. Let me see if I can stop you shivering. Your head has been bleeding and you are finding it painful. Oh yes. I see. A nasty wound. I will put ointment on it – and I have an ointment for these Cryptal burns on your wrists and ankles."

She sees well in this darkness, thought Ellen. *Of course. She's a Crystalmaker. I must be dreaming.*

"You also have some stomach pains. Has that louse raped you again?"

Ellen stiffened, her dreaminess shredding. *Who is this woman?* She had never told anyone that Redel raped her. Her mother and perhaps Lians Pethrie and Shivay, suspected and the deranged Lian Isoldé knew, but Ellen had never confirmed or denied it.

"Hold still, Ellen. Let me look after your head. I don't want to re-open the wound –"

"Who are you?" Ellen asked, the familiar use of her name finally forcing her voice box to work.

"Your grandmother." The woman paused. She held Ellen's gaze. "I am your grandmother," she said again softly. "Later we will talk. Now let me look after you."

There was no room to disobey, and no will on the part of Ellen to do so. The gentle hands spread comfort and warmth over her body, then held a cup of warm, milky liquid to her dry lips.

To the gentle hum of Cryptal song, Ellen fell asleep.

"Your mother was my daughter."

The statement wedged into Ellen's torpor.

Ellen focused more clearly on the woman who sat deep in the shadow of the overhang the Cryptals had used. It was difficult to make out her features. Long hair caught in a twisted bun in the nape of her neck, pale skin like Katherina had. She had on dark glasses and was dressed in olive green trousers and shirt. The clothes fitted her snugly, moulding comfortably to her slight frame. Ellen had the impression that the woman was old – and the woman probably was in Skyseeker terms. Ellen did not know much about Crystalmakers, but she had been told that they could live at least twice as long as Skyseekers. It had something to do with their close association with Cryptals.

"My lover and partner in life is Pedro, your tutor and your grandfather." The woman stirred the ground before her with a twig. "His family has always been a source of aid and strength to me. We became friends, then lovers, and your mother was our love child."

"With so much Skyseeker blood in her, I could not care for her belowground. Mylin would have killed her, and she would have hungered for light the way that Skyseekers do. So she grew up in Pedro's home. It would have been dangerous for other Skyseekers to know that Pedro associated with Crystalmakers, so we agreed upon a story that Pedro had found her abandoned as a baby. As it happened, he had adopted another child, so the claim was not so strange. Your mother, however, knew her heritage and I was with her and Pedro as much as I could be.

"I'm sure you've been told how Ülrügh Briani – your father – saw her once in Si'Em Square and was so taken by her beauty he demanded she become his wife. She was only seventeen but she made him a good wife. Your father also demanded that Pedro leave his home near Sinthén and become a tutor in the Si'Em City school."

The woman stopped speaking; the stick still moved over the ground.

Ellen had almost retreated back into the haze of her fever when the woman continued. "The presence of Pedro and your mother in Si'Em City was good for us – Crystalmakers and Webcleaners alike. They – Constance and Pedro – managed to smuggle many things out that helped us live less desperate lives. As you grew up, we hoped that you might influence the Ülrügh to make peace with us. Indeed, Constance had already managed to mollify the Ülrügh's behaviour.

"Your mother's –" the soft voice broke; the pale head bent forward, shoulders shaking with sudden, silent weeping. "Your mother's death – was a deep and painful blow. She was, as you sang at her funeral, 'grace and love and compassion and beloved of all'. You said, 'I miss her presence like days miss the sun in the sky.'"

"She told us she suspected that Redel abused you, and we did nothing –" once again the soft voice broke. "We did nothing," she repeated, as if not believing her own statement. "Instead we continued as if nothing had changed. Our decision – our inaction killed your mother."

Ellen's emotions twisted in her chest – constricting her breathing – the way they always did when someone faced her with the knowledge of what Redel did. It was such a shameful secret that she wanted to deny it out loud but, instead, she forced herself to concentrate on safer thoughts:

So. Pedro is my mother's actual father – my grandfather. Yes. I should have guessed it. I have been asleep for too many years.

Ellen closed her eyes. She felt too drained to speak and the woman's final statements had even sapped the strength to listen.

The cup of milky liquid at her lips woke her again. She sipped warmth and moisture into her throat. She looked up into an alabaster white face with mauve eyes that squinted in the uncertain light of a failing day. Now Ellen could see the resemblance to her mother's features: the oval face, the large eyes, the straight nose, the way tiny feathery strands of hair framed the forehead.

"What is your name, grandmother?" Ellen whispered.

"Elthán."

Small, strong hands laid Ellen's head gently back on the pillow. "I am taking you to a doctor. Two of my companions have arrived to help carry you into the tunnels. The Cryptals will have a sled to take us further. I have a mask for you and special clothing against Cryptal poison. I hope they will sufficiently protect you."

"I won't leave Rosa."

"The Cryptals will care for Rosa."

CHAPTER 2
Joosthin

NERVOUSLY.
 Carefully.

With trembling fingers, Joosthin opened the oven.

Inside, in the centre of the small, cubic space stood a vase with a bowl-shaped base and a fluted, intricately laced opening. It was flawlessly, non-reflectively transparent and he could not see it. He reached in, felt for the shape and lifted the vessel out, cupping it lovingly in his large, bony hands.

Had he made a virigin?

He tapped the delicate strands of lacework and they sang a soft, sad, melodious chord that echoed inside the bowl: A-flat major.

He allowed himself a small smile, daring to savour success. He lifted the vase to his cheek, feeling the smooth, hard surface against his skin. He held it for a second, love softening the grim lines of his face – then he opened his hands and dropped his creation.

The vase sounded a deep note of protest in B-flat as it hit the stone floor; the, before the note's vibration stilled in the air, it dropped a further semitone.

Joosthin folded his arms across his chest and closed his eyes to hold back the tears of disappointment.

Not a virigin.

He had failed again. A virigin did not lose tone. He breathed in and out, in and out, forcing control over his emotions. When he had pushed the threatening sob back down his throat, he snapped his eyes open. "Fool! Old man!" he admonished himself. He knelt and began searching for the vase, finding it resting against the side of a stone bench. Dust from the floor clung to its surface. Rising again, Joosthin lifted the vase so that it was between his eyes and the source of dim light in the room. Gently, he blew cool air on the lacework and watched it turn milky. The milkiness spread over the whole surface. The vase was clear no more. He breathed warm air on to the lacework, the milkiness faded. He touched a hot metal rod to the lacework. Within seconds the lacework glowed red then began to sag. He removed the rod, swallowing more disappointment.

Not even close to a virigin! *A virigin does not lose shape.*

Better heat control! He needed better heat control. Perhaps he had to make his oven hotter! But it was already much hotter. Nowhere else were the ovens as hot as those in The Deep – except in Trebiath, the traditional home of the crystal-making craft.

Joosthin touched the lacework; it had cooled enough for him to restore shape. He worked to achieve precision even though he was disinterested in the vase now. He set the ornament up on the shelf with other creations: bowls, figurines, plates, bottles. He could and did make all shapes. The most talented in his class, the undisputed master of this craft – a brilliant apprentice destined to become a brilliant Guild Master. He could have provided so much, given so much of his gift to Si'Empra!

Joosthin scowled. The older he became, the more bitter his memories. He thought he had cycled through too many starving winters to feel anything but bitterness. Sometimes he wondered why a spark of hope still glowed in him, why every time he made another crystal he dared to hope, and when he sat with other

Guild Masters he dared to speak of hope. It seemed to him that disappointment always answered.

In a sudden pique he wondered where Elthán was.

He strode to the doorway, thrust his head through a gap in the curtain and barked: "Zarl!"

The narrow hallway carried his voice to an adjoining den, causing the young man bent over a fibre-sorting tool to start.

Like everything else in the workroom, the sorting tool was old and worn. Several seemed to have collapsed on themselves so that even the finest Cryptal fibres could fit. Zarl had spent hours with Lara, Acolyte of the Weavers Guild and the only Crystalmaker left alive who had worked on the sorting tools, but neither could quite understand the techniques used in the times before The Destruction – and perhaps even before The Destruction, when the Crystal Makers Guild had known how to make virigins. Not even those from the Guild of Memory could help, though they studied their ancient tapestries over and over again to try to find the answers.

Zarl hurried to obey Joosthin's summons, but by the time he arrived the Guild Master had forgotten whatever it was he'd called Zarl for. Joosthin had heard the change in the WhiteŌne's tone; It was calling out a warning. Dread replaced Joosthin's pique.

Joosthin brushed past Zarl, snatched a coverall off a hook and tugged it over his clothes. He pulled a hood over his head and secured it, working gloves over his hands as he strode towards the exit to the Cryptal highway. "Get dressed!" he ordered over his shoulder. He thrust aside the heavy curtain door and hurried to the left, past several openings and down a slope worn smooth by the tread of millions of feet over millennia, towards the Source of Song. He slowed his stride, checked and re-checked the fit of his hood. Even through the thick, protective fabric of his hood he could smell the Cryptals.

The WhiteŌne, the Source of Song, sat where it always sat: a vast, pure white bulk in the middle of the cavernous chamber known as The Deep. A myriad of tiny holes radiated from that chamber throughout the Cryptals' underground world. The WhiteŌne was rarely silent.

The Source of Song was the heart of the Cryptal world. It gave direction. When It was silent, all who dwelt in that underground world felt alone and lost. The WhiteŌne's Song could be painfully beautiful, soothing or cajoling – and it could rise to a tone that struck terror with its message.

The WhiteŌne turned its large, round, faintly blue eyes in Joosthin's direction as he came to stand at the entrance of Its chamber, but the Song did not falter. Joosthin did not have to look at the WhiteŌne to understand the message; he came because he needed reassurance. It had been to The Deep and the WhiteŌne – the only Cryptal who was not poisonous – that the Cryptals had brought him and the ragged remnants of the Crystalmaker population more than sixty years ago, as Ülrügh Devi stormed through the Cryptal highways slaughtering Crystalmaker and Cryptal alike. In his anguish, Joosthin had touched the WhiteŌne and been embraced. It had given him comfort. He had never touched It or any Cryptal since. Such was not the relationship between Cryptals and Crystalmakers. But his embrace by the WhiteŌne had bound him to It. When he felt fear or despair he drew courage by simply remembering that embrace and listening to Its Song.

Now the urgent Song willed him to return to the other Crystalmakers and run! He retreated at a trot. A growl sounded behind him and he threw himself to the ground. Cryptals dashed over him, bounding between the tunnel walls in their leapfrog way. He came to his feet but staggered as the ground shook.

He dashed forward in panic, cursing himself for wasting time when the WhiteŌne had warned him that the earthquake threatened. He thrust the curtain aside, ready to bellow for everyone to follow him. He found the seven Crystalmakers pulling on their coveralls. Within seconds they crowded into the Cryptal highway behind him. Joosthin led them at a fast jog, the WhiteŌne's Song guiding his direction. Time and again the group dropped to the ground as Cryptals streamed over them, also driven by the Song.

One of the Crystalmakers, Cilla, was seven months pregnant and the repeated need to fall to the ground taxed her more than anyone else. She began to stumble. Zarl took her arm.

The earth shook again, more strongly, cracking a section of the tunnel before them.

The WhiteŌne's tone varied ever so slightly: *To the left! To the left!*

Joosthin groped along the dark walls and found another passage – smaller, more rough-hewn. He led his Crystalmakers into it, trusting the Song.

The group stumbled forward for half an hour; all that their sensitive eyes could see was the warm glow of each other's bodies.

Again the ground shuddered. Joosthin heard gasps of fright. Rocks fell behind and ahead. Several Crystalmakers cried out. The ground heaved and the tunnel was drowned in the sound of rock collapsing.

"Stay together! Stay together!" Joosthin screamed, frantically trying to hear more instructions from the WhiteŌne.

On! On!

Several Crystalmakers were crying out at once: "My arm! I can't free my arm!" Cilla's voice, grinding with panic, "Thyrol is gone!" Another voice – full of anguish.

Through the thick dust Joosthin could just see the red glow of Zarl's bent form, heaving at a black mass of rock.

"Guild Master! Joosthin!"

Joosthin started towards the cry. The WhiteŌne's Song stopped him abruptly.

On! On!

"I need help," Zarl grunted. "Pethrie– "

Cilla gave a cry of pain.

Another heave from the ground. Joosthin overbalanced, falling to his knees. Dust billowed from disintegrating rock, filtering through his mask.

On! On! The WhiteŌne's insistent Song sounded through the confusion. Joosthin scrambled to his feet. He could see two warm glows nearby. He lunged at them. "Go! Run! Don't stop here!" he yelled, pushing them both further into the tunnel.

"Zarl – leave!" Joosthin groped forward to where he had last seen Zarl. "Run! Zarl–" He made contact with Zarl's arm and was about to pull at it when Zarl said: "I've freed her. We're going!"

On! On! The WhiteŌne persisted.

Joosthin turned, seeking out the last of his party. "Heinie! There's no time to search–"

The ground groaned. Joosthin staggered as the earth tipped below him.

"Thyrol! We can't – Thyrol!" Joosthin could see Heinie frantically scrabbling at a wall of rubble. He grappled with her but she fought him off. "Thyrol! I have to find Thyrol!"

On! On!

The Song was urgent – so urgent.

Joosthin fled along the tunnel.

The ground shifted and groaned and rock cracked and tumbled from walls that undulated like cloth being shaken. The five Crystalmakers ran – blind, stumbling and injured – through twisting, narrow passages, helping each other, guided by the Song until – abruptly – the narrow tunnel ended and they were once again in a dimly lit Cryptal highway. Two Cryptals stood waiting for them, harnessed to a slender sled.

The Crystalmakers clambered aboard and the Cryptals galloped away from the earth's deep distress.

Drawing in sobbing breaths, the Crystalmakers clung to each other. Joosthin alone drew away from the companionship, wrapping his arms tightly around his chest, and weeping quietly behind his hood.

Oh Thyrol! Heinie! He had left them behind in the rock fall and he knew – knew by the crashing sounds that had followed their desperate flight – that they were buried now.

The Cryptals left Joosthin's group at the entrance to Illiath, where Thil, Acolyte of the Guild of Memory and Gate Master of Illiath, took them into his living space. They lay the unconscious Cilla, her arm a crushed, bloody mess, on to a bed. Zarl, with a deep gash to his head, sank on to another bed. Joosthin had escaped with no injuries. He stood apart, accepted a drink but otherwise rejected other offers of food or comfort.

A war of emotions pounded his heart and head: hatred for the Skyseekers, relief to be safe, fear for Cilla's life, grief for Heine and Thyrol – and exhilaration.

Exhilaration!

He knew that the others, in spite of their wounds, would be feeling the same surge of exhilaration. Mylin had seeped in great quantities into their blood – past their hoods – and drugged them. That was probably as well. Without the help of mylin, he doubted they could have endured the race to Illiath. In an hour or two he would lie on his bed and fall into a deep and restful sleep, waking nine or ten hours later feeling refreshed.

He looked around. People, walls, furniture, tapestries: everything was sharply defined. Colours were brighter, corners were sharper, curves more smoothly rendered. He could feel air on the bare skin of his face – feel it move in through his nostrils and into his lungs. He could feel every crease and seam of his clothes and the smoothness of the stone floor under his bare feet.

More intoxicatingly, he felt certain of himself. All doubts he had about his role as Guild Master and his relationships – particularly that with Elthán – faded. He felt sure that he could help secure the future of Crystalmakers. He felt certain that he should continue to speak directly to Elthán, in spite of her status as Webcleaner. He did not doubt that he would one day rediscover how to make a virigin.

This feeling of certainty, he knew, would fade.

He longed for it to stay. He visualised himself stepping into the Cryptal highway to breathe in a dose of mylin before working on the making of a crystal – perhaps a virigin – or stepping out into the Cryptal highway just before a Guild Master colloquy started so that he did not hesitate in his role as Guild Master.

No! No! No! Alarm knocked urgently at his thoughts. He shuddered, abruptly leaving the gatekeepers' quarters. He made his way through the lit hallways of Illiath towards his own sector of the belowground city. He passed passages carefully covered with thick tapestries; they were only faintly lit by phosphorescent moss, full of spider webs and home to albino insects and rodents. They were a part of Illiath that still showed the scars of The Destruction.

Joosthin knew that his once-closest friend still lived in these ruins of Illiath. He had given up trying to persuade Thren to turn away from his overuse of mylin. The last time Joosthin had seen Thren, he had clearly lost all sense of himself. He had been a disintegrating man who simply cocked his head slightly when Joosthin spoke to him, a frown fracturing the grime on his forehead, purple eyes flickering up and down as they inspected Joosthin without recognition. This man lived only for his next dose of mylin. Joosthin had turned away, tears spilling.

Mylin: Cryptal poison! All Crystalmakers needed it. In small, constant doses it helped them stay healthy and long-lived in their belowground world. In larger doses, it caused the body to corrode, inside and out.

Thren had stunk with a mix of body odour, urine and faeces. His filthy clothes were shredded beyond belief. The hood to his coverall that he never used hung at his back, filled with wisps of lank, greasy hair. Thren had once been charismatic, strong and generous – a foil for Joosthin's sombre and pessimistic temperament. In The Deep – after The Destruction – they had worked together to give hope to other Crystalmakers. Thren's drift into abuse of mylin had been gradual. At first no one noticed that he lingered more frequently in the Cryptal tunnels, pretending errands. When the drug abuse began to show in his eyes, his skin and behaviour, he melted into the uninhabited corners of Illiath, becoming one of the Overcome.

In the privacy of his own living quarters, Joosthin stripped off his clothes and pushed aside a curtain to the bathing chamber he shared with his closest acolytes. He lifted the lid covering the pool in a corner of the room and immersed himself in warm water. As the room filled with steam, the moss-covered walls glowed more brightly. The moss covered any wall that was continuously damp and glowed brightest with an increase in moisture. It was part of the duties of the Guild of Crystal Makers to keep the pads of moss contained in the specially constructed crystal sconces throughout Illiath glowing and healthy.

Joosthin relaxed, his senses wonderfully acute to the gentle, tugging current that moved continuously through the bath, fed by a warm stream that flowed below Illiath. The same stream flowed into the toilet areas, but that waste flushed out into a different channel.

Eyes closed, he winced as his mind's eye conjured that most recent vision of Thren. Then came a memory of another Thren: one that would not have abandoned Thyrol and Heinie, no matter that they were only Webcleaners.

"I see no sense in our despising Webcleaners!" Thren would argue when they were alone – never when others might hear because Crystalmakers would have turned upon him for such views. In childhood stories, those who cheated and lied, murdered and even ate people were always the Webcleaners. Thren had said: "Elthán and her people dare what we do not. They keep us alive and we treat them like dirt – no! Worse! We almost deny their existence! Why does The Order give them such a low status? I don't think The Order meant this to be the case."

It was the young Elthán who had supplied survivors of The Destruction with food, giving it to Thil's predecessor to distribute. Thren had met her in secret, thanking her and offering assistance. When she asked, he had provided her with Cryptal cloth and crystal. In time, Thren had co-opted Joosthin into also helping Elthán.

In the seventeen years since Thren's manifest disappearance from his life, Joosthin had continued his association with Elthán.

He covered his face with wet hands and groaned. He had done more than continue his association with her; he actually found himself sometimes forgetting altogether that she was a Webcleaner; sometimes he conversed with her as if she were a close associate.

Joosthin slid entirely under the water, scrubbing at his scalp to loosen dust from his short, white hair. Perhaps such closeness with a Webcleaner had been what had driven Thren to mylin.

He surfaced with a gasp, choking on guilt. Not long ago he had confided in Elthán, telling her of his deep disappointment at not being able to create a virigin. He had confided in her even though he knew – because the Guild Master of Memory reminded him and every other Crystalmaker – that Webcleaners had stolen the secret of how to make virigins. When Elthán told him some time later that Pedro knew of a book in which many of the rhymes of Crystalmakers were recorded, he had greedily asked her to bring it to him: perhaps one of those rhymes concerned the making of virigins.

Joosthin felt doubly guilty. The Guild Masters had determined, well before The Destruction, that written words were a danger to the existence of Crystalmakers. Learning how to read and write, two skills Skyseekers had offered to Crystalmakers before The Destruction, was strictly forbidden. But Joosthin had agreed – no! even asked – for Elthán to obtain the book.

Doubly guilty! Joosthin rubbed his face hard.

And yet. And yet! If he could make a virigin then the Crystalmakers could, once again, be more powerful than Skyseekers.

CHAPTER 3
Cheng Yi, Greçia, Phan, Müther

"On Si'Empra," Cheng Yi explained to the United States envoy, "we mostly mine elbaite, a kind of tourmaline, but we also mine other minerals. We are very fortunate in the variety of rock we have." The two men had just introduced themselves to each other, Cheng Yi having met the envoy at the lift to the gemstone fashioning workshops. The Ülrügh had asked Cheng Yi to show the envoy how Si'Empra's gemstones were cut, and then to escort him back for an intimate dinner party with the Ülrügh and other chosen guests.

"I'm Chuck Janson. Chuck – short for Charles. Just call me Chuck," the tall, rather bulky envoy had said in his initial greeting. "Really appreciate you taking the time to show me around here. I walked around your display room. Something else! Wow! You got some jewels here! I thought you just mined for gemstones and sent raw materials out. I didn't know you actually make jewellery too."

A small part of the operation, Cheng Yi had explained. Something his team was hoping to grow.

They now stood in a hexagonal space with panes of glass at each side that gave views of different rooms. Cheng Yi drew the envoy to the window into the gem cutting room and pointed to a woman bent over a bench. She wore overalls and ear protectors. "That person is using a diamond blade saw to take off excess material from a stone, preparatory to faceting a gem. That's the first stage of creating a jewel." He pointed to another person on the far side of the room. "That man is using a diamond grinding wheel to polish a stone."

"What? Do you just get a stone and then see what you make of it?"

"Often the useful part of the stone with colour highlights is buried within a crystal. But we are also guided by what we want to do." Cheng Yi led the envoy to another window with a view of four people drawing designs for jewellery. "We used to do only cutting of stone – often only to the point where the workable gem is exposed – and we still do much of that – but now we are also designing jewellery pieces, as you saw in the display room. So, often, now, we are looking for particular colours and shapes."

"Fascinating! So you are trying to add value to the raw material you're mining."

"Yes. Add value," Cheng Yi agreed. He continued to detail the stages of fashioning jewellery and the various uses of Si'Empra's gemstones but, alongside the familiar patter, his thoughts were predominantly occupied with the notion of 'adding value'. If only the Lianthem were more enthusiastic about his ideas for adding value, rather than just selling off the output of Si'Empra's mines. Quick money was their main concern, and there was little interest in his idea to invest in a sustained effort to build up the jewellery-making business.

Cheng Yi led the way out of the viewing room and the part of Si'Em City from which he managed the mining operations of Si'Empra – a business begun by his father but now his exclusive domain.

"I get lost in this city," Chuck remarked. "I guess you just think of these hallways like we think of streets, but I lose my bearings real quick. I'm forever asking people where I am and how to get to places."

Cheng Yi smiled. "I remember I was the same when I first came to Si'Empra. Now I use the artwork on the walls to get my bearings." He explained that, although the murals may appear as lovely random paintings, they actually provided 'you are here' directions about locations in the city, and which hallway to choose to go to which city section.

"Light. How do you light up these hallways?"

"Ah. In summer –" Cheng Yi pointed to small, bright holes in the ceiling, "light comes through those – the holes – reflected in from outside by crystals."

"You make those crystals?"

"Ah. No. That is an ancient technology; well before my time." To avoid possible questions concerning Crystalmaker crystal and Crystalmakers in general, Cheng Yi continued hastily. "You see those holes that are dark, that is ventilation. In winter we use ordinary electricity –"

"Papa!"

Both men turned at the sound of the call behind them. Cheng Yi's daughter, Gigi, hurried towards them. "Papa!" she said again in an aggrieved tone. "Have you seen Lian Ellen? Honestly! She is impossible!"

"May I introduce you?" Cheng Yi was pointedly polite. "This is Mr Charles Janson, the new US envoy. Mr Janson, this is my daughter Gigi."

Gigi glanced at Chuck, her black, almond-shaped eyes making a quick inspection. Cheng Yi could read her thoughts in the small lift of her eyebrows and the downward tweak of her mouth: *Old. Ugly. Uninteresting.* In spite of her apparent assessment, Gigi offered her hand as she'd been taught to do when introduced to foreigners and murmured a "how do you do" in English.

She was into her next sentence before even releasing the envoy's hand. In the language of the Skyseekers, she repeated: "Have you seen Lian Ellen, Papa?"

"Gigi, please mind your manners," Cheng Yi admonished, though he knew that his words would have little effect given that Gigi was in obvious high dudgeon.

"I was. I shook his hand. Have you? She promised she'd be around for a while and Katherina says she hasn't seen her for a couple of days and she went without saying where she was going and we've organised a party. She's not answering her phone and she's not even answering her emails. She is so frustrating! You know, Luman is going to be there. Papa you have no idea how protective they are of him – they hardly ever let him go out – and, you know, he hates it – he says that he thinks he'll become an adjutant – but he says that what he really wants is to concentrate on becoming better at schathem – and he's desperate to talk to Lian Ellen about it – even though she hasn't played in ages – I keep saying to her she should start playing again – people just love it when she does – just because – she's not sick anymore you know – it was weird the way –"

"Gigi!" Cheng Yi interrupted. As so often when Gigi spouted in this manner, Cheng Yi felt himself wanting to gasp, as if drawing a breath on her behalf. Gigi and Lian Ellen had been close friends since childhood, perfectly matched in their disposition for diving into action before considering the consequences – except that Lian Ellen had the cunning, intelligence and strength to forge rescue plans when consequences became dire, whereas guileless Gigi was unlikely to even recognise a problem until it was too late. Over the years, Lian Ellen had, to the relief of, especially, Constance, gradually exhibited signs of maturity, but Gigi continued to flit enthusiastically from one idea to the next – the current obsession being that some boys were utterly desirable and others should be ignored. Gigi was, nevertheless, completely endearing and Cheng Yi worried constantly that someone would take advantage of her and hurt her deeply.

"I have not seen Lian Ellen and I do not know where she is."

"Oh. Bother! She is just so-o-o hopeless!" Gigi turned on her heel and stalked away into the crowd of pedestrians in the broad hallway.

Chuck watched her go, a wide grin on his face. "Mind if I ask you what that was about?"

"Several things," Cheng Yi said slowly. "I am not sure I have the full gist of it, but basically she is displeased with who is and is not coming to a party she has organised."

"Very nice looking girl. I bet she turns quite a few heads – sorry, hope you don't take that the wrong way – I mean, I don't mean, you know, to be improper."

"No offence taken," Cheng Yi sighed. "I am aware that she turns heads. Unfortunately she is also fully aware that she turns heads and is given to flirting. But come, we had better hurry. The Ülrügh rather likes his guests to be punctual."

The men made their way through a part of the city's shopping precinct. Many shops were closed, their interiors dark and bare. Cheng Yi explained that they only opened in winter when Si'Em City was crowded with many more people. He greeted the proprietors of other shops who were closing up for the day, though he did not pause to introduce the envoy. The two men climbed the stairs to the Serai and along a corridor to the Ülrügh's private rooms.

The German and French envoys, who were the other guests at this dinner party, were already enjoying pre-dinner drinks and canapés with the Ülrügh, served by attendants dressed in formal suits. The dining room held a large table capable of seating twenty people, but it lay unset. Instead, a smaller table with seating for five had been laid with exquisite bone china, sterling silver cutlery and crystal wine glasses and tumblers. Soon the attendants bore away the canapés and disappeared through a doorway that led to the Ülrügh's personal kitchen, reappearing shortly afterward with bowls of bouillabaisse.

The men sat as the attendants poured their Pouilly-Fuissé wine. The Ülrügh played the perfect host and the group settled into a comfortable conversation that spanned discussion on world events and personal stories. The attendants cleared away the soup bowls and replaced them with plates of stuffed quail, served on a bed of mashed sweet potato with baby greens and attractive sides of melon salad; they replaced the white wine with a Cabernet Franc. By the time dessert arrived – a simple berry sorbet served with a Hobbs Semillon dessert wine and cherry-stuffed macaroons – tongues were loose. The Ülrügh began to relate a story of a recent adventure.

"You must understand, gentlemen," he said in flawless English, "that it is lethal to spend any time near our rivers – the midges that live there are ferocious. My good friend Stephan here –" he waved his hand casually in the direction of the French envoy, whose smile broadened, "was quite determined that we should photograph the spotted fantail. These birds love to eat midges so we had to go to the river. He assured me that some newfangled insect repellent he had brought with him would work."

"Did it?" Chuck asked, helping himself to another cherry-stuffed macaroon.

"No. The midges homed in on the stuff with unsurpassed glee. They didn't stop at our exposed hands and faces, they crawled into our clothing and – dare I say it – played with our most –"

"Ülrügh, Ülrügh," the French envoy interrupted with a laugh. "Surely all the details are not necessary?"

"Ha!" the Ülrügh put back his head and gave a hoot of laughter. Cheng Yi observed that the Ülrügh seemed in an exceptionally good mood this evening. He was tall for a Skyseeker, taking after his mother's side of the family. His body was lean and athletic and he liked to wear clothes that showed off his well-muscled limbs; tonight he wore relatively tight dark trousers and a raglan three-quarter sleeve tee-shirt – he was the picture of expensive casual. His dark brown hair, thick and shiny, was cut in the style of the day: the same length all over and parted on the side so that some hair fell slightly over his forehead. His squarish chin was shaven clean. When he laughed in this way, so obviously enjoying a joke with friends, it was very hard not to be charmed by him. "First aid. That was what we needed when we scampered out of that river valley. Only the threat of a flogging stopped my men from rolling around on the ground laughing."

"It is funny now," Stephan admitted. "I will not make the mistake of going to the river again. But," he said with a note of triumph, "we have a picture of the spotted fantail." He produced, from his shirt pocket, a photograph of a rather plump bird with a long, fanned tail. The breast of the bird was a glory of red spots on pure white; the spots were brightest at the neck and faded to a pale orange near the tail. The bird's wing covers were a moss-green.

"Good God!" Chuck said. "What an incredible specimen."

"My dear Chuck, that bird is only one of the many incredible specimens we have on our island."

"I'll say. I've seen pictures of that magnificent bird your sister, Lian Ellen, rides. I'm told you can see her riding sometimes. I've been on the lookout – but nothing yet."

Cheng Yi repressed a wince. *Am I the only one*, he wondered, *who notes the air has suddenly become colder?*

The Ülrügh of Si'Empra sat back slowly, bringing his wineglass to his lips. "You'd like to meet the Lian Ellen, Chuck, would you?"

Chuck glanced around the table, picking up on the changed atmosphere. "Well, Sir, just curiosity. It's really the bird, I'm interested in." He groped for another subject. "I tell you what I would really like to see: a Cryptal. Craziest creatures I've ever heard of. I'm told they move rocks around underground. I'm told they control all these hot springs on this island."

Oh, my friend, Cheng Yi thought. *Stop now!*

"And who has been talking to you about Cryptals?" the Ülrügh asked languidly, but in a voice that had become dangerously low.

"Eh? Oh no one in particular. All us ex-pats talk about them, don't we?" He looked around at his companions, but all seemed to have become preoccupied with their drinks or with morsels of food.

Cheng Yi shook his head mentally. Did they teach these envoys nothing about etiquette? Chuck had only been on the island for less than a week but the other two had visited Si'Empra before. At the very least they should have told the American that certain topics were best not raised with the Ülrügh.

"It is our friend, Cheng Yi, who moves the rocks on this island," Stephan said. "If you would really like to see something incredible, ask him for a tour of his quarries."

"We will do this tomorrow," Cheng Yi said, taking Stephan's lead. "Assuming there is no rain or fog." He raised his chin slightly in the direction of an attendant while flicking an eye in the direction of the Ülrügh's glass. The attendant hurried forward and offered wine. "With your permission of course Ülrügh. I always remember gratefully that it is your land from which I mine gemstones."

The Ülrügh waved the attendant away, sitting forward, thoughtful stare still fixed on Chuck. "What have you heard about the Cryptals?"

Chuck shrugged: "Not much, Sir – Ülrügh – Sir. I've been told they live in underground tunnels and you don't see them much."

"Why do you think this is the case?"

Chuck spread his hands in a silent plea. "Hell, you're asking the wrong person. I got no idea why you don't see them much."

"Jan?" the Ülrügh turned his attention to the German envoy.

"Ülrügh, I wish we did see them more. My country would pay much for more of their fur," Jan replied bluntly.

"Perhaps we should be more aggressive in hunting them. Chuck, would you like to join us on a hunt?"

Chuck's discomfiture gave way to eagerness. "Real hunting, my Lord Ülrügh?"

"Real hunting, Chuck."

The flat response sent a chill through Cheng Yi. He had no stomach for Cryptal and Crystalmaker hunts. *Barbaric!*

Ülrügh Redel smiled, indicating to the attendant – who still hovered nearby – to refill all the glasses. "Gentlemen. Let us withdraw to the Green Room for a hand or two of poker."

Cheng Yi relaxed. Sometimes, over apparently minor indiscretions, the Ülrügh would fly into a rage; not tonight. Perhaps because he loved to gamble and falling into a sulk would deprive him of that pleasure.

The men followed the Ülrügh into an adjoining room. Only Jan and Cheng Yi had been in the Green Room before. Stephan and Chuck delighted the Ülrügh by gasping appreciatively. All the furniture and fittings had been brought in from overseas: there were delicate oriental chests of drawers inlaid with mother of pearl; a round rosewood card table covered in green baize; glass-fronted cabinets of richly polished red cedar holding an assortment of small ornaments made of fine crystal, ivory, alabaster and other stone; fine Australian hardwood chairs with crushed velvet seat and back cushions; and a collection of miniature paintings, each worth a small fortune.

All this, thought Cheng Yi with an inward sigh, bought with funds that could have been used to fix up some of the disintegrating infrastructure of Si'Em City.

A BED. A CEILING. Sheets. Her head clearer.

Ellen looked for Elthán.

A tall, bony, dark-haired woman with thick-rimmed glasses over brown-flecked eyes, a striking aquiline nose and high cheekbones, appeared at the bedside. "Warmth and light, Lian."

Ellen noted the thick accent. She groped in her memory – *aah, yes*. This must be the Brazilian doctor who ran a medical clinic in Sinthén and now lived in Pedro's old home.

"Elthán put you into my care, Lian."

"Where is Elthán?"

"She left this morning – as soon as she was sure you were recovering. She has many things to attend to. May I take your temperature and feel your pulse?"

Ellen allowed the thermometer into her mouth and watched the doctor count the beats of her pulse against a wristwatch.

Greçia, Ellen recalled. *The people of Sinthén called her Greçia.*

As if hearing her name, the doctor smiled, one corner of her mouth rising slightly higher than the other. She released Ellen's wrist and removed the thermometer, glancing at it before making notes on a card on the bedside table. "Good," she said. "I've prepared some soup and pendle tea. Would you like some?"

Food! Yes, she did feel hungry.

But, more urgently, she needed to know: "Where is Rosa?"

"Just outside your window. She's been looking in frequently." Greçia frowned. "She taps the window each time I touch you. I – find it – disconcerting."

Ellen turned her head carefully and was rewarded with the sight of Rosa picking at a bale of hay. Her pet immediately noted the attention and stepped to the closed window, clacking and whistling happily.

"Can you open the window?"

"I'm somewhat nervous of her, Lian," Greçia said reluctantly.

"She is safe. She only wants to say hello."

Greçia unlocked the window and began to push it open, but jumped back with a yelp when Rosa forced her head inside. The bird craned her long neck toward Ellen. Very gently she began to nibble her sharp beak over Ellen's scalp, all the while emitting tiny noises, seeking reassurance.

Ellen buried her fingers into the soft feathers of Rosa's huge head, murmuring endearments in return. Then she whispered: "You stay outside now and don't eat everything in sight."

Rosa cocked her head, focusing one eye enquiringly on her mistress's face.

"Out you go, Rosa. Stay close," Ellen repeated more firmly.

Rosa withdrew obediently, shook herself to settle feathers and returned her attention to the hay.

Greçia closed the window with a quick, nervous movement.

"Thank you," Ellen said. "I apologise if she frightened you."

Greçia grimaced ruefully. "I'm not very good with animals," she admitted.

A troubled expression settled over her features. "But, Lian. May I ask you some questions? You're carrying old and not well-healed wounds, including an infected urethra. Are you taking medication for this?"

A memory flashed into Ellen's mind: lying in bed, hot and cold with fever, head turned to the wall with embarrassment, legs splayed for Lian Pethrie's examination while her mother stood next to the bed, face drawn with concern, fingers twisting the hem of her blouse; Lian Pethrie shaking his head with a resigned expression, "Please explain to your daughter that it is perfectly normal for girls of her age to bleed, especially girls with her condition. She has done herself damage. She has—"

Her mother attacked him, slapping him across the side of the head: "How dare you! How dare you! This has been done to her!"

Lian Pethrie had it right, though, Ellen had inflicted the wounds he inspected in her attempt to wash Redel out of herself. Lian Shivay, the second physician her mother had brought to Ellen's bed, gently cleaned the abrasions. "I don't know how this has come about," she said – she had said the words quietly and Constance had not heard them. "Lian Ellen please know that when you are ready for help I will do what I can," she had continued.

Ellen mentally scrambled not to drown in the sudden flood of shame Greçia's words released. *I am strong! I deal with the now! I am Lian Ellen! I ride Rosa! I am strong!*

Her gaze locked on to the sight of Rosa beyond the window.

I wonder who thought to give Rosa hay? The question zipped loudly into her mind, forcing an overlay to her emotions. *Where am I? Where am I?* She turned her focus from Rosa to her surroundings: not a large room, made of solid rock; a cloth embroidered with intricate hexagonal patterns of browns and oranges hung on one wall; a curtain hung over a doorway; another wall was made out of tightly woven leather and cane.

Hearing Greçia's slight intake of breath – preparatory to asking another question – Ellen's heart lurched. *Don't ask! Don't ask!* she wanted to scream.

She balled her fists tightly, searching more urgently for distraction: *I wonder how Elthán got me here! She said something about a sled and Cryptals and other Crystalmakers.*

"Are you on a course of medication and should I extend the treatment?" Greçia repeated.

Have I been in the Cryptal tunnels?

Out of the corner of her eye, Ellen saw Greçia turn and leave the room. She drew in a shaky breath, hugging herself tightly. *No tears! Control!* "I am the Lian Ellen. I am strong! I ride Rosa! I am strong!" She whispered the words over and over while her thoughts tumbled with embarrassment: *That was a stupid! Stupid reaction. All she did was ask a question. You behaved stupidly! Stupidly!*

But the mantra calmed her and by the time Greçia returned to her bedside with a steaming bowl of soup and mug of tea, Ellen had regained composure and had prepared a set of words should Greçia question her again.

But Greçia's question was different: "Will you eat something, Lian?"

"Yes. Thank you." Ellen attempted to push herself up but Greçia shook her head to stop her.

"Gently," she cautioned, setting the bowl and mug on the bedside table. She helped Ellen sit up, placing padding behind her neck to protect her bruised skull. Ellen lifted a hand for the spoon when Greçia held the bowl before her, but the smell and sight of the food made her hesitate.

"Lian?" Greçia asked in her soft voice. "The food is not to your liking?"

Ellen took a deep breath. "Sorry. Sorry I " Her words trailed away as she took hold of the spoon firmly and dipped it into the soup. She was determined not to make a fool of herself again. The food touched her taste buds and, in spite of her determination, she all but spat the liquid out. She swallowed quickly.

"Lian?" Greçia queried again. "The soup is not to your taste?"

"I'm sorry sorry. I'm just – just not very good with meat."

Greçia blinked her surprise. She looked down at the bowl in her hand then up at Ellen again. Her lips and eyes formed a warm smile as she moved the bowl away and took the spoon out of Ellen's hand. "Well, that is an easy problem to fix. I'll get you something else."

"I can manage," Ellen said, knowing that her protest did not sound convincing.

Greçia shook her head. "No. No. I pride myself on my cooking and will not suffer you to eat something you don't like. Perhaps some tea now and then I'll make you a more palatable meal."

Ellen drank the bitter tea, appreciating the moisture. When Greçia withdrew she closed her eyes. Her hunger had disappeared. She was unspeakably tired, and her head felt tight and swollen.

She didn't see Rosa, who had, all the while, watched the interaction between Greçia and her mistress, settle again beside the bale of hay and turn her attention to the man squatting nearby. The large bird bobbed her head and lifted the crest on the top of her head.

PHAN LOVED ANIMALS. HE understood them better than he understood people. Rosa's bob of the head and comb clearly signalled to him that Rosa had decided to trust him. His round face lit up with pleasure. Ever since Elthán had introduced him to Rosa he had checked on her welfare as often as possible. He had watched as Rosa peered fretfully into the windows of Greçia's home until she found her mistress. He felt sad when Rosa made small, concerned noises as she studied the prone figure, and noticed that the glasaur's concern peaked each time someone came close to Ellen's bed.

Hoping to help Rosa, Phan had selected a bale of hay from the winter storage cave and offered it. At first Rosa ignored it. Phan made snorting noises – the way he did when his goats were unhappy – explaining to her that it was his gift. She lifted her head high, towering above him, the crimson crest on her head fanning out, intense midnight eye with its bright blue ring fixed on him with indecision. Carefully, he had placed the bale on the ground and stepped back to watch.

Rosa had paced around, not touching the hay, alternately looking into the window and back at him. As the sun climbed to its zenith she settled to preen herself, her beak teasing out and smoothing the barbs on her long pinion feathers.

Interrupting his vigil, Elthán had emerged from the grotto with someone he didn't know. "That was a good idea to give her some food, Phan," she told him. He flapped his hands, pleased she had complimented him, but he had pointed at the uneaten bale, grunting his unhappiness. "You're worried she's not eating?" Elthán said. He nodded vigorously. "She might in a little while.

We need your help now, Phan, to select one of the chickens to kill."

Phan had snorted his protest. He loved eating and knew that the food came from the animals he looked after. Nevertheless, he did not like having to kill any of his flock. Forgetting Rosa for the moment, he had stumped dejectedly to the fowl enclosure. The chickens gathered around him as trustingly as always. He bent down and gently lifted one he had previously marked for sacrifice to the table. Cuddling it like a baby, he carried it away from its companions, carefully closing the fowl enclosure gate behind him. Through thick tears he killed the chicken and handed it to Elthán.

Elthán gave him a sympathetic pat on the shoulder and a big hug – which he always loved – and took the dead bird away.

Greçia had then called him indoors to eat. He had eaten quickly, filling his mouth with a thick goat and vegetable soup, and pancakes rolled around a layer of goat's cheese. All the time, he kept his eyes away from the strangers in the kitchen. They were working quickly, plucking the chicken he had killed and talking in low, anxious tones that made him feel nervous. He noted that Müther joined in their conversation.

Food finished, he had bolted outside to be with Rosa again, away from the strangers. He was relieved to see that she was picking at the hay now, though she was clearly still unsettled. He hardly registered Elthán's departure in his anxiety for the glasaur.

He leapt to his feet when Rosa suddenly turned to the window and pushed her head through. Phan saw Greçia jump back on the other side of the window. Rosa's wings drooped and fanned while her head was inside the room. When she withdrew her head she shook out her wings and tail and settled her feathers, but continued to stare through the glass when Greçia pulled the window closed. Suddenly, she seemed reassured, and had turned her head to give him this apparent invitation.

Phan dared to edge closer and Rosa did not rebuff him. Even when he touched her, she did no more than slightly lift the red crest on her head.

Her feathers were soft. They glowed iridescent in the cloud-filtered light, shining first blue, then green, then black as he stroked her. His hand traced down her neck and to the edges of her wings. He had seen pictures of birds that looked a little like Rosa. Greçia said they were called ostriches. But Rosa was much bigger than the picture birds: her neck was thicker, and her head and beak were more like those of a falcon than the picture ostrich – and she was much more beautiful! Phan gasped and muttered as he noted her broad chest and the layers of feathers: those underneath down-soft, those over the top stiff and smooth. Neither cold nor sharp rocks would easily penetrate such a covering. Rosa's back and pinion feathers were black, but when he gently lifted a wing, he saw that the underside was bright scarlet.

Rosa nudged him and he understood that she had had enough of his inspection. He withdrew, satisfied that it would be safe to leave her.

"Aak, aak, aak," he called to the goats in a high, nasal voice. They bleated in return, coming to him in ones and twos from inside their winter cave and all over the wide ledge stretching to the front and side of Greçia's home. He gave Rosa one more loving glance and scrambled away up the mountainside.

FROM THE WINDOW OF the large living area of her home, Greçia watched Phan's large, awkward frame laboriously but determinedly climb the escarpment into which her grotto was built, and on to the plateau above. Goats followed him, the kids gambolling in a happy tumble, the older animals picking their way more steadily over the rocky ground.

"Is he finally on his way?" Müther said.

"Yes." Greçia returned the phone handset to its cradle, ending her conversation with the clinic sister who had called to seek her advice.

"How is our patient?"

Four words, but Müther had managed to lace them with disapproval. Greçia chose not to react to the tone.

"She is asleep."

Müther sniffed. "We should be gone already," she muttered.

"Mmm." Greçia made the non-committal sound, not wanting to indulge Müther's grumpiness, even if what she said was correct. By this time of the year, Müther and Phan were usually safely in the Northern Lands, but their delay had nothing to do with the unexpected arrival of Lian Ellen. The snowmelt had been late this year and, because of the earthquake, Richard had decided to check the route to the Northern Lands before starting the journey.

Müther left her stool with an exaggerated sigh and made her way to the high-backed armchair with inbuilt speakers that Pedro had designed especially for her. She tracked through several programs loaded on a recorder before deciding on one.

Greçia settled to the paperwork she had brought home from the clinic. She ran two medical clinics: one in Sinthén, providing health services for those Si'Emprans too poor to afford treatment at the main hospitals in Baltha and Si'Em City, and another in the back of her home for Webcleaners.

"She's awake," Müther declared some time later, breaking Greçia's concentration.

She lifted her head to listen. Müther was right: there was a sound of movement in the bedroom.

Greçia found Ellen standing next to the bed, one hand on the wall for support.

"Lian?" Greçia closed a hand around a slender arm as Ellen's legs sagged.

"I need to go to the toilet." Ellen's voice slurred with effort.

Rosa's head appeared at the window. She rapped her beak against the pane.

"Lian, I have a bedpan for you. You would be well advised to lie still for a while longer."

Ellen drew in a deep, unsteady breath. Rosa rapped on the pane again.

Greçia gave the bird an anxious glance as she helped Ellen back into the bed. "Lian, she may break the glass."

Ellen frowned in Rosa's direction and waved a hand weakly at her pet. "Go away, Rosa. I'm alright." It was doubtful that Rosa could hear her through the triple-glazed window, but she appeared to understand and backed away.

Greçia eased Ellen's pants down and slipped a pan under her buttocks. Pretending not to notice Ellen's embarrassment, she pulled a sheet up to Ellen's chest and asked: "Lian, apart from hay, what does Rosa eat?"

"Eat?" Ellen echoed, confused by the question. Greçia noted the young woman flinch as she passed urine and wondered: *How long has it been since you have not experienced such a burn?* Remembering Ellen's earlier frozen response, she did not ask the question out loud but continued conversationally: "She's such a big bird; I wondered whether she survives entirely on grass."

"N-no – no. She'll eat anything – any scraps from the kitchen, seeds – she even eats meat –"

Greçia smiled. "Unlike her mistress." She passed Ellen a small hand towel to dry herself with, and covered the bedpan as she removed it from under the sheet.

"She – she – gets hungry – starts to destroy – things – unless you stop her – "

Greçia nodded, placing a hand on Ellen's forehead, as much to encourage her to stop attempting speech as to feel for fever. "I imagine your head's quite painful?"

"I b-bumped it."

"Yes. It is quite a bump. I'll give you a couple of tablets that will help to reduce the bruising. and perhaps this time you could stay awake long enough to eat and drink? I've made you some vegetable soup without a hint of meat."

CHAPTER 4
Webcleaning

*R*ICHARD HUNCHED INTO HIS coat, frowning into the night. Elthán was late. She had told him to meet her at the minor entrance to Illiath, but she was not here. He had waited all day, and now it was night and still she had not come. He had squeezed into the tunnel leading to Illiath and walked as far as the first Rest in the hope that he had misunderstood her and she had not meant to meet him aboveground but below. But she was not there either.

"Elthán," he hissed his worry for the thousandth time. "Where are you? Please be safe."

"I am here."

Richard swung around. He had expected her to arrive from the entrance to Illiath, but she was walking towards him down a slope from another direction. She moved quietly, placing her feet carefully. She would have seen him from some way off and, as always, underestimated his ability to see her in the dark.

He saw her teeth flash white in both a smile at his startle and in greeting. "My apologies for being late; I have been somewhat distracted."

"What happened?" He reached for her arm with concern, hearing the fatigue in her voice and noting the stoop of her shoulders. "I've pendle for you, and bread and paste."

"Aah, I am glad to sit, Richard," she sighed, accepting his hand to help her on to the mat he had spread over the soggy ground.

Richard lit a small fuel-fired camping stove and set a tin mug on it to re-heat. Next, he unwrapped flatbread made from berry flour, and spread it liberally with a cheesy bean paste. He rolled the bread and handed it to her.

Elthán sagged back against a boulder and nodded her thanks. "This is welcome. I ate something at Greçia's place but nothing since." She bit into the roll and continued, her voice slightly muffled with chewing. "I was on my way to Pedro's quarters to pick up a book Ellen was to give him when the Source of Song directed me to the shores of the Si'Em River. So urgently did the WhiteŌne want me to go that Cryptals carried me on one of their sleds. They led me out of their tunnels to where Ellen and that glasaur of hers were. She was sick to the death, Richard. I could not move her on my own to the tunnel so I had to wait for help to put her on to the Cryptal sled and we took her to Greçia."

"You mean Lian Ellen?" Richard was incredulous. "Is she still with Greçia?"

"Yes."

"Do you know what happened?"

"No. Not really. I suspect that brute of a brother had his way with her again, but she also has a nasty head wound and did not say how she got it. She was not yet awake when I left."

Richard shut off the stove's fuel valve, wrapped the heated mug in a cloth and passed it to Elthán. She took it in both hands, bending her face to breathe in the steam.

Lian Ellen, Richard thought.

Ordinary folk in Si'Empra idolised the Lian – something about her attracted people. It was not only her natural beauty and easy grace; perhaps it was something in her smile and air of honesty and sympathy. People called her 'Si'Empra Theolel' – the Jewel of Si'Empra. Richard had seen her in the couple of winters he had spent in Si'Em City. Sometimes she had been in the company of girls her own age, giggling and chatting as if she were just another child and not the Ülrügh's daughter. Most often, though, he had seen her when she performed as part of the entertainment that helped while away the long winter months. She sang, played musical instruments, told stories and made announcements with confident ease. Most of all he had admired her skill at schathem, Si'Empra's traditional climbing game. "Theolel! Theolel!" the crowd would yell encouragingly – Richard joining in as enthusiastically as the rest – as Lian Ellen swung from rope to rope across the ceiling over their heads, displaying great nerve and almost unbelievable strength and agility.

But that had been several years ago. It may puzzle others in Si'Empra that their Theolel now spent much less time in Si'Em City, chose not to play schathem and attended only a few official functions in winter, but Richard knew the reasons. Elthán had shared her distress at Greçia's table at each step of the tragedy surrounding Lian Ellen these last few years: first was the revelation by Constance that she believed her daughter was being abused by the Ülrügh; then the distress of learning that Constance had made a pact with Redel to become his wife if he promised not to touch his half-sister again; and, saddest, the tears when Constance died giving birth to the Ülrügh's child.

Richard had attended the funeral for Constance, standing among the crowd in Si'Em Square. Ülrügh Redel's eulogy had dwelt sadly upon the memory of his wife. Lian Ellen had stood by his side; her face a mask. She had sung a song of gentle praise for her mother that brought tears to everyone's eyes – even the Ülrügh had swiped his cheek. He had appeared sincere, holding Lian Ellen close at the end of the song – and she had not pulled away.

Seeing the open, brotherly affection, Richard had wondered, then, whether Constance had been wrong about her suspicions regarding the Ülrügh.

"Oh," Elthán had said bitterly when he told her about the funeral. "I think Lian Ellen is a good actress and Pedro tells me she does what she must to stop the tongues from wagging and making the situation worse for herself."

Elthán took a sip from the steaming mug. "I would like her to stay away from the Serai – from Si'Em City. I have asked Greçia to discuss this with her and offer her the option of travelling with you to the Northern Lands."

Richard paused in the act of packing away the camp stove. "Travel with us?" The possibility made him both nervous and excited. "It will be an interesting journey if Lian Ellen accompanies us," he murmured.

"I hope she agrees." Elthán took a sip of pendle. "I should be on my way. I want to see Pedro."

"About this book you mention?"

"Yes. And to ask him whether he knows what happened to Ellen."

"Do you think people will be searching for her?"

"I don't know. Pedro tells me that she is away from the Serai for such extended periods of time that people have become used to her absence."

"What is this book?"

"A book of rhymes. Pedro discovered it in the museum. It seemed to contain Crystalmaker rhymes. Pedro thought there may be words there that had been lost in The Destruction."

"I thought that Crystalmakers did not use writing."

"Pedro thinks that the words were written by a Skyseeker, one who understood the Crystalmaker language and who was intimate with Crystalmaker ways. He said it was very difficult to read because the person had used some form of phonetic alphabet, but he still hoped to translate it. I told Guild Master Joosthin about the book and he was most eager for access to its contents." Elthán took another sip of pendle and gave a small scornful huff. "He will have access to the contents and do his best to forget that his access was courtesy of the written word."

Words. Written words. Richard sat cross-legged in front of Elthán, whose wisdom and fortitude he admired immensely, and thought about the many battlefronts she faced simultaneously. The hostility of the majority Crystalmaker community towards the written word was just one of those fronts. They believed that the written word would trick people into believing that they had knowledge rather than just information. They also believed that the totality of knowledge should only be in the control of Guild Masters, who guarded the nature of truth and provided knowledge bit by bit to people when they were deemed ready to understand it. As Pedro had explained, such a belief had existed at the time of the Greek philosopher Socrates – which, Richard had learnt from Müther, had influenced many foreigners. In defiance of the Guild Masters, Elthán had decided that all Webcleaners should learn to read and write. It was only the contempt Crystalmakers had of Webcleaners – which forced Webcleaners to live in isolation and practice a form of 'invisibility' – that enabled Elthán to so blatantly disobey the Guild Masters.

"I have asked Greçia to ask Ellen about the book when she wakes up. Now – book and Ellen aside, Richard tell me – what have you found? Can you start the journey? Is the path to the Northern Lands passable?"

"Yes. The way is clear. An avalanche has scoured part of the Sith Cliff, but the path we use is undamaged. The team operating out of the Sith Chamber has started the harvest. Chris and Thimon are with them. Chris and Thimon will leave in four days and meet us at the Sith River."

Elthán nodded. She had a number of harvest teams. Four worked the highlands on the northern peninsula of Si'Empra, and a dozen worked the lowlands and its hinterlands. The lowlands provided more bountiful harvests but, because that was a favoured Skyseeker hunting ground, they were dangerous for Crystalmakers. Signs for this year's harvest were good despite the late start to spring. The past week of clear skies and sunshine and the lengthening daylight hours had hurried many bushes, herbs and grasses into production. A good harvest, well cured and stored, was the difference between a passable winter and hunger.

"Did you come across Cryptals in your travels?" Elthán asked.

"More than usual." Richard, though he was a Skyseeker, used both aboveground and belowground routes to move around the island. "They are busy above and below, moving and breaking a lot of rock. There was yet another earthquake a few days ago, deep underground. Thimon tells me that he'd heard The Deep was destroyed."

Elthán frowned. "Yes, I felt the shake of this earthquake, but I have not heard about damage to The Deep."

WRAP EATEN AND WARM drink finished, Elthán was ready to continue on her way. "I need to go, Richard. Please return to Müther and Phan and take them to the highlands as soon as you can – along with Ellen, I hope. I hope she is well enough to travel. She has the glasaur with her, of course, and that may make it easier for her."

Richard stood to bid her goodbye, placing his cheek into the cup of her palms in the gesture of endearment used by Crystalmakers.

She left, knowing that he would curl up to sleep, wrapped into a sleepsack and under a cover that he would rig against the inevitable rain. He would travel when the sun gave him sight again.

She climbed over a boulder and ducked under another. This entrance to Illiath had once been relatively large and easy to find. Now it was well concealed. She squeezed into a tiny opening into the ground. It was just large enough to fit a fully grown man but she was only a slight woman. She crawled forward on hands and knees for twenty metres through a cramped tunnel to a larger cave. There she opened her small backpack, took out a cream-coloured coverall and pulled it on. She settled the hood over her head and face, adjusting the two clear crystal-covered holes over her eyes. She fitted gloves over her hands, felt for the finger holds on the rock before her, and shoved it to the side. The rock rolled easily away on a worn track. Soft, warm air carrying the faint smell of mylin poured into the cave. Elthán stepped into the revealed tunnel and rolled the rock back into place. In the new dark, she groped her way to a smooth wall and sat against it, head back, eyes closed, breathing deeply through the hood she had not quite fastened.

Most of her life she had spent hours, days and weeks out of her underground world – without the help of mylin. She had become used to being aboveground, but sometimes every nerve in her body screamed protest. The first breath of mylin, even faint and stale as it was here, was welcome and to be savoured.

Elthán did not indulge herself for long. She sealed her mask, checked and rechecked that the seams of her robe were closed, and continued her journey to Illiath, one hand brushing the wall to guide her way.

Two hundred metres into the tunnel, the darkness gave way to a soft light emitted by curly bioluminescent fungi that covered the tunnel ceiling. Elaborately tended by Cryptals, these fungi grew in all the Cryptal highways, providing just enough light for the sensitive eyes of the underground dwellers to travel with ease. Elthán increased her pace but not so much that she could not appreciate the beauty of the way she travelled. She considered this part of the underground highway system to be one of the most spectacular. The countless rub of Cryptal hands and feet had polished the black walls to a high gloss. The black was shot through with glittering gold and veins of green in every shade. This type of colouring was the rarest in Si'Empra. The now abandoned labyrinth of Trebiath was hewn into this form of granite. In most of Illiath the rocks were in hues of pinks and reds.

Elthán's steps slowed, her eyes drawn to the glint of spider webs.

She hesitated, torn between the need to complete her journey and–

Just for a while, she promised herself. *I'll only do it for a while.*

She eased a small pouch she carried around her neck out of her coverall and extracted from it a crystal about the size of her small finger. She pulled a thimble-shaped cover off one end to expose two, fine, sharp-edged tines. Making a soft, buzzing sound with her tongue and lips, she approached a web. The tines of the crystal echoed her buzz – each prong sounding a slightly different tone. The spider – a white creature almost the size of her hand – moved to the web's centre at her approach; and there it stayed without moving while Elthán carefully picked the debris – insect husks and small bones of past meals – off sticky threads.

Each time she used her small web cleaner, tranquillity spread its arms around her. She had no idea why she was drawn to clean webs. Although Webcleaners belonged to the Crystalmaker peoples, most were born with this intense attraction towards cleaning spider webs. Sometimes Elthán wondered whether this primal urge was the reason why the Webcleaners were considered as a separate class of Crystalmakers. She would not mind if that was the reason, the puzzle she faced was why Webcleaners were also considered inferior. The Order, the code by which Crystalmakers organised their society, seemed to specify that Webcleaners should carry out all the most menial tasks. The day that old

Master Whyphoon, who had taught Elthán how to clean webs, pronounced her mastery, he had said: "This you have earned. By it you know who you are. By it you accept your part in The Order".

At the time, those words had made her swell with pride. "Oh yes," she had vowed, "I will play my part in The Order." In all her young life she had known nothing but servitude. It did not occur to her that she should feel demeaned by the way Webcleaners were, at best, ignored and, at worst, denigrated. It jarred her now to be treated so poorly by Crystalmakers, especially since there was no acknowledgment of what Webcleaners did for the whole Crystalmaker society. She had played her part for a long time and kept her thoughts largely to herself. At first she had only been focused on securing the future of the Crystalmaker population after The Destruction; afterward she had hoped that Webcleaners would gain status by being recognised for their work. But she had given up on Crystalmakers ever allowing Webcleaners true integration and, truth be told, Webcleaners themselves were so steeped in the norms of service that when she spoke of another way for them to exist as a group, very few were comfortable with the idea.

Lately, Elthán had been working on another idea for Webcleaners: independence.

"Master Whyphoon," she whispered to herself. "Much has changed since the day you gave me this little crystal tool."

It was on that day, the day she received her own tiny crystal web cleaner and permission to set out on her first solo excursion to clean webs that her world had changed forever. Ülrügh Devi, grandfather of the current Ülrügh, had invaded the Cryptal tunnels with his men and their bright lights, gas masks and guns, killing Crystalmakers and Cryptals by the hundreds.

She had heard them coming and seen the glare of their lights. Terrified, she pressed herself back into the narrow, short passage she had been working in, hiding her small body behind spider webs. Even after the age of shouts, screams, pleas and endless gunfire had died, she stayed where she was, afraid of the eerie silence. She could hear the spiders moving around their webs, seemingly as confused as she was. When she sensed a spider coming too close, she made the 'chuck chuck' sound she had been taught to make when a spider threatened, and it moved away.

Thirst had eventually forced her to grope her way back to Illiath through an unfamiliar blackness and a world in which, most terrifyingly, the WhiteŌne was silent. The smooth floor and sides of the Cryptal tunnel gave way to piles of rubble and, finally, a wall of collapsed rock. She felt around for a gap and saw the infrared glow of steam smoking up from a broken canal. Desperate for moisture, she sipped the warm water, gagging on its sulphuric taste. A voice moaned for help nearby and she located a faint warm glow half-buried in stone. She had found other people too; some were dead, others dying. All her efforts to help proved useless. Soon, she alone lived in that dark.

She had searched for some passage to take her deeper into the earth but all passages were blocked with walls of stone, so she travelled up – the way those with guns and masks had come – until she saw a faint glimmer of strange light. Even stranger than the light was the quality of the air. It was cool and thin. Cautiously, she released the cover over her face and breathed in a tangy sharpness that did not hurt her lungs. Little by little she had moved forward until she stood at the edge of her known world.

She had realised she was looking at a night sky; she had been told about 'night sky' and 'day sky', and 'sun', 'stars' and 'moon' and a place where colours were so bright that Crystalmakers lost their minds. She huddled against a wall and stared at the sky and the vast openness beyond the cave entrance. The openness was alive with warm bodies that darted up and down, appeared and disappeared behind dark masses that did not look like rocks; it had been her first experience of plants and aboveground animals. Exhaustion had dropped her eyes closed. Fear had shocked her eyes open when bright light flooded over her. She retreated into the tunnel. With tears leaking down her cheeks and desolation hugging her body, she stared at the light; it assaulted her senses. She could not confront it, but she could not go back into her familiar darkness.

Uncomfortable hours of thirst, hunger and wretchedness followed — then, the night sky returned.

In the world she had always known, light and shadows were constant. The changes she saw at the mouth of the tunnel were wondrous enough to encourage her to creep forward again to look out beyond her hiding place.

Something in the air told her there was water if she only dared to move beyond the exit of the tunnel. Even so, she might never have dared to go further, dying at the tunnel's entrance, had she not clearly identified one of the warm movements as a mouse; not white such as those that lived in the Crystalmaker labyrinths. This mouse was darker, but a mouse nevertheless. It stopped, lifted its snout and nibbled at one of the dark masses. She had realised that the mouse was nibbling at a berry. Without reflecting further, she scrambled forward, found a berry, picked it and shoved it into her mouth. Sweet, acidic moisture exploded against her parched pallet.

That berry had marked the beginning of her life aboveground. For days after that first scramble out of the tunnel, she had sheltered in the darkness of the ground during the day and foraged at night. She learnt to make sense of the uneven ground and of a world without walls. She had been shocked the first time water fell from the sky, sending her scurrying back into the shelter. Even more disturbing had been the moving air that whipped around her, pressing her clothes to her body and sucking out her body's warmth. She had learnt that too many berries made her stomach ache. She tried to eat leaves because they looked somewhat like food she was familiar with, but many of the leaves she tried were bitter and others left her gagging. At first she had been afraid of the animals that moved around at night, but they had no interest in her. After a few nights, she ignored them, especially since growing hunger made her increasingly desperate. It had been this inattention to her surroundings that caused her not to notice the man until his hand clamped around her wrist. She struggled furiously to free herself, but he was large and strong. He lifted her effortlessly and carried her to the entrance of a nearby cave. Keeping a firm hold of her, he reached into a bag, pulled out a flatbread and offered it to her.

That man, Pedro's father, had saved her from starvation and helped her to understand that not all Skyseekers, the aboveground dwellers of Si'Empra, were murderers.

Pedro's father had fed her berry bread, meat, cheese and pastes, and given her warm goat's milk to drink. When the night was finished, he gave her sunglasses and a hat, which made the light of day almost bearable. Over the course of the next few days, he showed her what was edible and what was not, and how to prepare food in the steaming water of a hot spring she had not noticed before. He spoke her language and she began to learn some words of his. He had not wanted to leave her alone, but, when he said he needed to return to his own home, she had refused to accompany him. Loneliness for her own people and fear of the strangeness of his people, the Skyseekers, chained her to the familiarity of her cave. He left her the rest of his food and promised to return.

Though he had left her in a better state than when he found her, it was not long before anxiety and raking pains in her body had confused her into a stupor.

"Mylin withdrawal," Elthán murmured as she picked away at debris in a web. Sometimes her memories of those days were so clear, all the rawness of those weeks seemed like yesterday's experience, not more than sixty years ago.

A Cryptal had found her within days of Pedro's father's leaving. It had led her from her tunnel, over ground and under night sky to another tunnel and down into a familiar world of passages, back to her own people.

Sixty years ago, Elthán reflected. Pedro's father was now dead. He had been so kind then and after. He had taught her much. And he had introduced her to Pedro.

Pedro.

At the thought of her life-partner, Elthán smiled. When they were together, she felt the same sense of peace and happiness as when she cleaned webs.

Elthán was cleaning a third web when she noted that the spider had abandoned it and was sitting in a newly woven one to the side.

Carefully she picked the abandoned web clean, gathering some of the debris into the thimble. When cleaned, she crushed the waste – using the blunter end of her tool. She brought the thimble close to the hood over her face. Quickly she released the hood, added a tiny amount of spit to the crushed debris, then fastened the hood again. She stirred the spit into the crushed waste with the tips of the tines and then used the moistened tips to release a gossamer thread where it attached to the rock wall. Holding the released end between thumb and forefinger, she pulled the thread gently forward until it tightened at the point where it joined another thread. She re-dipped the tine into the bowl and picked at the join. The moistened tip caused the glue between the threads to dissolve, releasing it. Dip, pick, release, twine the thread between little finger and forefinger; expertly she unravelled the web. Done, she carefully rolled the skein off her fingers, folded it and deposited it in a pocket of her coverall.

While she worked and remembered, she also listened to the Song of the WhiteŌne. The Song was not for her but it troubled her. Finally, its disquiet and Richard's news about The Deep leached away the pleasure of cleaning the webs and forced her to remember her duty.

"Others will clean you," she whispered in goodbye to the spiders who clung, docile and huge in the centre of their webs.

Over the years, she had taught others how to clean and unravel spider webs, knowing that it gave them the same pleasure it gave her; a relief from the often demanding, dangerous and menial work of Webcleaners. The biggest problem she faced was to find the tiny forks for trained Webcleaners to call their own. No one seemed to know how the Old People had made them. She had asked Thren once, and shown him her own web cleaner. To her surprise, his eyes had grown large with wonder: he had never seen one before. He said that the art of making such 'virigins' was lost, and told her never to show it to another Crystalmaker. She had found the tools that her people now used among skeletons in the abandoned chambers ruined in The Destruction. As Thren had advised, all Webcleaners now kept their tools carefully hidden.

She trained people in web cleaning, but when she gave a new graduate their web cleaner, she did not repeat the words of obligation intoned to her. She did not wish to bind her people to The Order.

Elthán arrived, finally, at the main entrance to Illiath, but walked past it into a narrow passage that led to a smaller, inconspicuous, curtained doorway. She pushed aside the curtain and entered the wide cavern that was the main living space of the Webcleaners.

A number of women, seated in a circle on a thick rug that covered the centre of the room, turned their heads at the sound of her footstep. They rose quickly to greet her. They touched her arms in a sign of welcome and to draw her in further, they helped her out of her coverall and indicated a cushion for her to sit on. One woman hurried out of the cavern to spread the word that

Elthán had returned. Another woman bustled to prepare food and drink for her. The rest sat, telling her how they had missed her presence and that she now made their lives complete.

Elthán let herself relax into the warmth of the familiar welcome. Several children ran into the room and sat on their haunches in front of her, reaching out to touch her arms as the women had done. She patted each of their hands, naming each child: "Pethry, you have grown two centimetres in my absence! Lonna, look at your fingers: they are grown elegant enough to pick a speck of dust from a web! My, my Jenjen, your hair is so white it will surely light the darkest alcove."

The children giggled, talking over each other to tell her about important events in the few weeks since she was last among them.

"Mistress, I have learnt how to mend the hem of a dress—"

"Mistress, we have been clearing the southern quarter and now have a wide area to practise aboveground directions—"

"Mistress, I have been writing a story—"

Thanin, who acted as her deputy in Illiath, entered the chamber.

"Ah, ah!" he interrupted the children with mock severity. "What are you children doing still awake? To bed with you! Let the Mistress alone. She doesn't want to hear your chatter."

"She does. She does," the children giggled, but scuttled back to give him room to sit close to Elthán. He poured her a cup of warm pendle and pushed a plate of small, stuffed buns towards her.

Of course she wanted to hear the children. She smiled at them and winked. She also wanted to talk to all the other people who crowded into the chamber to greet her. But most of all she wanted to ask Thanin about the disquiet in the WhiteŌne's Song.

He told her about the earthquake in The Deep and, particularly, about how Thyrol and Heinie had been left behind.

An hour later, after she had eaten a meal and listened to news from others who wanted her attention, she took her leave and made her way through the narrow tunnels that Webcleaners used to unobtrusively access the larger Crystalmaker chambers of Illiath.

At the service entrance to Guild Master Joosthin's alcove she paused to peer through a small peephole in the tapestry covering, wondering whether the Guild Master would still be awake at this late hour. He was seated at his workbench, head bent over cloths that he was, doubtless, fashioning for another crystal creation. She slapped the rock to the side of the entrance to signal her presence.

The Guild Master stood quickly and secured the curtain over the main doorway to his room. His first words were not a greeting but: "Have you brought the written words?"

She ignored the rudeness, taking a seat at the bench as a concession to her aching feet and tired muscles.

"No. I have not."

"Did the girl fail?"

The girl! Elthán felt a stab of annoyance. She disliked the dismissive way the Guild Master referred to Ellen – and to Skyseekers in general. She kept the annoyance from her tone, though, as she explained: "Redel has mistreated her again and she fled the city. The Source of Song bade me to look after her. I have taken her to be cared for by Greçia."

The Guild Master jerked. "You – The WhiteŌne? You are mistaken!"

"Then my mistake led me to where I could find her." Elthán almost snapped out the words but again managed to moderate her tone to soften the sarcasm. Joosthin always reacted with indignation when she mentioned that she could, at times, understand the WhiteŌne's Song. There was a belief among Crystalmakers that the WhiteŌne would only ever make itself understood to certain chosen Guild Masters. Guild Master Joosthin had been the chosen one for many decades now.

The Guild Master scowled but the glower did not quite cover the confusion in his eyes.

"I don't know if Lian Ellen found the book or not." Elthán made a point of emphasising both the title and name of her granddaughter. "If the abuse occurred after she obtained it, Redel may well have it now."

"Will he know what it is?"

"Skyseekers have long had the book and its information has, apparently, held no particular meaning for them."

"You said the book contains words?"

"Indeed." Elthán continued to keep her impatience at bay, aware that the Guild Master bordered on believing that written words had their own, living power. "Words without context are not information," she said.

"Only a Guild Master can decide on symbols for all to remember," he stated categorically.

Elthán chose not to debate the point. Among Crystalmakers, the Guild of Memory preserved history in song, rhyme and dance. Some songlines were rendered into the intricate designs of tapestries. It took years of practice and skill for initiates to memorise songlines and understand patterns in tapestries.

"Your duty—"

"Do not speak to me of duty, Guild Master."

She saw his face tighten. *Be calm, Elthán*, she scolded herself.

"Do not test me, Elthán!"

"I apologise for my shortness, Guild Master. I can do nothing about the book just now. When I see Pedro again I will discuss with him what to do. Please tell me what happened in The Deep."

For some seconds he seemed to consider whether or not to continue his conversation with her. Then he told her: "The southern routes from the Source of Song have been severely damaged."

"And the Source of Song?"

"The Cryptals have secured Its place in The Deep, but our chambers in The Deep have been destroyed. The Source was the one who guided me safely out."

"I have been told that you demanded Thil send a party to search for Heinie and Thyrol. Thank you."

Joosthin averted his eyes. No doubt Thil had been surprised by Guild Master Joosthin's request, given that Crystalmakers scarcely acknowledged the presence of Webcleaners, let alone learned their names. The Guild Master lowered himself to his seat, rested his elbows on his knees, and regarded his burn-scarred hands.

"Cilla has lost her child," he said woodenly.

"Not even The Deep is safe," Elthán sympathised.

"We – the Guild Masters – have decided to return to Trebiath."

"Trebiath?"

"We will fire up the furnaces there again."

"Trebiath is closest to the surface," Elthán worried, "and closest to Si'Em City."

"The Cryptals have closed most entrances from aboveground to Trebiath. I don't think Skyseekers can reach it any more."

Elthán came to her feet. "Well," she said. "I suppose you will want it cleaned and prepared. Trebiath has been abandoned a long time."

She was almost out of his alcove when she remembered the other news she wanted to give him. "Thren has died."

"How do you know?"

"Those who care for the Overcome found him this morning."

"You care for the Overcome!" The Guild Master's expression showed appal.

"Yes."

"But why? How?"

"They are still human, Guild Master, though their minds are gone. We give them food and, if they let us, we tend their sores and try to ease their pain. When they die we honour them by wrapping them in death cloths and giving them to the Cryptals to take to our final resting place."

"But they are despicable. They have chosen to leave us."

"Who knows, Guild Master, what causes Crystalmakers to prefer mylin to the companionship of their own kind. Whatever it is, it is a tragedy for them and I will not be the judge of why one group of people is more deserving than another."

Perhaps, Guild Master, we do this in the hope that one day other Crystalmakers will recognise that Webcleaners are not sub-humans, Elthán thought as she left the Guild Master's room.

CHAPTER 5
The Journey Begins

*E*LLEN PULLED OFF HER borrowed sleepwear and donned her familiar riding clothes: loose soft woollen trousers and shirt with a wide overlapping bodice over close-fitting thermals. She tugged a comb through her tangle of red curls before slipping on leather boots – cleaned and buffed – and tucked the bottoms of her trousers in before lacing up their sides.

Outside the window Rosa watched with anticipation. Ellen smiled and nodded at the bird. They were about to travel and the prospect of being in close company with her rider always made Rosa excited; she lifted the crest on her head and shook out her wings, giving the window a gentle few taps to indicate her impatience.

In the week of her gradual recuperation under Greçia's careful attention, Ellen had wondered what she should do. Having determined that returning to the Serai was not an option, she faced the life of a refugee. Friends and family at the Serai had become used to her very long absences in summer, but they would expect her to return for the winter months, and Redel would be furious because he would expect her to follow the usual practice of helping to make the crowded living in Si'Em City during the winter months a relatively pleasant experience. The latter concerned her least. During the past four years she had felt like an increasingly thin foil between the needs of the larger Skyseeker population – who held no position of power but just wanted to live their lives in relative comfort and security – and the excesses of the traditional ruling families. Particularly, she found she was steadily losing the battle against the adjutants, who seemed to think it their duty to threaten and imprison those who objected to their impoverished state.

Ellen toyed with the idea of overwintering at Thuls Refuge. It was the home of descendants of the small band of Lians who had opposed Ülrügh Devi's decision to destroy Cryptals and Crystalmakers more than sixty years ago. Thus far the exiles' sanctuary had not been discovered by the administrators of Si'Em City. She had almost decided upon this course of action and to simply continue her practice of visiting summer villages for the rest of this summer season, when Greçia had offered her another option.

"It is what Elthán wants," Greçia had explained. "I would prefer that you not make the journey yet, but the preparations are made and the party wants to leave in two days. We currently look after an exile. She stays with me over the winter months but in summer it is too dangerous for her here – sometimes people visit me. We can't hide her in the Cryptal tunnel behind this grotto because she reacts rather badly to Cryptal fumes. So she spends the summer in the Northern Lands. Elthán thinks that perhaps you would do well to go there also, then stay with us over winter and not return to Si'Em City."

The unexpected invitation intrigued her – or at least the prospect of journeying to the Northern Lands with people who were close to Elthán intrigued her. Ellen was keen to know more about her grandmother, and certainly curious about meeting the exile. Perhaps it was a person who was in the same situation as herself, though she could not readily call to mind exiles other than those at Thuls Refuge.

Before pushing aside the curtain to the bedroom which had been her sick room – and, it would seem, Greçia's bedroom, though Greçia had been sleeping elsewhere this past week – Ellen glanced briefly in the mirror. All her life she had been told she was a natural beauty and, as the Ülrügh's daughter, she had been schooled in the art of enhancing her features. Applying small touches to her clothing and deportment to ensure that she presented a strong, refined, confident, cheerful and untroubled person had become second nature.

Greçia, two men and a woman turned towards her as she left the bedroom, Greçia and the youngest of the men coming quickly to their feet.

Greçia began the introduction: "Lian Ellen, may I present Müther." Ellen did not know the name, but she knew precisely who the seated woman was. A surge of elation touched a smile to her lips. *This must be the exile! I would never have guessed!*

"I am honoured to meet Si'Empra Mayal," Ellen said

Müther started. Her shapely lips parted and her dark brows arched. She pulled her expression quickly into one of disapproval and snapped: "What do you know about the Songbird?"

Where Müther's eyes should have been there were lumpy scars; where Müther's hands should have been there were stumps. In spite of the deformities, Ellen had no doubt that this was the Songbird of Si'Empra – Si'Empra Mayal. Although the Songbird had purportedly died in an accident years before Ellen was born, there were many images of her in Si'Empra. "I know that Si'Empra has been poorer as a result of your absence."

"Is this Pedro's doing?"

"Pedro?" Ellen puzzled. Of course! This had, after all, been Pedro's home. Pedro must have known that Müther lived in this grotto. Ellen said: "No, Pedro has never spoken about you except as a legendary figure of our time."

Müther's lips pursed. She sat up very straight, her discomposure barely masked by her scowl.

Why scowl? Confused by Müther's reaction, Ellen turned her attention to the young man. Dark hair, dark eyes, high cheekbones and full lips: there was no doubt that this handsome person was a close relative of Müther. Ellen had seen him in Si'Em Square. He was usually bargaining for items that looked to her like junk, but she had long suspected that he engaged in the black market.

"May I present to you Richard, son of Müther," Greçia said.

"Warmth and light, Lian," Richard made the greeting with a small, courteous bow.

"Warmth and light," Ellen returned.

The second man, still seated, had turned his back to Ellen, but his head was turned so that he could steal shy, frightened glances at her. She recognised him as the man beyond her window who had befriended Rosa.

"And this is Phan," Greçia said.

"Warmth and light to you, Phan," Ellen said. "I have much to thank you for. You have taken great care of Rosa. She lets me know that she is very fond of you."

Phan turned slowly around, his small eyes growing quite round as a huge smile stretched over his face, swollen tongue lapping over his bottom lip.

Greçia laughed. "Phan will now follow you to the ends of the Earth. He is totally in love with that bird."

"Then we share a common interest."

"We are ready to depart, Lian," Richard said. He blurted out the statement, then seemed embarrassed by his abruptness. "The journey may take more than a week. We will cover hard terrain. Greçia said you could ride Rosa. We take goats and chickens. Will Rosa be alright travelling with goats and chickens?" His words tripped out in a fluster; colour crept up his neck and burned on his cheeks.

Goats and chickens? Ellen was intrigued. "Rosa will not mind goats and chickens," she said.

"We travel in the early hours of the day. That's when it seems to be the safest. Usually the patrols don't start until later in the day," Richard said.

The patrols were undertaken by Redel's rangers – part of his adjutants group. They patrolled with helicopters, looking for Crystalmakers and Cryptals to hunt.

"We know the route very well and should be safe, provided we get to each shelter by noon each day. The shelters give us enough cover to hide."

Ellen nodded her understanding.

Richard shuffled awkwardly. Müther shoved back her chair and stood. "Let us go then." She walked unerringly to the door; Richard pushed it open and a cold draft poured into the room. Pausing only to place the stump of her right arm on the doorjamb for balance, Müther descended the two steps out of the grotto.

Ellen followed, also pausing in the doorway, not for balance but to peer into the uncertain dawn light. Her eyes widened. A large trip of goats milled on a wide rock ledge. Many carried packs or cages holding chickens. The scene was so unlikely that she burst into a delighted laugh. "How wonderful!" She turned to Phan. "Are you the clever person who taught these goats and chickens how to travel this way?"

Phan practically capered with pleasure at her words, rushing to the nearest goat carrying a pair of chicken cages to show off how they were secured.

His demonstration was interrupted as bleating goats skittered aside to make way for Rosa. The glasaur had spied her mistress and was chirruping ecstatically. She seemed hardly to notice the goats as she strode among them, saddlebags dangling from a strap held in her beak.

She dropped the bags at Ellen's feet and lowered her head to rub her comb against Ellen's chest. Ellen put her arms around the great head. "Yes," she whispered so that only Rosa could hear, "I'm really glad to see you too." Then, more loudly, she said. "We have a journey to make."

Rosa picked up the bags and pushed them into Ellen's arms.

For Rosa the bags were an easily managed bundle, but they filled Ellen's arms and were too heavy for her to hold. She let them slide, and bent over one to remove a bundle of lightweight straps and a rectangular pad decorated by many loops. "I just need to put our harnesses on," she explained to Greçia and Richard, who were looking on with interest. She moved to a relatively clear patch of ground and the bird lowered herself to the ground.

"She's been carrying those bags around with her everywhere she went," Greçia marvelled.

Ellen nodded. She was unabashedly proud of her mount. "Yes, we decided that it was the only way to make sure we always had the harnesses and saddle, and our other gear, when we needed them. She can unsaddle herself and put everything away, but she can't saddle up by herself." Ellen worked quickly, Rosa helping with her beak to pull straps and fasteners into place. Finally, with Rosa saddled to her satisfaction, Ellen unfurled the sash around her waist and wrapped it across her back and chest. It was a fine, Cryptal cloth shawl, an heirloom from the days when Cryptal cloth was still available, and a good buffer against the cold. She had a coat, but left it packed away. Once she was on top of Rosa, the bird's body heat would give her sufficient extra warmth unless it rained. "You can get up," she told Rosa. The bird stood and shook her feathers into place. Ellen strapped on her own harness.

"We're ready," she said, only then becoming aware that Richard had been quietly relating the scene to his mother.

She saw Phan standing close by, transfixed. "Look, Rosa," she said. "Here is your friend Phan. We will be travelling with him."

Rosa reached her beak forward to Phan and gently gave his scalp a nibble. Phan hooted and snorted with delight, bringing his hands up to his head and rumpling his hair. He ran to Greçia and then to Richard, excitedly showing the top of his head to them.

"We should be away," Müther said. "I can already feel the sun."

"Phan will lead with his flock and Müther and I will follow," Richard said. "Lian, can you and your – ah – Rosa – follow?"

"As you wish," Ellen agreed.

"Let us go, Phan. Say goodbye to Greçia," Richard said.

At these words Phan began to cry. He took Greçia's hands and tugged at them, grunting and huffing.

Greçia shook her head firmly. "I'll wait for you to come back," she promised. "Go. Look, the animals want you to lead them."

With a bit more cajoling and pointing in the direction he should go, Greçia persuaded Phan to leave her. He trudged to the head of his flock, sobbing loudly and broken-heartedly.

Greçia bid Richard and Müther goodbye, taking their hands – in Müther's case, the ends of her arms – in her own and touching them to her forehead. "Warmth and light be with you."

"Stay safe," they returned, and Richard led Müther away to trail the goats.

Greçia turned to Ellen. "Lian, warmth and light be yours also."

Ellen did not extend her hands to Greçia, but crossed her arms over her chest. She bowed a little. "Thank you for your help, Greçia."

"Gladly given, Lian. Please take the medicines I gave you. They are to reduce swelling from the trauma to your head. And please – rest, lying down as often as you can. And if you begin to feel the return of infection, please take the antibiotics I put into your toiletries bag. Be careful with yourself."

Ellen gave a single, slight nod, a twinge of embarrassment at the oblique mention of her propensity to self harm. "Thank you," she said again.

She turned back to Rosa, snapped the pulley clip on to her harness and activated the small winch attached to Rosa's saddle to lift her up on to Rosa's back. "Just follow them," she instructed.

The path that led from the rock shelf up the steep slope behind the grotto became a track cut into a cliff that climbed slowly north. Out of the gorge, the ground – boulder-strewn but relatively flat – bloomed with vibrant grasses, herbs and small bushes. It was good land for goats to forage over.

Having established that the journey would be carried out at a slow walk, Ellen settled back on Rosa, adjusting straps to the side of the saddle, using loops on the saddle-pad and her own harness to create a seat with a backrest. Her head ached and, heeding Greçia's caution, she tried to give it support.

In front of her, Richard and Müther walked arm-in-arm, Müther surprisingly confident on the uneven surface. The goats bleated and the chickens clucked and fussed in their small cages. This was a strange procession indeed!

When the track ended at a rocky, deep gully, Ellen sat forward, intrigued to see how the handless, eyeless Müther would manage. She soon found out: with difficulty. Richard supported and lifted his mother, guiding her every move.

"Can you manage this, Lian?" he called back when he noted that Rosa was not following. "I'm afraid there are many places like this along the way."

Ellen urged Rosa forward. The bird easily negotiated the broken ground. "There is no problem for Rosa and myself," Ellen assured him when she was nearer. "But Rosa is quite capable of taking two people down and up this slope and, if Müther doesn't mind, she could ride Rosa with me and make this journey much easier for herself."

Müther, her face showing signs of exertion, snapped her head around in the direction of Ellen's voice. "What does she mean?" she demanded.

"I mean that you could ride on Rosa with me and she will take both of us through this gully and – even further."

Richard was eager. "It may mean we can go so much faster," he said, "and it would be easier for you."

Müther raised her eyebrows, scepticism in the grim line of her lips.

"She is safe," Ellen said. "Rosa is safe and I have an extra harness to secure you to her saddle so you can't fall off."

While Müther vacillated, Ellen dismounted and approached with the extra harness in her hands.

"What do you say, Müther?" Richard said.

Müther's nostrils flared. "I suppose it is worth a try," she conceded grudgingly.

"I'll slip the harness over your head and secure it," Ellen said. She touched the top of Müther's arm to forewarn her that the straps were about to be passed over her. "If you could lift your arms, it will make it easier for me to adjust the straps."

When the harness was secure she asked Richard to lead Müther to Rosa's side. "I will put my foot in a stirrup. You can put your right foot over the top of mine and stand against me with your arms wrapped backwards around me to give you balance. Richard, if you could hold me steady as the winch pulls us up, I can hold Müther's weight to the top, then, Müther, you need to lift your right leg up and over Rosa's back. You'll feel a pad – a cloth pad – on her back. That's what you'll sit on. You can't fall because I have you clipped on to the winch which pulls us up. So the worst that can happen is that we dangle from our harnesses."

It went fairly smoothly, with Müther floundering a little as she gauged the shape of Rosa's back and how to mount her. Richard reached up as high as he could to give Ellen support as she helped Müther settle. Rosa stood obediently still but watched the performance with a disapproving eye, neck craned around.

Ellen centred herself on the saddle. "I've secured your harness to the saddle so you can't fall when Rose makes sudden movements. Do you feel secure now?"

Müther nodded, clearly feeling anything but secure.

"Rosa, take us up," commanded Ellen.

Müther gave a yelp when Rosa made a long-legged leap up the gully's slope. Ellen closed her arms around Müther to keep her steady, leaning forward and encouraging her to do the same to give Rosa better balance.

Rosa was quickly among the goats and matching their pace and agility. She caught up with a heavily perspiring and panting Phan, who gave a cry of glee at seeing Müther mounted on Rosa. He flapped his hands, slapping them on his thighs as if he'd never seen anything so funny and wonderful.

"Oaf," Müther grunted.

"Wait, Rosa," Ellen said. "We've left Richard behind."

For a while Ellen could not see Richard, and then his head and shoulders appeared over the rim of the gully. Phan stumbled to him, gabbling, taking Richard's hand as soon as he reached him and pointing excitedly at Müther seated on top of Rosa.

Richard nodded, patting Phan's arm. "I know. I know. She's riding Rosa."

Catching up to where the glasaur waited, Richard grinned up at Ellen. "We'll be in the highlands in no time at this rate. How is it, Müther?"

"Less taxing," Müther said shortly, making no move to dismount.

An hour later, Richard stopped the group for a rest. He helped Müther and Ellen dismount, settled his mother on a rock and shared out small wads of flatbread made from a bean flour flavoured with berry paste. Müther held her wad firmly between her stumps, but she needed Richard's help to steady a canteen of water to her lips. Richard noted that this was their usual first camp, but they were making such good time that perhaps they should keep moving, especially since the weather was so good. Müther made a disgruntled noise in her throat but otherwise did not object.

THE JOURNEY BEGINS

The party stopped a couple of hours later in a charming saddle between two hills. A small spring welled up in the middle of the flat area, trickling into a rock pool before disappearing into the ground again. Between them, Phan and Richard relieved the goats of their packs, then, with speed borne of practice, fitted together pieces of cane into a frame and covered it with netting secured over a group of boulders and into the ground. They released the chickens into this temporary cage, and fed and watered them.

Müther knew her way around this area. While the men worked, she led Ellen to a rock overhang to the western side of the saddle. "We'll stay here the rest of the day," she said. "You should lie down and rest. Goodness knows Greçia told us often enough you should do so."

Ellen was glad to do as Müther suggested. Her head still ached uncomfortably and weakness jellied her muscles.

"We have travelled longer than we usually do, but we were making such good time–" Richard stopped as he entered the shelter.

Ellen opened her eyes.

"Lian you are not well." He was all concern.

In her mind, Ellen intoned: *I am Lian Ellen. I am strong. I ride Rosa. I am strong.* As with many of the pains that regularly afflicted her, she determined not to let the headache weaken her. "This is a pretty place. I don't believe I have been here before," she said.

"Yes." Richard looked about him. "Yes. It is. But please, let me find your bedding – in Rosa's saddlebags. Perhaps you would be more comfortable on bedding rather than just the ground?" He found and spread the bedding for her, encouraging her not to help but to sit quietly. Just as quickly and efficiently he prepared pendle. She sipped at the warm liquid, nibbled politely at the flatbread he gave her, then lay down and drifted into a doze that carried her through the rest of the day and deep into the night.

ELLEN WOKE TO THE cold dark and the urgent need to relieve herself. She moved a little away from the shelter, bumping into Rosa's warm, soft body as she did so. She finished her toilet quickly and groped her way back to her sleepsack, pulling the sleep mat and sack closer up against Rosa before crawling back into the warmth. But Ellen did not sleep again. She stared at the strip of dark grey sky showing between the roof of the overhang and the ground. She could hear the soft snores of Phan and Müther, the quieter breathing of Richard and the restless movement and sounds of goats all around them.

Her thoughts drifted to her brief encounter with Elthán. She also wondered whether her baby half-sister, Chrystal, was safe and loved. She had promised her mother she would look after Chrystal. She trusted that the faithful and kind Katherina was doing so. She was uneasy about the relationship Redel would establish with his daughter.

Ellen drew in a deep breath. Over the past few years she had taught herself not to dwell on the unhappy turns of her life, but just now, in the quiet of the night, she found it difficult not to feel despondent. She longed for her once simple, carefree life. It seemed a long time ago.

She mouthed the start of a poem that she had written about herself:

> *I lived a fairytale in my youth*
> *Beloved by the king and queen*
> *My beauty and charm were renowned*
> *Befitting my royal station*

THE JOURNEY BEGINS

I was the showpiece of the nation
Pearls and precious stones adorned my neck and ears
Jewels glittered on my wrists and fingers
My clothes were works of art
Dignitaries welcomed and wooed me
Over my smile and eyes songs were written…

Ellen grimaced into the dark.

"Mother." Her lips formed the word, and a lump of sadness formed in her throat, though her eyes did not water. She had moved beyond tears, glad that her mother no longer suffered.

For some time Ellen's thoughts stalled, depression gnawing, every failure in her life playing out in her mind. By the minute she felt herself becoming more worthless. As always when this mood overcame her, she felt the suffocating presence of Redel thrusting into her. She put her hands up over her face, fighting the urge to try, once again, to rub him out of her. Rosa stirred. Ellen felt the cool, hard beak of the bird press against her hands.

Ellen nodded in silent acknowledgement of her pet's sympathy and took a deep breath. *I am the Lian Ellen! I am strong. I look forward and not back! I do not pull others into my darkness.* She repeated the phrases over and over as she stroked Rosa's beak. By the time the sky became lighter she had folded her stifling emotions away behind the mantra of strength that was the vision of her best self.

She heard Richard's even breathing pause. The dark outline of his form sat up. He wriggled out of his sleepsack, stretched and moved to where he had set up a stove. She heard the tinkle of water being poured into a tin and the scrunch of plastic. "Time to rise," he said, a yawn muffling his voice.

Richard glanced shyly in Ellen's direction when she moved. "I hope you slept well, Lian." She assured him she had and asked what he was cooking. "Porridge," he said. "I'm afraid our fare is quite basic when we travel."

Ellen grinned. "It is less basic than when I go camping." She packed away her bedding, noting from the corner of her eye how Richard helped his mother out of her sleepsack and on to a mat. He passed Ellen a bowl of porridge and gave another to Phan. Richard fed Müther her porridge as he ate his. Phan carried his bowl around as he herded goats together and sorted the goats into those that would carry the chicken cages, those that would carry packs, and those that would be left free. With Müther's breakfast finished, Richard helped Phan catch the chickens and pack them – clucking in protest – into cages before dismantling their temporary confinement.

The whole business took more than an hour, the sky turning from hazy white to yellowish, then pink. It was November, the nights were rapidly getting shorter, Ellen observed. She washed herself at the small stream and changed her underclothes, Rosa's bulk giving her privacy. She saddled her bird and sat near Müther to watch the men work. From time to time she glanced at Müther, sitting still and patient, her luxurious hair, dark brown with a touch of gold when the sun shone, in disarray. There was a dribble of porridge on her chin. Müther tried several times, unsuccessfully, to rub the dribble away with a stump. Ellen would have liked to help but guessed such an offer would not be welcomed.

All the goats and chickens organised, Richard returned to the women. He helped his mother to her feet, and led her away to the little pool.

Ellen stepped behind Rosa and walked away. She heard Müther whisper: "Can she see us?" and Richard's response: "She's walking away with Rosa. Why?"

Ellen's lips quirked into a smile: was he really insensitive to the likelihood that his mother would feel awkward about being helped in the private matters of her toilet by her own son?

Well, it's probably the most natural thing for him. He's probably helped her all his life, thought Ellen. *He seems such a gentle person.*

It was tempting to compare him to Redel but she didn't want to do that. Redel had turned from being her best friend into a nightmare –

No! Don't think of that nightmare!

They set out soon afterward, Müther choosing to walk rather than ride, complaining of saddle soreness. Richard linked one of her arms through his and described the day to her: "The sky is very clear still. It would be wonderful if this weather holds for another week. Everywhere around us is very green and the grass long, Müther. There are thousands of hawkberry plants in bloom. Can you smell them?" Müther nodded. "It will be a good harvest here. I can also see the snapbush growing strongly among the rocks. Their leaves are bright red and catch the sun when they move –"

Ellen listened to his descriptions and their conversation. She drew in a deep breath, closing her eyes to try to imagine what Müther sensed. The smell of the hawkberry plants was indeed strong: *minty with a touch of rose*, she decided.

A few times, Müther and Richard broke into song, cleverly taking parts in harmony. Ellen smiled: mother and son were wonderfully at ease with one another. It must have been tedious for Müther to ride Rosa the previous day. Ellen had said barely a word, and then only to give Rosa instructions. She had not even considered that Müther might be interested to know what the world around her looked like.

Spurred further by Richard's intimate descriptions, Ellen also turned to observing her surroundings more closely. She had explored much of Si'Empra but had only visited this north-western flank of the island once, deciding it was an uninviting place to spend time in. They were traversing a narrow ridge between two river systems, the Sith on the west and the Charn to the east. The Sith River ran deep in a gorge it had carved for itself, while the Charn plunged along the base of an escarpment of gouged, broken and twisted rock faces that reared up to three hundred metres high. On top of the escarpment were the Charn Mountains, a jagged, hostile range often shrouded in fog and rarely free from a dressing of snow. Ellen had flown over the area in a helicopter with her father. The deep ravines, glaciers and fast-flowing streams dwarfed swards of green. To the north-east, the Antarctic Ocean battered the forbidding coastline, the cliffs and rocky inlets the home to thousands of migrating sea birds in the summer months.

Swarms of insects and flocks of small birds hopped, fluttered, whizzed, buzzed and twittered around the walkers, rushing to feed from carpets of tiny flowers, each singing their own vibrant colour. The herbs and bushes were already heavy with small, green berries. Uncertain summers and certain long winters demanded quick work from all Si'Empran wildlife. Hundreds of small rodents scrambled among the plants. These were a joy to Rosa, who snapped them up and swallowed them whole by the dozen, her grazing making her stride a jerky one.

After a few kilometres, the relatively open ridge-land became more rugged. Reluctantly, Müther climbed back onto Rosa. Richard walked ahead with Phan. The goats followed the men in single file, though the kids often broke ranks to cavort their enthusiasm. Rosa turned her attention from grazing on rodents to nibbling plants.

"I noted that Richard describes what he sees," Ellen said. "Would you like me to do the same?"

Ellen felt Müther stiffen. "You should not tire yourself," she said.

They progressed in silence. Ellen leaned back into her brace and tried to shut out Müther's resentment.

Almost as if to give her a focus for more pleasant thoughts, a snow falcon appeared above them.

The bird's black-tipped, long and narrow wings jutted out stiffly from her heavy body as she rode a thermal higher and higher until she was almost out of sight. Ellen was about to look away when she noted the wings suddenly work in a series of quick, shallow thrusts, increasing the raptor's speed as she completed a circle overhead before settling into a long, fast, shallow glide, stiffened wings slightly raked. Suddenly, the falcon plunged, plummeted a hundred metres to the ground, disappeared behind a pile of boulders and appeared again seconds later with a mouse hanging limply from her talons.

It was not the first time Ellen had seen snow falcons hunt.

> *Black tips that trace the speed*
> *Bringing doom with each repeat*
> *White gracing lines in the air…*

The lines played into her mind. She toyed with them, juggling them for the best cadence. Perhaps it depended on what the fourth line was: *dare, care, fare, spare, lair, pair – which word for the fourth line*, she mused.

"Kek, kek, kek, kek, wheeeeee." The falcon's call was distant but distinct. Müther sat up straighter, turning her face in the direction of the sound. Rosa, too, turned to look at the disappearing falcon, though Ellen did not doubt that Rosa had been watching the falcon's every move.

"Is it coming nearer?"

"No. It just killed a mouse and is probably taking it back to its young."

"Did you see him make the kill?"

It was a 'her', thought Ellen, but she replied: "Yes".

Müther opened her mouth to ask another question but closed it again, turning her face forward.

I can tell you about these birds, thought Ellen to the back of Müther's head. *I can describe how they hunt and where they nest and how they feed their young. I can tell you they are the only bird of prey on Si'Empra, apart from two owl species that have adapted to this island. I can tell you that they stay inland because the migrating skuas and gulls chase them away on the coastal areas.* She pursed her lips. *I bet you want to know. Why do you hold me away so much?*

Ellen wrinkled her nose. Well, she reasoned, perhaps the supposed accident had been manufactured and something had happened that was somehow connected to herself – though how that could be, she did not know. The Songbird had disappeared before she was even born.

The accepted explanation for the Songbird's disappearance was that she had accompanied Redel and a foreign visitor she had grown fond of on an exploratory trip into one of Si'Empra's mountain areas. The three had fallen into a ravine and only Redel had managed to save himself. The ravine was deep and efforts by rescuers had failed to recover the bodies. Ellen had heard murmurs that this was a highly unlikely story since it was well known that Müther did not like such outdoor activities. Pedro and her mother had always avoided speculating about the matter.

Ellen mentally shook Müther's rejection out of her head and recalled the poem she had started to compose, adding and discarding lines. Flocks of finches, fantails, sparrows and larks periodically rose and noisily scattered before them, coming to rest nearby and looking with bold curiosity at Rosa and her riders. Rosa returned their stare. She would have liked to dispatch them as simply as she did the small rodents she ate with such enthusiasm, but Ellen forbade the eating of birds.

Once again, they reached their day's destination well before schedule. Richard helped his mother and Ellen dismount. Müther gave a grunt of relief as her feet touched the ground. "I think I am more saddle sore from that bird than I ever was on a horse."

Ellen said. "You're probably sore in all sorts of different places because Rosa moves in quite different ways to horses. They could never climb the way she does."

A flash of irritation passed across Müther's features. *What did I say that offended?* Ellen wondered. A wave of loneliness began to crest in her diaphragm. She pushed the feeling aside firmly and followed her companions to their shelter. Like their shelter the previous night, it had a steep slope behind and a rugged drop in front, though this shelter was a cave rather than an overhang.

She drank from her water bottle while Richard unpacked the day's portion of flatbread and sweet berry paste. Phan began to unpack chicken cages.

Richard broke the bread into four portions and handed them around.

"You look well, Lian. You have not found today's journey as taxing as yesterday's?"

"I am well," Ellen said. Richard's words made her remember Greçia's medication. Her headache was marginal and the weakness in her limbs bearable. She reached into her pocket and fiddled for the tablets, breaking a couple from their seals and unobtrusively putting them into her mouth with the next mouthful of bread.

"We've made very good time. Usually at this time we would be only just finishing packing up to prepare for the crossing. We'll stay here the rest of the day, but if you don't mind I'd like the two of us to go and inspect the escarpment we have to climb tomorrow morning."

After setting up camp they headed off, Ellen riding Rosa, and travelled a couple of kilometres down an increasingly steep and difficult slope to a place that would be only just broad enough to hold the whole trip of goats. Richard pointed at the river below, drawing Ellen's attention to a thin black scar in the ravine into which the whole torrent of the Sith River disappeared. "Across the top of that ravine it's only fifteen metres wide. We sling a rope bridge over and cross there."

He pointed to a narrow line running up the cliff on the other side of the ravine. "The goats climb up the cliff that way – there's a narrow track they follow. Thimon and Chris will be waiting for us on top of the cliff; they will lower rope ladders for us and we'll haul up the chicken cages that way."

Rosa made a cluck-cluck sound and Ellen looked in the direction of her mount's attention. She saw two tiny figures on top of the cliff. *Thimon and Chris*, she guessed, when Richard waved at them.

"Thimon and Chris," confirmed Richard. "They've been watching out for us. See, they are waving too."

"Your eyes are good," Ellen said, squinting and perhaps seeing arms waving on top of the two distant dots. Her gaze travelled along the line of the escarpment and rested on an area broken by a landslide and the erosion of a waterway.

"Can Rosa follow the goats up that track? And – I wonder – the bridge is narrow. It's a rope bridge. We store it just near here and sling it across. The goats cross in single file, and Thimon and I carry the cages across. I just wonder whether Rosa can manage the bridge – or perhaps she can jump the ravine –"

Ellen glanced at the ravine again, then continued with her examination of the river valley. After some time, she shook her head. "Rosa can easily get Müther and me to the top of the escarpment, but we will launch from there." She pointed to a ledge further up the ridge from where they stood, almost opposite the landslide. "We'll make our way to that broken part of the cliff. Rosa will have better footing there than on the goat track. It will take her about half an hour to cross and climb."

"Only half an hour!" Richard's face lit up, and then he blinked. "Will it be safe for Müther? I know she is nervous – but, then, this crossing is always horrible for her."

"She will be safe. We are securely fastened to the saddle and the saddle is securely fastened to Rosa."

Richard stared first at the route Ellen had indicated and then at the bulk of Rosa, who was calmly snipping last year's seed pods off a nearby bush. He drew a deep breath. "Half an hour. We could be up on the escarpment and well into the foothills before noon. That is amazing. We are very exposed on this part of the journey so it will be very good to complete it quickly. We start everything at the first hint of light. Thimon and Chris, of course, with their Crystalmaker eyes, need very little light, but Phan and I need some. This is always such a nervous time for us."

They returned to the others, explained the plan to Müther and asked her opinion.

"I have no opinion. I will do what I must," she said shortly.

The party spent the rest of the day in and around their shelter, Phan constantly herding wandering goats back among rocks so that the likelihood of the herd being detected was lessened. Richard divided his time between helping Phan and reading to his mother from an e-reader he retrieved from his backpack. As Ellen did, he carried a small solar charger for the device. Ellen lay back on her sleepmat and dozed, rousing herself only to eat the meal that Richard cooked, and to prepare for the night.

CHAPTER 6
The Hunt

Phan and Richard worked quickly to pack up in the bare light of pre-dawn. There was no cooked breakfast. Müther settled on to Rosa and the party set off.

At the spot where Richard and Ellen had discussed routes the day before, Ellen instructed Rosa to climb to the targeted ledge. Once there, she said to Müther: "Would you like to climb down for a while? We have plenty of time. It won't take us long to get to the top of the escarpment and I would rather that Richard and Phan complete most of what they have to do before we start."

She helped Müther dismount and offered her a drink, holding the canteen to her lips when she agreed. In another attempt to gain Müther's approval, Ellen decided to describe what she saw.

"One of the people has come down from the top of the cliff. It looks like the person is pulling something across the ravine."

"Richard throws a rope across and Thimon pulls the bridge across and then they secure it," Müther told her.

"Ah, I see now. Yes. Goodness! That bridge is rather narrow. I imagine it's not very pleasant to cross."

"Unpleasant!" Müther confirmed shortly.

Ellen could not see Richard and Phan from her vantage point, only the person at the base of the cliff, moving among the rocks.

Probably securing the bridge, Ellen guessed.

"Ah, there is Phan making the crossing."

"He goes by himself because he's heavy," Müther said. "Then he goes up the ladder and to the end of the goat track to call up the goats. He takes a long time to go up the ladder. He doesn't like the climb. Thimon will put a rope on him in case he falls and Chris keeps the rope taut from the top of the escarpment. Sometimes Phan falls and then there's quite a bother to get him back to the ladder and climbing again. Richard will hold back the goats until Phan has finished climbing. Then the goats go across. Then Thimon and Richard carry each chicken cage across and all the packs. Then Thimon climbs the ladder and he and Chris haul up the cages that Richard ties to a rope."

"I've had all this explained to me many times – each time over the past two decades that we have made this journey."

"I see," Ellen murmured. Obviously Müther did not want yet another description, so Ellen watched in silence. Phan reached the top of the ladder and, soon afterward, Richard led the goats across and to the base of the goat track. He turned in her direction and waved his arms. She waved back. It was time to make her own preparations for crossing the gorge.

"If you don't mind, we'll change places on Rosa," she said to Müther. "When Rosa and I do this sort of thing, I usually direct where I want her to go. If I sit at the front it'll be easier for me to see. Also, because she'll need to do a lot of jumping and scrambling, we'll need to work with her, throwing our weight forward and back at the right times. If you sit behind me you can put your arms around my waist and hug me so you can move with me."

"Can Rosa fly?"

"No. Not really. But she's good at using her wings to help her when she's falling."

Ellen helped Müther back up into the saddle, strapped her in securely and directed her to test her seat by lurching sideways, forward and backwards. At first Müther was tentative with the movements but, at Ellen's urging, she pulled more vigorously.

Rosa turned her head to watch, fussing at having to stand still for so long. She nudged at Ellen, causing her to swing in the stirrup she was balancing on.

"Don't, Rosa," Ellen muttered absently as she steadied herself.

"What is it?" Müther asked nervously.

"Oh, Rosa is just grumpy." Ellen lowered herself to the ground, taking Rosa's head into her arms. She scratched the white, sensitive skin between the comb feathers. "You're so clever and beautiful," whispered Ellen to her pet. "No one in the world can do what you do and you're going to take us up the Sith Escarpment in no time at all, aren't you. I'll give you an extra long groom when it's all over. Alright?"

Rosa made small warbling sounds in her throat, all love and trust for her mistress.

Ellen swung back up into the saddle. "Could you put your arms around me and we'll practise moving together?"

Müther pressed against Ellen's back, wrapping her shortened arms around Ellen's body. Ellen closed her left hand over the stumps, holding them together.

"Forward, Rosa. Let's take a look." Ellen studied the cliff again. *This will be fun!* she wanted to say but she doubted that Müther would think so. Out loud she said to Müther: "Try to move as I do."

Against her back Ellen could feel Müther's soft breasts, and heart beating fast. The woman's fear was palpable but what interested Ellen more was her strength. The body that pressed against hers was well toned, not the usual physique of a middle-aged woman. In the past couple of days sitting behind her, Ellen had had plenty of time to admire Müther's thick, long hair – she'd wanted to plait it more tidily than Richard had done. She had also noticed Müther's strong and disagreeable body odour, probably a result of her inability to wash herself. With Müther's face now close to her own she realised that she must also suffer from decaying teeth.

The resentment she felt at Müther's surliness evaporated. She imagined how she would cope if she herself had no eyes and hands. She repressed a shudder.

"We start by going down. It will be a series of jumps. We'll land with a thump then we'll go again till we're in a spot to leap to the other side of the river. You'll probably be jolted around a bit because Rosa might slip a bit when she lands, but she doesn't really need to be steady, just needs a bit of purchase to make another jump."

Giving Müther no time to respond, Ellen commanded: "Let's go, Rosa!"

Rosa launched forward. Ellen gripped Müther's arms harder as she leaned back to balance Rosa's movement. Müther gasped.

Down they plunged, Rosa spreading her wings to slow their fall, great talons reaching for the ledges that Ellen guided her to. She struck each ledge, bent her long legs like springs and snapped them straight to launch forward to another ledge. She negotiated two successfully but the third gave way when she landed, sending her slipping down the slope with legs and wings flaying. Ellen threw herself forward, gripping the front of the saddle to pull herself and Müther down as much as possible. She grunted with the effort but her voice – as she gave Rosa instruction – remained calm and firm: "Fly forward! Not your feet! Wings! Now your feet down! Up! Big wing beats! Bigger! Down – left! More! Jump!" Rosa's feet struck another ledge. It held and she regained balance but hardly paused, reacting almost instantly to Ellen's instruction to "Jump!"

Müther gave a thin, terrified moan as her arms slipped from Ellen's waist in the explosion of movement. Ellen reached back with both arms and pulled Müther's body against her own. Müther's arms wrapped around Ellen's waist again, hugging with all their might.

Though she steadied Müther as best she could, Ellen was totally focused on guiding Rosa. They made six more bounds, scrambling and sliding, once even hurtling end over end to plummet twenty metres before Rosa's wings arrested the fall.

Ellen whooped, eyes alight with the thrill of the ride. She would have laughed but there was no time; Rosa needed to be told where to land. No good trying to go for the spot she had originally aimed for, better to glide to a lower point.

"Keep height Rosa. Fly!"

"She can't! She can't!" Müther wailed.

Ellen squeezed Müther's arm to reassure her while she continued to urge her mount not to lose height.

Rosa beat her vast wings, breaking her silence with a protesting trumpet.

At the sound, Ellen did laugh. "You're clever! Clever!" she praised. "Drop! Now! Land!"

Rosa banked slightly to slow as she set her feet down, tipping forward only the slightest bit as she balanced.

Perfect!

Ellen let Müther's arms go as she leaned forward to stroke her pet's neck.

"Clever. So clever," she crooned.

Rosa's chest heaved, hooked beak open, eyes snapping open and shut as she recovered.

Ellen straightened and winced as a sharp pain gripped the back of her neck. Behind her, Müther was breathing in uncomfortable gasps. Ellen swivelled to look at Müther and, in spite of the spots that had begun to dance before her eyes, she almost laughed again to see the pale face and the lips that moved soundlessly. She was glad Müther could not see her probably misplaced mirth.

"That's as bad as it gets, Müther." She tried to sound sympathetic. "I'm sorry you got thrown about a bit. We slipped. Now we only have to go up. I've got a strap I can put behind you so you can lean back. It'll feel a bit like you're sitting on a chair being hoisted up – only, of course, it will be a bit bumpy. But not like what we've just done."

"I can't," Müther whispered as Ellen reached to adjust the brace.

"What you must already have achieved in your life is infinitely more than a mere roller coaster ride on this cliff face," Ellen said. *BlackŌne's beard. I don't feel too good*, she thought. In fact Ellen had the strong urge to vomit and, by the second, strength was leaching out of her.

But now was not the time to be weak –

"A roller coaster ride!" Müther's voice was thin and high. "Is that what you think this is? This is madness! I want no more of it!"

Ellen looked up at the cliff towering above them. "Twenty minutes," she said. "Another twenty minutes and we'll be on top. Tolerate what comes." She infused command into her tone and had no doubt that Müther would obey – which she did, setting her lips in a grim line and pressing her arms against the straps holding her in the saddle.

Ellen squeezed her eyelids together, trying to shut out her headache. "Let's go Rosa. Up!" She leaned her body forward over the base of Rosa's neck, tucking her hands into the harness around the bird's chest for extra support.

Rosa chirruped and clacked in protest but did as she was told, hopping and leaping, using talons and beak to pull herself up, and wings to steady herself when she slipped. Each jolt in Rosa's climb wedged pain further into Ellen's neck until even her mantra of strength became a jumble of nonsense and all her will focused on keeping herself from slipping into a gathering blackness.

"Look at that!" the ranger chortled. He stared again through his binoculars to double-check what he saw and turned to his companion. "Focus on that section of the cliffs."

His companion, still lying in his sleepsack, sat up. The pair were camped on a bluff jutting over the part of the valley where the Chess and Sith river courses were at their closest. They had an unobstructed view of the Sith Escarpment, the Northern and the Central Lands, including Sinthén. Behind them on a narrow strip of cleared land, sat the bright yellow two-seater helicopter that had brought them to this lookout point. The men had been camped on the bluff for the past few days. During daylight hours, they continually scanned the landscape for signs of Crystalmakers. At night they whiled away the boring hours by watching movies on their small electronic devices. The Ülrügh had told them to stay on the bluff until they had something interesting to report to him and they were close to believing that nothing more interesting than the endless move of nature happened in the areas they surveyed.

The second ranger put his own binoculars to his eyes and grinned when he saw the string of cages being hauled up. A little to the left, he saw a long line of goats also making their way up the cliff.

"What do you reckon is going on?" asked the first ranger. "Recon they're Crystalmakers?"

"Doubt it. Haven't heard of Crystalmakers having goats. They just pick berries and stuff." The second ranger scanned further along the cliff, his attention caught by another movement. He whistled softly. Making her way up the cliff was the unmistakable bulk of Lian Ellen's glaaaun.

"Now that is much more interesting. I have a feeling our Ülrügh would be interested in that!"

"... AND SO NONE of you thought you should listen ... just showing off... idiotic." The angry, shouted phrases became louder and less disjointed as Ellen gradually became more aware of her surroundings.

"I think you have made your point, Thimon," a calming voice said.

Crystalmaker language– aahh, my head hurts!

She remembered reaching the top of the cliff, Richard running towards them, his face open with an admiring laugh, Müther saying: "Get me on to the ground!"

But then her memory went hazy. Had she helped Müther off Rosa?

"…Greçia said not to shake her about – what in the BlackŌne's name do you call that!" the angry voice continued.

"I forgot." Richard's voice: contrite.

"We all forgot." Müther now, sounding sulky.

"Forgot! Forgot–"

"Thimon. You have made your point. Let us now concentrate on what to do now." The calming voice again.

But you are right. I ignored Greçia's advice.

"We need to move." The angry voice: a man; a little more controlled.

"Greçia said that if bruising appeared around her eyes we shouldn't move her," Richard said, unhappy.

"We can't stay here. We are exposed. The whole of Si'Empra can see us!"

"Perhaps not, Thimon. Look. Clouds are rolling in. They will hide us." The calming voice; a woman's voice; very close. Ellen caught a whiff of the same pungent smell that Elthán had: a Crystalmaker – Chris?

"You think this is better? We stay here without shelter?"

"We can't move her, Thimon. Look at her. There's even blood coming out of her ears. We can put up a cover before the rain comes."

"Are you mad! That would be making us more visible!"

Ooooh! Ellen thought miserably. She understood now that the party must be close to where Rosa had topped the escarpment; a high point that was visible from many points on the Central Lands. *Yes. Yes. We have to move. Just give me a few more minutes – then I can do it –*

"Greçia said she gave Lian Ellen tablets that would reduce inflammation in the brain. Perhaps we could give her those," Müther said.

"Where are they?" the kind-voiced woman asked.

In my pocket – please just be quiet for a moment – then I can tell you –

"I think she keeps them in her pocket. I've heard her fiddling with them," said Müther.

A series of clacks and a rustle: Rosa.

"Uh, uh," Phan grunted.

Rosa's clack mixed with a warning warble.

"What is it? Phan, can you see something?" Richard.

"What do you see? My eyes are useless in this light," said angry man – Thimon?

"Helicopters," Ellen found her voice. "Rosa is telling us she can hear helicopters."

A hand touched her brow. She opened her eyes. "Helicopters," she whispered again, looking into a woman's face.

"We have to go!" Thimon said.

"I see it." Richard stood with his back to Ellen, binoculars to his eyes. "It's heading away from us."

"What mischief are they up to?" A small man wearing a wide-brimmed hat came to stand next to Richard. His movements were tight and twitchy. "They might have seen us on the cliff," he said. "They might be going back to Si'Em City to tell the murderers."

He turned and fixed his gaze on Ellen. "We have to go!"

"Yes," she agreed weakly and tried to sit up. The woman pressed her back. "Thimon, she is too ill."

"Then we leave her here – the glasaur can look after her. If we stay, we are dead."

"No!" Richard shook his head adamantly. "Elthán said to look after her. We can't leave her."

Thimon whirled on him. "What do you suggest then? Are you going to carry her?"

"Yes – yes. I'll carry her."

"There may be another way." Müther spoke from somewhere outside of Ellen's line of sight. "I can mount Rosa again and I can hold her. She can lie against me."

Ellen took a deep breath and made another attempt to sit up. The woman lowered her gently back down again. "We will not move her until she has had Greçia's tablets and some colour has returned to her face. Thimon, you go on with Phan and the goats. We will come when we can."

"We go together," Thimon growled. As he stumped away, he added: "And we die together."

Lian Chithra, Chancellor of Si'Empra, was a large woman: tall and fat – unusual features for a Si'Empran. She lived close to her office in the Serai and rarely attempted the thousands of stairs in Si'Em City that kept other Si'Emprans slim. Mostly she dealt with the administrative details that Redel found unbearably tedious but now and then she insisted on giving him information that she thought he needed to know.

Redel understood her motive, but really! She had droned on for more than an hour now!

He yawned ostentatiously.

This is just for the benefit of the Lianthem. She thinks I care what they think. He lounged further into his deep armchair, legs splaying out. *The Lianthem knows she takes care of all of this.*

Keeping just enough attention on her report in case she

said something interesting, Redel studied the sky outside the one window in the Lian's spacious office: *Clouds getting thicker. Weather turning.* His eyes roved over walls lined with shelves, most full of books. He wondered what it would be like to have a brain like Chithra's. He knew she had read every book in her office but rarely consulted them a second time because their contents – and probably the details of every discussion and bit of information she had ever read or heard – were fixed in her mind. Her recall was faultless. He laughed to himself when he compared her brain with her stature: *Full of fat!* Well, he thought smugly. *She might not admit it but I am cleverer than she is because she works for me.*

She had even allied herself with him against his father when it became clear that Briani would name Ellen as his successor. Redel felt a twist of hate at the thought of his father's betrayal. Briani had deserved his death!

"We could face a fuel shortage this winter. I have contacted our suppliers and they have informed us they will only make an extra delivery if we pay fifty per cent upon ordering. They demand full payment before they pump into our storage tanks. I have, therefore, made the deposit and instructed Lian Cecil to collect taxes as soon as possible. Nevertheless, we are likely to fall short of funds. It may be necessary to borrow from members of the Lianthem – again – perhaps even Cheng Yi. They are likely to cry poor. I suggest that we offer to pay a higher rate of interest – loan to be repaid by next midsummer with the first proceeds of gemstone sales next year. That should make them feel less poor. Nevertheless, I regret that it may be necessary to postpone the purchase of another stallion for your stable."

"That's not fair!" His last stallion had broken its leg on a gallop through the mountains and had to be put down. The stable now only held mares. "What about payment from the gems this year? A shipload went out yesterday. You said that would pay for the fuel!"

"You may recall that we took advance payment for that shipload to cover the cost of purchasing a third helicopter."

"That helicopter was vital for hunting Cryptals!" He had explained this to the Lianthem. *Fools! I am surrounded by fools!*

"Do we really need the fuel?" He knew the instant he asked the question that he should not have. He didn't need the slight rise of Chithra's brow to tell him that without the fuel Si'Em City and Baltha would likely not survive winter. He slammed his fist onto the arm of the chair.

"How often do I have to explain to those fools on the Lianthem that if they concentrated on getting rid of Cryptals we wouldn't have this need to buy fuel? Thermal energy. We are sitting on enough thermal energy to give us all our energy needs. Yet, every time we try to harness it, the Cryptals sabotage our work.

"You know? I suspect that some of the Lianthem even collude with Crystalmakers and Cryptals. Fools!"

"It did occur to me that we should increase the price that we sell our fuel for, Ülrügh, this may help the Lianthem to recognise reason. The extra revenue would be another way for us to increase income. After all, you make all the arrangements for the fuel's purchase and delivery, and barely gain any return from making fuel available to the population."

Redel considered Chithra's suggestion, temper calming.

Finally he heaved a long-suffering sigh. "Might do. I've also been thinking that we need to think of a cheaper way of providing heating. Coal is cheaper than diesel. Until we get rid of the Cryptals – and the Crystalmakers – let's start using coal."

"Indeed, Ülrügh. A brilliant idea. Shall I have Lian Thobias look into this?"

"Sure. Sure. Do it."

His eyes settled on Chithra's breasts, hoping to see the amusing way they wobbled at her slightest movement, but she kept still, a slight twitch to her lips the only indication that she knew his thoughts and was teasing him. He saw the adoration in her dark eyes. *She will do anything for me*, he thought smugly.

An urgent knock on the door made them both start.

"Ülrügh! Ülrügh! We have found her!"

Redel vaulted out of his chair and yanked open the door. "What are you talking about, man!" he demanded.

"Ülrügh. We have found her. She is on the Sith Plateau. We are ready to take you."

ROSA WAS NOT HAPPY. Ellen tried to reassure her but the glasaur refused to be appeased, stopping at likely shelters and nudging at Ellen to dismount. "What is she doing?" Müther asked, the third time that Rosa stopped.

"She's found a shelter and wants us to go into it," Ellen explained. To the bird Ellen said: "Rosa, no. Not now. Keep going."

"Why?" Müther asked.

"She – she – when I'm not well she doesn't like it when I ride." Ellen made a feeble attempt to sit up but Müther's arms tightened around her. She relaxed her head against Müther's breast again. "You have to keep going, Rosa," she repeated, her voice barely a whisper. She took a deep breath and said with more force: "Go, Rosa, or we will fall further behind."

A mist dulled light and landscape. When Müther and Ellen had first mounted Rosa, Richard had wrapped a poncho around them, but tiny, cold droplets touched Ellen's face and she shivered. She closed her eyes, invoking her mantra of strength: *I am the Lian Ellen. I ride Rosa. I am strong.*

"I can't hear the goats. Are we following them?"

Ellen dragged open her eyes. "I can't see – aah – aaah!" A cramp clutched hard at her lower belly. She lurched against Müther's arms. Her headache flared.

"What! What?"

Rosa jerked to a stop, swinging her head around to look at Ellen.

Not now! Not now! Ellen begged uselessly, pressing her hands hard against the cramp. She felt warm moisture spread between her thighs.

Rosa nudged at Ellen with her beak.

"BlackŌne's beard! Tell me what you are doing. Chris! Where is Chris! Richard!" Müther's strong arms tried to force Ellen to lie back.

After some minutes, with Müther still pulling at her and demanding answers, and Rosa nudging her, the cramp eased enough so that Ellen could speak. "I – I just need to get off for – for a minute. Just need – need to clean up –"

Oh! Oh! My head!

"What do you mean? You just lie back here! What do you mean clean up?"

Rosa made a low, warbling, clacking sound, dropped her head and swayed it in a slow arc over the ground. The bird's signal sent alarm shooting into Ellen's muscles. She could see nothing. Mist swirled around her, shredding to show strips of pale blue overhead.

Again Rosa repeated her warning. Ellen struggled against Müther's arms "Where are the others? We have to warn them," she stammered.

"I don't know! What is Rosa doing? What's going on–"

"Rosa! Run! Find them! Run!" Ellen struggled free from Müther's arms, everything forgotten but the urgent need to warn every one of the danger.

Rosa's legs stretched into a sprint, wings opening to increase her balance.

The whap-whap-whap of helicopter blades shattered the air.

"BlackŌne's beard!" Müther gasped, her arms wrapping around Ellen in a clutch of terror.

Everything happened fast: the mist parted, showing Thimon and Phan side by side threading their way up a slope followed by the goats. Ellen screamed, "Take cover! Take cover!" Goats and humans turned startled faces towards her.

Thimon reacted first, shoving Phan aside.

The dark hulks of three helicopters roared overhead.

Rosa dropped to the ground and lay still. Ellen pulled Müther down, "Don't move! Don't look up! Don't move!"

"What's happening? What's happening?" Müther's words were snatched into the howl of engines.

Through the noise Ellen could faintly hear Thimon and Richard shouting, and the goats bleating in frightened confusion. A disembodied voice bellowed: "Where is she! She was with you! Where is she?"

AT THE SOUND OF the voice, Richard looked up to see the Ülrügh standing in the doorway of the largest helicopter. He was dressed in bright yellow and red, a hailer to his mouth.

"Where is she!" Throwing the hailer aside, the Ülrügh snatched up a semi-automatic rifle and pointed it down. Richard dived for cover behind a rock. Thimon hurled himself at Phan, who was calling the panicked goats to him, and dragged him under the overhang of a boulder. Bullets chipped at the ground and rock in bursts, interspersed with more shouts from the Ülrügh. The guns fired and kept firing. Goats scattered and bawled.

MIST FOLDED AROUND THE helicopter, hiding the ground. Redel punched the back of a seat in frustration, demanding the pilot land the craft. The pilot turned his face to look at Redel, eyes wide with fright. He shook his head. "Impossible," he pleaded. He concentrated on the controls again, gaining altitude to release the craft from the mist.

Redel glared into the whiteness below him. It was becoming

thicker. He pointed his weapon down and fired a long burst, lips set in a snarl. "There are Crystalmakers down there. There are traitorous Skyseekers working with Crystalmakers!" He had recognised the ridiculous wide hats and sun glasses that Crystalmakers wore. Ellen – his sister! – was down there with these traitors!

She is the traitor! He thought savagely. *After everything I have done for her! How could she betray me by being with Crystalmakers!*

RICHARD SAW PHAN FREE himself from Thimon's hold and burst out of cover, calling "Aaak! Aaak! Aaak!" for his goats. Richard dragged himself to his feet and tried to see into the hazed-out landscape for the shape of his Rosa and her riders, the noise from the now invisible helicopters addling his thoughts.

Two frightened goats appeared suddenly, careening into him and sending chicken cages awry. He fell heavily, the goats' hooves cutting into his arm and leg. A chicken cage burst open. Birds and feathers detonated around him.

Noise. Pulsating noise!

A long, long burst of gunfire; Richard hugged the ground.

The engines grew fainter.

"Richard!" he heard his mother gasp close by. "The guns – where–"

A dark mass moved. Richard made out the outline of Rosa and saw his mother's silhouette sit up and Ellen swing her legs to one side to dismount. He stumbled forward and reached up to help Ellen. When her feet touched the ground her legs sagged. "Oh Rosa," he heard her gasp. "Help me!"

Rosa swung her head around, knocked Richard to the ground and swept Ellen under her wing. She then lifter her head and pushed at Müther, who was still fastened to the saddle.

Müther flailed at Rosa with her stumps, calling: "Lian Ellen! What's happening– stop it Rosa! Lian Ellen where are you! Lian Ellen – stop it Rosa!"

Richard stood. Rosa hissed at him, threatening to strike again. He held his hands up. In a placating tone he said: "Steady. Steady." Slowly, he moved to the side of the bird, away from the wing protecting Ellen. "Steady. Steady," he repeated. "Rosa, I'm only going to let Müther down."

Rosa glared, watching his every move. "Stay very still, Müther," he told his mother quietly as he reached up to release a clasp. Rosa hissed again but did not strike him. He grunted as he reached up further, across Müther's lap, to undo another clasp, releasing her from the saddle. She fell sideways into his arms.

With venomous clacks and trills Rosa pushed the pair away. Richard staggered back, keeping a firm grip of his mother, and kept moving until the bird stopped threatening him. Through thickening rain he saw Rosa turn to look under her spread wing. She chirruped softly: concerned, enquiring.

CHAPTER 7
Rescue

ELTHÁN INSPECTED THE HALF empty shelves of the storage room, worry creasing her brow. There had been good years in the past five decades, especially the last two, when Crystalmakers had had enough to eat. For many, hunger was a nightmare of the past, evident only in the stunted bodies of some adults who had been children in the years of deprivation. Cryptals had found ways to stop the deep raids underground by Skyseekers.

Believing themselves more secure, Crystalmakers rebuilt their city and their rich culture. The number of acolytes in the Guilds grew. The Guilds produced ever-finer cloths, crystals and tapestries, and they rebuilt structures that had been destroyed or fallen into disrepair. The lesser crafts also blossomed and Illiath filled again with comfort and art. At the end of each waking set of hours, there were several sites around Illiath where people could go and listen to stories told by members of the Guild of Memory: stories of the past, stories filled with fantasy, others of romance and others still that thrilled listeners with fear or tears. There were places, too, where people could go to listen to or make music or to dance.

All of this existed for Crystalmakers, not for Webcleaners. They lived apart, doing as best as they could with minimal aid from the Guilds. The Guild of Crystal Makers, through Thil – who was the intermediary between Webcleaners and Crystalmakers – provided regular light sconces to replenish those that were spent, and the Guild of Structure kept the waters for warmth and sanitation flowing through the Webcleaners' spaces.

In Elthán's childhood Webcleaners had scavenged for their needs, making do with what other Crystalmakers no longer wanted. As Elthán grew in confidence, borne by her association with Skyseekers, she encouraged her people to learn how to make the items they traditionally scavenged. Doing so directly challenged The Order, which minutely regulated what various sections of the Crystalmaker community could do: from weaving cloth to harnessing light, to making music and even who was entitled to learn the practice of midwifery. Thus far, no one had challenged the Webcleaners' growing skills in supplying many of their own needs, because no Crystalmaker ever entered Webcleaner spaces or associated with them in a meaningful way. Although it rankled Elthán that Webcleaners were ignored and regarded with contempt by other Crystalmakers, she appreciated the freedoms Webcleaners gained as a result.

To continue to be ignored, Webcleaners needed to keep serving as always: they were the invisible force that kept spaces and clothes clean.

But we have taken on one more duty we never had before, Elthán thought. *We are feeding Crystalmakers and Cryptals.*

"Not much has been harvested yet." said Tharyl; he was in charge of the storage room that Elthán was touring. "I'm told the harvesters work longer hours and gather higher into the hills, but it seems to be a bad season."

The fine twin lines between Elthán's eyebrows deepened. She had heard the same story last year – and the year before – but knew the season was not bad.

"The earthquakes have also prevented harvesters from going into new areas."

"You mean, don't you, that no one wants to work any distance from tunnel entrances."

"The Skyseeker hunters are active," Tharyl said unhappily.

"I know," Elthán said, regretting her rebuke. Only a few, a very few, Webcleaners were as brave as Chris and Thimon and dared to go far from their escape tunnels. She provided Webcleaners with training that should help them with aboveground navigation, and how to cope with the open spaces and light, but it was hard for the majority to overcome their fear, especially when there was the added threat of hunters.

She patted Tharyl's arm sympathetically. "But we will need to think of something if we are to harvest enough."

She walked out of the storage cave into another cavern. A group of people were at work weaving the tough stems of sedge, gathered from the midge-infested banks of rivers, into thick coils.

"I don't understand why the harvest is so poor," Tharyl lamented.

"Because we harvest too much," Elthán said.

"I don't understand."

"The berries, bulbs and seeds that we take are what make new plants. The more that we take, the less there are to make new plants. That's why I want the harvesters to work in a different place each year." She had explained this before, but it made little difference because of the reality of the danger.

Elthán was about to take her leave to inspect another storage area when the tone of the ever-present WhiteŌne's Song changed. All work in the room stopped.

"Is it – an earthquake?" Tharyl's voice was hushed and fearful.

Elthán held up a hand for silence so that she could hear the WhiteŌne more clearly. Her heart skipped a beat. "Hunters!" she breathed.

The WhiteŌne sang on. Elthán frowned, concentrating. *Ellen. Something has happened to Ellen?*

"Thimon, Richard, Chris, Müther, Phan!" Elthán gasped out the words. *I've got to go!* She turned to run from the room, but Tharyl caught her sleeve.

"Mistress! What is happening?"

She grabbed his arm, pulling him along with her. "Go. Tell Thanin that hunters have attacked in the Sith Ranges – he knows what to do." She left Tharyl to pass on the news and hurried to an exit to the Cryptal tunnels, tugging on a protective garment snatched up from a shelf.

She pushed aside the curtain over the exit and almost collided with a Cryptal. It backed off to protect her from itself. A second Cryptal, harnessed to a sled, sang a note for her attention and she understood that they wished to transport her.

Elthán climbed aboard and the Cryptals immediately broke into a gallop. It took them less than hour to reach the junction with the route to aboveground on the Sith Plateau – a journey that would otherwise have taken her several hours. The Cryptals changed places in the sled's harness and had barely started up the long upslope when a man came running towards them.

"Mistress! Hunters!" he panted. "They attacked Thimon's group. Hunters have shot all the goats and chickens and Richard is dying."

"Dying? Richard! And the others?"

"Thimon didn't say. He just said he needed help. He didn't want to stay in our cave in case the hunters followed him. We – they're getting together some supplies. They sent me to raise the alarm."

"Thanin is on his way. Get on the sled."

The Cryptals left Elthán and her companion at a Rest then continued on. *Where are they going? There is only aboveground that way,* thought Elthán. While preoccupied with the needs of the moment, she nevertheless puzzled about the strange behaviour of the Cryptals: *Why do they appear to be concerned about Ellen? They have never transported me except when Ellen is involved.*

Inside the alcove, Elthán found a dozen Crystalmakers busily cooking food and packaging up medical supplies, and dry clothing and wraps.

"Mistress," they greeted her in surprise. "We did not expect you so soon."

"Please continue your preparations."

"You," she said, pointing to the tallest male. "Come with me."

Without waiting for the man to join her, she left the Rest, following in the wake of the Cryptals. The tunnel soon opened into a large cave with a high, shadowy ceiling and walls so far apart they disappeared into the dark. Light filtered into the cave from an opening at the top of a rubble slope. Elthán skirted a number of covered baskets containing seed, mushrooms and berries, a pile of dirty roots, and bundled long stalks of grass ready for threshing as she made for the slope.

The man she had singled out clambered up next to her into the daylight and rain.

"Where are they?" Breathing hard from the climb, she fished sunglasses from a pocket so she could see in the obscene brightness of aboveground.

Her companion also shoved on a pair of sunglasses. He peered around uncertainly. "I'm not sure."

Elthán faced the young man, only then realising that she did not recognise him: he was not a Webcleaner. But there was no time to ask why he was with her harvesters. *Richard is dying?* "How far away are they?"

"Ah – ah – I'm not sure. Thimon ran back – he – he didn't say."

"So what *did* he say?"

"That the hunters had–"

"What is your name?"

"Sam. My name is Sam."

"Sam. Think clearly. Tell me exactly what Thimon did and said. Never mind about the hunters."

"We heard Thimon running and shouting for help. We were in the Rest – we had been working at the harvest. I dug up roots – then the rain started so we went back to the cave. Thimon came. He said something about an attack by hunters and by – by – goons or guts – I don't know the word – the others tell me they make a loud noise and can kill – they explained it to me – I don't know what they are – a loud noise. Thimon – I think he said goats were dead and someone called ... Rich – Rich –"

Hunters. Guns. Richard. Of all the people for her to pick to accompany her, why did she pick this one with no knowledge of the aboveground? "Where did he say he was?" Elthán repeated.

"He said he didn't want to stay at the cave because these – aah – these hunters might follow him there. But he said he needed dry clothes and warm food, and he went away."

"Sam," Elthán forced herself to be patient with the youth. "Did Thimon say where he was going?"

"He –" Sam frowned. "He said something about – ah – rif – riffs – and also something like vail – no valt – something like that – and a shelter."

Shelter. Elthán sorted through the garbled information. *Shelter. Shelter near here.* "You mean a shelter in a rift valley?"

Sam nodded enthusiastically. "Yes. Yes. That was what he said!"

"This way." Elthán led the way down the slope and into a gully that had formed in a rift between two rock formations. Within minutes they were both rain-soaked but she pressed on, driven by anxiety.

Thimon appeared before them out of the rain.

"Warmth and light, Mistress," he greeted, his cool-headed greeting flooding her with relief. *It can't be too bad!* "I'm glad it's you making all this noise and not a pack of hunters with their dogs."

"Ah. Apologies for the noise. I should have been more cautious."

"I doubt it was you. Sam is the noisy one."

"What has happened, Thimon?"

Thimon led them further down the gully, briefly describing the encounter with Ülrügh and his rangers.

"We left many goats behind and many chickens. It was more important to be safe than to round them all up. They were too panicked to come to Phan's call. We found many wounded or dead. Those too wounded to walk we killed. We'll go back and round up as many live ones as we can once we have Müther to safety."

"And Richard? How badly is he hurt?"

"Not too bad. He has a few wounds from goats' hooves."

"Goats' hooves?"

"No doubt in time there will be jokes made about that," remarked Thimon dryly. "Here we are."

Richard and Chris came to their feet as she entered the shelter. Richard had bloodstained bandages around an arm and leg and a grazes on his face but otherwise seemed fine, as did Chris. Phan was huddled on the ground, sobbing brokenly. Müther sat against the back of the shelter on a mat, her head moving slightly this way and that as she tried to understand what was going on around her. Everyone was muddy and, except for Thimon, had the disoriented look of those in shock.

"Where is Ellen?" Elthán said.

"We left her–" Chris began, but Thimon interrupted. "The bird of hers would not let us anywhere near her. It was too dangerous for us to stay. We had to leave. As far as we know she still –" His voice faltered when Elthán snatched off her sunglasses to stare at him in disbelief.

"Mistress, it was too dangerous to stay in the open – we were so exposed – there was no shelter," he protested.

Elthán pressed her lips into a grim line.

She looked around again, this time to assess the security of the group. The goats were crowded outside the shelter in a natural scoop of the valley. The chickens were in their larger cage. Everything was wet and rivulets were forming along the valley floor. If the rain kept falling, a stream would start to flow.

"Why would Rosa not let you near Ellen?" she asked Chris.

Chris shook her head unhappily. "Lian Ellen is ill, Mistress. After the climb up the escarpment she lost consciousness. We tried to get her to safety, but the helicopters came and then Rosa put her under a wing and we couldn't get near her."

"Something happened just before the helicopters came. Ellen wanted to do something – something about cleaning herself," Müther spoke up from her mat. "Then it is as Chris says. Rosa would not let us near her."

"Still, you should not have left her! Thimon and Richard, pack up and get yourselves out of here before flood waters sweep you out. Go up the rift to the cave. Use the cave to dry out your gear and get yourselves ready to journey on."

"Is that wise?" Thimon said carefully. "We may be followed."

Müther also made a noise of protest, shaking her head. "I can't go into the Cryptal tunnel!"

Ignoring Thimon, Elthán said: "Müther, the cave is large and has very good ventilation. It will fit all the goats, chickens and yourselves. Cryptals do not use the cave. Their scent will be faint."

Richard knelt next to his mother. "She is right about this cave, Müther. I have been in it. The smell is like that of the Crystalmakers. There is no poison."

Elthán gestured to Sam. "You will help here and go to the cave with these people, and you and the others are to provide them with everything they need to continue their journey."

Sam nodded.

Elthán took Chris's arm. "Show me where Ellen is."

Chris led the way but it was Elthán who set the pace, following closely behind when they travelled single-file, or edging forward when they walked side-by-side.

A dead goat lay to the side of the path in a dark pool of blood. Elthán paused to inspect it.

"Richard cut its throat. See, its back leg is broken and a bullet hit its thigh," Chris said.

Chickens clucked nearby, nervously pecking at the ground, unused to their freedom.

"How many chickens did you lose?"

Chris shrugged. "I don't know. Twenty. Thirty."

"And goats?"

Again Chris shrugged. "Maybe twenty. Maybe more."

They walked on, past another dead goat and a few more chickens. Elthán stopped again, frowning. There was too much food here to leave – too much to leave when the current harvest was faltering.

"We are close," said Chris, wiping her dark glasses. Her hat stopped a lot of the rain from hitting her face, but the damp air fogged the lenses of her glasses. A shiver shook her body. Elthán winced, realising that Chris must be close to exhaustion. She led Elthán past a tumble of boulders and into the area where the shooting had occurred. Broken chicken cages lay strewn around, some wedged between rocks, others still tied to the broken bodies of goats. Rain had washed blood to a pink stain over the gravely earth.

"Over there," said Chris, pointing.

Elthán peered into the rain. She saw movement. The two Cryptals who had transported Elthán shuffled out from a rock ledge.

Chris saw them too. "Cryptals!" she exclaimed softly. "What are Cryptals doing here?"

"I'm not sure," Elthán said, but she thought: *They are here because of Ellen.*

"Where is Ellen?" she asked Chris.

Chris pointed again. "You can see Rosa – see her move?"

In the uncertain light the bird had been another dark form on the boulder-strewn ground. As the women approached Rosa reared her head threateningly.

Chris put a restraining hand on Elthán's arm. "She will hurt you. She would not even let Phan come near. He has a bruise on his shoulder where she struck him."

Elthán was about to walk forward despite Chris's warning when one of the Cryptals began to sing. Rosa turned her attention to the ancient creature. She wagged her head unhappily, chirruping a protest, but the Cryptal sang on and Rosa submitted. She folded her neck over her shoulders and did not move as Elthán stepped forward, though she emitted a worried warble as Elthán lifted the spread wing to reveal Ellen's still form.

"The WhiteŌne's mercy," Elthán gasped. From waist to knees, Ellen's clothing was stained with blood. Rosa's protection might have kept her warm but she was wet through and smeared with mud.

Chris knelt next to Elthán. "She is not conscious, but she breathes. Mistress, if we move her we must be careful. She has problems with her neck and – see – the leakage from her ears–"

Both women jumped at the sound of pebbles grinding. The Cryptals were pushing their sled towards them.

"Do they mean us to put her on there?" Chris asked incredulously.

"Yes. They do," Elthán said. She turned her attention back to Ellen. "Hold her head and neck as I turn her over. The Cryptals want us to take her to the cave, and they will transport her to Greçia's home."

"Why? Cryptals do not help in this way. What does she mean to them?"

Elthán shook her head. "I don't know. But I am glad of their help. Take whatever clothes and toiletries Ellen has in those saddle bags. Is there a sleepsack in her gear? And maybe a mat?"

They spread the mat on the base of the sled, lifted Ellen on to it and covered her with the sleepsack and a waterproof groundsheet. The sled was not ideal for transportation aboveground but it was surprisingly light. The women each picked up an end and started back to the Cryptal cave.

As they left, one of the Cryptals approached Rosa with a warble and a trill. "Just a minute, Chris. I want to see what they do with Rosa."

Rosa unsaddled herself and packed her harness into the saddlebags, using her beak and talons, even managing the magnetic clasps holding the saddlebags closed. Under more instructions from the Cryptal, Rosa picked up the saddlebags in her beak, gave a last look in the direction of Ellen, and disappeared into the rain.

The Cryptals followed the women, jumping and crawling over the ground like lumbering, broken beasts, ungainly outside the tunnels they were born into.

The women spoke only to determine how to manage their burden over the most difficult sections of their journey. Increasingly they needed to stop to let Chris rest. By the time the party reached the cave, light was beginning to fade and Chris's movements were almost as ungainly as those of the Cryptals.

Elthán left Chris with the sled at the entrance and scrambled down the rubble into the now crowded cave, smelly and noisy with wet goats and chickens. She instructed Richard, Thimon and Sam to fetch the sled and help Chris manage the scree.

"Be careful. Don't let Ellen slip."

As the trio left she peered at the others in the cave. "Are there any dry clothes?"

"We've brought all the clothes from the Rest," a woman said, bending to a basket at her feet.

Elthán sorted through various bundles and found what she needed for herself, Ellen, Chris and herself. . A clatter of stones announced the men returning. "Everyone into their coveralls –

two Cryptals are about to come in. Put Müther into a coverall and take her to the far end of the cave," Elthán ordered. She pulled the groundsheet over Ellen's face to protect her.

Once the Cryptals had passed through the cave, Elthán and two of the women stripped Ellen of her clothes. A bucket of warm water appeared at Elthán's side. She sponged Ellen clean as quickly as she could, noting that she was still bleeding. Someone passed her an absorbent pad, which she adjusted into place before redressing Ellen's still limp form in a coverall, carefully checking and re-checking to ensure that all seams were closed. "Take her to the tunnel," Elthán said.

She stripped off her own sodden clothes and redressed. She was just about to close the seams to her coverall when Richard appeared at her elbow with a mug of fluid and a rolled cake. "Drink and eat, Elthán. You need to keep up your strength."

Elthán almost refused, her sense of urgency high. But she took the food and drink and gulped them down, remembering the instructions she needed to give. She said to the Webcleaners: "There are goats and chickens at the place the hunters attacked. You need to go tonight, all of you – Thimon, you show them the way. Round up the live ones and butcher the dead. We need the meat. Leave the hides. We need the meat. When the help Thanin is sending arrives, they can help take the meat to storage. Richard, you and Phan continue alone with Müther and the beasts as soon as you can. Thimon and Chris – when she is rested – will join you later."

With that she pulled the hood over her face and hurried to the tunnel at the end of the cave where the Cryptals were waiting to take Ellen back to Greçia's care.

CHAPTER 8
Redel's Betrayal

Elthán stirred, waking from a deep sleep. She found herself slumped in a cushioned armchair near Ellen's bed, feet resting on a footstool. Someone – Greçia probably – had covered her with a blanket and slipped a pillow beneath her head.

"Sorry. Didn't mean to wake you," Greçia said softly. She was standing on the other side of the bed.

Elthán slowly pushed herself up, and let her breath out in a sigh as her back, arm and leg muscles protested against the movement. She didn't remember having sat down. She flexed her fingers and realised some were bandaged, blisters stinging under the dressing.

"How do you feel?" Greçia asked.

"Fine. A bit stiff." Elthán tilted her chin inquiringly towards Ellen.

"She's coming around. The bruising around her eyes is less and the discharge from her nose and ears has stopped. Good signs."

Ellen's eyelids fluttered, stilled, and flickered open. Her gaze roamed the room, rested briefly on Greçia and focused on Elthán.

"I had a strange dream," Ellen murmured.

Elthán leaned closer to the bed. "What was your dream?"

Ellen took a while before she answered in a half whisper: "I dreamt that I met the Songbird of Si'Empra and took her on a journey on Rosa. We were travelling to a safe place. There were – she had a son and another man who – his name was Phan – and goats and chickens –" She paused, perhaps puzzled by the clarity of the dream. "We climbed the Sith Escarpment," she finished.

Elthán nodded slowly. Ellen studied her through half-closed eyes.

"It was not dream," she breathed, eyes closing. "And the shooting was also real."

"A few goats and chickens were shot but the party is safe."

The muscles around Ellen's eyes relaxed. "Good," she mouthed.

Greçia touched Elthán's shoulder, motioning for her to follow. "I have prepared a meal for us both in the kitchen. Let her sleep."

"How is she?" Elthán asked, seating herself at the table. More thirsty than hungry, she sipped gratefully at a hot mug of pendle.

Greçia shrugged. "Remarkable, really. She seems to be recovering much faster than I could have imagined possible; even her bleeding has stopped."

"Constance said she has something called en – endo –"

"Endometriosis," Greçia finished the word for her. She nodded. "That explains the heavy bleeding and pain."

"Is there really nothing that can be done for this endo – whatever?"

"She's very young to have this problem –"

"Could it be because of what Redel has done to her?"

Greçia shook her head thoughtfully. "No. As far as I know the cause is unknown. She probably suffers from pain and heavy bleeding each month."

"Yes. Constance said that was the case."

"I looked through her toiletries and found that she has medication that she can take for the pain. For some women, once they have a child the condition improves. Although falling pregnant is often a problem. But I don't think that endometriosis is the only problem Lian Ellen has. I tried to talk to her about it, but she's clearly uncomfortable with such a discussion. I do believe that she has not been kind to herself – and that is likely to be more dangerous at this stage than the endometriosis."

"Yes – yes. Constance told me that she started being obsessed with cleaning herself. But – but I thought she didn't do that any more –"

Greçia wrinkled her nose. "Poor girl. That is, no doubt, a consequence of Redel's abuse. In any case, the most immediate problem is her head. I don't want her to move out of that bed for at least a month. She should never have left a bed in the first place. The bruised eyes and nose discharge indicate damage to the base of her skull. She needs to rest and let's hope she'll heal without long-term effects. She should be in a hospital."

"Then her brother can have his way with her again."

"You should at least give her the option to choose whether she wants proper treatment. I have to go to the clinic soon. I've told Tham and Phiet what they need to do to care for her. Tell her to stay in bed and lie as still as possible."

Elthán picked up the sandwich on her plate. It was made from wheat bread and had been layered with butter, cheese and tomato, with a sprinkling of cracked pepper. The food was luxurious, not the sort of fare that most Crystalmakers even dreamt of tasting. Greçia's larder was filled with food given to her by grateful patients too poor to pay a fee for her services, but wheat bread was a rare gift, especially fresh.

"Dr Thrake, the orthopaedic surgeon at Baltha hospital, gave me the loaf of bread and tomatoes," Greçia said to Elthán's unspoken question. "I was there this – no, yesterday morning. I go to visit him from time to time. He sets aside some equipment and medications no longer useful to him for me."

"Does this Dr Thrake know you treat Crystalmakers?"

"I doubt it. I do take care that no one knows."

"Have I ever told you that we are very lucky in your generosity to us?"

Greçia smiled her lopsided smile. "Not once, not twice, but a million times," she said.

"Then I have not said it enough."

"It's my pleasure." Greçia rose. "You would do well to get a bit more sleep, Elthán."

Elthán nodded. "I feel it." She flexed her fingers, a worried frown settling on her brow as she recalled what she had been busy with before racing off to rescue her granddaughter.

Greçia saw her expression and paused in the act of settling her medical bag on her shoulder. "Problems? More than Lian Ellen problems?"

Elthán shrugged slightly. "We are such a fragile community."

Greçia tipped her head to one side, studying Elthán with her bespectacled eyes.

"Is it twenty years since I first met you?" It was a rhetorical question. Elthán knew that she was referring to the night she had brought Müther to this grotto. Pedro had fetched Greçia from Sinthén to tend to her.

"Müther was incoherent, alternately screaming in pain and moaning that she could not see. She begged to die. You held her in your arms and told her that time heals and no one knows what the future brings. You told her that death cheats opportunity.

"Nowadays I use those words with patients who are in despair. I also think that Crystalmakers have dragged themselves up from ruin on the back of your words. You are so much less fragile than you were."

Elthán smiled at her friend. "It is relative," she agreed. "But hunger and terror are not things you ever want to revisit."

"Crystalmakers fear hunger. Skyseekers fear hunger and cold."

"And the hunters – we fear hunters."

"Ah, the hunters." Greçia's voice held disgust. "You mean the Ülrügh and his butchers. I have treated more than one woman – men too – who have been victims of the adjutants. Our Lian Ellen is not the only one who has suffered rape."

"You say that in Brazil there are also problems among people?"

"Yes. In Brazil it is also so. There are poor people and rich people. There are people who are happy and unhappy. There are sick people and healthy people. There are bad people and good people. Only there are no people who live underground and there are no Cryptals." Greçia pulled on a rainproof poncho. With an "I'll see you tonight", she walked out into the steady drizzle of the outside world.

Elthán stared for some time at the door Greçia had closed behind her, reflecting on why Greçia had left Brazil: a dead son and a relationship she could no longer tolerate; she had taken a job on a cargo ship that had called into Si'Empra and decided to make the island her home. Pedro had once shown Elthán a map of the world and pointed to Brazil – a part of a landmass so vast that it was possible to walk for years and still not find the end. By contrast he had shown her where Si'Empra lay on the map: a speck on the uniformly blue part of the bottom of the map labelled: 'Southern Ocean'. He said that it was many thousands of kilometres south-east of Brazil on something called the Pacific-Antarctic Ridge – an earth fracture that was the reason why Si'Empra experienced earthquakes – and south of large islands called New Zealand and Tasmania. Greçia sometimes described how warm Brazil could be and how lush with trees parts of Brazil were. It seemed so different to Si'Empra that no explanation Greçia provided helped Elthán to understand the doctor's decision to stay in Si'Empra.

Shaking her head in puzzlement, Elthán returned to Ellen's bedside to find her awake, with Tham, one of Greçia's nurses, checking her temperature and pulse. Tham bent slightly from the waist towards Elthán to show respect. "I have washed her and given her the doctor's medicine, Mistress," she said.

"Thank you for your help, Tham." To Ellen she said: "You have regained a great deal of colour."

Ellen waited until Tham had finished her ministrations, and slowly rolled on to her back.

"I am not in the same room," she noted.

"No. This room is at the back of Pedro's home. It is one of three that we call the hospital. Crystalmakers who need Greçia's care come here." Elthán should have said Webcleaners, but she let the distinction pass.

"Where is Rosa?"

"Rosa?" *Does she think of nothing else?* "The Cryptals care for her, I think. As for your care, Greçia believes you should be in a proper hospital under proper care."

Ellen shuddered. "I am comfortable." She closed her eyes and ended the conversation.

Elthán made herself stay with Ellen, though she was anxious to return to her responsibilities. Tham and Phiet by turns nursed Ellen, encouraging her to drink and eat, and helping with her toilet. After Greçia returned and, she watched on as the doctor checked on her patient. As she and Greçia ate their evening meal Greçia remarked again that Ellen was recovering with surprising speed. That night Elthán slept in a hospital bed next to Ellen's.

The routine of close care continued the next day. When Elthán had told Greçia that she intended to stay until she was sure her granddaughter was well on the path to recovery, the doctor had given her magazines to read to pass the time. But Elthán left them unread. Although she was a competent reader of the Skyseeker language, she had never liked doing it for pleasure. She associated reading with winter days and nights alongside Pedro and Constance in this cosy home. Pedro was the one who read, and mother and daughter had listened, letting Pedro's voice take them on adventures around the world or into the romantic lives of others.

Elthán shut her eyes tightly as sadness caused tears to gather. Her times with Constance had been precious. She had never regretted her love for Pedro, but she had regretted that their half-caste daughter had not been able to tolerate mylin–

"Mylin!" whispered Elthán, her eyes opening wide. She studied Ellen's face, her thoughts a sudden whirl.

Ellen was deeply asleep; long, brown lashes feathering from relaxed eyelids, soft breath slightly but rhythmically raising and lowering her diaphragm. She looked very much at peace. The bruising around her eyes – ugly smears barely twenty-four hours ago – was almost gone, and her cheeks had gained a soft pink colour.

"Are you using mylin?" Elthán breathed. That would be astonishing. How could a Skyseeker use mylin? Pedro said that the whole of Si'Empra was infused with mylin and it affected Skyseekers by tying them to the island, causing them to feel anxious at the thought of leaving. But Skyseekers exposed to fresh mylin became ill. Even Constance, who was half Skyseeker and half Crystalmaker had not been able to tolerate much mylin, let alone use it as Crystalmakers did to help them heal and become stronger.

"No. You are just young and the young can recover quickly. Nevertheless, there is a puzzle here. The WhiteOne has never before told me of a hunt. Usually I need to wait till I have word from a runner. Cryptals also rarely offer to transport us. But with you – you they seem to pay special attention to. What hold have you over them?"

As if hearing the whispering, Ellen's eyes fluttered open. She blinked several times; green eyes focusing.

"Good morning," Elthán said. "Are you feeling a bit better?"

"Yes. Thank you."

"Breakfast?"

"I'll just get up to –"

"You'll do no such thing. If Greçia finds that you've lifted your head off that pillow she'll probably never let me into her clinic again. Phiet is here and she'll help you with whatever you want – even give you a wash – if you like. In the meantime I'll warm up the breakfast Greçia has prepared for you."

Breakfast was a thick porridge into which Elthán stirred sweet, dried berries.

"Would you like me to read to you? Or would you like to sleep some more?" asked Elthán when Ellen had settled again on her side – seemingly the most comfortable position for her.

"Will you tell me how Müther came to live here?"

Elthán sat back into the armchair. "Yes. I can tell you that story. There is a place not far from Baltha where Skyseekers leave unwanted things, including their dead. Do you know it?"

"You mean The Shoals? Where we give our dead to the sea?"

"Yes."

"I found her there. I brought her here to Pedro."

"What were you doing at The Shoals?"

"I spent a lot of time there once. Skyseekers throw out much that is useful to needy Crystalmakers. I sometimes also saw Skyseekers scavenging there. The first real treasure I found there was Phan."

"Will you tell me about Phan first and then about Müther?"

"It was night near to summer's end and the sea at low tide. Usually that is a safe time to be at that place – though only if the wind blows, otherwise the midges are torture. On this night I heard the cry of a baby and saw a tall person, shining a light, come to the edge of the water. I saw the person lay down a crying baby. She or he – I think it was a she – knelt next to the baby, fussing with its covers, speaking to it very soft tones. Then she stood and began to walk away. I think it was hard for her to leave the baby. She returned several times and picked it up to try to soothe its crying. Once she picked up a rock and lifted it over the child's head. I thought she would murder it, but she threw the rock away and ran away.

"When I was sure she was gone, I picked up the baby. A Sky-seeker baby. I couldn't take it back into our caves but I couldn't leave it there to be swept into the sea either, so I brought it to Pedro."

"You walked with the baby over the road to Sinthén to here?"

"No. No. So brave I am not. There is a path that leads from The Shoals to Pedro's home. It is not a clear path, but it is a path I often used when coming here to Pedro's home."

With her eyes closed, Ellen asked. "And Müther?"

"I'll tell you after you have rested."

When Ellen woke again and had drunk the milk prepared for her, Elthán returned to the story of Müther.

"She came to The Shoals with two men in a car. I had been inspecting a large iron tub that had holes in it to see how I could use it. I saw the car coming and hid behind the tub. She stepped out of the car with two men. One man was very tall with very black skin and the other man was Redel. They stepped out the vehicle and walked towards the sea, the black man carrying a light that he held high above his head. I heard Müther say: 'I can't see anything here that is so remarkable that you need to drag me out here'. She did not sound at all happy. Later she told me that Redel had told her and the other man that he had found something at The Shoals over which she could write many songs. She said she was very fond of the other man. I saw Redel turn back to the car and he pulled out what looked to me a long wide stick – but Pedro said it must have been a sword. He ran up behind the black man and shoved the sword into his back. Müther turned around and attacked Redel, shouting. He fell back with her on top of him and they struggled. He took hold of her wrists and forced her off him. They were shouting at one another. A lot of words I have never heard before. He held her down with a knee on her cheek, fiddled with something he had in his pocket and stabbed it into her eyes. She screamed." Elthán shuddered. "An awful scream. I can still hear it sometimes. Redel stood up and she put her hands up to her face. Redel's face was full of blood – I think from where she scratched him. He kicked her and told her she was a filthy lowlife and that she had hurt him. He picked up the sword he had dropped and pulled one of her arm straight and put his foot on it." Elthán hesitated. In spite of the years, the scene she had witnessed was still horribly clear. She did not usually tell this story with such detail, but somehow she felt compelled to tell Ellen.

"He took off her hands. It was Redel who took off her hands," Ellen murmured sadly.

"Yes. Yes. 'You'll never scratch me again!' he shouted at her. Then he dragged her and the black man close to the sea and went back to his car and drove away."

Throughout Ellen's childhood, Constance, knowing Müther's story, had often expressed her unease to Elthán concerning Ellen's close friendship with Redel. Seeing the distress in Ellen's expression now, she wondered whether it was because she was being told yet another story of Redel's cruelty.

"Aaah –" Ellen breathed out the sound – so soft but it could have been a scream with the emotion it held. She whispered: "Then he went back to the Serai and wept a story to my father that there had been a terrible accident." For some time she was silent, her stare focused on other things than what was before her.

"Müther said that she had been complaining a lot about Redel and saying that he was unfit to be a future Ülrügh and she thinks that's why he tried to murder her."

Ellen closed her eyes, soft breath even. Elthán wondered whether she was using her measured breath to control emotions. She studied her granddaughter. *She is like a too-perfect painting* thought Elthán, noting the symmetry of her features, the smooth flawlessness of her skin, the soft shape of her lips, the curve of her nose and the glorious deep, gold-red colour of her curl; all details dwarfed when her large, spectacular, green eyes opened and the smile, which seemed ever ready in spite of the turns of her young life, lifted her features into even greater display.

Ellen asked: "You helped her then?"

"I tried. When I was sure the men had gone. I tried to help by stopping the bleeding. She had on a wide skirt and I tore at it and bound up her wrists and sponged at her eyes. Then this man came – another man – a young man. He was there before I realised it. He was panting hard as if he had run a long way. I thought he would kill me but he knelt next to me. He had a medicine kit with bandages and other things. He wrapped up the stumps and her eyes. There were tears in his eyes. He asked me if I knew of a safe place. I showed him the path to Pedro's place and he carried her. He was strong but she wa no easy load. He carried her until she started to regain consciousness. Then he laid her down, said he couldn't do any more, and left.

"Müther walked the rest of the way. She leaned on me but she made herself walk. She was very brave. Müther has always been brave. Many months and months and months she suffered terrible pain. But I think the worst pain was knowing that she would never see again or have hands to use again. Pedro did many things around his home to help her."

"You look after her very well – you and Greçia – and others."

"She deserves to be looked after. She has given us so much. I have never met anyone so accomplished. Pedro had but to read something to her once and she would remember its details exactly. She knows so much about Si'Empra – and about the world.

She knows even more than Pedro. He would listen to her and learn from her. They would study books together in languages so foreign I wonder how they get their tongues around the sounds. Aaah – I remember the first night she sang for us."

Later – in the afternoon – Ellen wanted to know whether Richard was always with his mother.

No, Elthán said, Richard carried out many tasks. He visited small villages around Si'Empra to trade items the Crystalmakers made in return for food and goods they needed. He also traded in Si'Em Square, but never with Crystalmaker wares. The black market for Crystalmaker goods operated well away from Si'Em City. "He is also very good with any technological or mechanical things. He makes many things for us from bits and pieces he finds and puts together."

For a while they were silent, Ellen with her eyes closed. The Ellen said. "Thank you, Elthán, for helping me. Thank you for answering my questions. If you need to go, please do so."

And so I am dismissed, Elthán thought, bemused. *Authority sits easily with this child.*

CHAPTER 9
Reality

Something about the Ülrügh's enthusiasm for the hunt made Chuck feel uncomfortable.

Chuck had learnt how to hunt on his parents' Texan cattle station. During the past few decades he had broadened his childhood experiences by hunting animals in India, Africa and Canada. His experience in foreign lands had been a significant factor in obtaining this posting as envoy to Si'Empra.

Chuck's uneasiness with the Ülrügh began when he had chosen a .22 calibre rifle from the array of guns on offer in the well-stocked weapons room of the Serai. The Ülrügh had raised an eyebrow quizzically. "I don't plan to be so subtle," he said, lifting a sub-machine gun out of its stand.

"We are after Cryptals, Ülrügh? Are they bigger than our bears?"

"Oh my word! Imagine the grizzly bear of your nightmares," the Ülrügh had laughed. "But no matter. Your weapon will be quite sufficient. Come. Let us go to our waiting transport. In Si'Empra we have to seize the opportunity when it presents itself. The weather over the north of the island has finally cleared. My men and I were hunting there a few days ago when the weather closed in. I suspect that we will have an excellent time if we go back." He had flashed his engaging grin. "Come, our transport is ready."

Setting aside his unease, Chuck gripped his rifle more firmly, ducking his head as he ran after the Ülrügh into the largest of three waiting helicopters. Two wolfhounds bounded in behind him and pressed themselves against the Ülrügh's legs as he clipped short leads to their collars.

"Puck and Muck," the Ülrügh shouted over the roar of rotor blades. He patted the dogs fondly and they sat adoringly at his feet. "They are my two best hunters." He turned to the pilot and gave a nod.

In just half an hour the helicopters had delivered their passengers to the site of the hunt in the Sith mountains. There were eight men, including Chuck and the Ülrügh, and the two dogs. Almost immediately, the Ülrügh and his men found butchered goat carcasses, a few shattered packs and cages, and clusters of feathers.

"Good. Good," the Ülrügh muttered.

"Part of the skill in this endeavour," he explained to Chuck, "– as I said before – is to complete our hunt before the weather beats us again and our transport can't pick us up. Since the weather is wildly unpredictable, we are taking a chance here! Hey ho, what fun!"

"It looks like there was a bit of a battle going on here," Chuck said. "Was this the site of your last hunt?" When the Ülrügh's only response was a wry smile, he continued: "What exactly are we looking for, Sir?"

"Footprints, my dear man. We are looking for footprints."

"What type of footprints?"

One of the men shouted: "Ülrügh!"

Chuck followed the Ülrügh to where the man crouched under a rock overhang.

"These footprints, my friend, these footprints will do quite nicely," the Ülrügh said softly, squatting to study the large prints on the dry, dusty ground. "See what very few see."

Chuck settled beside him.

"Three toes to the front and two to the back. Almost like some birds'. See here? The deeper impressions? Those are claws. Long, wicked claws."

"Cryptals, Ülrügh? Good God, these footprints are bigger than a lion's – or a grizzly bear's! How dangerous are they?"

"Dangerous in many ways, my friend. They can kill without touching you with their poison – don't worry, we have the equipment to guard against that. They can also kill with these claws and they can crush you."

"Are they carnivores? Would they hunt us?"

Ülrügh Redel laughed. "Now that would make our hunt more interesting. Unfortunately they are skulkers, living mostly underground. As to their diet – of that I have little information. I have never thought to ask. It's time to see what Puck and Muck can do."

The hounds growled as they sniffed the prints, hackles rising. They prowled, stiff-legged, to a tumble of boulders overgrown by thick, bright green moss. They sniffed around a boggy, disturbed area, seemingly confused, alternately wagging their tails and growling. The Ülrügh studied the behaviour for a while, then scanned nearby bushes. "Interesting," he murmured, retrieving a soft, bright-red breast feather from a tangle of twigs. He twirled it in his fingers for some seconds then whispered: "Rosa," and other words Chuck could not understand.

"Ülrügh?"

Ülrügh Redel turned to Chuck, his good humour seemed to have dissipated. "It would appear I was not mistaken in what I saw. They hide well, that bird and her."

Before Chuck could ask another question, the Ülrügh whistled to his dogs and flung out an arm in command: "Find them! Find them!"

The dogs leapt forward, unerringly following in the footsteps of Elthán, Chris, the Cryptals and the Crystalmakers who had followed Elthán's instructions to butcher the goats and collect the chickens. The men followed – Ülrügh Redel the most agile and focused of them all, carrying his weapon as if it were nothing more than a light stick.

One thing Chuck had learnt about Si'Emprans was that they were oblivious to the effects of gravity – or so it appeared. They climbed up and down steep slopes as if traversing flat ground, as sure-footed as goats. He had always prided himself on being a fit man, but there was no way he could keep up with the hunting party. He slipped further and further behind and would have lost the group altogether had not one of the rangers stayed by his side to show the way.

He caught up, sweating and breathless, to find Ülrügh Redel and his men donning overalls. The two dogs were a little distance away, staring intently into an opening at the base of a massive boulder.

"Ah, my dear man," the Ülrügh said quietly, pausing in the act of pulling up a zip that extended from the crutch of his overall to his neck. "My apologies for leaving you behind. I confess to having been rather carried away." He waved to a bundle on the ground next to a number of open backpacks. "There is your overall and mask. Please put them on. We must be quick. If we are lucky they have not heard us arrive." He indicated to one of his men to help Chuck.

"Overalls, Lord?" Chuck panted, setting down his rifle. The Ülrügh's man flicked the bundle out and held open the foot of the garment, indicating to Chuck that he should put his foot – boot and all – into it.

"Indeed. If there are Cryptals inside that cave, then we will have to guard against their odour." The Ülrügh pulled a hood over his head and adjusted a gas mask over his face as Chuck's helper pulled the coverall up and Chuck slipped his arms into the sleeves. "Come, we have delayed enough. Silence is paramount." The Ülrügh's voice was disembodied behind the mask. He crouched next to the opening, fondling the dogs' ears and giving a soft command that caused them to drop to the ground.

Chuck hastily pulled on his mask while the man adjusted the hood. No part of his body was now exposed. "Careful not to block light," his helper cautioned. Chuck noted how the Ülrügh and his men manoeuvred themselves through the crevice, pressing hard against the sides and entering one by one. Chuck gripped his gun, heart knocking deliciously in his chest in anticipation of closing in on the quarry. Beyond the crevice the area was fairly open, though the ground was uneven and felt loose underfoot. He stood still to give his eyes time to adjust to the gloom. From somewhere below he could hear what sounded like voices – it could have been singing – he was unsure. The sound was hollow, as if made in a vast space.

Before Chuck could make any other observations, a powerful light stabbed the dark, probing swiftly until it found the source of the sound some thirty metres below. Several startled animal eyes stared blindly and unmoving into the light. Chuck's excitement surged. *Cryptals! Man oh man! This is—*

He drew in a sharp breath as he recognised what was actually trapped in the light.

Not Cryptals! People!

The people were sitting in a circle around a large, shallow basket – their frozen arms reaching into the basket – their faces white masks of shock.

"Wha–" Chuck began, bewildered, but Ülrügh Redel's hiss interrupted: "Take them!" More lights flared. The men around Chuck bellowed as one, leaping forward. "Jesus! No!" gasped Chuck, jerking back, but the Ülrügh grabbed his arm and pulled him along. Chuck's feet stumbled on to a steep, rubbly downslope. He slipped and scrambled, fighting for balance. He heard shouts of alarm, screams of terror – some cut off in sickening crunches.

Chuck's feet found firmer ground and the Ülrügh let go his arm.

"After them!" Ülrügh Redel yelled.

Chuck saw two figures, tracked by light beams from torches mounted on the foreheads of rangers, racing into the blackness at the end of the cavern. The Ülrügh sprinted after them.

Chuck did not have a light of his own and the departure of the men left him in the dark. Stunned, wondering whether he had just been a witness to murder, he stood unmoving. A light turned towards him and its owner rushed back. Once again Chuck felt himself being dragged forward by a grip on his arm. He struggled away:

"What just happened! What did – are these Cryptals? – What –"

"Not Cryptals, Sir. Crystalmakers. Hurry! We must hurry! The Cryptals are warned. Hurry!"

The urgency in the voice pitched Chuck into a run more than the sustained pull on his arm, but he continued to question: "They're people–"

The man apparently decided it would be best to abandon Chuck. He let go Chuck's arm and began to run at full stride. "Wait! Wait!" Chuck shouted, chasing after him. The man slowed fractionally but stayed ahead of Chuck, giving him just enough light to see. They ran at speed for two hundred – three – four – five hundred metres. Chuck's legs ached with the strain, and his lungs heaved. He dropped his gun and put his hands up to remove his mask, which felt like it was suffocating him.

A mind-numbing roar – deeper and louder than any lion Chuck had ever heard – blasted down the tunnel, closely followed by rapid gunfire. Chuck fell to his knees, terror overlaying shortness of breath. The roar cut off in an agonised shriek. A voice wailed. More gunfire and – into the silence that followed – a shout of triumph. Hands hauled Chuck to his feet and he stumbled forward into a pool of light. Ülrügh Redel's masked face turned towards him. "You've bought me luck!" The Ülrügh gave Chuck a hearty slap on the back then turned his attention away. "You! You!" He pointed at two of the rangers. "Go back down the tunnel: make sure you keep our exit clear." Chuck had bent double, hands on his knees, whooping for breath and glad of the mask because it hid the tears that had begun to flow. The Ülrügh thumped him on the back again. "We have to be careful now not to be trapped by them! Look, my dear man! Look what we have."

At the Ülrügh's feet lay a huge, long-haired beast. Its head was a third of a metre across. It had high-set, light-brown eyes, open in death and staring in an eerily human way. One side of the head was a red mash of bone, flesh and blood. "The question is whether we press our luck or skin this Cryptal and go. At the very least I'll be able to give you what you came to Si'Empra for, my dear chap."

"Wha– what I – I came f–for?" Chuck stammered in confusion.

"You have not said, but I am sure that you have been sent to Si'Empra to find Cryptal products," Ülrügh Redel said. "A rare commodity nowadays, but we should be able to give you at least a Cryptal hide – for a price, of course."

Chuck straightened, fighting to control his weeping. *What about the people!* He wanted to scream.

The Ülrügh ummed and aahed, shaking his head, his masked face turned towards the tunnel before him. Chuck reeled back when he saw the corpse of another person: the head was half blown away, an arm was flung up and half dismembered; red holes punctured the back.

Chuck retched inside his mask. "Jesus, Mary and Joseph!" he sobbed. "What sort of hunt is this?"

Ülrügh Redel's hand grasped his arm. In a happy voice, apparently oblivious to Chuck's distress, he began to point out the features of the Cryptals. "See how widely spaced their limbs are. They move through these tunnels by pushing their way along the sides, vaulting along – I think you'd say. They use those hind claws to tear at rocks and those massive arms and large hands move the rock. Their skulls are very thick and they use them to batter rock to smash it–" He interrupted his explanation to growl at the two men who were skinning the Cryptal; they had spilt blood on to the honey-coloured fur of the beast as they hacked at the hands.

"My Lord. Those people – back there–"

A roar of crashing rocks sounded from further into the tunnel.

"God in heaven! What is that?"

"Oh, that's just the tunnel collapsing. Cryptals collapse their tunnels when they are threatened. Come." Without waiting, the Ülrügh began to jog back. "We have done enough in here."

Chuck staggered after him.

He caught up with Ülrügh Redel in the main cavern. "Four dead but this one lives," he heard someone say.

"Bring him along. And relieve the others of their clothes." To Chuck, the Ülrügh said: "The clothes are made of Cryptal cloth. The fabric will also fetch a good price."

"My Lord, who – who – are these people?" Chuck whimpered.

Ülrügh Redel stirred one of the bodies with the toe of his boot: "Crystalmakers," he said with disgust. "They are ground dwellers and the scourge of Si'Empra. They sabotage our every effort to live decent lives."

"But why – why–"

"Why sabotage? To that question I have no clear answer. Our past is littered with indignities because of Crystalmakers. My grandfather had it right when he finally confronted them."

"No – no – I mean – you killed them–" Chuck hurried after the Ülrügh, who had turned away and was striding across the cave.

"Of course," Ülrügh Redel said in an off-hand way. "My grandfather should have finished the job. Ah well – it does provide us with some sport now. An excellent hunt, wouldn't you say? Excellent. Of course it would have been better if I had also found my sister. Be that as it may. I will do that also."

Chuck's scramble up the scree slope was less adroit than the Ülrügh's, so that by the time he had squeezed out of the crevice the Ülrügh had his mask off and was stripping out of his overalls, his dogs at his side, tails sweeping in welcome.

Chuck fumbled off his mask, took a deep breath and choked. Fire poured into his lungs as he desperately tried to fill and empty them simultaneously.

Ülrügh Redel glanced at him with mild interest. He flipped his hand at one of his men: "Take him away from the skin," he said. To another man he said: "Call in the helicopters."

Gagging and gasping, Chuck fell to his knees, hands over his blistering face and smarting eyes. A hand clamped something moist and sticky over his mouth and nose, and the searing pain in his lungs eased a little. He heard the helicopters, felt himself being lashed on to a stretcher that swayed and bucked under him. As the final shreds of consciousness left him, he heard Ülrügh Redel give a whoop of triumph: "My dear chap! I have just seen how I can find every Crystalmaker exit on this island!"

CHAPTER 10
Finding Religion

CHITHRA BENT OVER THE papers on her desk, matching data in columns to information she had compiled on her laptop computer. No matter how she moved the data around on the screen, the information presented a dismal figure.

"My dear Chancellor, your face is positively ferocious!" Ülrügh Redel's voice was cheerful.

Startled, Chithra heaved herself to her feet to pay him the respect that was his due. "Ülrügh, I did not hear you enter."

"No, indeed!" He waved her into her seat. "You were far too angry at the computer. Dear Lian, you will give yourself stress distress if you allow yourself to be quite so serious."

Chithra lowered herself back on to the seat, unsettled by the Ülrügh's cheerfulness. Past experience had taught her that such a mood did not necessarily herald good news for her.

"Ah," he grinned, dropping into the armchair he favoured. "Before you think that I might be here on business, let me assure you that this is a social visit. I have had a most wonderful couple of days!

"First of all, I can see now how to more easily find the exits to the tunnels Crystalmaker's use. Do you know that, at their entrance, the vegetation looks different – from the air it looks more bare. Ha! I will hunt every bare patch on Si'Empra."

He burst into a laugh. "And, do you know, I have just had a most interesting session with that North American envoy. You know, the one with the – oh so American – name of Chuck. Chuck. Chuck. Chuck."

His merriment increased. "In Australian English, to chuck is to vomit. Imagine being proud of a name 'Chuck'! Well – it would appear that he is very sensitive to Cryptal fumes. A single whiff of a dead skin and his lungs and skin are a mess. The physicians have him on oxygen." The Ülrügh's mirth bubbled up again. "I thought it would be polite to visit him at his sick bed and he presumed to tell me I had done a bad thing. He used that English word 'evil'. You should have heard him. He can hardly speak but, gasping like he had just run up Si'Em Gorge, he tells me I should not have killed the Crystalmakers. What do you think of that?"

Chithra had heard of the hunt. She had come to accept that ridding Si'Empra of Crystalmakers and Cryptals might be necessary, but did not understand the pleasure that the Ülrügh apparently found in the killing – though she was always careful to hide her discomfort. "And did he tell you why he found the killing so 'evil', Ülrügh?"

"Aah. This is why I thought I would come to you, my dear Chithra. I thought you might enlighten me as to his reasoning. It would appear that God – you know how these foreigners often talk about their Gods – tells Chuck what to do. His God has, apparently, said –" Ülrügh Redel switched to English to make the quote, "'Thou shalt not kill.'"

He waved his hand to forestall comment and continued.

"I know, of course, that these outlanders are wont to practice religion, which takes many guises, but I always thought they were entertainments, opportunities for putting on grand clothes, and for people to come together to chant and sing. I was so bold as to ask him why he thought our hunt this morning was objectionable when, from what I have read and heard, his kind hunt and kill all the time. He told me that this God of his – the Christian God that I had to learn about when I was at school – tells him when it is right and when it is not right. He then went on with some justifications which made no sense to me. Apparently it is alright to kill people when there is a war – but he did not consider the killing of Crystalmakers as justified under that rule. He wasn't at all concerned about killing Cryptals, since they are apparently animals by his God's definition. I am now quite curious why he is so fervent about this God. Obviously there is no such thing as a God. Yet he believes it so fervently and was quite put out when I laughed at him and wanted to know how he knew about God. What do you think, Chithra, why is he so adamant there is a God?"

Chithra smiled. She cherished these times when Ülrügh Redel threw himself into the armchair and sought to engage her in discussions. It used to happen much more in the past, especially when he had had a disagreement with his father.

"There is an interesting theory, Ülrügh, put forward by this man." Chithra made her way to a bookshelf behind her desk. She plucked out a book without any need to search for its whereabouts: a talent that always astounded anyone watching. "The author says there is evidence that deep inside the human brain is a part that controls what he calls 'religious fervour.'"

Chithra opened the book to the exact page. "He quotes the work of a scientist who conducted experiments and found that there is a part in the brain that governs this religious fervour. The theory is that humans have evolved this quirk to stop the rational brain from overriding the irrational brain."

Chithra had not exactly offered the book to him, but Redel took it from her hands and inspected the cover. "Are we talking about left brain-right brain stuff – left brain rational; right brain irrational?"

"That is a simplistic notion of the way the brain works. Only some of what the brain does localises to one or other part of the brain. But we are talking about parts of the brain controlling other parts."

Redel opened the book, flipped through several pages of closely written text, studied a few graphs and pictures and decided he would prefer to have Chithra tell him more. He set the book on a nearby coffee table. "Explain to me, Chithra."

His chancellor resumed her seat. "The author begins his argument by noting that most of our behaviour is determined by the way our genes coordinate behaviour in the brain. Humans have a particularly strong reasoning capacity and sometimes this reasoning capacity can get in the way of survival. For example, humans sometimes ask the question 'why do we exist?' It may be that there is no rational answer to this question, so humans could conclude there is no need to strive to continue to live. To prevent such destructive thoughts, genes have evolved a fail-safe method by not allowing the rational self to control behaviour, especially behaviour that has to do with survival and propagation. Essentially the irrational brain – a spirit gene – feeds the rational brain with a fantasy."

The Ülrügh took up the explanation: "To keep the rational brain from protesting, the irrational brain convinces the rational brain that the fantasy is in fact wisdom from a rationally unfathomable source – the supernatural – something like a god."

Lian Chithra nodded, smiling.

"Could there be truth in this, Chithra?"

She shrugged. "I believe it is simplistic. The idea of a spirit gene is interesting and may explain some behaviours but I should think there is greater complexity in explaining why humans are drawn towards believing in a supernatural – in other words, explaining why humans appear to be spirit-hungry."

"In fact," Ülrügh Redel said slowly, though clearly his mind was racing, "such a state of mind is ripe for accepting the hypocritical complexities of religions that outlanders seem to adopt."

He sat forward, absorbed in his thoughts. Chithra almost gasped with pleasure at seeing how noble he looked – his smooth skin soft over his high cheek bones, his dark eyes under their perfect brows reflecting a glimmer of light – as his wonderful mind focused on the information she had provided. It had been some time since she had seen him like this. When he wanted to – when he was interested – he could think very clearly.

"But Chithra," he continued eventually. "Do you know, Chithra – from what I discern of outlander religions, they all have fantastic social coordination powers – huge numbers of people spread over vast geographical spaces adhere to incredible sets of rules without anyone forcing them to do so – just the threat of punishment or reward after death seems enough to persuade people to make incredible sacrifices." He lounged back again. "Let me see. I think religion operates in this way: someone in a group provides an explanation for something that no one else can explain, something like why the universe exists or why humans exist. The explanation, however, has at its core this notion of a supernatural thing, which our friend Chuck calls 'God'. Now, because as you say humans are naturally spirit-hungry people, they accept the description because the notion of a God doesn't seem irrational and the explanation answers their need for an explanation."

"Now." The Ülrügh's face lit up with an expression somewhere between excitement and amusement. "So, some people claim to be so attuned to what this God is thinking and wanting that they gain high status among the group. You know, outlander history has all sorts of stories about prophets and high priests and the like. So – so – these people become very important in the community. Imagine if these important people are also leaders – just think of the power they have! Think of that, Chithra. A leader who says they know what God wants could get people to do whatever he wants. And people would have to do whatever he wants because they believe that he is speaking on God's behalf."

FINDING RELIGION

Ülrügh Redel beamed at Chithra. "I think I should invent a religion for Si'Empra and make myself a prophet. I would be very powerful."

Chithra could not hide her surprise. This was not the conclusion she had foreseen.

"Ah, Chithra. We could then achieve so much more with much less pain – and you would not have to work so hard at the desk."

Chithra responded in a way he would not be able to fault: "It would indeed be an interesting exercise, Ülrügh. Should we adopt an already-established religion and simply begin with the announcement of your conversion to the belief system, or should we invent a totally new one?"

"Well, Chithra, since we have no religion –" Redel stopped, drawing in a sharp breath.

Chithra nodded almost imperceptibly. "Why do you think your father was so intent on destroying Cryptals?"

Redel stared at her. "Cryptals," he breathed. "By the BlackŌne. No wonder so many people don't like hunting Cryptals. Si'Emprans have elevated Cryptals into their spiritual masters."

He was still for a long time, then he said: "I think I can use this to benefit. Christians have a devil as well as a God. I do believe that the Cryptals are devils." He smiled at Chithra. "How very convenient."

Chithra's skin prickled with goose bumps; trepidation caused an unhappy taste in her mouth. *BlackŌne's beard, I do not know whether I like what I hear! This may entirely change who we are on Si'Empra.*

CHAPTER 11
Fadil

*E*LLEN LOUNGED BACK AGAINST the saddle brace, one knee crossed over the other, free foot swinging idly to Rosa's motion. She was contented to be on her way again, finally released from Greçia's care after a month of inactivity.

She frowned at the page clipped against a plastic board that rested against her thigh. She tapped the end of a pencil against her bottom lip as she inspected the page. The writing was rather haphazard, given the unstable surface. She grumbled to Rosa about 'movement' from time to time, drawing aggrieved glances from the bird when she did so.

Muttering, Ellen added a few more words, wrinkled her nose and carefully erased what she had just written. She tapped the end of the pencil against her lip again then sighed dramatically.

"Listen to this, Rosa. It's in no way finished, but listen anyway." Ellen cleared her throat and began to read what she had written. She was not two sentences into the story when she wrinkled her nose with distaste. It was not good at all.

This is nonsense!

She looked over the top of her knee to check for Rosa's reaction. Rosa stretched her neck forward and plucked at a rather delectable-looking herb growing between two rocks. "As I expected, you didn't listen to a word," Ellen huffed. "You could at least pretend to listen! Just because you think I should stick to reading and forget writing you shouldn't ignore me. I like writing – so a bit of encouragement would be appreciated."

Storytelling was a well-loved pastime for Si'Emprans. Some of Ellen's earliest memories were of sitting on one or other parent's lap and listening to skilled storytellers take her into the lives of other people and events. When she learnt how to read, especially when she learnt how to read in the English language, she discovered an even greater universe of stories. Her desire to become a storyteller had blossomed early and her tutors had indulged her, as had foreign visitors.

Her father had been less enthralled.

"Your duties are to learn leadership," he reminded her time and again.

Ellen focused on the page on her lap again. "Of course," she muttered. "I should think of another–"

Rosa dropped to the ground, making a soft warbling sound. Ellen stilled. Without moving her head, she scanned her surroundings. To her right a slope rose steeply toward the sky and, as far as she could tell, nothing moved on it. To her left, the slope dipped to a degraded cart track – about 200 metres away – that she and Rosa had crossed fifteen minutes ago and gradually moved away from. Slowly, Ellen turned her head to get a better view. A group of men were facing toward her. From the way they behaved, it was obvious that they did not have a clear idea of what they might have seen. One of the men was pointing in her direction.

With minimal movement, Ellen unclipped her harness. One man pulled a backpack off his shoulders, dropping it to the ground. The others turned towards him.

In that instant of their distraction, Ellen slipped behind Rosa's black back. She crept past the glasaur's shoulder and peered carefully over the outstretched neck. All the men were looking up again. The one who had been pointing was again gesturing, his head close to a man with binoculars to his eyes.

This would be a test! Ellen glanced at the sky. It was its usual overcast self. If the sun broke through the clouds, chances were Rosa's black bulk would be recognisable. In the more uncertain light, Ellen was confident that Rosa would be well camouflaged. Not that it really mattered if the men did see her, she just preferred it that Redel did not have word of her whereabouts.

The man with the binoculars shook his head, lowering the glasses. Ellen recognised him from his bulk and movements: Lian Cecil.

The man who had pointed began to move up the slope. It was a steep climb but physically possible. If they all climbed then she and Rosa might have a chance to slip away as the men disappeared temporarily behind a drop-off. If some stayed behind then any movement Rosa made would give away her position.

The climber paused; there appeared to be a discussion and he scrambled back down. The party set off again along the track.

Ellen let out the breath she had been holding, and made sure they were well out of sight before standing.

"Now where do you think they might be going, Rosa? There's only Fadil at the end of this track. It's as poor as winter sunshine. Why would Lian Cecil want to go there?"

She knew the village of Fadil well. It had not been her intent to visit it now, but now she decided to do so.

Keeping away from the track, Ellen and Rosa arrived at the outskirts of the valley fronting the grottos that made up Fadil. Ellen tugged a nondescript, knee-length raincoat out of a saddlebag and dismounted, telling Rosa to stay hidden. Shrugging into the coat and pulling the hood up to shade her face, she made her way down a slope into the valley.

A goatherd sat on a bench near one of the grotto entrances, surrounded by about thirty restless goats. small clusters of people stood outside other entrances, whispering worriedly to each other. A larger group, peering anxiously into the gloom of the cavern that served as the community's meeting space, was silent.

The herder was the first to see her. He stood up quickly and bowed respectfully.

"Are those men here to collect taxes from you?" Ellen asked.

"Yes," the man said unhappily. "Ghuy is protesting that we have nothing to give them if we are to live. But he has been busy at it for some time – but they are insisting.

"I would like to listen to this conversation. May I wander through your halls to enter the meeting space from the inside?"

As she made her way through the Fadil labyrinth, some people followed, obeying her caution to do so quietly. Motioning that she wanted to enter the meeting room alone, she slipped past a curtain, pleased that she had remembered that this entrance was usually quite dark but had a good view of the central area.

Lian Cecil had set himself up behind a table. In front of him stood Ghuy, the leader of Fadil. Lian Cecil was tapping a large sheet of paper on the table with a pen.

"There are fifty-three people in this village. Only nineteen of them are children too young to produce. I know your people have been in the city and have exchanged goods for money. This amount you have handed over is nothing."

"Lian," Ghuy protested. "Other money we had has been used to purchase things we need for winter."

Lian Cecil rejected the argument. He threatened to have his men search every grotto and confiscate what he said was the "Lianthem's rightful due", unless Ghuy produced whatever amount the Lian seemed to have decided the village should provide.

Over the course of the next quarter hour, Ghuy surrendered an amount of money that he swore was all there was in the village, as well as goats and chickens, sacks of provisions and a goat cart to hold the provisions, and still Lian Cecil argued there must be more.

With each concession that Ghuy made, Ellen's disgust rose. What was surrendered might seem little to Lian Cecil, but Ellen knew that each item was crucial for the survival of the villagers. Ghuy advanced this argument but Lian Cecil merely told him to take his people to Si'Em City for the winter. The fact that the villagers had not been able to afford overwintering in Si'Em City for some years obviously escaped him altogether. It did not escape Ellen though. It had been an issue that had troubled her for some years.

When she was barely ten years old she had asked her father why some Skyseekers, especially those who came from summer villages to overwinter in Si'Em City, were crowded into small apartments or even had no apartment accommodation at all, while others had so much space. Her father had told her that it was just the way it was. Redel had been even more dismissive: "They don't deserve more. It is enough that we provide them with shelter and warmth and things to do, otherwise they'd probably destroy the city in winter, they are so boorish." Neither answer had satisfied Ellen. Over the years, as she came to know the poorer folk of Si'Empra better, and concluded that they were neither undeserving nor boorish, she probed further. Lian Chithra had hinted that the root cause of the problem was because the villagers had given up their rights to own private accommodation. It was Pedro who eventually provided a full explanation of the dilemma facing the homeless.

"Well, it is both complicated and simple," he said. "In the olden times, every family had a place in Si'Em City that they could use in winter. Many places were empty in summer when the families went to their summer villages, except when some member of the family came to Si'Em City to sell produce or, sometimes, some family members who were too old or sick to travel to the summer villages would stay there. Sometimes, there were arguments about how much space belonged to a family group; mostly this happened if arrangements for the allocation of space wasn't worked out before a marriage took place. The Lianthem would then sort out these problems.

About twenty years before you were born, the Lianthem decided on a different way to organise people. They said to each family that they now owned the spaces but could sell them or sell parts of the spaces they didn't use. This seemed like a good idea and there was a lot of buying and selling. Some people were clever about what they bought and others were not clever about what they sold. The not-so-clever ones only saw that they could make money by selling their places and didn't think that the money would run out and they would have nowhere to live in winter. They just thought that they had a lot of money and they could make more money in the summer time and in the winter they could just rent the spaces they needed. The clever ones used what they bought to make their own places bigger and rented out places to people who didn't have spaces. Some set up apartments that foreigners could use all the time and many spaces then just stopped being available to Si'Emprans. Each year, the people who owned the spaces made the rents higher so that you had to have more and more money to be able to afford to rent an apartment. It got harder and harder for people who didn't own spaces to find a place they could afford, especially because the people from the summer villages weren't making as much money as they used to."

The Fadil villagers had been one of the groups to fall foul of the new system of ownership.

Ellen's lips clamped tight as she continued to listen to the negotiations. She had never had a high opinion of Lian Cecil. As far as she was concerned, he was a greedy, self-serving man whose ambitions ran no further than to ingratiate himself with the most powerful in Si'Empra. He would probably pocket a percentage of the proceeds he gathered from his tax-collecting ventures. Her gaze flickered over the men who stood behind the Lian with their guns. Guns! *Since when have Si'Emprans even needed guns against each other!* These men were not Redel's adjutants. They were likely a cohort of bullies Lian Cecil had recruited to help intimidate the villagers.

Forgetting her resolve to make her whereabouts unknown, allowing the disgust she felt to propel her forward, and with only the vaguest of plans, Ellen strode into the room to confront the Lian.

"Lian Cecil, Ghuy is deceiving you. He has failed to mention this village's most valuable asset and he will deprive the Lianthem of it if you take what he has offered you now."

All the men jumped as Ellen's clear voice rang out. She threw back the hood over her head, ignoring the guns that snapped their barrels in her direction and then wavered away. Lian Cecil rose, ducking his head in a deferential bow. "Lian Ellen, I did not know you were here," he blurted, managing to sound both confused and peeved.

"I note you are about the very important business of raising taxes," she said. "You have come to a very isolated village for this. I am in awe of your dedication."

"The Chancellor – ah – Si'Empra has need for provisions for winter. The people have – are hoarding what they have and the Lianthem – the Lianthem has – ah – ah – declared that in fairness to all, the administration must take the hoards and redistribute them. And – there is – there is also a need to fight back the – aaah – the assault of the Crystalmakers and Cryptals – yes – assault."

Ellen nodded. "The Lianthem is wise. There is little doubt that many will suffer in winter unless the Lianthem is firm about how food, clothing, warmth and shelter are distributed among the people. I have been to this village a number of times and I have been listening to Ghuy's excuses just now. He offers a paltry amount when, I tell you, he could do much better."

Out of the corner of her eye, she saw Ghuy's eyes widen in shock. From the entrance, voices began to murmur. But she knew she had an innate skill of sweeping people along with her ideas, a skill her father had helped her to hone. "When you start a negotiation never show that you are uncertain of yourself," he had advised. She continued to focus on Lian Cecil.

Lian Cecil shifted his stare, trying to avoid her eyes. "I am on the point of ordering a search of all dwellings," he explained.

"That is hardly likely to reveal anything. Tell me, have you visited other villages to raise these taxes?"

Ellen could see that the Lian was recovering from his initial surprise. He was probably beginning to wonder whether she had a right to ask him questions at all. She made sure her steady, uncompromising gaze did not waver.

"We have visited others."

She turned on her heel, striding towards the entrance. "Let me show you what these villagers are hiding from you."

People stood aside to let her pass, and the Lian and his men followed her. Ellen crossed the valley, walking too quickly to afford an opportunity for anyone to ask questions. At the farthest, southern section of the valley, she stopped at the base of a series of terraces cut into a steep slope. Many terraces were unkempt but some had been tilled and grew summer vegetables.

"This is their greatest asset," she announced. "From these terraces, this village used to feed at least another two hundred people, as well as growing lithilian berries for wine. Now look at the number of terraces that are not tended. They are only concerned with feeding themselves. Those lithilian vines," she pointed to terraces of tangled vines, "will produce juicy berries ready for crushing in another month, but there will be hardly enough to press a few vats of wine – which these villagers will keep for themselves. Do you remember the Fadil vintages, Lian Cecil? My father used to speak of them quite fondly. Each time I visit this village I have noticed these people becoming more lazy."

Ellen heard a woman's voice gasp.

"Lian Cecil–" one of the gunmen began.

Ellen cut across him. "I believe that with relatively little effort these terraces could, even this summer, produce an abundance of produce. All these terraces need is a little investment of materials and time."

In the past Fadil had indeed produced much food for Si'Empra. The shape of the steep slopes around the valley formed a warm microclimate, letting in sunshine and moisture and keeping out the harshest of weather. Nevertheless, encouraging the crops to grow required constant applications of rich nutrients and much labour. Goat herders from many parts of Si'Empra used to sell their manure and other rich compost to Fadil. Now, however, Si'Emprans produced much of their food in hothouses that occupied the relatively flat fields close to Baltha, or they obtained supplies from overseas. The falling demand for their produce had forced the villagers to gradually abandon more and more of their terraces.

Lian Cecil shifted uncomfortably. "We don't need food from here. The hothouses produce our food."

Ellen raised an eyebrow, making plain her surprise at his words. She drew breath to speak, glanced at those who stood around, then settled for a conspiratorial expression. She placed a hand on Lian Cecil's arm and drew him aside, dropping her voice so that others could not hear.

"Lian, I have not been privy to the discussions that have you making this, doubtless, uncomfortable journey to this isolated village. However, I did hear you say that the Lianthem is running low on provisions for this winter. I am aware that our fuel supplies for the hothouses are running low again and we do, indeed, need to find other sources to restock our winter supply rooms."

Not inclined to put him on the defensive and, therefore, unwilling to cooperate with her, Ellen surged on.

"May I say that I have been travelling around the summer villages for some time now and, as I'm sure you have observed, it is evident that the villagers are becoming increasingly selfish in their attitudes towards the greater good of Si'Empra. My father worried about this. Lian Cecil, I think it is possible for you to double and even triple the contribution of all people to Si'Empra. I think you could made a significant return on the investment you make—"

"Investment! What investment?"

Ellen looked apologetic. "I'm sorry. Let me take a few steps back. I am so excited that I have quite run ahead of myself! I have been thinking about this for some time but I don't have your experience to take the idea further. Like I said, this village used to produce a lot of food and wine. Do you think it would be possible to get them to do it again and for you to sell it in Si'Em City? I know that it costs a lot to produce food in the hothouses and to buy it from overseas. It must be cheaper to do it here."

Lian Cecil was condescending. "The food I collect is in lieu of taxes due."

"Oh. Yes. But I was thinking: what if there was more food than just what's due in taxes? There must be a way of making money from extra food if there's such a shortage."

As she'd anticipated, Lian Cecil's greed began to take hold. Ellen knew that it was not only the poor who dealt in the black market, and Lian Cecil likely shadowed his hands in that economy as well.

"How can we be sure that the villagers can deliver? What would it take?"

Ellen walked over to the villagers huddled in a worried group. She explained what she had been discussing. "Impossible," Ghuy protested.

Ellen shook her head firmly. "You mean to tell me that this village that has prided itself on having the best farmers has suddenly lost its capacity to produce?"

"No. But, Lian Ellen, many of our tools are broken and we are too poor to purchase new ones or to afford the services of those who might mend them. We only have three goat carts – and those men are taking one. The track is very bad and in many places we have to carry the carts over sections. It takes a long time to reach Si'Em City and when we have tried in the past our produce has spoilt. We also do not have enough seed–"

Ellen held up her hand. "This is what we will do. I will continue to talk to Lian Cecil and his men. I will raise at least two hundred dinars from them, get your cart back and other things they've so far collected from you. While I'm doing that, I want you to think about what you can do to increase production – and what more you will need. Don't worry about transport. We'll work that out later. It is very important that you act confident that you can make these men rich. Trust me. I will make this work. I know people who can help with this."

There was fear in the villagers' eyes, but Ghuy nodded slowly.

Ellen returned to Lian Cecil. "Yes. Not a problem," she said. "There are a number of issues, however, that we need to work through."

After an hour of discussion, with Lian Cecil becoming increasingly excited by the idea of the new enterprise he had conceived, Ellen managed to collect an 'investment' of two hundred and thirty-five dinars as well as a return of all the money, items and livestock that Ghuy had previously negotiated away.

In the meantime, Ghuy and the villagers, in spite of their continued misgivings, had done as she asked: they had concocted a plan to restore some of the terraces and increase production, along with the start of a list of essentials. While she talked to the villagers, Ellen saw that Lian Cecil was busy with his men. Having drawn him into the clandestine adventure, Ellen left him to sort out the details of how to ensure his henchmen committed.

"Your task for the rest of this evening," Ellen told the villagers, "is to give these men a good time. Give them your best wine; turn on your best entertainment and food. Don't hold back. I want lots of good feelings from your guests when they leave in the morning."

The villagers did their best. Ellen wove in and out of kitchens that were suddenly busy preparing a feast with food the people could scarcely find, reassuring worried cooks that all would be well. She told everyone she was confident that she could call on the help of friends to ensure the villagers would not suffer. In the meeting hall, she sat with the men who were suddenly business partners, encouraging banter and goodwill, every bit the hostess and Ülrügh's daughter. As the food arrived, she called for music, knowing that a few of the villagers played the samira and drums. The samira was old and missing strings, but it was still possible to pluck out a tune of sorts and the drums were lively. She, herself, played the clarinet. People asked her to sing. She had a sweet voice and had been taught how to use it. She sang for them, and danced as she sang. Si'Emprans loved to sing and dance – and sing and dance they did – old and new songs: some to dance by, some to sway sadly by and other to lustily laugh with.

When the last of the guests had dropped his head in sleep, Ellen and Ghuy left the meeting hall to sit on a bench where they could converse without being overheard. It was early January, the summer sun had dipped to the horizon, touching the earth but would not settle more deeply. The sky had taken on a yellow-grey hue. A breeze trembled the leaves of bushes. Two grey, thick-furred solnis slunk out from behind a pile of stones. They blinked their yellow-green eyes at the two humans, dog-like snouts lifted to the breeze, black noses twitching, and small, rounded black ears pricked.

"Those two!" Ghuy growled.

The solnis turned their lithe bodies in a flash, their long black-tipped bushy tails the last to disappear.

"They've taken two of our kids," Ghuy said.

Ellen rested her head back against the wall behind her, closing her eyes. "I would not have thought they were big enough."

"They won't take a full-grown goat but they're as big as a new-born kid and they'll take a kid up to twice their size. Pesky hunters! Clever too. We're sure they've got a den with pups but we can't find them and they've managed to miss our traps."

Ellen smiled. She'd heard similar grumbles from other goatherds. They all had a love-hate relationship with the pretty solnis. On the one hand they appreciated the way the solnis helped keep down the number of rodents that exploded every summer on the island. On the other hand they resented that the solnis also took young kids. Ellen counted herself fortunate enough to have been able to watch the extended families of solnis at play: the pure white pups gambolling in happy oblivion to dangers from hunting sea birds and humans; adult solnis by turn taking watch duty while others lay among the pups and tolerated their play.

"Lian, we have consumed half of the food we stockpiled for winter in this one night," Ghuy said.

Ellen cracked open her eyes and took a deep breath to push away her exhaustion. Ghuy was sitting forward, elbows resting on his knees, eyes focused on the point where the solnis had disappeared. He had a rather flat face with a thin mouth that was drawn down at the corners. A two-day stubble covered his square chin. The stubble was grey but his hair, cut short, sat thatch-like on his head, was black. He had large hands–

Ellen shook her head, realising that her musings over Ghuy's appearance were simply a prelude to falling asleep. She lifted her head and forced her eyes fully open.

"Some of Lian Cecil's men may wake up thinking that they have struck a bad bargain," she said. "It's important that we stay really positive when they wake up and treat them as business partners. Perhaps it might even be a good idea for you to discuss some of the ideas that you have, to indicate that our plans will work. If we can figure out a way of enabling Lian Cecil to turn an early profit – perhaps by having produce that he can immediately sell – that would be good. From what I hear, there are a number of rich families who are looking to increase their own stores and not just rely on the general Si'Em City stores."

"Do you propose we sell the other half of our winter's supply?"

Ellen sat up straighter. She had known Ghuy since her childhood. As one of the foremen in the hothouses, he had indulged her by picking the tastiest fruits and vegetables for her to sample when she visited. His parents were the previous village leaders; when they died he had given up his position at the hothouse to take over leadership of Fadil when his parents, the previous village leaders, had died. He had done this even though his income from the hothouse work had been a significant source of funds for the village. Leadership was a grim task. Fadil eeked out a subsistence existence, overwintering in grottos that were not as safe to live in as those of Sinthén. Each winter, the villagers lived in dread that an avalanche or earthquake would damage their homes.

"I have been coming to this village for four years, Ghuy – ever since you took charge. You have told me that you could improve the prospects of this village if only you had more resources. Now you have them."

Ghuy did not look at her. "You do not mention, Lian, that we have promised everything we produce. Only by doing that will we be able to meet the promises you have made on our behalf – and even then I am not sure we can do it."

"I will make sure that you have enough."

"How?"

"I am not completely without resources and friends."

"I'm not sure that you understand. As Lian Cecil pointed out, there are fifty-three people in Fadil. I came back to this village because eighteen, not counting the children, are too feeble to do more than help themselves out of bed and to the dining tables. Only six of the children in this village have fathers alive, the rest are children of widows–"

"Ghuy, these numbers may go round and round in your head but they are meaningless. My father liked to quote me this: 'If you give people opportunity and hope, they become strong.'"

"If he believed this then I do not know why he and his father before him were bent upon taking all hope from us. Better the Si'Empra we had before the foreigners gave the Lianthem ideas that changed everything. At least in the past we all had a share and there were not the likes of Lian Cecil to come demanding taxes to make themselves or the Lianthem more comfortable." Ghuy's tone was bitter.

Ellen pursed her lips. There was truth in what Ghuy said, but it was not the whole truth. "The foreigners introduced us to great opportunity, Ghuy. Don't romanticise what life was like in the past. Ülrügh Devi was brilliant in the way that he used foreigners to lift us to better living–"

"Some of us–"

"The problem was that he fell out with the Crystalmakers–"

"But he did fall out with them and he decided to make war on them and decided that it was better to make some people well-off and make others poor."

"But Briani – my father – was considering ways to make peace with the Crystalmakers."

"He hunted them as much as Ülrügh Devi did."

"Not in the last few years. Less and less after he married my mother."

"Be that as it may, the current Ülrügh has no intention of making peace and he funds his war by making us poorer."

To that, Ellen had no answer.

For some time they were silent, then Ellen promised: "I will not let you down, Ghuy. We will make this enterprise work. Fadil will be better off. As I said before, I am not completely without resources. When we have created the benefit from this enterprise, I want a promise from you: that you will abandon Fadil in winter and return to Si'Em City."

"If we make this enterprise work and we can afford it, we will gladly overwinter in Si'Em City."

"Plan to do it this winter."

Ghuy shook his head. "Fifty-three people, Lian. Even the smallest apartment in Si'Em City is not possible."

"It might," Ellen argued, though she realised that she did not really know how much it cost to live in Si'Em City.

After a long silence, Ghuy said: "The rumour is that Ülrügh Briani had chosen you as next leader of the Lianthem. Is this true?"

Ellen frowned. "Redel is first born and the Lianthem chose him. There is no need to argue against their choice."

Ghuy swivelled his head to face her. "The point is, Lian Ellen, that you do and he does not have an interest in how Si'Emprans live. He only has his own interests. You do not think that we have not all heard the rumours of why you spend so much time away from the Serai."

Ellen stood, her heart suddenly bouncing erratically. *I am not defined by what he does! I am Lian Ellen. I am strong!* "What we can do at this time," she kept her voice even, "is to improve the situation of Fadil. I intend to do everything within my power to bring this about, and I hope you will do the same. I trust that you'll see our guests off when they awake with much goodwill and promises. I'll be back within the week."

Ghuy looked up at her, though he did not straighten his posture. He nodded slowly. "You are right, Lian Ellen. I apologise if I have offended you, but should you consider becoming Ülrügh, I think you would give many of us real hope."

CHAPTER 12
Norm Tucker

Norm Tucker watched as Cheng Yi reached across the small table to pour coffee into his mug. He pushed a small jug of milk towards Norm. "Raw goat's milk. In Si'Empra, I'm afraid, that is the only milk. An acquired taste." Norm had introduced himself to Cheng Yi only minutes before, and asked if he could join him at his table. Cheng Yi had courteously invited him to take a seat and asked the teahouse's proprietor to bring another mug and more coffee to share.

"Yeah. That tea – what do they call it?"

"Pendle."

"That's right. That's got to be an acquired taste as well."

Cheng Yi gave a single nod of his head. "Sweet and bitter at the same time but quite stimulating once you are used to it. It is made from the leaves of the pendle berry bush. Sometimes it is served together with the berries. But the berries are tiny and even more bitter. I must admit that you have to be born to Si'Empra to enjoy their addition to the tea. Please, try the cake."

Norm picked up a slice of cake from the plate Cheng Yi indicated. "Funny colour. What's this made from?"

"A combination of grass seed and berry flour. Si'Emprans harvest grass seed and pound it, then add the dried pulp of a rather tasteless berry to the flour to give it that solid texture. The colour in the cake is made from a combination of berry juices."

"Seems berries are used for everything."

"Indeed. This island has an incredible diversity of berries. They are indeed a staple."

Norm chewed reflectively, taking in the scene before him.

The two men were seated on a small platform outside a teahouse on Si'Em Square, where people wandered between makeshift stalls selling a variety of foods, goat hides, clothing, furniture, baskets, ornaments, and odds and ends. *There's no buzz in this market*, Norm observed. When he remarked on it, Cheng Yi explained that the Lianthem preferred goods to be sold to a central storehouse for distribution.

Norm raised an eyebrow at this information: "Does the Lianthem make a tidy profit on the way?"

Cheng Yi inclined his head non-committedly.

"Is the cake to your liking?"

"Yeah. Not bad. Funny texture, but it's not bad."

"I'm pleased, Mr Tucker. There are also more conventional foods, if you like."

"Norm's my name. No – this is good. Thanks."

No curiosity from the Chinaman either, Norm thought as he continued to inspect the market. All morning he'd attempted conversation with people. The well-dressed ones understood English well enough and were polite in response, but seemed to be totally uninterested in him. The ones who looked less well-off just stared at him vacuously when he spoke to them. He'd been warned that Si'Emprans would not warm to him easily. Unfortunately, the Chinaman seemed just as taciturn as the rest of the mob.

"Pretty amazing place," Norm said. "Never seen a city carved into a cliff before."

"Yes. It is an amazing city. One of the most beautiful I have had the pleasure of seeing. If you have not walked through it yet, you should do so. Stairways will lead you all the way to the Serai. I believe that some of the lifts are even working today."

"Yeah, I walked through and I'm impressed. Know a thing or two about art, these people. Got an eye for detail with all that rock carving on the walls and the way they work the colour and the crystal in. I didn't take the lifts. Got told you could get stuck between floors."

"That is sometimes a problem."

"So how long have these people been living here?"

"I believe thousands of years. There is a publication on the history of Si'Empra. I believe the main stores within the city complex have it available. Otherwise, there is a very good little library with a museum attached."

"I went there. Seems they've run out of copies."

"Ah."

"Anyone who might show me around?"

Cheng Yi smiled. "Mr Tucker, if no one has offered thus far, I fear your chances of having someone show you around are slim. Si'Emprans are slow to accept strangers."

"Yeah. I get the feeling. What about you?"

"I am but a guest in this country."

Norm took that as a "no". He wasn't getting anywhere fast. He watched a young, dark-haired man stop at a stall and begin a conversation with the stallholder. A passer-by stopped and joined the conversation. A girl shoved her way into the group, her loud, raucous voice pitched to ask a question. One of the men gave her a small, impatient shove and she left the group, calling out something to him over her shoulder.

"Got any Si'Empra crystal?" Norm asked.

Cheng Yi's eyebrows arched. After some seconds he said, "I do not trade in crystal, Mr Tu – Norm. I trade in gemstones."

"Do you know who trades in Si'Empra crystal? Anyone in this market?"

"Only the Lianthem is permitted to trade in Si'Empra crystal."

Norm's lips twitched in frustration. He stretched out his long legs and tugged a tobacco pouch from the pocket of his khaki trousers. He offered to roll a cigarette for Cheng Yi.

"No, thank you."

"Do you mind if I do?"

"By all means. Go ahead."

Norm creased a rolling paper between thumb and middle finger and added loose tobacco. As he licked and sealed the cigarette closed, he said: "I've got a ketch, see. A lovely two-masted job. *Westrunner*'s her name. She's hove to just over the way." He waved in the direction of the sea. "I got my men to drop me off here this morning – early – because I'd heard that I might be able to do some good trading here – if I catch the market when there's a bit of sun about. I'm willing to bring stuff to this island in return for a bit of Si'Empra crystal. I've seen the glass and I quite fancy having some of it –"

Norm stopped, speech interrupted by the girl who had been rejected by the men around the stall. She had made her way to the teahouse platform and was calling out something to Cheng Yi, her hand gesturing to the contents of a cart full of open bags of various types of dried berries. A goat, tethered to the cart, tossed its head, flicked its long ears and folded its legs to settle on to the ground.

Cheng Yi waved the girl forward, asking her a question in the melodic Si'Empran language. The girl pushed cracked and oversized, tinted glasses further up her nose, brushing lank hair off her forehead. The glasses seemed to do nothing to improve her sight because she felt for the height of the step to the platform with her foot and then bumped into the leg of a bench as she came towards Cheng Yi. She held out five different types of dried berries in her grubby hands, saying something to Cheng Yi. It sounded like she was talking up the attributes of the produce.

Cheng Yi frowned, making a clucking sound with his tongue. He picked up a rather juicy-looking raisin to examine it more closely.

The girl hawked and spat a purplish glob expertly off the platform into a planter box, causing the teashop proprietor to shout at her. She ducked her head, muttering what sounded like an obscenity. She sucked at her stained teeth and moved something in her mouth so that her cheek bulged out.

Cheng Yi said something in a sceptical tone, holding up the berry and pointing at others. The girl drew herself up straighter, her lips pursed, brows pulled together, clearly offended. She took back the berry from Cheng Yi and launched into a flow of words. Cheng Yi held up the palm of his hand, laughing, and said something in a soothing tone. She sniffed, frown still in place but body a little more relaxed. Back and forth between Cheng Yi and the girl went clipped words.

"Is she trying to sell you these things?" Norm asked.

"Yes. She is. These dried berries are rather precious in Si'Empra. Our hothouses and drying platforms produce something like this, but this girl and her father," Cheng Yi pointed his chin in the direction of one of the more active stalls in the market, "turn up a few times each summer with a cart-full of these dried fruits. They somehow have found the means to sun-dry them and their sweetness is superior to the usual fare."

The girl interjected, her tongue having difficulty with the only word that Norm understood: "Chinese". She peered in Norm's direction, trying to see him better past the crack in her glasses.

Cheng Yi shook his head. "She is asking if we are speaking Chinese," he explained. "English," he said to the girl, and continued in her language.

After more to-ing and fro-ing, the girl examined Cheng Yi thoughtfully before feeling her way back off the platform to the cart.

"For Si'Empran crystal I could bring all sorts of dried fruits – from all around the world," Norm said.

"Then you should speak to the Lianthem – or perhaps the Chancellor." Cheng Yi kept his tone quietly polite.

"Yep, I tried that. They say they're not interested. They've got their own suppliers. But I've been talking to some blokes back home. They tell me there's a bit of a black market–"

The girl returned and addressed Cheng Yi in her husky voice, holding out another selection of dried produce. Cheng Yi shook his head in resignation and handed over money. She returned to her cart, put a careful selection of her wares into a small woven basket, and laid them out on the table. Chen Yi asked a question and she looked offended again and said something that sounded rude. Cheng Yi chuckled good-humouredly. She looked at him quizzically, hawked again and was about to spit, but – with a quick glance at the watching teahouse proprietor – thought better of it and swallowed whatever vile fluid she had chewed out of the leaves still distorting the sides of her cheeks. She plunged a hand into one of the deep pockets of her oversized, greasy, shapeless overcoat. As if doing Cheng Yi a favour, she took a wrapping of moss from around two, small, grey-speckled eggs and spoke, for the first time, in a gentler tone.

Cheng Yi parted with more money for the eggs and the girl returned to her cart and made a fuss over the patient goat, which had come to its feet at her command. She wandered off with the goat following placidly, calling out her wares in her jarring voice.

"Did you get a good deal?" Norm asked.

"I think I did. It's hard to tell. From experience I know that if I displease her too much I simply find myself with fruit that doesn't taste the best, or has some other defect. The fact that she offered me eggs probably means I haven't offended her, though she said I did." He smiled as if he'd enjoyed the way the girl had treated him.

"What are those eggs?"

"Swallow-tit eggs. The nests are almost impossible to find. Si'Emprans, in general, love the taste of these eggs – though I do not. These are for my wife. Josephine will have no problem selling whatever supply of eggs she has in those pockets."

"Josephine. That's that girl's name? She could do with a bath and an eye doctor," Norm remarked.

"Many of them –" Cheng Yi swept his gaze over the people in the square, "could do with better care. Not many of them have the means –" He stopped himself abruptly, as if regretting his words. *Gawd!* Norm thought. *He's as tight-lipped as the rest of them.*

"She can see good enough to spit."

"I think Josephine sees what she wants to see," Chen Yi said with a smile as he packed his purchases carefully into a paper bag the teahouse proprietor had given him.

"You have a Si'Empran wife, have you?"

"I am fortunate enough to be thus blessed." Cheng Yi rose. "I must go, Mr Tu– Norm. Please excuse me. The bill is taken care of."

"Oh, thanks mate. So. You can't help me, mate?"

"I'm afraid not. I do have everything that I need. You see, Mr Tuck– Norm – I have ships that go back and forth with my cargo all summer long. I can and do order what I like."

"And your ships bring the Lianthem's supplies too?"

"A bulk of them, yes."

Norm nodded, standing. "Thanks, mate. Yeah, I'd been told – you know, I've got mates who have been here, to this spot of land – they told me you had a pretty good arrangement. I thought we might be able to do a deal."

"I wish you better luck with others, Norm."

Norm lit his cigarette, drew deeply and let out the smoke through an open mouth. He stood up and wandered over to a group of men clustered around a stall. They fell silent as he approached.

"Anyone here speak English?" he asked.

The men looked at one another and back at him. The stallholder said something unintelligible, indicating his wares – an assortment of electronic goods – and raised his eyebrows inquiringly.

"No, mate, I don't want to buy anything here. Most of this is junk. I'm after crystal – virigin." He'd been taught that word by others who had visited Si'Empra. He thought he'd made a good go at pronouncing it the way Si'Emprans did. It was obvious these men understood because suddenly they became very nervous. The stallholder held up both hands, palms up, and shook them, motioning that he did not have virigin. He pointed to the top of the Si'Empra City bluff, at the Serai. "Virigin," he said, pointing up at the Serai again and repeating the word, "virigin".

"Yeah. Yeah. I know mate. The Lianthem's the only one who sells it. But they don't have any – or so they say. Anyway, I'll settle for some crystal and that nice cloth if there's some begging. I hear word that I can get some if I ask around. Anyone around here speak English?" Again: blank looks. He nodded. "I'll be on my way then." He turned to go and almost fell over the dried berries girl, Josephine. She had stopped quite close to the back of his legs and was busy sorting her wares. She scowled and spat out words at him.

"Jesus!" he retorted. "You didn't need to park it behind my feet!"

Her brow knitted as she pushed the useless glasses up her nose, opening her mouth to say something more.

Norm forestalled her by dropping a coin at her feet. "Yeah, yeah, whatever," he muttered, stepping around her goat and stalking away.

RICHARD, WHO WAS ONE of the group of men Norm had just spoken to, finished negotiating the purchase of an outdated mobile phone, said no to batteries the stallholder pressed him to buy – knowing they would be flat – and took his leave.

Out of sight behind a huge crane used to lift cargo off ships, he scribbled a note to the sandy-haired Australian, nominating a time and place for a meeting. Walking back into the market area, he saw Josephine sitting on the edge of the goat cart, inspecting the coin the Australian had given her. She jerked her head up as he neared and hastily tucked the coin away. *A useless piece of metal on Si'Empra, but fascinating to a girl like her*, Richard thought. She immediately began to describe the attributes of her dried fruits to him.

He listened politely and agreed to buy a handful of dried pill-berries. He told her he would buy the handful for the first price she offered – without haggling – if she would agree to secretly deliver a note to the Australian.

She stared at him, jaw opening to reveal the glory of her stained teeth. She peered around the square and fixed on the figure of Norm, now talking to another group of people. "Him?" she asked.

"Give it to him so no one else sees the note," Richard said. "If you do that I'll buy another expensive handful from you after you've done it."

She gave him a handful of dried berries – he noted it was not a big handful – but he took it and simultaneously placed the note he had written for Norm Tucker in her hand. She closed her grimy fingers over the paper, deposited it in her coat and held out the hand again. "Quarter dinar."

"What! That's outrageous!"

"You want I ask someone what the note says?" she threatened.

Richard rolled his eyes. "You're a thief."

She hawked and spat. "Quarter dinar."

He gave her the money. "Can I trust you?"

She nodded. "For quarter dinar, yes. For half dinar definitely."

Richard pursed his lips, wondering whether he had chosen the right messenger. It was dangerous enough at the best of times to do business in the square. Her price, however, bit deeply into his tight budget.

"The next handful will be quarter dinar," she said.

CHAPTER 13
Ellen's Hide

"How do you think I can find Elthán?" wondered Ellen. She ducked her head under water, surfaced with a whoosh of air and began to scrub between her legs again.

A warning chirrup – almost a bark – stopped Ellen's hands. Rosa, several metres away and standing in warm mud on the downslope of the steaming pool in which Ellen bathed, was staring at her intently.

Ellen slowly raised her hands and put the soap she held in its holder. *It's alright!* She told herself, her chest constricting with a sudden mixture of panic and shame. *I just forgot for a minute because I feel quite anxious. It's alright, I haven't hurt myself.*

She buried her face in her hands, her thoughts scrambling to distract from the embarrassment of her unconscious action and the memory of him – him! – him!

"Shit! Shit! Shit! I'm a worthless idiot! How on earth am I going to fix this mess I've created!" she hissed.

Rosa, frozen in the act of pulling up the bulb of a reedy plant with one of her feet, regarded Ellen speculatively.

"Not by whining. Not by whining!" Ellen took a deep breath. "Not by whining." She moved the fingers of her hand apart so that she could look at Rosa. "I have the beginnings of a plan. I need to talk to Elthán, though. I can fix this. I think I can fix things if I can talk to her."

Rosa pulled up the bulb ate it, though her attention remained focused on Ellen. She emitted a disapproving guttural sound.

"I know! I heard you," Ellen said. "I'm getting out."

She stepped out of the water and reached for her towel. "I could go back to Greçia's and I'm sure Greçia would know how I can get in touch with her. But she's looking after a lot of people. Redel's been hunting – it's awful!" She reached for her towel. Looking down at herself, she saw that her skin was rubbed almost raw. She padded herself dry, averting her gaze from the damage. "Elthán's probably busy too. But I won't take up much of her time. Actually, if I see any Crystalmaker I can probably work things out, so maybe going back to Greçia's place is the best thing." She picked up a large tube labelled 'Nirvana: specially formulated to heal and soothe'.

She smoothed the ointment on carefully, keeping her attention firmly on the issues concerning the problem she had created.

"I've got two villages in trouble now and I've promised both I'd make sure it was alright." She almost groaned as she said this. Her promises had tripped off her tongue so easily. All she'd felt at the time was a surge of excitement about the challenge she'd set herself.

She had left Fadil more than a week ago and made her way to Thuls Refuge. As in Fadil, the Thuls Refuge villagers were expert horticulturalists. They sold a very small portion of their wares twice a year in Si'Em City, sometimes with Ellen's assistance. Ellen had explained to them the needs of Fadil, and the Thuls Refuge villagers had agreed to help. Only a few days after leaving Fadil she had returned with four strong men and women, their tools and many well-established seedlings.

Reality had since set in and as the days passed she had grown increasingly anxious about how she find the means to make good on her promises.

"Mother often said I was impetuous. But the reality is that by helping Fadil, Thuls Refuge is depleting their winter stores. What I've really done with my bargain with Lian Cecil is make two villages need extra supplies for the winter." She scowled. "I'm seriously, seriously, worried I've created a mess I can't wriggle out of. So, how am I going to feed two villages over winter because everything – and I mean EVERYTHING – they now produce will be the property of Lian Cecil and those men of his."

She replaced the cap on the ointment and put it into her toiletries bag. She picked up the soapbox and snapped it closed as if it had offended her. "And my toiletries are running low. I've got to visit my room. Katherina always makes sure there's stuff there for me to pick up. I should have done it yesterday when I had the chance."

She gasped, stilled for a moment by a new thought. Slowly she bent over to pick up the clothes she had been wearing for the past couple of days. "Wait a minute. Wait a minute. I think I know how to contact Elthán. There's a little tunnel at the back of Mother's room. Now that I know that Mother used to see Elthán – I bet that's how they used to meet – through that tunnel. It must lead into the Cryptal tunnels – I've just never followed it far because it becomes quite narrow and uncomfortable."

She stood up, taking courage from her developing idea.

"Redel was hopeless in the tunnels, you know." She said the word 'Redel' very deliberately. She glanced at Rosa, who had returned her attention to pulling up roots. The bird did not even appear to hear the word. "Redel," Ellen said again, certain that if she could say the word as if it were any other name, and think and talk about him as if he were just another person in her life, he would not have power to frighten her.

Ellen stuffed the clothes into a weatherproof plastic box, made sure the lid was tightly secure and pushed the box carefully out of sight between clumps of twiggy bushes under a narrow rock ledge. "Redel and I used to explore the tunnels together and he'd get lost. He always got annoyed that I didn't get lost. I wonder if that's why he's been blocking passages since our father died – so he won't get lost in so many. But it is a nuisance that he keeps blocking passages. It's harder to get around the Serai and Si'Em City without people seeing me now."

She looked around.

The area around her pool was a small oasis of thick, moss-covered boulders over boggy ground carpeted in sphagnum moss, ferns and small plants with tiny, white, star-like flowers or clusters of pink, small-bell flowers. Here and there brown gelatinous-looking mushrooms peeped through the ground cover. Over the years, she had widened the place where the warm spring welled out of the ground, gradually working past the mossy mud into the gravel underlay to create a bath of clear, warm water deep enough to lie in. Not far from the pool, she had, with Rosa's help, created a small shelter that was large enough for her to sit and lie down in. Plastic sheeting on the walls and floor helped to keep out drafts, and thick wads of rugs buffered her from the cold ground. Plastic boxes that doubled up as a form of furniture held stores of food, extra toiletries and clothes, writing materials, books and other items that made her predominantly outdoor existence of the past few summers relatively comfortable. When she left her shelter for any time, she rolled a rock over the small entrance to discourage animals from taking up residence.

In all of Si'Empra, this was the place where she felt most secure – even though it was so close to Si'Em City. To get to Ellen's Hide, as she called it, a person had to first cross the Overshot gorge then sidle along the top of the cliff and finally into this small, secluded valley with its steep, rocky slopes – or they had to go through a narrow tunnel that started just above her shelter to the cliff edge below the Serai and climb the rock face up to the open area in front of the Serai. There was a third way, but that meant a crossing at the headwaters of the Si'Em River at the base of the Si'Em Glacier.

Rosa presented the top of her head and Ellen gave it a fond scratch. "I do believe the Cryptals wanted me to find this place." She paused, a small frown forming on her brow. "Now why would Cryptals do such a thing? What a funny thing for me to say."

She picked up the discarded towel and laid it over the boxes in the shelter.

"Maybe Elthán asked them to – she seemed to know how to talk to them. Do you think they talk? Must be. They told her how to find me – that's what she said."

"Anyway. I've packed things away so it's tidy here now. I've decided to see whether that tunnel behind Mother's room is what I think it is. Don't eat all those reeds. Go and find some rodents to eat." She gave Rosa a final scratch, climbed a little way up the valley slope and, turning herself sideways, squeezed into the tunnel.

In the darkness she finally – finally! – felt the return of the sweet thrill of anticipation and adventure that challenges usually gave her.

"Better," she murmured. "Much better than whining and hurting yourself."

JOOSTHIN PACED HIS ALCOVE restlessly. His latest inspection of Trebiath had established that two of the crystal-firing ovens were substantially intact. Three others were damaged but the stonemasons said they were repairable. Under the guidance of Auchust, the Guild Master of Structure, stonemasons were also creating new benches and repairing chamber walls against the leak of mylin from the Cryptal tunnels. Sara, Guild Master of Weaving, and her acolytes had designed new curtains for the entrances; he had seen the curtain they had already finished for the main entrance and found it especially magnificent. The design was, of course, by the talented Tharnie, Guild Master of Design.

The pink, red-and-brown-shot rock walls of his Illiath alcove looked insipid when compared to the magnificent black, gold-and-green-shot rock walls of Trebiath. Illiath had become the present home of all Crystalmakers only because it had suffered the least damage during The Destruction. Ülrügh Devi had had little interest in plundering there because it had predominantly been the dwelling and working place of the Guild of Memory and many of the lower craftspeople. It was the city in which everyday necessities were taken care of, or materials were made ready for transformation by the Guilds.

Joosthin stepped towards his bench, with its litter of designs for the making of crystal wares. For some hours he forced himself to work. No one disturbed him; his acolytes had learnt that when his mood was foul, it was best to leave him alone. He was eager to move to Trebiath and found that the confines of Illiath increasingly stifled his creativity.

The problem was that the living quarters in Trebiath were a putrid mess. The disturbed bones of Crystalmakers lay among the debris of broken chambers and the sanitation channels were filled with rubbish, many of them blocked. Elthán was stubbornly resisting demands for Webcleaners to attend to the task of cleaning up. The woman had failed at so many levels lately that he seriously thought of never helping her again. He still smarted at the loss of the book. Apparently that granddaughter of hers had deposited it behind a bench, but it was no longer there.

As if in response to his thoughts, the slap of a hand on rock warned him that Elthán was outside the room. Quickly he secured the room's main entrance. When he turned, Elthán had already stepped inside.

"Richard has a buyer for crystal," she said without preamble. "He has negotiated the sale of five pieces."

Joosthin frowned; her familiarity further ignited his already smouldering irritation.

"Sale in return for what?" he growled.

"Food."

"Food?" That was an unexpected answer. He could not remember that she'd ever wanted crystal to trade for food.

"That does not appear to me to be a good use of crystal. Aboveground has always provided enough food – even when our numbers were far greater. Are we falling back into the trap of relying on Skyseekers?"

"We have never stopped relying on them." A weariness he had never heard before underscored Elthán's voice. "Without Phan and Richard and a place to winter the goats, we would have no meat or dairy products. Without Richard and Pedro we would not have the basics to carry out and cure our harvest."

Joosthin shook his head. "The Creation Song tells us that we did all of this before the Skyseekers came."

"The Creation Song also indicates that all Crystalmakers once roamed aboveground throughout summer and were not hunted by Skyseekers."

"It is more likely that over the decades Webcleaners have put aside traditional ways of providing food. There were not always goats on Si'Empra. They were brought by Skyseekers when they first landed. The Guild Master of Memory is restudying the archive of tapestries. We believe that it would be better if we completely sever ties with Skyseekers." He did not add that there had been a lengthy discussion about the incompetence of Webcleaners who had progressively reduced Crystalmaker dominance on Si'Empra by firstly destroying the knowledge for making virigins, then forgetting how to serve Crystalmakers without the help of Skyseekers.

He met her gaze as she studied him. Spots of colour had appeared on her cheeks.

"I suppose we could live on mushrooms," she said, her voice so controlled it held no expression. "I've tried the moss that grows in all the damp areas of our city but it makes me nauseous, so that is probably not an option. Perhaps we could more actively hunt the rodents that share our underground world. The insects could also be an option – perhaps even the spiders–"

"We did better than that in the past!" he snapped. "Perhaps it might do for you to revert to ways that were more successful than the ones you now practice."

The spots of colour on her cheeks deepened and her eyes narrowed. "I am willing, Guild Master, as I always have been, to take advice I can use. However, it does occur to me that I have not heard in the Creation Song anywhere that says Webcleaners are responsible for supply of food. Nor do I know of it in The Order."

"That is not an issue you have the right to determine. Nor have you the right to co-opt Crystalmakers and have them killed."

Elthán flinched. She began too turn, as if to leave, but brought herself around to face him again, the hand that held the bag for the crystals she had come for balled into a tight fist.

"Guild Master," she began icily, "Thil has already taken me to task about Sam's death. The fact is that the youth joined our harvest team without my knowledge. Of his own volition, he sought out the harvesters. Out of respect for Crystalmakers, they allowed him to stay."

"As soon as you discovered his presence among your people you should have returned him to safety."

"Safety? Ah – Crystalmaker safety – I momentarily forgot that Webcleaners don't need safety. I have been somewhat preoccupied–"

"Preoccupation seems to be distracting you from a number of your duties. Being at the beck and call of your granddaughter should not be your first priority. There is Trebiath–"

"Let me tell you about my preoccupations, Guild Master." The tremor in Elthán's voice edged her quietly-spoken words with the threat of explosion.

"Do not–" Joosthin flared, meaning to interrupt her in turn, but she softened her voice further and continued.

"In the past six weeks, since the incident that saw Sam – and others – killed, I have held in my arms twelve more dead bodies: twelve harvesters; and twenty-seven others lie gravely wounded in their beds. Four Cryptals have also been killed. These are my pre-occupations, Guild Master. Trebiath is not high on that list."

"Twelve killed! Twenty-seven – aah – why? How?"

"The Skyseekers have somehow found a way of identifying the areas we harvest in. They kill and wound with guns and dogs, as always."

"But – but you – surely you still harvest?"

"Oh, we do our best. We harvest during the darkest hours, but at this time of year such hours are still brief and the harvesters can only endure so much cold, rain and wind. Perhaps, Guild Master, Thil has failed to mention that our supplies, which were already low, are now dangerously low."

BlackŌne's beard! Joosthin's heart beat faster with alarm. *I had no idea! Has Thil reported this?*

"I have asked Richard to take the risky step of increasing his efforts to find us alternative means of supply. The crystal I am asking you for will bring us such supplies. Unfortunately, not until next summer, but it is at least some insurance."

What would Thren do now, Joosthin wondered. With difficulty he kept his face emotionless. It would not do for Elthán to see his consternation. The thought came to him that Threvor had indeed been informed by Thil about the problems the Webcleaners were facing: *this is why Threvor is suddenly so interested in finding traditional means of providing food.* Her sudden fervour for examining the archives had surprised all the Guild Masters, but they were used to her irascible and unpredictable ways and had not questioned her motives. *How is it that we allow Threvor to keep us so ignorant of what really happens! Should I discuss this—*

"What do you think, Guild Master, would it please you to part with a little crystal or shall I simply call in the harvesters, ask them to clean Trebiath and start breeding mushrooms and, perhaps, set traps for rodents and crickets—"

"Don't play with me, Elthán. I have heard you. I will give you the crystal."

RICHARD STOOD AS ELTHÁN re-entered her alcove. She passed him the bag of carefully wrapped crystal. "Five crystals as requested," she said. She was still too angry to trust herself to be pleasant, so she slid on to the seat behind her table to continue the task she had been busy with when Richard had come with his request.

"Thank you. I wanted also to report that the exit to the eastern fields was overrun yesterday. Skyseekers—"

"I know," Elthán said. "I've asked the Cryptals to make new exits to aboveground. Leave me be, Richard."

"Warmth and light," she heard him murmur.

Alone, she gasped in a deep breath. And another. *I cannot do this any more!* She slumped over her desk. When Richard had come into her room with news about his deal with the foreigner she had had a small spurt of hope. But when he informed her that he had, so far, been unable to find supplies for this winter, the hope all but died. Her strategy for somehow increasing the use of the black market was not working well enough. Richard promised he would continue to investigate other opportunities. He had tried finding supplies in Skyseeker villages but it seemed that most people were struggling to hold on to what they had; the Lianthem was confiscating ever-increasing amounts.

Through her despondency she heard the WhiteŌne's Song change and understood the Song was meant for her. After some minutes of listening she began to make out the Song's intent and sat up with a jolt of indignation.

"Ellen! What do you mean?" she demanded. "I cannot spend my life running after her! I have done enough! Why is she in trouble?"

Whether or not the WhiteŌne understood her protest she could not tell. The Song did not change, simply repeating that she should leave now to urgently attend to Ellen.

Fuming but compelled to obey the WhiteŌne's call, Elthán caught up her protective clothing and dressed as she made her way to the Cryptal tunnels. "I have a matter to attend to," she told someone she passed. "Tell Thanin."

She was not surprised to find a sled waiting for her. She knew that Ellen had left Greçia's care, but when she realised that the sled was taking her in the direction of Si'Em City, her exasperation deepened.

"What are you doing around here, Ellen?" Elthán muttered as she clung to the speeding sled. "You are supposed to stay away from Si'Em City."

The Cryptals stopped outside a Rest at the beginning of the labyrinth under the Serai. Inside, Elthán found Ellen huddled in a corner, struggling to draw breath past swollen lips, gloved hands over her face.

Elthán grabbed a pot of salve, a bowl and a cloth from a shelf. She slid back the lid to the hot water source in the room and filled the bowl. Opening the pot of greasy salve, she scooped out a little and dropped it into the hot water, swirling the water to dissolve the grease. She soaked a cloth in the water, checked the temperature and gently pressed it over Ellen's face.

"Breathe through the cloth. Try not to cough. Breathe. The pain will ease," she said when Ellen instinctively drew away from the cloth.

After some minutes Ellen's breathing grew less laboured and she opened puffy eyes. Elthán resoaked the cloth and replaced it over nose and mouth. "Hold it yourself. Press it against your eyelids." She continued to check Ellen's body for any openings in the clothing that might have let in mylin, and spread salve on blisters around her ankles and wrists.

Finally, she sat down on a bench that doubled as a bed and simply studied her granddaughter, keeping her fury carefully in check.

Minutes passed as Ellen alternately breathed through the cloth and pressed it carefully over her face and neck. "I came to find you," she finally rasped.

"You have found me. What do you want?"

One of Ellen's eyebrows twitched up. Over the top of the cloth her green eyes, made small by the red-rimmed swollen eyelids, met Elthán's glare with an enquiring gaze.

Elthán allowed her frustration to show, lips pressed into a tight line. *Yes, granddaughter. I am angry with you.*

"I apologise for disturbing you," Ellen said after long seconds of silence, her voice muffled by the cloth. "I found a tunnel behind the wall of my mother's room. I thought if I walked long enough I would find Crystalmakers who could tell me how to find you. When I realised I was being affected by Cryptal poison I tried to turn back but a Cryptal appeared and led me to this cave."

"It is called a Rest. If you are going to start wandering these tunnels, you might as well know what different places are called," Elthán said sharply. "By the look of you, any more time in the tunnels and you would have died. Did your mother and Pedro teach you nothing? Why are you here?"

Elthán was slow to anger but when she did, people generally flinched. Ellen, however, simply regarded Elthán speculatively before speaking. "I hear that Redel's hunts have become more effective."

"Did you come into the tunnels to say that? Have you not seen the flow of people to Greçia's rooms? In fact, why are you not with Greçia?"

"I had business to attend to. She was certainly very busy and declared me healthy enough to travel. I came to find you for several reasons. Perhaps the most important just now is to say that I have heard a rumour that a Crystalmaker male has been captured alive and is being kept at the Serai."

Elthán jolted upright, staring at Ellen. "What!"

"Oh – you didn't know?"

"Captured? I thought Redel only killed – and–" Elthán stared for a moment at Ellen, her eyes narrowing. "How do you know this, Ellen? How do you hear rumours? Surely you have not returned to the Serai."

"Not exactly. Anyway, I know my way through much of the labyrinth under and behind Si'Em City and the Serai. If a Crystalmaker is kept in the Serai I could probably find him and it may be possible to get him out."

Ellen moved the cloth away from her face again and tried another breath. She cleared her throat carefully.

Elthán, feeling suddenly profoundly exhausted, took the cloth from Ellen. She resoaked it. "One more time, Ellen. Breathe in the steam from the cloth as deeply as you can." She leaned forward, inspecting Ellen's face. "Your face already looks less inflamed." *In fact, remarkably so!* "Nevertheless, it will take a couple of days before your lungs and skin will be well enough for you to venture into the tunnels again."

"I will sleep here and leave when I feel well enough," Ellen declared. "It is not necessary for you to stay. I imagine you have many tasks to attend to and my intrusion on your time is obviously not something you need just now. I do, however, have a number of requests. I would be grateful if you could show me the proper way to protect myself from Cryptal poison. Also, can you tell me whether Crystalmakers have crystal and Cryptal cloth in any quantity with which to barter for goods?"

"Requests! BlackŌne's beard, Ellen, what are you about? You can't just wander these tunnels. What do you mean, barter?"

"I know there is demand by foreigners for crystal and Cryptal cloth. The Lianthem has confiscated all crystal and sells it for a high price. I don't think they have much left – and you told me once that you give Richard some that he sells secretly. There is a foreigner who has just landed in Si'Empra. I hear that he has been asking around for crystal and is willing to exchange the crystal for goods. I'm thinking that if Crystalmakers have crystal – and cloth, then I can persuade the foreigner to deliver some goods for friends of mine – and perhaps Crystalmakers may want some items too?"

"Is this the foreigner who Richard is just now dealing with?"

"What is he dealing?"

"Five pieces of crystal for delivery of goods next year."

"Five! Next year? Why so little and – next year?"

"The problem is the time it takes for the foreigner to return to his land and back again. He says he will be caught in sea ice if he tries this year. There's also the problem of removing a large amount of goods from the harbour without being noticed."

"Ah," Ellen said, flicking fingers in the air dismissively. "I think we can overcome both those problems. How much crystal do you have – and Cryptal cloth?"

"I have none. The Guild Masters control crystal and cloth. I am able to persuade one of them to give me a little crystal for Richard to trade. I have a little cloth that we make for ourselves."

"The Guild Masters–" Ellen's eyes took on a thoughtful look. "Okay – I'll speak to the Guild Masters."

"You! Speak to the Guild–" Elthán caught herself. She had automatically reacted as if the notion was absurd – but Ellen was highborn.

"Who are these friends of yours and, given our own circumstances, why should Crystalmakers be concerned about helping you to help your friends?"

"How bad are your circumstances?"

"Dire."

"Alright. Then I will help Crystalmakers in return for having the opportunity to help my friends. If I am to speak to the Guild Masters it will have to be in the next few days. Perhaps you could make up a list of your needs – Greçia tells me you are in charge of all of that sort of thing – and I'll see what I can do with whatever crystal and cloth the Guild Masters give me. Actually, do you think it might be an idea to talk to Greçia about what's available in foreign lands because she probably knows – or do you know?"

Elthán almost laughed at Ellen's naivety. "Ellen," she said. "I am uncertain the Guild Masters will meet you, let alone trust you. And what makes you think you can do better than what Richard has done. He has been busy in this business for a long time."

"It's worth a try," Ellen said, as if Elthán had not spoken condescendingly. The girl's gaze was focused on nothing in particular, but Elthán could practically see thoughts racing around under the red curls. "When is Richard due to meet the foreigner again?"

"Very shortly, I imagine."

"Mmm. That's a nuisance. He might have been able to pass on a message. No matter. I can do it another way. I will need to meet with the Guild Masters in three days' time. Is that something I can arrange through you?"

"The Guild Masters," Elthán began slowly, feeling she had stepped into a surreal situation: *Why am I discussing this at all!* "The Guild Masters are wont to set their own terms."

"Really?" Ellen sounded intrigued rather than cautioned. "Well, we can only do our best. I'll be – ah – I don't know where the place to meet them will be. Tell me where I should be in three days time. Will the Guild Masters come here?" She grinned at the look of horror on Elthán's face. "No? Well. Tell me where I need to be."

"This is going a little too fast for me, Ellen. I need to think about this."

"Alright." Ellen removed the cloth from her face. "While you're thinking, would there be something I could eat and maybe I should have a sleep. I don't know whether this stuff I've been breathing in is doing it, but I am really, really sleepy – and hungry."

This child is full of surprises! She is indeed able to tolerate – and – perhaps – even use mylin! Her reaction to mylin is more like that of a Crystalmaker than a Skyseeker. Who is this child?

"I'll prepare you some food, Ellen, then you will sleep."

CHAPTER 14
Webcloth

*E*LTHÁN GRIMACED AS SHE removed her boots. She wriggled her toes with relief, then pulled her left foot over her right knee and bent to inspect her heel. Sure enough, there was a blister. Among Crystalmakers, only harvesters covered their feet. The smooth floors of the Crystalmaker world meant people did not need to use foot covers. She had long become used to wearing boots and usually had them on even when she had no intention of visiting aboveground. But the boots she had on when the WhiteŌne called her to attend Ellen had worn thin and did not fit as well as they used to.

She sighed, set her foot to the floor and slumped back on her bed. While Ellen had slept long and deeply, Elthán had mostly passed the time cleaning nearby webs. When her granddaughter awoke she had been very business-like, asking questions and making preparations to return to aboveground. Elthán showed her how to use the ablution facilities of the Rest, explained how tunnels, Rests and living spaces were organised underground, gave her a spare protective garment and showed her how to use it properly. Ellen had all but dismissed Elthán's caution about re-entering the tunnels so soon after her heavy dose of mylin, and Elthán had not pressed the point. It was astounding enough that Ellen seemed able to tolerate mylin; it was deeply worrying that she appeared to be using it – though she seemed oblivious that the drug was possibly the source of her strength. Elthán warned her about the effects of overuse, describing the awful consequences of the Overcome. "That's interesting," Ellen had responded nonchalantly. "Don't worry, I'm not really attracted to being down here, you know."

Ellen had left the Rest to climb her way to aboveground and Elthán had walked three-and-half hours to return to Illiath. No Cryptals had appeared with a sled. She had grumbled more than once to the WhiteŌne that there was an injustice in only ever providing transport to rescue Ellen, but the WhiteŌne's background song had not even hesitated to acknowledge her grumble.

"I have bought you pendle and a meal, Mistress."

Elthán started out of her doze. "Oh, Thanin," she grunted, sitting up. "Thank you."

"You left us in a hurry," Thanin said, setting down a glass and plate on the edge of her workbench. He was too polite to ask directly, but waited hopefully for information.

Elthán took a sip of the pendle. "Yes. My granddaughter again, Thanin. Somehow she had found her way into the Cryptal tunnels without good protection. The Cryptals were anxious for her safety."

"She has not suffered too much, I trust?"

"She is a remarkable girl. Yes. She recovered quickly with the help of a little salve."

"The Cryptals seem to pay her great concern."

"Yes. Yes. They do." Elthán drew in a deep breath and sighed it out. "Thanin, I am not sure where she and the Cryptals are dragging us to. I am not sure that she is even aware that the Cryptals are paying her special attention. I don't think that we have much option but to allow ourselves to be – ah – dragged."

She shook her head. "Thanin, she has charged me–" Seeing the surprise on Thanin's face, she smiled. "Indeed Thanin, that is the type of person she is. She has charged me to arrange a meeting between her and the Guild Masters."

Thanin's eyes grew rounder. "With the Guild Masters, Mistress? Surely they will refuse? How will you do that?"

"They may not refuse. I will try to arrange the meeting initially by simply telling Thil that she wants to meet the Guild Masters. Let's see how far we get. Would you be good enough to find out if Thil is in a position to meet with me sometime soon – very soon?"

"Of course." Her deputy turned to leave.

"Thanin." He turned to her again. "Have you ever heard the Guild Masters talking to one another?"

Thanin glanced nervously at the opening to her chamber. It was forbidden for a Webcleaner to be in the presence of a Guild Master.

"No one hears us but the WhiteŌne, Thanin."

"Yes, Mistress. Frequently. I often clean their workspaces. But I am not there."

Elthán nodded, understanding. Webcleaners were required to serve and simultaneously pretend not to be present.

"They speak to one another as do others in the Guilds."

Elthán drained the last of her tea and set her glass down.

"May I ask the reason for your enquiry, Mistress?"

"Yes. Yes, of course. Ellen's questions regarding this had me wondering too. I told her that she speaks the Crystalmakers' language the way Webcleaners speak it. I thought it better if she could speak in the way of the Guilds. I gave her some examples of how they speak – you know – more formally than we do. Then she asked me how the Guild Masters address one another."

Elthán's lips twitched into a smile as she remembered her response to Ellen's question and then Ellen's reaction:

"The Guild Masters? Ah – when you speak, you must keep your eyes to the ground, head bowed. You will not speak to them directly. It will be through a mediator who will interpret their wishes. You must not address the Guild Masters directly but allow the mediator to guide your requests to the Guild Masters. If you have questions you must pose them quietly to the mediator who will ask the Guild Masters."

Ellen had raised her eyebrows incredulously, and then actually given a hoot of laughter. "I shall keep your advice in mind," she had said, giving Elthán the uncomfortable feeling that 'in mind' was all that she would do with the advice. "How do they address one another?" Ellen had asked again.

And it had dawned on Elthán that she had never heard the Guild Masters talking amongst themselves.

"It occurs to me that Ellen aims to speak directly to the Guild Masters as an equal," Elthán said.

"An-an equal!" stuttered Thanin.

"She is, after all, highborn – I think that Ellen will do what she will do, Thanin, and I fear that she will not take my advice in the matter. Could I impose upon you to meet her and bring her to the meeting we might arrange? And as you accompany her – I have asked her to meet us at the minor entrance to Illiath – could you please tell her everything you know of the way that Guild Masters address one another."

Thanin had barely left and she had only taken a few mouthfuls of the meal he had brought her when a small, bent form shuffled timidly into her room and waited to be acknowledged.

Elthán rose immediately and helped the crippled woman on to a seat.

"Hochhein," Elthán stroked the woman's arm, feeling thinness under the cloth. "I am honoured by your visit." It hurt Hochhein to be on her feet. The fact that she had made the effort to come to Elthán's chamber must mean she had a significant reason.

"I apologise for disturbing you, Mistress. I have been waiting for your return. Mistress, I have something to show you." With that Hochhein drew out of her pocket a small, rolled piece of cloth. Carefully, with slender fingers – the most beautiful feature of her emaciated body – she unrolled the cloth and laid it flat on Elthán's workbench.

It took Elthán a few seconds to comprehend what was on her desk. She bent to take a closer look and her mouth dropped open in wonder. The finest material she had ever seen, translucent but tightly woven, lay on the cloth. The material looked so fragile that she thought a movement of air might cause it to disintegrate, but Hochhein lifted a corner with her nail and picked the material up. "It is quite strong," she said, handing it to Elthán. "Feel it."

So light. So fine. So silken. Elthán had never felt anything quite so wonderful. Tears pricked her eyes. "You made this from spider webs." It was a statement, not a question, because the material felt as familiar as breath yet she had never seen its like before.

Hochhein's face was alight with happiness, the pain she lived with every day wiped away by Elthán's reaction.

"I have never seen anything so beautiful, Hochhein. How did you do it? How could you have conceived it?"

"I've been working on it for a long time," Hochhein admitted. "There were so many balls of spider thread that others would bring back from cleaning webs. I liked just touching them. Then I thought I would try to clean off the gum from the threads and spool them. It took a long time." Hochhein gave a small, deprecating laugh. "When others saw me do it, they thought my mind was deforming as well as my body. But it amused me so I continued to do it. I had to thicken the threads by twisting several strands together. I will show you the tools I used. Sometimes I thought my eyes would die with the strain of trying to see the threads –" Another small laugh. "Oh, mistress, I will not bore you now with the details, but I have been working on this for years. I have made other little scraps but this is one that I finally think I can show someone."

"I am full of wonder, Hochhein. What are these tools you speak of?"

"They were Master Whyphoon's, Mistress. He kept them wrapped up in a piece of cloth. He showed them to me one time and he was very sad. He said to me that our past is littered with needless tragedy. But he never told me what they were for."

Hochhein was Master Whyphoon's only surviving child. She was of Elthan's age but had been severely injured in The Destruction. She had taken over the alcove that had been the one allocated to her parents those many many years ago. Elthán had never visited the alcove, though she had been told by others who helped to care for Hochhein that she kept it spotless, each item that reminded her of her parents carefully displayed and cared for.

"Hochhein, what do you wish me to do with this?"

"Mistress. I – I – Mistress, I am afraid that the Guild Masters will take it from us. This knowledge that I think we had."

Why would they? Elthán wondered. But then Master Whyphoon had even kept knowledge of the tools from other Webcleaners. Why? "Is this something you would like to develop further before it becomes something to share?"

Hochhein nodded shyly. "Mistress, I would like help to improve what I do. I – I am restricted in what I can do."

"In this, Hochhein," Elthán praised gently, "you have done more than an able-bodied person could ever hope to achieve."

CHAPTER 15
Lian Achton

Tiny flakes of skin rolled away as Ellen rubbed her face. "Do I still look all red?" she asked Rosa, who was seated on the ground to give Ellen access to the saddlebags. She zipped open her toiletries bag. "Let me see." She held up a small hand mirror. "It's looking a bit better. Still a mess, though. Blast! Let's see what I can do."

Carefully she applied a thin smear of make-up, inspected herself again and pursed her lips with distaste. "Well. It will just have to do."

A cool breeze ruffled her hair, touching her cheek with uncomfortable damp. She pulled the weatherproof coat more securely around her neck, glancing up at the grey sky. At least the light rain had stopped falling and the chances that Lian Achton would take his dogs walking were a little more hopeful. "I suppose I'd better make myself useful while we wait," she murmured, adjusting the fastening of weatherproof over pants on the ankle of her boots. She reached up to a second saddlebag and extracted a plastic box. "You can get up now. But keep out a sharp eye for visitors. And don't move about too much, because I haven't secured that flap."

Rosa rose, giving herself a shake to settle her feathers.

"Hey! I said not to move about too much!"

Rosa gave a dismissive cluck. Ellen frowned with mock severity. "Well if things fall out, you'll have to help me pick everything up."

She was about to head for a bush dotted with small yellow berries when Rosa stepped in front of her. Ellen reacted quickly, trying to push past the long leg, but Rosa simply shifted her weight a little and trapped Ellen again.

"Brute!" Ellen gasped, pushing at a scaly shank.

Hardly acknowledging the efforts of her mistress to shove her aside, Rosa snaked out her long neck and delicately plucked a berry from the bush.

"It's mine!" Ellen protested. She squeezed between the bird's legs and leapt for Rosa's head, taking hold of it in both hands. "Drop it! Drop it!"

Rosa gave a gentle shake of her head, lifting Ellen off her feet, berry still held in her beak. Stifling laughter, Ellen kept up a display of indignation, squirming and lunging to get hold of the berry, which Rosa cleverly managed just to keep out of reach by arching her neck, swinging her foot forward to unbalance Ellen or pushing her away.

The two were so engrossed in their play that neither noticed the two long-haired yellow dogs bounding up the slope towards them. The hounds barked in unison to announce their presence and entered the melee. Rosa dropped to the ground, legs folding, and Ellen disappeared under a furry body, her yelp of surprise followed by a burst of giggles as she warded off first one and then a second exuberant tongue. "I've had a bath! I've had a bath!" she exclaimed. "Stop licking me!"

After some more chaotic rumbling over the ground, Ellen managed to disengage from the dogs. She looked around to see Lord Achton sitting on a boulder a little way off, a broad grin lighting up his craggy face.

"There is a strong trait in your family of empathy with animals. Briani and Devi, as well as Redel and yourself – all animals come to adore you. I sometimes wonder whether my dogs, given the choice, would rather follow you than me."

Ellen picked herself up off the ground. The dogs tried another lunge at her. "Enough!" she commanded in a growling voice while frowning severely. The dogs turned to Rosa and lavished attention on her, licking her beak as she swayed her neck back and forth gracefully, cooing affectionately with eyes half-closed, the berry in her beak comically forgotten but still held gently.

Ellen wiped dog saliva from her face with the back of her sleeve as she walked towards Lord Achton. "My overclothes were clean at the beginning of this day," she said ruefully, attempting to brush the mud off her clothing.

"Warmth and light, Lian Ellen."

"Warmth and light, Lian Achton. I was waiting for you, hoping that you would take your customary walk this way."

"I am glad I decided upon it. You would have been welcome to my home."

"Ah. Openly calling on friends is a little tricky nowadays. I'm not quite sure whom I may meet."

"You mean you may meet your brother?"

"Well, yes, or an adjutant or two. How is Lian Isoldé?"

"She is well at this time. She is rather preoccupied with a guest that we have. Her more insubstantial companions seem to have become less important for the time being. She tells me some companions have decided to return to the Serai."

Ellen searched Lord Achton's face for a hint of bitterness but found only resignation. He was one of her oldest friends. He had taught her a love of music, guiding her fingers over the strings of the thordilones, an instrument that seemed designed to test even the most aspiring musician. "You must love this instrument," he had told her, "and then it will sing for you. Your fingers must only guide the song, not pluck it from it strings." He had been Si'Empra's chief musician.

At one time his wife had also been a significant member of the Lianthem. Lian Isoldé had been largely responsible for the astonishing achievements in education under Ülrüghs Devi and Briani. But a mental illness now scrambled her mind. Even before Redel had become Ülrügh, Lord Achton had started isolating her in their stone house five kilometres from Baltha. There he lived out most of the year with half-dozen or so others who helped to care for their needs. Friends called from time to time. Ellen had been a frequent visitor, always enjoying Lord Achton's company, and always gentle with Lian Isoldé, who never failed to engage in heated discussions about Ellen's future with her group of invisible companions.

"I wonder if you would be able to help me in two ways," Ellen said.

"If I can, it would be my pleasure."

"The first is that I need to make contact with a gentleman who has recently come to Si'Empra for the first time. I believe he is Australian and has been trying to buy crystal."

"I have heard of such a man. I thought he had left."

"I think he is still in Si'Empra. I want to meet him. Could you arrange such a meeting? I thought maybe in two days time at the grotto you use for your goats in winter."

Lord Achton raised an inquiring eyebrow.

"Of course people will be curious that you search out this stranger and bring him to your home. Perhaps you could develop a ruse that Lian Isoldé developed a fancy to meet with the man."

The old musician's eyes crinkled in bemusement. "I see. My doing so will cause even more tongues to wag about Isoldé. I'm sure that people are already hotly discussing how she insisted on seeing the Crystalmaker and bringing him to our home. They will be most curious when they learn that she also wants to meet a foreigner."

All thoughts about arranging meetings with the Australian fled from Ellen's mind. She asked slowly: "There is a Crystalmaker in your home?"

"A very sick one. I don't think it will be much longer before he dies."

"Is he injured?"

"Oh. He was. But his wounds have almost healed. Isoldé believes that he sickens because he needs to be belowground. She is probably right but the Ülrügh has forbidden it."

"Where do you keep him?"

"In the darkest, most enclosed room of the house."

"What does he do?"

"He stares at a wall and rocks back forth. Isoldé remembers a little of the Crystalmaker language and tries to soothe him. She takes food to him and he will eat a little and drink a little when she offers it. If anyone else approaches him he becomes very agitated."

"Why did Redel suggest you take this Crystalmaker?"

Lian Achton gave a rueful smile. "Isoldé heard of the Crystalmaker's capture. She would not let the matter rest but I had to take her to see the wretch. Redel let her meet with him, and agreed that we should take him and keep him prisoner."

Ellen's thoughts raced: tomorrow she was due belowground. Would Lian Achton release the Crystalmaker? There was a chance he might not.

Best not to compromise him.

She gave a little shrug, as if losing interest in the Crystalmaker. "Will you bring the stranger to the chosen meeting place in two days time?"

"May I know why?"

"I wish to trade with him."

"What will you trade?"

"Crystal and Cryptal cloth."

Lian Achton pursed his lips as he studied her. He gave a tiny shake of his head and his shoulders moved in a small shrug. "I will do my best. And the second task?"

"Second task?"

"You said you had two tasks for me."

"Ah. Actually I said that I could do with your help in two ways. Bringing the stranger to me at the grotto will suffice for now." She turned from him. "I will let you continue on your way in case someone begins to wonder why you are taking so long. Besides, I think it's going to start sleeting again, and you should be inside to avoid getting too wet."

"And how do you avoid getting wet, Lian Ellen?"

"I, too, should move on to my shelter."

Both dogs had settled next to Rosa, who had laid a wing over their backs. The dogs, tongues lolling from happy mouths, stared at the humans. Rosa, with her eyes coyly half closed, was focused on the dogs. "Oh Rosa," Ellen giggled, "You are such a tart. Come. Up you get. It's time we moved on. We've things to do."

Lian Achton rose, whistling for his dogs. "Warmth and light, Lian Ellen," he said.

She gave the dogs a final pat. "Warmth and light, Lian Achton."

"What is this about, Elthán?" Joosthin asked.

Elthán shrugged. "I met with her and she tells me she wants to speak with the Guild Masters. I said I would pass on the message."

"Thil has told the assembled Guild Masters that she has a proposal to provide us with food and other supplies."

"Ellen didn't tell me the details of her plan. I told her our food supplies were low. She said that if she has crystal and cloth she could barter for supplies."

"I thought that Richard was your emissary in this?"

"Indeed, but I believe that her plans are more grand than those of Richard."

"It is not right that Skyseekers walk our tunnels."

"The Cryptals not only allow her passage but show her the way, and even sled her."

Joosthin's head jerked up. "What do the Cryptals want with the girl?"

"I don't know. I only know they give her passage and favour her." Elthán turned to go but stopped in the act of leaving his room. "I think you will find her quite remarkable," she said over her shoulder.

CHAPTER 16
Lian Isoldé, Redel, Mary

*I*SOLDÉ DRAGGED CUSHIONS OFF a settee and laid them in front of the gate to the Crystalmaker's prison. "You have to stay awake," she told the boy who took a seat at the edge of one of the cushions. "I need to sleep now." The boy was sulking. He thought that he should be allowed to sleep, but she pointed out that he had been asleep most of the day and it was her turn to rest. "You have to look after our guest. I promised Achton. He had to go away on some urgent business. He said I had to look after the prisoner while he was away. You have to help me."

She felt particularly anxious for the Crystalmaker tonight. All afternoon she had tried to engage him in conversation and encourage him to eat, but he was not interested in food and seemed only to want to sleep. She had tiptoed out of his prison and begun trawling through the many books in her library, desperately trying to find information on Crystalmakers. Books now lay open on every table, chair and bench in the room, spilled on to the floor and even out of the door. Every book was open at a page. She had joined the pages together with a long, thin string, taped to words she believed would give her the information she needed. Now, as she settled on to the cushions, she carefully taped the end of the string to her ear in the belief that, while she slept, the words she had joined together would slide along the string and into her brain to give her the knowledge to heal the Crystalmaker. "But I have to lie very still," she murmured.

The boy woke her from a deep sleep to tell her a person had come to see her. She sat up with a start, the string falling off her ear. Out of the corner of her eye she saw all the words that had been laboriously making their way along the string fall on to the floor. But she did not have time to be concerned about the fate of the words. Before her was an apparition to which she needed to pay homage. "Oh, My Star," she gasped, her hand coming up to shield her eyes from the bright light. She scrambled to her feet and contorted her thin limbs into a curtsey.

The bright apparition tipped her head slightly to the side. Isoldé flustered, wondering whether it was surprise or anger that touched the features of the apparition's face.

"Lian Isoldé, I have come to take the Crystalmaker." The voice tinkled.

Lian Isoldé felt a stab of desolation. "Has he died, then?" Lian Isoldé turned to the boy, tears welling into her eyes. "I told you to look after him." Then she dropped her face into her hands. "I beg your forgiveness," she moaned. "I gave in to sleep. Oh, Achton will be disappointed that I have neglected to care for our guest."

"Hush! Lian Isoldé, please do not disturb the household. I will simply take the Crystalmaker with me."

Through her tears, Lian Isoldé looked pleadingly at the light that spoke. "Will you take all of the Crystalmaker? Will some part of him remain with me?"

The apparition hesitated a long moment, a frown forming on perfect features that were almost hidden in the radiating brightness. Lian Isoldé began to shiver with fear, wondering if she had angered the wraith. But finally the beautiful light said: "I will leave you his essence, but I will take his physical self. Please now open the door."

The door? Which door? Isoldé looked around. She could see three doors. One had the string running out of it and a cluster of words on the floor around the doorway trying to clamber on to the string to make their way back to the books they came from; that door was already open. Another door led to the room Achton always tried to persuade her to spend her nights in; it was also open. A third door led to other people in the house. It stood half open. She could see a trail of light through that door and guessed that the Star had walked through it. "My Star, the doors are open," she murmured unhappily. "I see no other doors to open. I am locked in this world. I do not see what you can see."

Again a slight frown on the perfect features; Lian Isoldé's legs almost gave way in her terror.

"Please lead me to the Crystalmaker. You need to put his hand into mine so that his essence stays with you."

"Oh!" Lian Isoldé's relief burst from her. Sometimes these apparitions were so hard to understand! She waved away the boy – he had not even had the decency to stand before the Star! She muttered an apology to the apparition about the boy's bad manners as she dragged the cushions away from in front of the prison gate and searched among them for the large iron ring on which she kept the single key to the prison. She hoped the Star would notice how careful she had been to ensure that everything was properly taken care of. The Star would, of course, know that a jailer's key must always be kept on a large ring. She inserted the key into the lock of the gate, pushing at the iron bars. She gave a little grunt because the gate was heavy to move.

Light spilled into the dark prison. She thought she saw a stir of movement but dismissed it as a trick of the light. Everyone knew that the dead did not move.

The Star walked past her and directly to the dead Crystalmaker. In the dim light, Lian Isoldé saw the Star kneel before the figure and sing a low song. The Crystalmaker sat up slowly.

The dead are reluctant movers, Lian Isoldé noted. She whispered these words to the boy, who had not spoken for a long time. *He is afraid that I will scold him for letting the Crystalmaker die*, she thought. She wondered if it would be the right thing to do to scold him. Really! She did not have much experience with boys. It was such a trial that she now had responsibility for this one!

– but she mustn't be distracted, she had a task to perform. She knelt beside the Star and, taking the Crystalmaker's hand, she placed it into the Star's hand. Again the Star sang a song – she recognised it as the Crystalmaker's language, but spoken so fluently that it became a song – and then the Crystalmaker sang back. His song was cracked and broken. He gripped the Star's hand. Lian Isoldé could feel his desperation. She still held one of his hands, reluctant to let go in case his essence decided not to stay with her. *Poor Crystalmaker. The Star must have just told him that he's died and now he's upset.*

The Star helped the Crystalmaker to his feet.

"Lian Isoldé," the Star said – the light shining from her lit the room so brightly it was hard to see anything. Lian Isoldé peered into the light. "Please stay in this room with his essence. He begs me to thank you for all the kindness you have shown him. He says he does not know how long his essence can stay with you. Probably until morning."

Lian Isoldé took a seat at the end of the mat that the Crystalmaker had died on. She still held the hand but it had lost its warmth. She felt at peace, now, with the death, knowing the Crystalmaker had appreciated her care.

The boy came and sat with her. They sat quietly in the dark together. Every now and then the Crystalmaker's essence would sing softly to them in the flowing words she had heard the Star sing.

IT REQUIRED QUITE SOME effort for Ellen to hold Sam upright as he shuffled forward down a hallway leading to the front door of the house. He whimpered in pain with every step. At the door, she helped him struggle into a long, heavy coat she found hanging on a hook, pulled a plastic poncho over his head and shoulders and pushed open the door, stepping out with her burden into the driving rain. The door slammed shut behind them. She winced but hoped that the general noise of the weather would cause others in the household to discount the sound.

In the half-light of the Antarctic summer midnight, she forced Sam forward towards an outhouse behind which Rosa waited. At the sight of Rosa, Sam's courage seemed to desert him altogether. He cried and tried to pull away, but he was so weak that she only had to wrap her arms around him to keep his close. "Sam. Listen to me. I said I would return you to your people and I will do so. This glasaur is my creature. She will help us in any way I ask her. Your body is ill and my glasaur and I can help you in your weakness. But you must help by keeping your mind strong. Sam, I want you to hold on to these thoughts: Your will is what rules you. Your will has let you live to now. The pain you feel is not what rules you. The fear you feel is not what rules you. Your will rules and it can overcome fear and pain. Trust me, Sam. Let me work with you so that we can both be quickly and safely away from here. Do you hear me Sam?"

He stared at her with large, pale, bloodshot eyes sunk deep in their sockets. His breath came out in short, uneven huffs.

"Trust me, Sam. Let your will rule."

She felt his resistance yield and he allowed her to lead her closer to Rosa. She attached a harness to him and commanded Rosa to lower herself, not trusting Sam to be calm enough to let himself be hauled up by the pulley. She pushed him up on to Rosa's back and he managed, with some more coaxing, to lift a leg and straddle the saddle. With a helpful shove by Rosa, Ellen clambered on behind him and fastened them both to the seat.

"Let's go, Rosa."

Sam jerked in terror when Rosa came to her feet. Ellen hugged him to her. "Lean against me Sam. There is nothing to fear now. Rosa will take us to your people."

Sam's body shook with sobs then seemed to lose all strength, becoming a dead weight against her. Ellen decided he had either lost consciousness or fallen asleep. Either way he was now totally dependent upon her and Rosa. She adjusted the poncho more securely around him, tucking it around his dangling legs. The rendezvous point with Crystalmakers would take some hours to reach and Rosa had gullies and slopes to clamber over to get there. Reaching behind her, Ellen adjusted her seating to give her back more support, then bowed her head further into the hood of her coat to better shield her face against the rain and settled to doing her best to support Sam throughout the journey.

Satisfied for the moment that she could do nothing more for herself or Sam, she thought about her encounter with Lian Isoldé.

A most strange encounter.

She had accurately located the room to which Lord Achton had alluded and been surprised to find Lian Isoldé stretched out on cushions before it. Unable to enter without disturbing the Lian, she decided to try to persuade Lian Isoldé to help her free Sam – though to do so, given the Lian's unpredictable reactions, carried risks.

Hoping that Lian's Isoldé's first reaction would not be to yell loudly and waken the household, Ellen whispered her name softly.

Lian Isoldé had sat up with a jolt, seemingly distracted by something behind her, then she had thrown up a hand as if shielding herself from the sight of Ellen.

There followed a most strange conversation: Ellen had leapt from one guess to another, trying to appropriately react to whatever it was that Lian Isoldé's deranged mind was conjuring. A star? A star to take Sam's dead body away?

Ellen wrinkled her nose. She did not feel good about duping Lian Isoldé in the way that she had. But at least she now had Sam, and, hopefully, he still had enough strength to recover from his ordeal.

REDEL JAMMED HIS THUMB hard on a button on the game controller. The monster showing on the monitor jerked, and blood sprayed over a grey wall behind it. Green teeth showed in a menacing snarl as flame erupted from its mouth. An agonised yelp sounded and the scene blanked. The words: "You died. 2150 points. Best score 272,000. Better luck next time!" scrolled across the screen.

"Shit of a game, anyway!" Redel muttered, hurling the controller away. It hit the wall with a satisfying crack.

The corners of his mouth turning down with disgust, Redel surveyed the oversized desk with its array of monitors and controllers. He used to enjoy playing computer games. He'd linked up with other players around the world, spending hours in blissful distraction with virtual people as he pitted himself against ever-faster, more ferocious and gory beasts.

Lately, though, he quickly became bored. It wasn't just the frustration of the Internet suddenly dropping out – which apparently had to do with not paying bills on time: why Chithra couldn't sort that out he could not fathom – it was that something more profound was happening to him, and he was feeling his way to that 'something' with both trepidation and gratitude.

So much about his life was becoming clearer to him. These days he found that he was better able to interpret the unsettling clamour of his thoughts; they were settling into murmured revelations he could make sense of.

For the first time in his life Redel felt the glory of the energy of purpose; he was beginning to understand he had to take matters in hand and shape Si'Empra – indeed, he was increasingly convinced he needed to save Si'Empra! To save Si'Empra from the devil!

Redel sank deeper into his armchair, chin pressed down to his chest, computer games forgotten, eyes lowered. For some time, he let his thoughts wander, but gradually he gathered them to concentrate. To battle the devil he needed to have his wits about him. He had to plan carefully. The devil had infected the brains of even his most trusted people; especially, he had to be careful with Chithra.

Oh yes! He had seen the shock on her face when he had started telling her about his renewed sense of purpose. He had been quick to realise how tainted she was by evil. He had covered his words by smiling at her in the way he knew melted her into a doting admirer.

"Ülrügh, there is much in the Bible and in the Koran that is full of wisdom," she had told him in that annoying way she had of forever trying to tutor him. "Over more than a thousand years, the words in these writings have been studied and debated. Context is very important to understanding their meaning, especially when applied to different cultures. The words in these books can be used – and have been used – to justify almost every cause for and against the way that people live, love and socialise. My studies of these religions lead me to conclude they come from a tradition and a vastness of land that we, in Si'Empra, can only try to imagine. They come from a tradition that believes that there is some fundamental message that needs to be spread among all humans."

For someone he had always believed to have a brilliant mind, she proved the narrowness of her understanding with her words and her witless caution. He could almost see her tongue fork as she spoke.

Everywhere he looked he could see the devil at work in Si'Empra. He particularly saw it in the way that women, like Lian

Chithra, could command respect and wield power – align the powerful against him – even though *he* had been chosen by God to save Si'Empra.

His journey to these realisations had taken many weeks. At first he had laughed when Chuck told him about the devil and about hell. But Chuck's words had made more and more sense and he began to hear God whispering the Truth to him. Now he understood – with a horror that kept him awake at night – that Si'Empra was the maw of hell's pit. His few attempts to share his revelation with others had drawn puzzled frowns. It would take time. Perhaps some force would be needed. He had begun to convert the more willing of his adjutants: his disciples – his apostles.

Oh, yes. He had to be careful. Somehow he had to make others see how evil women were, how women dragged down the true potential of a man and made them serve the devil.

Redel's brow creased into a frown as he contemplated the nature of women. He did not altogether feel comfortable with his ruminations. *Not all women are evil*, he thought. No. In the Bible, some women were clearly chosen by God to give birth to the pure and chosen few.

Redel picked up the well-thumbed copy of a Bible on the table near his armchair. He opened the book, turning to passage 20 of Genesis. He read Abraham's words about his wife, Sarah: "she is indeed my sister, my father's daughter though not my mother's; and she became my wife". Sarah bore Abraham a son, Isaac, who founded the nation of God's chosen people.

Redel knew that, like Abraham, he had been chosen to lead Si'Empra to God. Like Abraham he needed his sister to be his wife.

There had been so many signs pointing to the truth of this prophecy. The first had been their natural attraction to one another, the way Ellen had trusted him entirely when she was a child. The second sign had been the way she had confided in him about her most private problems, especially the physical pain of menstruation and how she had been told that the pain might pass after her first child. Then it had been the way she had accepted his rightful position as Ülrügh and stood ready to be by his side.

When he had become Ülrügh, he had finally felt able to tell her what he had known all along what he should do: give her the child she needed. He had not known then that his gift to her was what had been foretold – was what God had intended all along. He had just known the rightness of it.

It was still hard not to feel the smart of rejection when she had, at first, laughed at his offer, then recoiled in horror when she realised he was not joking.

But, even in the face of her rejection, he had steadily persisted, instinctively knowing he was on the side of God. He regretted that he seemed to hurt her in his attempts to love her as he should. He had puzzled over the adrenalin rush of pleasure he felt when he saw her pain but now he realised – no – it had not been pleasure in seeing her pain, it was pleasure in knowing that he was carrying out the will of God. He only regretted that the devil's claws were so deep into Si'Empra's sensibilities that he had to keep his relationship with Ellen a secret.

Yes! Even Ellen knew it was right because she, too, kept their most sacred acts a secret.

But it would not always be so! One day, they would reign openly and lovingly together.

Redel's frown deepened. His lips drew back into a snarl.

The Cryptals – creatures of the devil – thwarted him constantly. They had taken Ellen from him. All Si'Emprans were doomed unless he could find a way to destroy Cryptals. If he did not save Si'Empra, the evil would spread across the whole world. Already there were more strangers visiting Si'Empra. The devil would infect them and they would take the contagion back to their countries.

Mary swayed as she came to her feet. Chithra steadied her, gently grasping a thin arm. "Enough," she said. "It's time for you to take a rest."

Mary smiled tremulously. "Oh, I'm alright. Just low blood pressure."

"You shouldn't be working."

"Of course I should be working. I'm not sick. I just don't react well to chemotherapy."

"Your definition of 'sickness' is somewhat unique." Chithra used her considerably larger presence to manoeuvre Mary towards an armchair and press her back into it. "Let me make you a coffee."

"Oh, not coffee," Mary said. In spite of her show of bravery, the nausea that dogged her for days after a treatment was evident. "Perhaps a little weak pendle, if you have some."

Chithra bustled to a bench on which she kept the small number of appliances for making herself snacks and drinks. She boiled the kettle, selected the best of her china, and set the pendle to brew. All the while, she was acutely aware that she was making every excuse not to look at the shadow her companion had become.

"There has been no problem with your medication?" she asked, setting a cup and saucer on the arm of Mary's seat.

Mary's eyes had half-closed. They snapped open and Chithra gave herself a mental reprimand for not noticing Mary's doze. But Mary smiled her easy, serene smile. "Of course. You know the doctors and nurses are in terror of you. I am treated with such consideration I am the envy of every patient."

"You deserve it."

"No more than anyone." Mary sat up a little straighter, taking the cup and saucer on to her lap. She sipped carefully then looked as if she were about to retch. She tried to hide her discomfort, saying: "That dress suits you well. I have always liked that colour auburn on you. It goes well with the reddish brown in your hair."

"Then perhaps I should choose grey. There is more than a little greyishness in my hair nowadays."

Mary grinned. "I would have more than a little grey if I tried to keep all affairs of state in my head the way you do."

Her own position in the government of Si'Empra was not where Chithra wanted to take the conversation. "How is Marthin?" she asked. "I haven't seen him for some time."

"Marthin is doing well. The Ülrügh has him training the adjutants how to do fighting sort of things.'

"You said to me once that something very deep was troubling him. Do you still think so?" Chithra could see that the tea was not giving Mary any relief, so she reached forward and took the cup and saucer out of the woman's lap.

Mary frowned a little. "Yes. Something does. But he won't tell me. When he looks particularly troubled, I ask him. All he says is that life takes some funny turns and it's difficult to know how to make amends for the past. I really don't know what amends he needs to make. I think he's always been such a good man. He has always worked faithfully at his work and he is still so diligent."

Chithra nodded. She didn't doubt that Mary believed what she said, but she, herself, did not trust Marthin. She did not know why, but she did not trust him.

"Have you ever told him our tale?"

A smile. "No, Lian Chithra. I made you a promise and that promise I will keep. Our tale goes with me beyond my death."

"There may come a time when it is better to break the promise."

"There will never be a time when I will break the promise I gave to you."

Chithra covered her face with a pudgy hand to hide the prick of tears in her eyes. "Ah, Mary, what have I done to deserve you?"

Mary shrugged. "We are friends, are we not?" she said softly.

"I have no truer friend," Chithra murmured behind her fingers.

Mary straightened the scarf she had wound around her bald head. "Well," she said, levering herself forward. "This is not going to get that dress of yours sewn before the festivities begin. Once I have finished making the adjustments we decided upon today, I have in mind a lovely pattern to go from your left shoulder and down to wrap around your right hip."

"Given the metres of material that stretches through the span you describe," Chithra said wryly, "I hope you don't intend to make the pattern too intricate, or you won't be finished before winter's festivities the year after this one."

Mary's chuckle made her heart break. They both knew there would be no 'next winter' for the seamstress.

"Well," Mary said practically. "You had best take the dress off so I can take it back to my workroom. Shall I undo the clasp at the neck?"

"I'll manage just fine. Sit there a moment longer." Chithra stepped out of the new gown, careful not to dislodge the pins Mary had inserted, and folded it. As she buttoned herself into another dress, she walked to the door leading into her office, opened it and called out to her administrative aid. He presented himself promptly.

"Jon, please accompany Mary back to her residence." Chithra handed him the folded gown to carry before bending to help Mary to her feet.

"Oh, don't fuss, Lian. This is quite unnecessary."

"It is the least I can do, my friend." Chithra took Mary's cold hands into her own warm ones and brought them to her face. "Look after yourself," she said tenderly.

"The Lians Dane and Julian have arrived," Jon announced as he stepped back to let Mary pass through the doorway. "Shall I show them in?"

"Please attend to Mary. I'll see them into my office."

Chithra turned her mind from festive gowns and her dying friend to affairs of state. She picked up a folder of papers from her desk before stepping into Jon's office to invite the two waiting men into her meeting room.

"I apologise for keeping you waiting. I had not the heart to hurry Mary."

Dane, a man in his early fifties with clear blue eyes and a balding pate but handsome, strong proportions to his lean frame, nodded sympathetically. "I saw her pass. She is failing. I am surprised she is working at all. Anne has been unable to obtain her services for some time."

"I am quite privileged," Chithra agreed. "Julian, you are well?"

"I could complain about the arthritis in my joints." Julian was a cheerful man, though forceful, and a nephew of the late Ülrügh Devi. Arthritis had bowed his back to a stoop and he shuffled when he walked, though the physical defects had not diminished the respect he commanded among a majority of the ruling families. "But I think that today I will simply count my good fortunes."

Chithra enjoyed the company of these men. Each week they met to discuss issues confronting Si'Empra – this in lieu of the increasingly infrequent meetings of the Lianthem.

She closed the door of the meeting room before lowering herself into a reinforced seat at the table. She started to open the folder containing papers she had put together for the meeting, but Julian forestalled her.

"Something is troubling the Ülrügh?" he enquired.

Chithra shot him a glance, caught off-guard. "Why do you ask?

"There has been a significant change in his behaviour. Dare I say that he appears to have – ah – matured."

Chithra relaxed. Julian was one of the wealthiest men on Si'Empra. When Ülrügh Devi had first persuaded the Lianthem to adopt a modern economic system for Si'Empra, Lian Julian's father had been quick to seize opportunity, eagerly absorbing advice from the foreigners. Most significantly, he had persuaded the Lianthem to introduce the private property system that had changed so much of the way people were accommodated in Si'Em City and the ownership of businesses. Julian's family had benefited greatly from the changes, buying up property from those who spent half of their year in summer villages and converting the properties into rental accommodation, or into opulent residences for rich ruling families. Julian now owned two residences for his own use. One was in Si'Em City directly below the Serai. It took up a space that had previously accommodated twenty other extended households. The other residence was in Baltha. Chithra had been to both and was particularly impressed by the Baltha home, which was surrounded by extensive gardens that included trees.

Dane and members of his family owned a number of hothouses and orchards. The hothouses consumed a major portion of the diesel imported each summer. He had tried, several times and, at significant expense, to tap into the hot artesian waters that seamed the island, but each time he tapped a source it petered out. He had no doubt that the Crystalmakers or Cryptals were responsible for closing the thermal source. Of all the Lians, he was the most likely to join the Ülrügh in a hunt – though less and less as the years set more bulk to his waistline.

Dane chuckled. "I am most pleased to note that our Ülrügh has become much more strategic in his battle against our aggravating underground beasts."

"Nevertheless, I am concerned that he seems to have withdrawn significantly. I am told that he has been speaking of a higher purpose. Do you know what he means, Chithra?" Julian asked.

"I should imagine that he is talking about the welfare of Si'Empra," Chithra replied carefully, "though he has not spoken of this with me."

"Seems to me that our welfare has never been better," Dane said. "Compared with what our forefathers had, we are much better off. We live longer, eat better, have better health all round, enjoy more comfortable living conditions, have more variety in our lives. I could go on. Our biggest problem continues to be dealing with the Crystalmakers."

Chithra nodded slowly. She had been feeling increasingly uneasy about the future of Si'Empra, finding her thoughts drifting to arguments made long ago by her sister, Grace. A past member of the Lianthem, Grace had been most forward in pointing out that their Lianthem was failing Si'Emprans.

"Yes," Chithra said, her tone more emphatic than intended as she once again attempted to dismiss doubts that her Ülrügh was the best leader for Si'Empra. "I wanted us to discuss something else, though. Somewhere on this island there are, apparently, those who still deal with the Crystalmakers. I have now had several accounts of foreigners obtaining crystal. Cecil also tells me that, in his recent visits to summer villages, he has found people wearing cryptal cloth and possessing items that are not available in our stores. The people claim that the stock is old – handed down from long ago. Cecil has confiscated all such cloth."

"We should bring such people in for more extensive questioning," Lian Dane said.

"Perhaps," Julian cautioned, "we should just let it be known that, in future, anyone found to be wearing such cloth will be brought in for more extensive questioning."

"I fear all that would do is make those who deal in the black market more cautious," said Chithra.

"These Crystalmakers continue to be a significant drain on us. I wish Ülrügh Devi had succeeded in wiping them out –" began Dane in a querulous tone, but Julian interrupted him:

"Some people are whispering that, perhaps, we should try to make peace with the Crystalmakers."

"Useless!" Dane snapped.

"I agree. My father often told of the times when he and the Ülrügh tried in vain to negotiate with the Guild Masters for less crippling terms for the Cryptal cloth and crystal – and then for them to stop sabotaging our efforts to extract gemstones from the ground. All they did was harp on about The Order."

Chithra eased back in her chair as she listened to the men engage in one of their favourite subjects. She wondered if ever they did more than scan the information that she gave them that told of the affairs of Si'Empra. Lately, especially since the Ülrügh had become icier towards her, she had come to realise that unless the Lianthem – and the Ülrügh – significantly changed the way they governed the affairs of Skyseekers, the wellbeing of everyone would be in danger.

She wondered whether she should talk about her misgivings to these, her friends.

But she did not, staying faithful to her deepest feelings of love for – and, therefore, trust in – Redel.

CHAPTER 17
The Guild Masters

*I*T WAS WITH RELIEF that Ellen saw the two Crystalmakers approach her cautiously.

"Warmth and light," she greeted. "I am Lian Ellen come to have audience with the Guild Master."

"Warmth and light, Lian Ellen," returned the older and smaller of the two. He took a few more steps towards her and bowed deeply. "My name is Thanin. I will lead you to our dwelling and into the care of those who will take you to the Guild Masters. My companion is Sira."

"Thank you Thanin and Sira. We will be a party of four. I have one of your people with me and he will need all our help. He was taken prisoner by Skyseekers. I have managed to release him and bring him here with the help of my glasaur, but, unfortunately, he is quite ill and has lost consciousness."

Thanin snatched off his dark glasses at her words, staring at her with rapidly blinking eyes. "What – what is his name?"

"I believe it is Sam." Ellen beckoned them to follow her toward where Sam lay under Rosa's wing.

Thanin hesitated upon seeing the enormous bird, but when Ellen indicated that Rosa was safe, he approached Sam and looked down into the pale face. "Ayee!" he moaned in a mixture of relief and distress. "This is indeed Sam. We believed him dead."

"I am afraid there's not much life left in him," Ellen said softly. She eased her aching shoulders; the Crystalmaker had been a dead weight in her arms throughout their journey to this meeting place.

Thanin let out puffs of anxious breath as he tried to determine what to do. He bent over Sam.

"He is very mylin depleted," he muttered, noting the sweatiness of the skin and the way that Sam's limbs twitched even in his comatose state.

"Let us take him into the Cryptal tunnels and give him mylin, then," Ellen suggested.

Thanin nodded slowly. "Yes. Let us get him into the tunnel, but we must not expose him too soon. Lian Ellen, may I impose on you to help Sira and myself carry him?"

Once the three had made Sam as comfortable as they could a short way into the Cryptal tunnel, Ellen and Thanin left him in the care of Sira, and hurried towards the arranged meeting with the Guild Masters.

"Immediately I am able, I will bring help back to attend to Sam," Thanin said.

There was just enough light in the tunnel for Ellen to be able to make out Thanin's form beside her and the space of the tunnel around her.

Thanin continued: "Lian Ellen, the Mistress instructed me to tell you everything I know of how Guild Masters address one another."

"Thank you."

He licked his lips nervously. "You should perhaps it is useful for you to know that no – I mean that I did not hear – that no one, except their closest apprentices, hears the Guild Masters conversing with one another. I mean – I hear but I was not present – they don't know I am present."

Ellen frowned, absorbing and sorting this muddled message. "Ah. You mean you would not like it to be known that my knowledge comes from you. If so, I will certainly never let your name pass my lips."

Thanin nodded then began to speak rapidly, relating each conversation he had overheard. Ellen listened intently, sometimes interrupting briefly for clarification, not sure whether and how any of the information would be useful, but certain that the more background she had for this meeting with the Guild Masters, the better.

They had been walking for close on two hours when Thanin stopped mid-way through a story. At this point, the tunnel widened. To one side hung the heavy curtains of an entrance. Thanin pulled a cord next to the curtain several times then began to withdraw, murmuring, "I will leave you now, Lian." He disappeared into the gloom.

The curtain shifted aside and before her stood another Crystalmaker male, taller than Thanin, younger and with a haughty bearing.

"Enter," he said, holding aside the curtain.

Ellen stepped into a large cavern that was somewhat brighter than the tunnel, though still too dark for her to comfortably make out details. At intervals around the walls, a soft glow spilled from bowls in crystal sconces that caught and amplified the glow into light. Here and there, dark arches hinted at entrances to other areas of this dwelling place.

"My name is Thil," the Crystalmaker said, removing a light coverall over his head. She peered at him, wondering whether her eyes were playing tricks in the relative dimness. But no. Thil had dyed his short hair blue and coloured his lips and ears to match. She saw, then, that his clothes were also in hues of blue. Each part of the long loose smock he wore over loose trousers was a different shade: one sleeve dark blue, the other light blue, the front almost white and the back almost black; one trouser leg was almost green, the other almost purple. Each trouser leg was caught at the ankles with a bright yellow ribbon; no doubt as an amusing counterpoint.

Repressing a smile, Ellen pushed back the hood of her own coverall and shook out her red curls. "Warmth and light, Thil."

Thil's aloofness slipped; his mouth fell open slightly. Obviously, if his appearance had caused her astonishment, her appearance was equally startling. She wondered if he had ever seen a Skyseeker before. With an apparent effort he gathered himself. "The Guild Masters will see you in due course. You are early. You will have to wait. You are not expected for at least another hour."

Even from his few words, Ellen noted that he spoke slightly differently to Elthán and the other Crystalmakers she had met. She listened carefully to his cadence, hoping he would say more. He led her into a small room and, with gestures and few words, invited her to sit on one of the half-dozen cushioned benches. "I will arrange refreshments. You are free to make use of the facilities." Thil pointed to a doorway towards the back of the room.

"Thank you," she said.

He left her alone. Ellen immediately made her way to the bathroom. She extracted a torch from her backpack and set it up on end to give herself more light. As in the Rest in which she had met Elthán, the bath was covered with a slab of stone. She rolled the stone back, quickly undressed and lowered herself into the luxuriously warm water, washing away the accumulated sweat, dirt and worry of the night and morning.

Not wishing to be caught in the bath, she climbed out, dried herself with a folded cloth that appeared to be laid out for her to use, dressed herself in dry undergarments, applied cream, fluffed her hair and made herself as presentable as she could. It was good to be out of her damp clothes: no matter how tightly she closed her rain clothes, some water always seemed to make its way through.

When she re-entered the waiting room, she found a tray of pendle tea, cakes and cheese on a low table. She drank the tea thirstily and made short work of the food.

"I wonder how long they'll make me wait," she murmured. The bath, food, the warmth of the room, its relative darkness and, most of all, the exertions of the past twenty-four hours made her feel sleepy. *Well, no doubt I'll be woken when they're ready.* Ellen removed the cushions from two benches, placed them side-by-side on the floor mat and lay down, letting herself fall asleep.

Thil's voice woke her. "The Guild Masters will now see you." She levered up on one elbow, blinking into the darkness as she re-oriented herself. The luminous dials on her watch told her she had been asleep for more than two hours.

"Thank you Thil," she said, in as neutral a tone as she could manage. "Excuse me one moment." She stood, picked up her pack and turned toward the bathroom.

"The Guild Masters will not appreciate being kept waiting," he said.

She paused, turned a little towards him and simply said: "I understand," and continued to the bathroom.

It was hard to judge Thil's reaction to her words in the darkness of the room. She thought he stiffened slightly. He did not respond. She did not keep him waiting long, however. When she returned from the bathroom, he held the curtain aside for her to pass through.

She shouldered her backpack and followed him through the cavern, noting that there were quite a number of Crystalmakers standing in clusters. They whispered to one another and turned their heads in her direction. She studied them in turn. Like Thil, they were ostentatiously made up and dressed, noting like the simple plainness of Webcleaners. Some people had on long sparkling gowns that entirely covered their bodies, others had on barely any clothes at all but had tattooed their bare arms and legs and further adorned their limbs with bands of cloth, still others had on tight suits over which hung tassels that blinked in a kaleidoscope of colour. Almost everyone had elaborate hairstyles, dyed to exactly match the clothes they wore. Ellen smiled at the pleasure of seeing the artistry and would have loved to stop and examine each outfit in turn. Skyseeker clothes were drab indeed beside the imagination displayed by the Crystalmakers!

Thil led on without pause, radiating stern purpose.

Another curtained entrance led them into a long tunnel. Here the walls not only held sconces but were adorned with sparkling stones and floor-to-ceiling tapestries. Ellen itched to take the torch out of her bag to inspect the images. She had seen Crystalmaker images before on her visit to the Lost City and would have liked to make comparisons.

But Thil led on doggedly – and silently.

The tunnel ended at a large, ornate doorway. Even in the half-light, the curtain over the doorway was breathtakingly beautiful, glittering with inlaid crystal arranged in a pattern around images of people engaged in the crafts that were fundamental to Crystalmaker culture: shaping crystal, weaving cloth, creating design, and forming structures. Behind the guildspeople were others. Ellen guessed that these figures depicted the Memory Masters.

Ellen frowned a little, the magnificent weaving stirring a memory. She had seen these images before, but it had not been so complete – and yet something seemed to be missing.

The curtain parted, evenly lifting on both sides without disturbing the highest folds. Light poured out of the room behind the curtain. She saw Thil flinch, eyes blinking rapidly. For Ellen the light was a relief, easing the strain of gloom. Fleetingly, she thought that the increased illumination was a courtesy meant for her Skyseeker eyes. But then she saw the Guild Masters, seated on high-backed thrones on a dais at the far end of a long hall, looking stern and noble. She realised, then, that the light was an attempt to demonstrate power.

All you have done, Guild Masters, Ellen thought, feeling the thrill of a challenge, *is to remove the advantage you could have had with your more light-sensitive eyes. If you want a show, I can give you a show!*

Thil stepped forward, indicating with a tiny movement of his hand that Ellen should follow. He stopped ten metres from the dais but Ellen did not stop with him. She heard Thil gasp and saw the Guild Masters stiffen. Thil's hand grasped her arm. She turned to him, first looking impassively into his eyes, then at the hand that held her arm. His fingers lost their grip and she made to move on again. He grabbed her again and a Guild Master growled: "Be still!" Thil's clutch tightened.

Ellen stopped but this time did not acknowledge Thil's grip. Instead, she focused, her features still holding no expression, on the one who had spoken: an old woman. Even in her seat her back was slightly stooped. She wore a shapeless smock, richly embroidered at the right side with the figure of a rather androgynous person delivering an oration. Her thin hair had been died black and was woven up and through a small, bright yellow trellis on her head.

Thanin had described and told her the names of each of the Guild Masters. This old one must be the Guild Master of Memory, Threvor, the oldest and perhaps the most powerful of the Guild Masters.

She returned Ellen's direct gaze with a glare full of distrust. Ellen waited silently, not averting her eyes.

"I – I present to you this Skyseeker," Thil stammered.

"And why do you do so?" the Guild Master of Memory asked.

"She has sought an audience. With your permission I will interrogate this Skyseeker."

"Permission is so granted."

Thil turned to Ellen. "By order of the Guild Masters I am charged to demand why you have sought to be brought into their presence," he intoned.

Ellen ignored him. She shifted her gaze from the Guild Master of Memory and studied each Guild Master by turn, continuing to keep her features inscrutable. The first eyes she met were those of the Guild Master of Crystal, Joosthin. Elthán had spoken of him and her clandestine alliance with him. He wore a plain, white robe, belted at the waist. His white hair was short; there was no attempt by this man to display himself. The second Guild Master she turned her attention to was clearly the youngest: a small woman dressed in a flowing gown with a complex weave of colours radiating from a wide waistband. The hair on her head was looped with a network of plaits, each plait a different colour. The end of each plait hung loose to her shoulders, giving the effect of a rainbow collar. This was the Guild Master of Weaving, Sara. Next, Ellen's gaze moved to the Guild Master of Design. He was a slim male of middle age. His mauve eyes were large and fringed with long, pale-brown lashes, the skin of his face was almost too soft to belong to a man. His long hair, glowing a lemon yellow, was caught in a single, thick braid and draped over one shoulder. His name was Tharnie. The last was the Guild Master of Structure, Auchust. His strong-looking hands were folded on his lap; short, platinum-coloured hair sat in spikes over his head. He wore plain grey trousers and shirt. His deep-set eyes stared at her speculatively.

Behind the Guild Masters sat a man and a woman. They were dressed exactly alike in a pleated white robe that fell straight from shoulder to floor, hiding their arms and legs. Their heads were covered by white clothes so that only their faces showed. Ellen guessed them to be acolytes of the Guild Master of Memory. It would be their task to remember each aspect of this meeting and, perhaps, to commit it to a poem.

The silence stretched. Thil still had hold of her arm. "You are charged to tell me why you have sought to be brought into the presence of the Guild Masters," he repeated, the nervousness in his voice more pronounced.

Having finished her inspection of the Guild Masters, Ellen looked carefully at the dais. The Guild Masters sat around a massive elliptical stone slab that seemed to glow with its own light. On top of the slab lay a glittering crystal sceptre. Her eyes lingered on the sceptre a few seconds – it seemed faintly familiar – and then her eyes were drawn to the wall behind the dais. Shadows that ran into grooves cut into the stone gave the impression that the whole of the vast audience hall either exploded out from the wall or was collapsing into the wall. It was a clever trick of perception: she blinked and all lines in the room seemed to converge; she blinked again and all lines ran out to form the hall.

Since the Guild Masters had still not addressed her, she continued her study of the chamber. All the walls were highly polished and smooth. First impressions were that they were pink, but, actually, they were shot through with many colours: a black streak, sparkling with tiny crystals, bulged and contracted from floor to ceiling on the left of the dais; a claret-red mark showed up clearly on the ceiling and seemed to have thrown drops of itself on to the walls and floor; white, cream and brown patches – some tiny, some as a wide as a hand – showed up irregularly, some with a homogenous colour, others with gradations of colour. Brown, black, red and even yellowish lines scribbled randomly through the rock. No arrangement of colour or shape was repeated anywhere. Ellen had grown up surrounded by smoothly polished granite surfaces: for walls, ceilings, floors and benches, granite was the most-used construction material in Si'Empra, but never had she seen rock that seemed so alive. The floor-to-ceiling tapestries that hung at intervals on the walls were almost unwelcome interruptions.

From the corner of her eye she could see that a sheen had formed on Thil's upper lip. The acolytes on the dais stole uncertain glances at one another. The Guild Master of Memory's face had reddened; a vein began to pulse on her temple. The Guild Master of Design tipped his head slightly, a slight smile forming at the corners of his mouth as he contemplated her. Guild Master Joosthin's lips tightened as his brows lowered.

Finally, with a snarl, Guild Master Joosthin commanded: "Speak!"

Ellen's attention returned to the dais. She began to draw a breath to respond to his command when the crystal sceptre echoed: "Speak, speak, speak," in a pure tone.

Ellen barely managed to mask her surprise, keeping her gaze steadily on the Guild Master's face. Her thoughts, however, raced, remembering the missing item in the museum. *This is a virigin! This is the Guild Sceptre! It does exist!*

Once the virigin was silent again, Ellen released her indrawn breath. Making eye contact with each Guild Master by turn, she spoke in a clear voice, using formal words but not attempting to hide Webcleaner cadences.

"I am Lian Ellen. Daughter of the half-caste Constance and Ülrügh Briani of the ruling house of Skyseekers." She did not know which words of power the virigin would repeat so she chose her words carefully, not wishing the virigin to distract from her speech until she wanted it to. "My grandfather was the Ülrügh Devi who, angered by the intransigence of the Guild Masters and then with the Cryptals for denying warmth to the city of Si'Em, invaded the Cryptal tunnels and engaged in the wholesale slaughter of Cryptals and Crystalmakers. I am the mistress of the glasaur Rosa, gifted to me by the Cryptals. In bestowing the glasaur to me, the Cryptals importuned me to help Crystalmakers and Skyseekers alike. It has come to my attention that Crystalmakers will face a winter of hunger. I have come to offer my assistance to broker a deal which will provide Crystalmakers with the provisions they need. For this I need the crystal and cloth that you, Guild Masters, have the power to provide. I stand before you ready to be of service."

She made sure her facial features remained impassive but authoritative as she observed the confusion her words caused the Guild Masters: almost as one they had started when she revealed Ülrügh Devi's motivation to engage in The Destruction; their jaws had dropped at the mention of the glasaur; they had looked sideways at one another when she revealed the implicit pact she had made with the Cryptals; and they now stared at her.

Thil released her arm.

"Glasaurs no longer exist," the Guild Master of Memory stated, breaking the silence with a reedy, ancient voice.

Ellen fixed her gaze on the speaker. Waited until she was sure the Guild Master had nothing more to say, and returned "You are wrong, Guild Master of Memory. Glasaurs are creatures fashioned by Cryptals and can be created at any time by the Cryptals."

"There has been no glasaur for centuries – millennia!"

To this, Ellen needed to say nothing.

The Guild Master surged to her feet, bringing up her arm and pointing. "Your tongue speaks the falsehoods of Skyseekers! What plot is this that the Scourge of Si'Empra now brings to our world? Your plot is to destroy us entirely!"

The Scourge of Si'Empra. Ellen wondered who that might be: Redel? Skyseekers in general? She watched as the old woman turned to her fellow Guild Masters. "She will destroy us entirely. We must hold her and destroy her."

The other Guild Masters were clearly taken aback by their colleague's outburst but, perhaps to show solidarity, they hastened to their feet and confronted Ellen with stern looks.

"There are indeed a number of factors that we must consider," the Guild Master of Crystal said. He waved a hand dismissively in Ellen's direction, directing a command to Thil.

"Leave us now—"

"Leave, leave, leave," echoed the virigin, interrupting him. Joosthin shot it a venomous glance. "We will call you when—".

"Call, call, call."

Joosthin's lips closed into a thin line. Colour flooded his face.

And you should blush, Ellen thought. *Fancy you, Guild Master of Crystal of all people, forgetting how to use a virigin to emphasise rather than interrupt your directives.*

Before Thil could touch her, she turned on her heel and indicated with a slight nod that she was ready to follow him.

He led her to a small room not far from the entrance to the main chamber. He did not come in with her, but held the curtain aside and dropped it closed as soon as she entered, plunging the small room into darkness. Ellen groped her way to a seat. "Well," she murmured to herself. "That was short and sweet. I had wanted to make an impression but it seems like I may have overdone the impression bit. Do they really not know about Rosa? Is there such a divide between Webcleaners and other Crystalmakers? Well, at least that's interesting to discover."

She swung her backpack off, rummaged around for her torch and wound it vigorously to charge the battery. She shone the torch around the room. Unlike the grand chamber, the walls here were relatively bare. She felt around in her pack again, looking for a purse in which she kept a stock of lozenges and other sweets. Even though the mylin in the chambers was faint, it was beginning to irritate her throat. She remembered Elthán's warnings about overdosing on mylin and wrapped a scarf around her mouth and nose.

She looked around the bare room again and sighed. She had a feeling she might be waiting for a while. *Might as well read a book.* She took the novel she had packed into her bag out and laid it open on her lap, but her thoughts strayed.

I might not be able to swing a deal with these Guild Masters. That means I can't help Elthán – or Fadil and Thuls Refuge. I need to think of another plan. Ellen felt a strong urge to have a bath and hated herself for it, then buried the urge and hate with a shake of her head. *Another plan!* she told herself sternly. *The spread on my bed at the Serai is made from Cryptal cloth. I could use that. And – oooh, Ellen, this would cause quite some stir: I can steal some crystal out of the Serai too. There are still a few bits and pieces around, especially in Redel's Green Room.*

A CRYSTALMAKER CHILD DENIED mylin could learn to live without the drug. An adult with a lifetime of mylin exposure could not. After a few weeks without Cryptal poison, feverish muscle cramps shook the body, followed by a process that caused wasting much like rapid ageing, leading to death within a few months. Only Sam's youth and, probably, Lian Isoldé's intense ministrations, had kept him alive.

Though Sam needed mylin, he would die if he breathed too much too soon. Those Crystalmakers who worked for any period aboveground had experienced the unpleasant rush of pain and illness that came with too much mylin too soon. For Sam, at his advanced stage of deterioration, even the amount of mylin that a Skyseeker might, with practice, tolerate, would probably kill him.

Elthán and her companions first dressed the unconscious Sam in protective clothing, checking and re-checking seams, before carrying him further into the Cryptal tunnel and lying him just at the point where the first wafts of fresh mylin affected the air. Within half an hour he began to stir. Elthán murmured soothing words, but glanced worriedly along the length of the tunnel. She had sent a message to Thil asking him to send someone close to Sam; someone who could help to keep him calm. In his initial confusion he would likely consider any stranger, even another Crystalmaker, as a threat.

Sam moaned. To her relief, two figures emerged from the depths of the passageway. Elthán rose to meet them. They stopped as she approached. She recognised them as two of the Crystalmakers in charge of the vast Illiath communal kitchen. They stood back from her, not returning her greeting, clearly unwilling to communicate with her. Ignoring the body signals, Elthán explained what they were to do with Sam and why. She had barely finished when a third person arrived, breathless and flustered.

"Master Thil demands your attendance!"

Elthán swore under her breath. Sam had need of her attention but Thil's summons must have something to do with Ellen. She glanced at her companions. She had taught all her people how to revive those starved of mylin, but the problem was whether the newcomers would heed their instruction.

"I recognise you as Serge and Con from the Illiath kitchen. My companions are Sira and Sonia. It is very important that you listen to them and do as they instruct, or Sam will die."

"We will not take instruction from them," came the unsurprising response.

"Then Sam will die," Elthán warned. "And he will die in great pain. I strongly urge you to think of his welfare."

"You should not have touched him," Serge snapped.

"How then could we bring him in from beneath the sky? Should we have left him there for you to bring in?"

"He should never have been aboveground–"

Con put a placatory hand on Serge's arm. "Let us do as she says, Serge. We should do what is best for Sam."

Turning to Elthán, she said. "We will work with your people." She knelt next to Sam and took his hand. He moaned again, moved his head restlessly from side to side and muttered words she did not understand. Elthán translated: "He is saying Skyseeker words, they mean 'good' and 'sick.'"

"Do you know what he has endured, Elthán?"

Elthán's eyebrow twitched in surprise at being called by name by the Crystalmaker.

"I don't know beyond that he was taken prisoner and that my granddaughter freed him."

Con gave a single nod and turned to Serge. "Come and sit by your brother and let us do our best for him. I have missed his laughter and would like to hear it again."

With that assurance, Elthán departed. An hour-and-a-half later she entered the conference room Thil used, and found him standing at a desk. "You did not tell us she has a glasaur," he said resentfully and without preamble.

"Glasaur?" Elthán blinked and stared at Thil, eyes widening with incredulity. "It never occurred to me that this was not common knowledge."

Thil drew himself up straighter. To emphasise his distaste for Elthán's granddaughter he continued: "I have seen her in the waiting room. She reads!"

"Most Skyseekers read."

"It is forbidden!"

Elthán closed her eyes. *I tire of being treated in this way*, she thought. "By the BlackŌne's beard!" she said as evenly as she could manage. "I have left a grievously ill man because you sent a message saying I was urgently needed. Is there nothing more than inane observations to your urgency?"

Thil's face flushed red with anger. "I am commanded by the Guild Masters to demand that you provide a full account of the glasaur and of this Skyseeker person. She has spoken directly to the Guild Masters, grievously offending them and has put forward a proposal and they –" Thil hesitated. Elthán felt like finishing off the sentence for him: *and they don't know what to do!*

Ellen has seriously rattled them! Elthán almost smiled, curious now to find out what had happened in the audience room.

Reigning in her temper, she said in as humble a tone as she could manage: "How may I be of service?"

Haughtily, Thil interrogated her about Rosa and how Ellen came to be mistress of the glasaur. He detailed Ellen's proposal and demanded that Elthán explain the situation of the Crystalmakers regarding provisions. Elthán answered his questions carefully, guessing that her answers and cooperation could make the difference between the success and failure of Ellen's plan.

CHAPTER 18
Striking a Bargain

*E*LLEN WASHED HERSELF CAREFULLY but quickly in the water of a stream that trickled from a thin crevasse. She towelled herself dry, creamed her body and pulled on clean clothes. It would have been good to wash her hair as well, but the water was too cold for that. Using a damp washer with a drop of perfume, she rubbed her curls vigorously.

She inspected her reflection in a small pocket mirror, noting with satisfaction that her skin had entirely lost its puffy, red look.

"Well, that's the best I can do," she murmured and packed her toiletries away.

Well before the appointed time, she positioned herself and Rosa slightly up the hill, where she could see Lian Achton's goat grotto but was herself out of sight.

Lian Achton – his dogs at his heels – and the foreigner appeared; the stranger was a head taller than the Lian. He walked with the easy gait of a strong, confident man. Lian Achton opened the door to the grotto, and men and dogs disappeared inside.

Ellen waited until the appointed time. "No one else around?" she asked Rosa. The bird stayed relaxed. Ellen rose, tucking a bundle under her arm. "Stay close, Rosa. Tell us if someone comes."

Fifteen metres from the grotto, the dogs began to bark. The door opened. She expected the dogs to bolt out, but Lian Achton commanded them to sit at his feet. They extended their noses eagerly towards her, tails sweeping the floor.

"Warmth and light, Lian," Lian Achton greeted.

"Warmth and light, Lian Achton," she returned. "Thank you for helping me in this way."

"I am hoping you can return the favour by telling me where the Crystalmaker in my charge, and a rather prized coat, has disappeared to." There was an edge of ice to his voice.

"Has Lian Isoldé not told you already? As for the coat, here it is." She passed him the bundle.

Lian Achton took the coat from her, though his ice did not thaw. "She told me the Crystalmaker died and has been taken by the star of light."

Ellen was unfazed by his annoyance. "Aah. I have been wondering what she saw. She didn't seem to recognise me. I thought maybe it was because it was so dark." In acknowledgement of his displeasure, she continued. "Neither the Ülrügh nor you had the right to hold the Crystalmaker, Lian. I have returned him to his people."

"And by whose authority did you do that?"

"By the authority of decency that I was taught as a child, by you, among other people –"

"Is this a private party, or can anyone join in?" the foreigner interrupted.

Lian Achton stiffened. He moved one of his legs back to turn side-on so that Ellen could see into the room.

The Australian sat at a small table, face turned towards the door, elbows on the table, a steaming mug of tea clasped in his hands. At the sight of Ellen he put down the mug and pushed himself slowly up to his feet, emitting a low whistle: "Will you look at that! They weren't half wrong when they said you're a stunner!"

"Norm Tucker, may I present Lian Ellen." Achton's tone growled slightly with disapproval.

Norm Tucker bowed in a mocking way. "G'day, milady."

"How do you do, Mr Tucker. I hope we may do some business."

"Yea. That's what I'm here for," he said, his voice slow and distracted. His deep blue eyes flickered in open admiration. His gaze dropped to her feet and began to slowly travel up the length of her body. She bore his inspection by studying him calmly in turn.

He was a lean man, perhaps in his mid-thirties. Long-limbed. Although his speech was uncultured, even bordering on crude, his appearance spoke of vanity. His sandy brown hair, though short, had been neatly trimmed and recently combed back into place, with a part to the left. His face was smoothly shaven. He had a longish face with creases just under the cheekbones running almost to the sides of a sharply defined chin line. *You use cream on your face because you don't have that dry scaly look that some men get.* His clothes were practical: loose fitting but well cut. The long, dark-olive trousers were made from a tightly woven fabric, probably water repellent. There were pocket openings at the hips and two zipped pockets at the sides of the thighs. There was no belt and the shirt, made of a lighter fabric – the colour a lighter shade of olive and matching the trousers – was tucked neatly into the waistline. His rolled-up sleeves exposed brown arms with a dusting of dark hair, and the open shirt collar showed part of a hairy chest. A coat hung over the back of his chair. It was probably reversible: the outside was a dark brown but the inside looked bright yellow. *Yellow probably more suitable for wearing out at sea; brown on land so as not to stand out.*

Norm Tucker's eyes met hers. He blinked. His mouth, which had been slightly and loosely open, tightened into a grin, showing carefully aligned teeth – a left eye-tooth capped in gold. *For show?* Ellen mused.

"Sorry, Princess. Don't mind me giving you the once-over. I'm just a lowlife sailor. Don't get to see girls as pretty as you too often. You reckon you got business with me. I'm reckoning you want passage off the island. Gossip's got it life hasn't been all roses for you, Princess."

Gossip? Ellen stepped into the room, not showing any reaction to his words. *Interesting. So you have been talking widely, as I guessed you might.* She had assessed that Norm Tucker would be a man who aggressively — and probably ruthlessly — sought out opportunity to combine richness with adventure. *Let me see how I can use your hunger for my need.* The flicker of anticipation that had stimulated her thoughts all morning burned more brightly at the challenge of matching her wits with those of this foreigner.

"Thank you, Mr Tucker, but I am not interested in passage off the island. I believe I have a more interesting proposition to discuss with you."

He resumed his seat, sitting sideways on the chair, one elbow on the table, the other across the back of the chair and an ankle resting on a knee, as if to say: "I'm all yours — nothing to hide".

"Interesting proposition, eh? What would that be, Princess?"

"I have Cryptal cloth and crystal, Mr Tucker. What have you got for me?'

"Depends on what you want and how much you got."

Ellen stepped further into the room, drew several pages from an inside pocket of her coat and handed them to Norm Tucker. Behind her, Lian Achton closed the door.

Norm Tucker flicked through the pages: a list of provisions to last a long winter.

"This isn't just a bit," he said finally, placing the pages on the table beside him. "It's going to cost plenty and I'm going be stretched getting this together and carting it here. Season for boating's nearly over so it'll be November — maybe December — before I can land this. And I'll want to be paid up front."

Ellen gave a small shrug. She reached for the list. "Then our potential business partnership is over, Mr Tucker. Those terms are useless to me."

"Whoa. Whoa." Norm brought his large, tanned hand over her small, white one. Ellen covered her involuntary flinch by drawing her eyebrows together to intensify her gaze. Firmly, but unhurriedly, she drew her hand and the pages out from under Norm Tucker's hand.

"Why don't you sit down," he said, fingers tightening for a flash at the edge of the withdrawing pages before letting go. "Let's talk about this man-to-man. It's sort of hard to think with you standing and me sitting." He turned to Lian Achton, who still stood at the door. "You sit down, too, Lian Achton. Perhaps you'd like a warm cup of something, Princess. I think there's still water in the thermos we brought. Why don't you take off your coat?"

"Thank you for your thoughtfulness, Mr Tucker. I do not need refreshments and my coat is not uncomfortable." *Ah – but perhaps I am beginning to make you a little less certain? Good. Good.*

"Well at least sit down. It's hard for me to think when I have to deal with people standing around."

Ellen shifted a chair as if to sit opposite him, but she stayed standing, her hand on the back of the chair.

"You'd better tell me what you need and I'll see what I can do. And Norm's my name. Just call me Norm."

"Thank you, Mr Tucker. I believe that you will be quite pleased with what I have for you." She set the list on the table again, spreading the pages. She knew the list intimately and knew what she could negotiate away and what she could not. "What I want is on this list, Mr Tucker. But before we talk further about what I want, I would be most grateful if you could give me some confidence that you can deliver. I do not want to burden you with the impossible and nor do I want to waste your time. I believe that you are a very experienced sailor and have a lovely boat."

Norm gave a small dismissive huff. "Oh my boat's good alright. And I can deliver; no worries. Just got to be realistic."

Good, thought Ellen. *Now tell me all about yourself and what you really can do and what your real limitations are.* "Perhaps you could reassure me by telling me a little about how you run your enterprise."

"Yeah, no problem. I got my boat about seven year ago. Me and a mate. I've bought him out since. Always been a sailor, I have. Learnt it from my dad."

"In your blood," Ellen remarked, eyes softening to show her understanding.

Norm Tucker grinned. "You could say that: it's in my blood."

With these types of small nudges from Ellen, Norm Tucker settled into telling her about his boat, his adventures and how he delivered cargo all over the world. Ellen settled into the chair she had pulled out, leaning slightly towards him as the story of his exploits unfolded. She took note of every detail, sorting elements into an order that would help her negotiate a good outcome, her questions deliberately feigning randomness, but, in fact, quite targeted.

"I can get stuff to places no other ship can get to, see. I can hove to a bit out of the way and drop a good-and-stable inflatable runabout with the cargo to get it to shore," he told her, his gold tooth flashing as he grinned.

"I specialise in giving people what they need. Like, just a few months back I dropped off a load of stuff to Somalia – you know – Africa. Some governments – they don't always get it, right. You know yourself, Princess, you just got to look around this island and you can see some people just need things. I don't know whether you're going to sell this stuff–" he flicked a finger at the pages on the table "–and make some cash for yourself. Don't blame you if you are. But I reckon you want it to give this stuff away. That's how I read you. That's why I'm interested in working with you, see. I reckon you've got a good heart."

STRIKING A BARGAIN

"You do indeed have a very interesting profession, Mr Tucker. But doesn't sailing in these Antarctic waters cause you concern? I have heard such horrific stories of ships being caught in sea ice and crews freezing to death."

"Aw," Norm scoffed. "Them that's happened to are plain inexperienced. I've been down in these waters when they start getting chewy. You have to know how to keep yourself out of trouble."

"And do you have work colleagues in other countries?"

"Sure I do. I've got the best equipment on board my boat and I can get fellows in Australia and New Zealand – even bottom of Argentina – to help me out if I want to. We help each other out all the time."

"That affords me a great deal of relief, Mr Tucker. Perhaps it could be possible to have them come to your aid to help deliver my needs before the seas become impassable?"

Norm's eyes widened. He stared at her a second then barked out a laugh. "You've got a quick mind, Princess. I can see I'll need to watch my Ps and Qs."

And so the negotiations began. Ellen showed Norm small samples of the cloth and crystal she could supply but was firm that she would only pay a deposit, reasoning that she did not have the means to carry the amount of crystal and cloth to do more than pay a deposit at this time, and besides, it would be dangerous for him to carry such a large quantity of crystal and cloth into Si'Em City. They talked about quality of the supplies he needed to deliver, how he might obtain them at such short notice, and how to land the goods. She showed him a map of Si'Empra and told him where she wanted the goods landed: a shoal at the mouth of the North River within a bay enclosed by the Northern and Central Lands. "My observation is that this bay contains ice floes for much of summer but they are small and drift in and out depending on the wind. A freeze at the entrance to the bay generally begins by about May. Thus, it will be necessary to complete the landing before then."

"Jeez, Princess, that only gives hardly more than a month!"

"I am most grateful that you are willing to consider this timeline, Mr Tucker. I hope that your friends will be suitably impressed by the crystal and Cryptal cloth you can provide them."

When Ellen was satisfied that she had covered all necessary details, she left the hut to fetch two crystal urns and a bolt of cloth as down payment. Norm took the ornaments from her and inspected them keenly. She guessed that he was comparing them to those Richard had provided, and knew their quality was much higher.

"You don't have a virigin somewhere, do you?" he said. "I'll trade the whole cargo for one virigin."

"No, Mr Tucker. I don't have a virigin."

"Norm. You should call me Norm, now that we're business partners."

Ellen made a non-committal movement with her head. Turning to Lian Achton, who had seated himself at an opposite corner of the table and been silent throughout the conversation, she said in the language of the Skyseekers: "Thank you, again, Lian, for your help." To Norm she cautioned in English. "You should know that if any part of this deal becomes public in Si'Empra – including Lian Achton's involvement – your payment will be forfeit, as is any future business dealing I might have with you."

"Mum's the word," Norm Tucker promised, tapping the side of his nose. "No one's better than me at keeping secrets." He grinned again at her, standing when she did and holding out his hand to shake on the deal.

She put her hand in his, forcing herself to return his firm shake, though inwardly she rebelled at the touch. She smiled at him as she took her leave, but her thoughts did not reflect her smile: *I do not like you, Norm Tucker. I do not trust you. I would prefer not to deal with you and will cease to do so as soon as I can. Otherwise, I fear, you will do Si'Empra great harm.*

CHAPTER 19
Promised Deliveries

Norm delivered, as promised. After the meeting with Lian Ellen, he had taken quick leave of Lian Achton, politely declining an invitation to take a meal with the old man at his home. They had called in there briefly before meeting the young Princess, and Norm had been distinctly uncomfortable with the way Lian Achton's wife had looked him up and down and muttered darkly. He didn't really want to see her again.

As his ship set sail north, Norm busied himself in the communications room, contacting associates most likely able to help him. It took several calls and a few days of haggling and promises, while *Westrunner* continued to beat against currents and winds, before he finally found one group that had the capacity and willingness to purchase the goods he wanted. He spent the next few weeks visiting ports along the coast of South America to take on parts of the cargo until he had bought all that he wanted.

With a sharp eye on the weather, he and his crew dodged and ran before storms back south east to Si'Empra. He was surprised to find that it was Richard and not the Princess who met him at the shoals. The young man had a group of funny looking people with him, but they were strong and efficient, and Richard had the crystal and cloth, just as the Princess had promised. As luck would have it, the wind turned and started blowing onshore halfway through the operation of loading and unloading. Norm Tucker handed rubber suits with inbuilt boots to Richard and a small, chunky man, who seemed to have some authority, rubber suits with inbuilt boots and the two men stood waist-deep in the water, pushing away ice floes to enable the heavily laden inflatable to make landfall and take off again.

With the trade done, Norm Tucker and his crew wasted no time to set the course of *Westrunner* away from Si'Empra towards New Zealand. The wind was behind them, but it blasted such an icy temperature there was barely comfort in it at all. "Better than having it against us, Ian," Norm said. In spite of his exhaustion, he felt well satisfied.

Ian Sewell, who had been Norm's partner on more than a few adventures, snorted. "We'll be lucky to get home without getting caught in this slush." He took one hand off his steaming mug of thin soup and waved it at the window to indicate the mush of ice that was beginning to form over the grey, pitching ocean. Ian preferred tropical waters.

"We'll be lucky not to be snap frozen." The third member of the crew was Joe, a tall, thin man with eyes hidden behind deep furrows of skin formed by years of staring into glaring sea distances. "This haul you got had better be worth this trip." Like Ian, Joe had expressed doubts about trading in Si'Empra, but he felt more at home on the ocean than on land and would take on almost any venture, especially when combined with good rewards.

"It's worth it," Norm assured. "Gees, it's worth it. We can sell this stuff they gave us legitimate and live like kings. Even better. I just know we can get more. The people on that island are going to screw that Ülrügh of theirs. Mark my words. They're not only going to want food. They'll want more of what we can get them – and I bet they'll pay top dollar for it. Not the Princess. I reckon she'll just go icy on me if I mention guns and stuff. But the people who came to get the cargo from us – you know those little ones with sunglasses and hats and skin like white tissue paper. I have a feeling in my bones they'll deal with us – maybe that Richard bloke too."

"Yeah, what about that Richard bloke? I got a surprise when he showed up. I thought he was another dealer that you talked to," Ian said.

"I don't know what that was about. Whatever the arrangement he and the Princess had, he did his job okay. He was particular about checking everything before handing over the pay, though. I think he'll be doing more deals another time. I gave the Princess my phone number and email address – him too – told them to contact me when they want to deal again. I think she or he – they'll contact me. Now that we know what they've got, I reckon we can do even better next time."

"Where was she anyway? I was sort of looking forward to seeing her," Ian said. It had required all of his considerable skill to make the multiple shore landings of cargo. Each time he waited for the cargo to be unloaded, he had scanned the rocky shore for a glimpse of the woman Norm had described in eloquent detail.

"Yeah. She's a looker. Speaks English like a native. I met the bloke who had a hand in teaching her. He lives in Bali now. He said she was a fast learner. He's the one who told me about Si'Empra. He's got a virigin too. Showed it to me. You could sell your soul for a virigin and still come out rich. It's a bit like this crystal but stronger and hard to see unless there's a pattern. It can say things back to you."

"What's he do with it?"

"He had a few. Kept one for himself and sold the others. Lives like a king now." Norm picked up a piece of Cryptal cloth and fingered its softness. It radiated warmth into his hand. He felt the crystal pendant he had decided to claim for himself swing against the skin of his chest as he moved, feeling its strong smoothness. "Oh, we'll find a way to deal some more," he repeated. "That Richard – his English is okay – good enough."

WHILE RICHARD, THIMON AND other Webcleaners helped to unload and transfer the cargo to Illiath, Ellen and Rosa helped the people of Thul's Refuge and Fadil to carry their produce to the outskirts of Baltha and into a barn in which Lian Cecil's family, in times past when they were goat herders, had overwintered their flock. Lian Cecil had demanded that all activity around the barn occur only at night and in secret. It took two weeks and several trips – Rosa loaded with heavy baskets of brassicas, beans, and vats of pressed juices, and the stronger villagers carrying dried vegetables and fruits in their backpacks – to transfer everything Fadil and Thuls Refuge had managed to grow and cure.

Lian Cecil was present at each transfer, inspecting every load and matching it against the deal he had negotiated with Ellen.

Ellen was also present at each of transfer: her only aim being to ensure that Lian Cecil did not cheat in his calculations.

What Lian Cecil did with the produce once she and the villagers had deposited it into his care, she did not know, nor did she want to know. She guessed that he had already found the means to distribute it for a profit.

Once the dealings with Lian Cecil had finished, Ellen made her way to the Cryptal tunnel entrance where she had asked Richard to leave that part of the goods meant for the villagers. The entrance was in the Central Ranges, a few kilometres from Thuls Refuge. Even as she entered the tunnel, Ellen had no idea if Norm Tucker had managed to make his deliveries. The relief at seeing the boxes and bags of goods weakened her knees so much she had to sit down.

"I think I've managed to pull all of this off," she murmured.

She sank her head between her knees and her body shuddered with released tension.

Usually she felt a sense of elation after an adventure that taxed her ingenuity and daring. This time, however, she felt only plain relief. Never before had her flirtations with reckless action involved the welfare of so many others. In spite of all her self-talk and forced relish as each part of the complex operation she had engineered came together, a part of her had continued to thrum with unpleasant anxiety.

The Guild Masters had required delicate handling. They had managed to obtain more information about Rosa and herself – from Elthán, as she found out later. When recalled into their presence after being banished into the anteroom, Ellen set about impressing the Guild Masters into believing that they were in full control of negotiations and that their gains and status were unquestionable.

The Guild Master of Memory had required the most delicate handling; she had continued to be suspicious, pouncing on every word that might be interpreted as a slight against Crystalmakers, or a hint of Skyseeker superiority. Ellen took the utmost care in her communication with the Guild Master, because it would be the Guild of Memory – the acolytes in attendance listening with intense concentration to the discussions – that the Crystalmakers would rely upon to remember what had been agreed.

The Guild Master of Weaving fluttered about, by turn squeaking uncertainly about matters to do with how much cloth and the value of the cloth she could make available, and falling into a deeply knowledgeable presentation about this or that type of cloth.

Ellen's greatest ally was the Guild Master of Crystal. It was clear that none of the other Crystal Makers were aware of his association with Elthán, but it did not surprise Ellen that he had the clearest idea of the worth of the offerings of Crystalmakers.

Though she had spoken mostly with the other three Guild Masters, Ellen had been intrigued by the Guild Masters of Structure and Design. After initially inviting her to join them on the dais – a move that had clearly not pleased the Guild Master of Memory – they had stayed mostly silent, but she did not doubt their interest. The Guild Master of Structure kept his thoughts carefully hidden, but the Guild Master of Design's effeminate features had changed subtly but constantly to reveal emotions ranging from amusement to admiration. Ellen was aware that he was reading her manipulations very well. Had he been the only Guild Master she needed to deal with, Ellen believed she would have been quite relaxed in her discussions.

Lian Cecil had also required careful handling. She did not trust him and had decided that the only way to ensure that he did not renege on the deal he had struck with Fadil was to find a way to blackmail him. It had taken some dedicated clandestine snooping in his private quarters in Si'Em City to find information that she could use. He was, she had discovered as she trawled through his office, a meticulous accountant. He kept two sets of books: one that was public and for the eyes of the Lianthem, and one for his own use. The latter tallied, in neat script, money he had gained from dealing in the black market, including taxes he had gathered and not declared. She focused the camera of her smartphone and recorded images of pages in his book.

"This is just security in case you decide to cheat," she had told Lian Cecil, showing him the photos on her phone. "I have backed up these photos. They will become publicly available unless we operate honestly with one another."

He'd been furious. Purportedly he now had surveillance cameras installed in his office.

"Too many surveillance cameras. And if Redel keeps closing up tunnels, I might just not be able to do that sort of thing in future," Ellen murmured. She drew a deep breath, lifting her head, her eyes falling again on the cargo from Norm Tucker's boat. "Anyway, it looks like you've pulled it all off. There's still this stuff to move. I tell you what, though, once I've helped move this stuff, I am going to plumb for such a peaceful existence no one will know I exist!"

Her mind free from anxiety, and clear for the first time in months of the need to scheme, she mounted Rosa, sat back and allowed herself to daydream as they travelled to Thuls Refuge. She led the villagers back to the Cryptal tunnel entrance, and with Rosa's help moved everything to the refuge, then helped transport a promised portion to Fadil. When all was done, she headed to Ellen's Hide. There was one last task to do before going to Greçia's home for the winter.

CHAPTER 20
Tharnie's Questions

Tharnie joined Joosthin at his meal table. The tables were set in twos, fours and sixes in the vast Trebiath dining hall. The section where Joosthin dined was partially screened, set aside for the Guild Masters and their acolytes. Joosthin sat at a table for two, his back to the room, signalling his preference to dine alone. The Guild Master of Design ignored the signal.

"Our dining room is most comfortable, is it not?" Tharnie said.

Joosthin sat back a little from his meal, placing the spade he had been using on the side of his plate. "Mmm."

With a suitable portion of the city having finally been repaired and cleaned, the Guild Masters – except for Threvor, who stayed in Illiath, the traditional home of the Guild of Memory – and a major number of Crystalmakers had moved into Trebiath some days previously.

"I hope that one day this dining hall will be as full of our people as I believe it once was," Tharnie said. "Although very pleasant now, it is the people who are the real beauty."

Joosthin gave a small snort. "I can appreciate places with or without people."

Tharnie's smile accentuated the beauty of his features. He was a strong male but moved as gracefully as a woman. He was charming, competent and, Joosthin admitted grumpily to himself, totally likeable.

To distract himself from his – rather too intimate – thoughts about Tharnie's effeminate nature, Joosthin turned side-on on his cushioned bench to inspect the dining room.

The entrance was close to the section partitioned for the Guild Masters and acolytes; basically, the entrance was the end of an arched tunnel from which many parts of the Trebiath labyrinth could be accessed. Two large, crystal sconces, shaped as welcoming hands, marked the entrance. From the entrance, the roof of the dining room vaulted three metres overhead. Some light sconces, set at intervals around the room, were fashioned to throw light on to this ceiling, picking out sparkling crystals and runs of gold and vermillion in the rock. Odd shots of steam or swirls of air as people walked by the sconces caused the light to sway and, for a while, the ceiling would seem to come alive.

The dining room itself was an oval shape. At one end was an open kitchen at which cooks and kitchen hands prepared food. Most of the steam from the boiling water pits used for cooking and cleaning funnelled up through openings, but sufficient escaped to feed the luminescent moss that covered the kitchen walls and provided the area with light. Though useful for lighting, the moss growth in the humidity of the kitchen was also a nuisance, constantly having to be scrubbed off surfaces used for food preparation, storage and cleaning.

Food was served on platters and in bowls along a wide groove cut into the wall opposite the entrance. A tapestry hung above and over the length of the groove. The tapestry was an attempt at depicting the aboveground. Tharnie had designed it, drawing from a study of other tapestries with similar depictions. In a conversation with Elthán, Joosthin had asked her about the tapestry. Elthán had smiled. "I think that Skyseekers would call it abstract art," she said. "It is true that the sun is round and very yellow, but when it is visible it sits in a blue sky and not in a green and white landscape. However, Guild Master, the tapestry is breathtakingly beautiful and full of colour that is often aboveground. I would not change a thread, though I hope that Crystalmakers do not believe it really shows what aboveground looks like."

Other tapestries hung around the walls of the dining room. Some were ancient, rescued and repaired by Sara and her acolytes. Others were new. All depicted some part of Crystalmaker history or life.

The Guild Masters – with Guild Master Threvor the exception – had decided against hanging tapestries telling the story of The Destruction in the dining area, deciding the space should be one that brought comfort and peace.

The runs of carpet laid in squares over the polished stone floor each told a favourite Crystalmaker story. The one closest to Joosthin and Tharnie told the story of the landing of the first peoples on Si'Empra: the first panel showed people flung about in swirls of dark foam and water; the second showed Cryptals and glasaurs standing over people lying on the ground; the third showed people riding glasaurs being brought into caves by Cryptals; and the fourth panel showed people and Cryptals exchanging gifts.

"Indeed," Joosthin said. "The dining room is most satisfactory. You are satisfied?" His question, however, was really: *Why do you sit here?*

"Lian Ellen has delivered us not only food, it would seem, but also leisure to prepare our home."

"So it would seem." Elthán had certainly been more cooperative about preparing Trebiath once she was no longer preoccupied with finding food and other materials. Joosthin cut into a steaming bun and forked out the meaty stew inside.

"What can you tell me about this Lian Ellen?" Tharnie asked.

"I know little more than you do, Tharnie. What do you wish to know?"

THARNIE'S QUESTIONS

"Why did she need to consult the Webcleaner to determine our needs?"

Joosthin's attention shifted again from the food on his plate to Tharnie's face. Lian Ellen's insistence had caused a great deal of consternation among the Guild Masters. After much discussion and interrogation of Thil – who had further to consult elsewhere about the glasaur – the Guild Masters had finally decided that their best course of action was to deal with Lian Ellen. They had called her into their presence. Cool and composed, and determinedly assertive but polite, she discussed her plan and explained what she needed from the Guild Masters. The quantity of cloth and crystal she asked for was significant but not beyond the stores they had. Truth be told, Joosthin had been quite excited at the prospect of providing so much of his crystal for her purpose. This was how it had been when he was a youth – before The Destruction. Sara, too, had bustled with pleasure for weeks after being given the task of organising the delivery of so much extra cloth. She and Ellen had had quite an exchange about the type of cloth and, before Threvor cut short further discussion, had agreed upon plain, cream-coloured cloth with a light and firm weave.

The difficulty had come when Ellen had turned to the issue of what precisely should be ordered in exchange for the crystal and cloth. The Guild Masters had no idea about what should be ordered and Thil, who had continued to stand attentively at the foot of the dais, indicated that he, too, would be unable to provide the information. "Perhaps Elthán could tell us?" Ellen suggested.

"Who is Elthán?" Guild Master Threvor had demanded.

"My grandmother," Ellen answered.

Confused, all Guild Masters had turned – Joosthin copying the movement hastily to hide his knowledge – to Thil who, flushing a deep red, had stammered: "She is Mistress of the Webcleaners, Guild Masters."

When Threvor had recovered from the shock, she had drawn away from Ellen as if confronted by a toxic substance; her suspicion of the Lian turning into vehement rejection. "A Webcleaner! You are granddaughter of a Webcleaner!"

Sara, Auchust and Tharnie had been surprised but not revolted by the revelation of Lian Ellen's heritage. Calming words from Tharnie and, surprisingly, Auchust – while Lian Ellen looked on with a hint of bemusement in her eyes – had finally resolved the matter. "If you can bear to be in the presence of a Webcleaner," Guild Master Threvor had finally said. "You may consult with – with – it." Threvor had then pushed herself up out of her seat, indicating discussions were at an end. "Thil, you will ensure that this matter is carried further." She jerked her chin at Lian Ellen. "You may now leave our presence."

Lian Ellen had risen elegantly from her seat. Unhurriedly and, with a slight incline of her head, she bid each Guild Master "warmth and light". When she had gone from the audience chamber, Guild Master Threvor had collapsed back into her seat and spat: "That explains why she speaks like a gutter slug!"

Joosthin mentally shook his head. Tharnie had been the only one of the Guild Masters who had demurred, noting quietly that the Lian had shown a grasp of ideas that did not diminish because of her manner of speech.

"You were there, Tharnie, at the discussion. What more is there?" Joosthin asked.

"Yes. Yes, of course. But I am still puzzled that Thil, apparently, could not help at all in the matter of our supplies. I thought that it was part of Threvor's remit to care for such matters?"

"You should discuss this with Threvor."

"Did you know that the Webcleaners are in charge of our stores – our most basic supplies?"

Joosthin hesitated. It occurred to him that Tharnie reminded him, in some ways, of Thren. "Yes," he admitted cautiously.

THARNIE'S QUESTIONS

"So they collect the stores and they take care of the stores."

"Yes."

"And they have always done this?'

"Whether 'always' you would have to ask our Guild Master of Memory. As far as I am aware, the Webcleaners have been in charge of supplies since The Destruction."

"Why have you never brought this matter to our attention?"

"It is no secret. Threvor is quite aware of the arrangement."

"Indeed? It is most curious that neither you nor Threvor have ever mentioned this matter or the fact that we were in such a parlous state in terms of our supplies. I would have thought this was precisely the sort of matter that we Guild Masters should discuss in our colloquies."

Tharnie smiled. Joosthin wondered what the smile might mean. Before he could reflect further, Tharnie continued: "I am sure that you each have your separate reasons, but–" and now he chuckled. "Lian Ellen must indeed have found us curiously ignorant when we barely acknowledge the presence of those upon whom we entirely depend."

Joosthin frowned. He is not offended by how the girl played with us. He finds it amusing! He knows how to laugh at himself – just as Thren knew!

Tharnie bent to his food. Joosthin continued with his own meal. For some time they ate in silence – Joosthin apprehensive about the next subject Tharnie might raise.

Sure enough, the subject arose: "Have you ever met this Webcleaner whom Lian Ellen says is her grandmother?"

"I met her at the time of The Destruction. The Cryptals herded us all together, regardless of our standing."

"Yes. I was not born, of course. Tell me about it."

"Threvor has a better memory for these matters than I."

"Mmm. I hope you will not find me offensive if I observe that Guild Master Threvor's reaction towards Lian Ellen and about

Webcleaners at that meeting has made me wonder whether her memories are – shall we say – rather selective."

"That you will have to have out with her."

"I do not currently have the stomach for that. She can be rather – ah – prickly – as can you. I would appreciate it if you could tell me what you know of the Webcleaner."

Reluctantly, Joosthin said: "As far as I know, she made her way to aboveground after The Destruction and found a way to live there. The Cryptals returned her to us and, for some time, she worked with them to bring food to those few of us who were left. We then moved back into Illiath and she continued in her role of provider of food and taught others of her kind the necessary skills."

"How did she come to mother a child with a Skyseeker?"

"I imagine that she meets Skyseekers from time to time."

"Why was the daughter left with the Skyseekers?"

"There are no half-castes among Crystalmakers."

"Of course. Mylin would kill them. But I am curious that the granddaughter is of the ruling class. How did a Webcleaner meet one of the Skyseeker ruling class – and why?"

"I do not know."

"Do you ever consult with the Webcleaner?"

Justin raised his eyebrows, widening his eyes in feigned shock. He was relieved when Tharnie apparently assumed that he did not meet with Elthán.

"Ah, a shame. She seems, to me, like a worthy person to meet."

"Tharnie you tread dangerous ground."

"So Threvor would have me believe. But I wonder, Joosthin, how much you actually are not saying."

REDEL STARED IN DISBELIEF at his computer screen.

For months and months all this past long summer and autumn, Redel had not heard from Ellen, or even heard from others where she might be. He had asked Lian Cecil if he had heard any news of Ellen on his visits to summer villages. Lian Cecil assured him he had not. Redel had even visited many villages himself and interrogated villagers; sometimes he'd lashed out with threats of violence when he thought a villager might be lying, but to no avail. No one had been visited by Lian Ellen this summer, though they admitted she had visited in previous summers. Increasingly, Redel panicked that his beloved sister might be lying injured somewhere, or even dead.

The last did not bear thinking about! He could not imagine a future without Ellen.

As summer drew to a close and winter snows painted more mountains in white, Redel's fright turned into distracted foreboding. With Crystalmakers and signs of their harvesting suddenly disappearing altogether from the landscape, he spent more time in one of his helicopters traversing Si'Empra for signs of Ellen or Rosa. In response to Chithra's and other lians' attempts to draw him back to his duties as Ülrügh, he snarled that his only duty at this time was to find his sister.

Redel closed his eyes, took a deep breath, closed the laptop, carefully looked around the room to reassure himself that he was not in the grip of a vision sent by God, and opened the laptop again.

The email was still on the screen:

Re: Overwintering somewhere else

Hi Redel

I've decided to overwinter somewhere else. Hope all goes well with winter in Si'Em City and your team gets lots of goals in schathem.

Ellen

Redel had instructed the IT people to notify him immediately there was a signal from any of Ellen's electronic devices. Her computer had lain untouched in her room for all the time she'd been away. As far as Redel knew, she only had a smartphone with her, but that had not emitted a single signal – until now.

Redel looked up at the young man who had brought him the message that they had finally detected a signal. "Have you traced the phone's whereabouts?"

"The signal was only live long enough to send this email, Ülrügh."

Redel smashed his fist down on the desk.

He had been so, so, so worried about her and this–

THIS!

This was the only message she sent!

He could see her laughing, the way that she used to when they were in the tunnels around Si'Em City; laughing that he was lost. He could see her now. She had to be somewhere near, otherwise she could not have sent the email, but he knew that there was no way he could find her, that every tunnel he knew about had already been sealed.

Another thought grabbed hold of Redel's heart, forced his fury to dissipate and caused him to almost double over in pain.

"Cryptals," he gasped.

"I beg your pardon, Ülrügh?"

"The Cryptals have got her soul."

The young man looked surprised. "Cryptals, Ülrügh? Soul, Ülrügh?"

Only the restraining hand of God, which Redel felt fall softly on to his shoulder, stopped him from launching himself over the table and taking a stranglehold of the disbelieving idiot who stood in front of his desk.

"Patience," God whispered. "This man has yet to learn. Harming him may turn others who do not yet know you are the Chosen, against you. Learn the lesson of what happened to Jesus when he revealed his deep wisdom before others were ready to receive and understand."

"Thank you," Redel said out loud, his voice choking with the effort of controlling his roiling emotions. "It would appear that we shall not have the pleasure of Lian Ellen this winter."

As the young man left, Redel turned to the window and looked out at the faltering light beyond. He wondered whether there was enough light to do a pass around the Si'Em Bluff on the off chance that he would see Ellen exiting some tunnel or other. He dismissed the idea almost before it was born, acknowledging that he had no idea where to look, and such a pass, with the wind and cold picking up by the minute, would be futile.

Redel fell to his knees and clasped his fingers together in prayer. "Keep her safe, my Lord, my Saviour. Keep her safe this long winter in body and soul. Look over her and give her strength to continue to fight the devil till she is once more safe in my arms."

PART TWO

SONG AND DANCE

CHAPTER 21
Winter Begins

---

*D*ISTASTE TWISTED THE LINE of Ellen's lips. She frowned at the words on the page in front of her: *Too much. I need to make it less saccharine. What about if I start differently–*

Müther's frustrated voice – suddenly loud and silencing the singing in the next room – sliced into Ellen's musings.

"Can't you hear that contraption squeaking, Josie? How often do I have to tell you to stop playing it when it goes out of tune!"

A minute of silence followed this outburst. Then Müther – voice more composed – said: "We'll start that song again, starting from the second chorus. Bachar, you sing the solo."

Ellen looked speculatively at the heavy curtain that separated Müther's classroom from the living room in which she sat. This was not the first time she had heard such an outburst.

Two weeks ago, he had sent the email message to Redel from just beyond the wall of the Serai, at the point where she could pick up an Internet signal, then hurried back to the cliff edge, made her way down the cliff and into a cave in the cliff, then hastened through the tunnel back to Ellen's hide to where Rosa waited. She forced the increasingly uncooperative glasaur – whose main pre-occupation had become where to settle for her winter hibernation – to race through near darkness, driving sleet and bitter cold along the Overshot and Si'Em river gorges, over The Shoals and up Elthán's path to Greçia's home, where she had promised Elthán she would spend the winter. She had arrived near frozen, but did not give in to Greçia's demands to take a warm bath and tuck into bed till she was sure that Rosa was properly accommodated.

During the course of the two weeks, Ellen had gradually learnt the pattern of each day: in the morning, Müther, with the help of Richard and adult Crystalmakers, held classes on reading, writing and maths; after lunch, the topics became more general, including science and geography; and in mid-afternoon, Müther conducted a music class, mostly on her own.

Ellen was not expected to contribute in any way to the winter business of the household, and she revelled in that freedom. Never before had she experienced a time when nothing was expected from her. In Si'Em City, the Ülrügh's daughter was always to either lead or be a part of some form of activity, whether summer or winter. Each hour, even the hours of leisure, had been carefully calculated – and argued over – by the range of tutors that surrounded her, or by her parents or the lians who organised the city's activities. Only when Ellen physically removed herself from the Serai had she felt able to relax into self-indulgence.

Ellen revelled in the freedom she was granted in this comfortable household, though, simultaneously, she felt guilty that she was not contributing in some way. Particularly, she bridled when she heard Müther lose her temper with the unfortunate Josie.

"Josie is not able to sing," Greçia had explained when Ellen raised a curious eyebrow at the first such outburst some days ago. "She had an accident as a child. Müther includes her in the singing class by having her play an instrument, but something seems to go wrong with the instrument."

Ellen had offered to help, but Müther had told her that there was no need.

Noting Ellen's attention now in the direction of the classroom, Richard said, with a note of resignation in his voice: "Müther and I tuned the samira that Josie is playing last night but the strings seem to loosen quickly. I wish I could do better. Poor Josie."

Ellen studied Richard for a second, wondering whether she should discuss the matter with him. The problem of the instrument was easy to solve. Müther's flat rejection of her offer to help chafed her. She set aside the pad and pen she had been working with, rose and crossed the room to the curtained doorway.

All heads, except the blind Müther's, turned towards the chink of light that fell into the room when Ellen moved the curtain aside a little. Fifteen children sat on mats on the floor. Today's general lessons had been broad-ranging, so eleven adults had also attended class and stayed for the music lesson. Ellen saw Müther's shadowy head twitch in reaction to the change of sound from voices that had suddenly turned away from her. Ellen put a finger to her lips and indicated that everyone should face the front again.

Ellen located the child who had offended Müther. She sat hunched over a samira. Ellen crooked a finger at her, indicating her to come forward quietly and to bring the instrument. The child moved almost silently but still Müther twitched again, her hypersensitive hearing on high alert.

Shielding her eyes, the child came into the living room. Ellen dropped the curtain closed. Richard stood hurriedly, picking up a pair of sunglasses. "This is Josie," he said quietly, placing the glasses over the child's eyes. "Josie, Lian Ellen has invited you into this room."

"Warmth and light, Josie," Ellen greeted. "I have been hearing you play. It is good playing."

The child tipped her face up to Ellen. Thick, lumpy scald scars disfigured the right side of her head, neck and shoulders. Scald scars were common enough among Si'Emprans but Josie's accident must have been particularly traumatic. One side of her mouth had fused shut and it looked as if part of her neck had been hollowed out. Ellen guessed that singing would be only one of the many difficulties this child faced.

"I have an instrument for you that you will probably find less cumbersome to play," Ellen said, taking a thordilones from its cradle on the wall. She had discovered the instrument during her convalescence. In the many hours she spent alone while Greçia was at her clinic, she had alternated between honing her musical skills on the thordilones, writing stories and poems, and reading the many novels and magazines that crammed bookshelves around the home.

Behind the sunglasses, Josie's eyes grew round. She had seen the thordilones and Müther had spoken about its sweet tones, but there had been no one with the skill to play it since Pedro's departure. Richard, too, looked surprised. "Can she manage such a complex–" he began to say, but stopped because Ellen was quickly and expertly taking the instrument apart, stripping it to the sound box and strings. She set it before Josie. "I think you will find this much the same as the samira you've been playing. Please try it, but softly so that it doesn't disturb those in the next room."

Müther's voice sounded next door, singing several notes of a song. The combined voices of the children and adults repeated the tune.

Josie began to pluck the notes gently from the strings of the thordilones but stopped almost immediately, her quick intake of breath showing her obvious delight at the sound. Ellen smiled. "Your ears are very good; so is your touch. I need just to tune it slightly. Later I will show you how to tune it yourself."

When Ellen had finished tuning, she told Josie to quietly resume her seat among the children and, when appropriate, join in play again.

"Lian Ellen," Richard cautioned. "Müther likes to be in control of her lessons."

Ellen shrugged. "Müther will do what Müther must do," she said. She picked up the samira Josie had left behind and began to fiddle with it as Richard helped Josie quietly back to her place in the next room. He then disappeared into the alcove that was his bedspace and brought out two broken samiras.

"I found these at the market and hoped to be able to make one good one. Unfortunately, I have not enough knowledge of the instruments to know how to repair them. It would appear that you have the skill and knowledge."

"Perfect!" Ellen said.

A flurry of sound from wind instruments started up and, coming in at precisely the right time, the thordilones joined the sound. Voices rose and fell in harmony.

At the end of the song there was a long silence, then the curtain swept aside and Müther stood in the doorway.

"Lian Ellen." Müther's voice was very quiet. Richard winced. Ellen looked up from her work.

"I am here," Ellen said.

"I take it you play the thordilones."

"I do."

"Was it necessary for you to take apart the instrument for the child?"

"I have heard her play the samira. She has a fine touch but I did not think she had the skill to play all of the thordilones. Stripping the instrument to its simplest elements seemed a good compromise."

Silence. Then, "Where is the samira she was playing?"

"It is here on my lap."

"What are you doing with it?"

"Richard and I are cannibalising two broken samiras for parts to make this one work."

"What is wrong with it?"

"Two of the keys are incorrect for the strings. The sound box was slightly warped but Richard has managed to ease it straight. It now sounds fine to my ear."

"Is it now workable?"

"Almost."

"Finish it."

Müther stood still, listening intently, head slightly to one side while Ellen and Richard worked. When Ellen declared the samira workable, she said: "Richard give the samira to Josie and bring the thordilones in here. Lian Ellen, I would be grateful if you could restore the thordilones and join me in the music class to play it." With that, she stepped back, letting the curtain fall. The whispering and giggling in the classroom came to an abrupt halt. Soon after, singing started again.

Ellen kept her face carefully emotionless when Greçia caught her eye. She re-assembled the thordilones, tuned it and joined Müther as instructed. Richard followed her in. Müther indicated that Ellen should take a place next to her. Richard rigged a small lamp to shine on the thordilones.

At first, Müther simply asked Ellen to accompany the singers, then to play the introduction to well-known tunes and repeat parts of tunes she wanted the children to practice. Other adult Crystalmakers drifted into the room, attracted by the new sounds. Finally, a few asked Müther to sing one of her own songs. She required little encouragement.

The Songbird chose one of her own compositions; an early arrangement that had become popular.

"Do you know how to play 'The Island's dream', Lian Ellen?"

"I do." Ellen rubbed her fingers over a number of strings, producing a sound akin to a C chord made by a violin, and followed that chord with a melancholic arpeggio in A minor. As her fingers moved to another sound, Müther took up the melody:

> *The moon, the moon*
> *Light in the midnight sky*

WINTER BEGINS

Spills, it spills the earth
The low and the high

Müther drew a breath to continue with the next lines, but before she could, Ellen sang:

The moon, the moon
Light in the midnight sky

Müther's head jerked with surprise.

Ellen smiled mischievously. The song Müther had chosen was usually sung as a duet, but, obviously, Müther had not expected a partner to sing. Ellen replayed and re-sang the bars to cover Müther's hesitation.

Then Müther sang:

With the power of birth
Aah skylight, mother of hope
Bearer of sun, father of life
Tonight your face revealed
A glimpse, a dream

The song swelled, the two voices playing against each other, sometimes in harmony, other times echoing. Ellen could hear that, after recovering from her initial surprise, Müther's reaction was to challenge her to perform. She introduced variations to the harmony and Ellen had to react quickly to hold the flow of music. Luckily, the game Müther played was one that Ellen's music teacher had often engaged her in. Rather than being intimidated – which she suspected Müther was attempting – Ellen enjoyed the test.

IN THE DEEP, THE WhiteŌne fell silent, enthralled by this new sound in Its world.

Beyond The Deep, the BlackŌne raised Its head, It's large, dark brown eyes intent. It had not heard this sound of beauty in a long time.

When the duet finished, children and adults slapped the floor and walls to show their appreciation. Müther held herself stiffly. It had been almost twenty years since a skilled musician had accompanied her.

But why does it have to be this girl! The blindness of Ülrügh Briani to both his son's sadistic tendencies and the deterioration of the fabric of all that made Si'Empra unique had seeded distrust in Müther of the Ülrügh's family. Seeing how her sister had also been tainted by association with the Ülrügh and the young Redel, Müther found it hard to believe that Lian Ellen could have escaped contamination. Müther viewed with suspicion each of Ellen's interference with the past twenty years' established pattern of survival and living. She expected that Ellen's true motives would reveal themselves in time and she braced herself to absorb yet another blow in her life.

She drew her lips into a stern line and turned to Ellen: "How do you know how to accompany me in that song?"

"I used to dream of singing with you. I have listened to every recording you have made and done my best to learn every part suitable for my voice."

Taken aback, Müther was again silent for some time. Then curiosity won over her reluctance to share anything with Lian Ellen. *Just how skilled are you?*

"Shall we sing The Song of the Albatross?"

A ripple of laughter sounded. Müther cocked her head, trying to discern the cause of the mirth.

Lian Ellen explained: "Apologies. They are laughing at me. I made a face in fright at your suggestion. I will do my best to play and sing with you."

"You do not like The Song of the Albatross?"

"On the contrary. It is the most beautiful of all songs. But it is somewhat challenging."

Müther could hear that while Lian Ellen spoke she also fiddled with the thordilones to prepare it for the song. The fiddling stopped and Lian Ellen said: "I am ready when you are."

"Lead as you should," Müther said.

The strings of the thordilones hummed gently in unison. Into the sound Ellen's voice breathed:

Air sighs

The voice faded together with the sound of the strings. And when silence settled, notes rippled into the room from delicately plucked strings.

Water murmurs

Lian Ellen sang softly.

Before that sound also died, Müther let her voice take flight, infusing it with joy and longing:

I come. I come.

The murmur of notes from the thordilones swelled. In her mind's eye, Müther saw Lian Ellen rub the palm of her hand over several strings as she sang:

So close she glides. A touch of air above water

Müther continued, her tone still full of happiness:

I come. I come
Winter's solitude is past
Summer's love is ours

Lian Ellen narrated:

On bended wings she glides

Müther again:

I'll find you there upon the land
where summers past we formed our bond
Year-upon-year, our bond for life
    She glides
    On the wind she glides
I'll match your welcome with aerial grace
I'll see my joy in your eyes' glow
    On wings of winter skies

Müther stopped listening for Ellen's part, giving herself to the song. She became the albatross: full, vibrant and joyous, hearing Ellen's words only as those that set the scene for her story.

We'll find that ledge to share our young
Like summers past our dearest charge
Together
    She lifts her wings
    Drifts higher
    Higher
I'll see you soon
I'll hear your voice
    She presses the sky
    White speck on blue
I see our land
Below it lies
We'll claim our ledge
I am come
I look for you
    Thousands of birds
    Thousands of greetings
    Summer's labour is begun
I am arrived
Hear my call
I listen for yours

WINTER BEGINS

She settles and rises
Each time with hope
Hear my call.
I am arrived.
I listen for you
    Thousands of birds
    Thousands of greetings
    Sunset
    Sunrise
    Each day is longer
Summers past we were together
All winter long I dreamed of you
Alone I flew and dreamed of you
of summer's bond each year renewed
Alone I flew but dreamed of you
    Upon her roost
    Among a thousand sounds
    She sits quite still
All is empty: the sky and sea
The air is still without your voice
    Her wings do lift
    She drifts from land
I'll search for you
to hear your cry
to feel your touch
to form out bond
Our bond for life
    On wings of winter skies
    She glides
I'll find you then upon the sea
    She glides
    Over waters blue and lands of green and brown
    she glides.

High and low
through storm and heat and ice
she glides
A wraith from winter skies
I see you there in waters deep
I hear your call
I come
I come
    She sits quite still on tossing waves
I hear your call
I come
I come
    Water murmurs
Together
We are together
Our bond forever

The melody that had played in the background faded into a ripple of notes and stilled with a slow stroke of the strings.

    Air sighs

The hum of the thordilones gradually died and for a long moment there was only silence. Müther found she was trembling, her emotions a barely controllable riot: to sing so freely accompanied by a thordilones, to hear those notes – it was a something she had never thought would happen again.

She took command of her emotions, remembering that, above all, she was a performer and her audience was what mattered! She moved her head slightly this way and that, trying to catch a sound from them.

"Everyone is just staring at you," she heard Ellen murmur. "I think you absolutely stunned them."

Müther started: she had forgotten that it was Lian Ellen who had accompanied her. She snapped: "You should think less about how you are playing and more about the emotion of the song—"

A hand stroked her arm. Then another hand stroked her arm. "I've never heard anything so beautiful," a soft voice said. It was Chris. She felt people gather around her.

"So sad. So lovely," another voice said as another hand touched her.

Müther shuddered with the effort not to sob. She drew herself up and began to tap her foot loudly. "Pick up this beat," she commanded, "and see if you can pick up an accompaniment to this ditty."

As soon as the tapping began, giggles sounded and the press of people around her retreated. Hands began to clap in time. When the thordilones and hands were all beating enthusiastically, Müther bent at the waist, facing her audience and began:

> *Tilly Billy Silly Dilly*
> *Don't you know this land is hilly*
> *Tilly Billy Silly Dilly*
> *Don't you know this land is chilly*
> *You are hot but we are not*

> *On a plain so flat and sandy*
> *Sat a goat inside a boat*
> *I look grand I look so dandy*
> *I can gloat, I am afloat*

Enthusiastically, everyone repeated the chorus.

> *Tilly Billy Silly Dilly*
> *Don't you know this land is hilly*
> *Tilly Billy Silly Dilly*
> *Don't you know this land is chilly*
> *You are hot but we are NOT*

Müther drew herself up, arm crooked over her forehead as if to shade her eyes. She swivelled her head around as if searching the horizon. Accompanied by giggles and enthusiastic singing of the chorus after each stanza, Müther sang of how the goat convinced himself that midges, which swarmed irritatingly around him, had marooned his boat on sand. The goat's efforts concentrated increasingly on eliminating the midges, blinding him to the increasingly dire state of the boat.

At the end of the ditty, as she pranced back and forth swiping at imaginary midges while the Crystalmaker children and adults shouted out the chorus another time, Müther heard Ellen's burst of laughter.

"That's a wonderful ditty," Ellen said when the excitement had died a little. "But I am glad my father did not hear that song."

Müther turned to Lian Ellen. "Why do you say that?"

"Oh, I have been told that Lian Thea would sometimes call my father Tilly the Goat."

Müther sniffed contemptuously. "I lost my sight and hands because that song irritated not only your father but others. It would appear that they are still swiping at midges and not the real issues that confront Si'Empra."

After several seconds of silence, Lian Ellen said softly, "Ah, Müther, I am sorry. I would have thought you more astute. Few people like being made fun of."

Astute! How dare she! The audacity of this child! How dare she!

"Who taught you the thordilones?" Müther demanded.

"We had the same tutor, Müther."

For the third time that afternoon, Lian Ellen shook Müther's world. She drew in a deep breath to steady herself. She wanted to end this interchange with this most aggravating of all people – but – but – she longed to know –

"How is Lord Achton?"

"I saw him less than three months ago. He is well."

"And Lian Isoldé? I hear she is – her mind is no longer–"

"Her mind wanders in worlds we don't always understand," Ellen said. "She is otherwise well and they both live all year quite peacefully in the summer home."

"I want you to teach Richard how to play the thordilones."

"I am not skilled enough to teach him, but I can be your eyes and your hands."

CHAPTER 22
Schathem

MARTHIN HAD BUILT a table for Mary over which she could stretch a gown and embroider. He bent over it now, carefully working a needle around an appliqué to secure it. At the other side of the table, Mary pinned another appliqué, setting it slightly away from an embroidered line.

"These are the last two," she said. Her fingers trembled. Her voice was barely more than a whisper. She sat back, closing her eyes. She did not try to be brave in front of Marthin.

Marthin straightened to inspect his work. Sometime in the last few months, he had started to help Mary with her work. At first it was only to help lift the fabric and reposition her tools of trade, but when even a needle became too heavy for her, she taught him how to stitch. At night, after a full day at his own work as city steward, he toiled with needles that his large, powerful hands could hardly hold.

No matter how hard he tried, he could always see the difference between his stitches and hers. "You have a gift," he would grumble, and she would laugh that gentle laugh of hers.

He moved now to secure the leaf she had just pinned, giving her time to gather the trickle of strength that might return to her muscles. When that leaf was also secured, he turned to her to find her smiling fondly at him.

"You look so serious when you sew," she teased.

"I'm terrified by the task," he admitted.

"It's finished, Marthin. Could you put the gown on the hanger and deliver it to Lian Chithra. I am sorry to use you as a delivery boy."

Marthin hung the gown. Then he lifted his frail wife into his arms, took her to her bed and tucked her under the bed covers. "I'll be back soon," he promised.

"Oh no, Marthin! You should go to the winter feast. I will be perfectly fine. In fact, after a short rest, I might even go myself."

"In that case, I would not dream of letting you go alone. I will come back for you and we will go in grand style together."

Mary pursed her lips but returned the smile in his eyes, acknowledging that her ruse would not work.

Marthin doubled Lian Chithra's gown over his arm and made his way to the Chancellor's chambers. She responded to his knock in person. He could see that she had already dressed for the feast, clearly not expecting Mary to finish the gown. At the sight of it she winced. "I did not want to trouble her."

"She apologises it was not ready before now and hopes you will enjoy wearing it." He held the gown up for her to see.

Chithra's gaze roved over the pattern of flowers and leaves that hung off a single embroidered vine stretching from a complexity of colour on the right shoulder to finish in a few bright leaves that drooped over the fabric that would cover her hips.

"It is beautiful!' she exclaimed with a short intake of breath. 'It is truly beautiful." She took the hanger from Marthin.

As he turned away, she asked, "Marthin, how can I thank her?"

Marthin hesitated. He glanced over his shoulder at her. "Lian, you could wear the gown tonight and have someone take a photo of you wearing it for her to see."

"A photo!" Lian Chithra recoiled. Then she nodded. "Yes. Yes. I will do as you suggest. Thank you Marthin."

The thick fabric of the new gown fell over Chithra's large frame, hiding the many folds of flesh. She remembered Mary saying that the colour complemented her hair. She stood before the mirror and lifted her hands to rearrange her hair; perhaps remove the single plait that she had earlier wound into a bun at the back of her head and have it hang over her shoulder? But reflecting back at her was a large face flattened by excess. It made little difference how her hair looked. The gown was all the beauty she could display.

Chithra let her hands fall, and wondered whom she could ask to take her photograph. Jon? Unfortunately, it would have to be Jon. She went to his office, grimacing with distaste at the thought of posing for a portrait, but he had already left. Everyone would, of course, be assembling for the grand feast that marked the official beginning of winter in Si'Em City.

Oh well, at some time during the night she would have to allow her photograph to be taken.

She locked the door to her chambers and started the long walk to the Layamlé. The lifts, unfortunately, had not been working for some time, and the required spare parts had not arrived on the last ship to land cargo before winter ice closed the shipping lanes. However, the Layamlé was below her chambers; going downstairs would tax her little and when she sweated her way up the stairs at the end of the festivities, no one would be in a state to notice her labours.

The Layamlé's domed ceiling was thirty metres at its highest point. The centre – a huge crystal disc some thirty-five metres in diameter made by Crystalmakers in the time before – was lit from behind, radiating a pale yellow glow that illuminated the whole chamber. An intricate web of ropes, kept aloft by hooks and anchored at ten points spaced about five metres apart, laced over the area of light. A rope hung from floor to ceiling at each of the anchor points. A broad staircase with an intricately carved stone balustrade and thickly carpeted steps led from the Serai to the floor of the Layamlé. Three stages, spaced evenly around the Layamlé, had been cut into its walls, and were now curtained off. Almost at ceiling height was another room, its face covered with a trellis that allowed its occupants to observe the Layamlé without being seen.

The walls of the Layamlé –indeed most walls in Si'Em City – were covered in murals. Removing and recreating murals was a favourite wintertime activity; small teams, led by a qualified artist, were a common sight throughout Si'Em City. Which murals should be removed and what the theme of new paintings should be was guided by an elaborate nomination and voting system that the Lianthem guided but in which the whole population could take part: the system triggered as much heightened emotion and gossip as any major sporting event.

The Layamlé was the city's heart, especially in winter, when Si'Emprans valued its space in lieu of access to the outside world. Increasingly, it was also a place where those who could not afford otherwise, spent their nights when the ceiling light was turned off for ten hours. This use of the Layamlé as a sleeping room was tolerated as long as all bedrolls and personal effects were not in evidence when the light was switched on again. Marthin had allocated a room where people could store their possessions, and he and his team rigorously policed the rules of Layamlé use.

During the official opening of the winter season, the usual park-like play equipment and seating of the Layamlé, and places where people could purchase food and drink, were replaced by rows of trestle tables and benches – enough to fit the entire city's population. The night began with the serving of free meals and continued with the opening of schathem, Si'Empra's ceiling games competition. The competition remained a weekly, standard fixture throughout winter, drawing Si'Emprans into the Layamlé every week, with the finals again accompanied by a free feast.

Chithra was as enthusiastic about the games as any other Si'Empran, though she only attended the opening and closing games in person – happy otherwise to listen to the commentary broadcast over Si'Em's radio channel. She made her way down the staircase in the company of others who lived in the Serai. Ülrügh Redel, she noted with surprise, was already in his seat. In past years he had waited until the hall was almost full, then declared his entrance by showing off his athleticism: running down the stairs and vaulting into his seat over the table, enthusiastically shouting something like: "The drama is about to begin. Si'Emprans. All! Welcome to another exciting winter of tournaments, feasts and – I hear you groan – education!"

Now he sat quietly in his seat, his daughter Chrystal on his lap. She was dressed in frills and bows, obviously enjoying his attention and that of the people who stopped briefly before her father's chair to pay their respects. The seat to the right of his had a large cushion on it. This would no doubt be Chrystal's when she was not on his lap, though it should, of course, have been occupied by Lian Ellen.

Chithra bowed her head in acknowledgment of the Ülrügh and took her own seat. This year it was not on his immediate left side, as had been customary since the death of Lian Constance, but one seat removed. At the Ülrügh's left tonight was a man who had arrived with the last ship: a priest by the name of Augustine – Father Augustine, he liked to be called. He was an elderly man with a large, balding head, a prominent nose and a thick lower lip he was in the habit of tugging. He always dressed in a long, brown robe, tied at the waist with a cord. Apparently he had no intention of stepping outdoors this winter, because his only footwear appeared to be open sandals.

"This all looks rather exciting," the priest said as she filled her seat. Among the many other features that Chithra found irritating about the man was that he was Spanish and spoke poor English. The reason she found his Spanishness irritating was because once he discovered she could speak his native tongue, he had sought her out at every opportunity.

"It is an important event," she returned, her tone borderline polite.

"Now. I am told that this is the most important event of the year," he said, unfazed by her lack of enthusiasm.

"Probably the melting of snow at the end of winter is a contender," she murmured.

"If I understand the Ülrügh correctly, you start a tournament at this festivity."

Chithra's eyes swept the Layamlé. The last few years had seen a drop in the number of people attending the Grand Feast. Notably, some of the ruling class were no longer taking their winter residence in the Si'Em City complex, but stayed in their summer houses in Baltha or, like Lian Achton and Lian Isoldé, other parts of Si'Empra.

In some ways, this was good, she reflected, because it relieved the pressure on Si'Em City's resources. In other ways it was not good because it meant a break with the long tradition of all Si'Emprans coming together for the winter to renew acquaintances and their bond as a people.

Chithra picked out the figure of Lian Dane. He sat with his extended family at a large square table closest to the high table. Lian Julian, also seated at his own table with his family, raised a hand to greet her. He had Cheng Yi and his wife, and that flibbertigibbet of a daughter of theirs, Gigi, as guests at his table. Chithra had heard that the girl had made quite a fuss when she heard that Lian Ellen would not be spending winter in Si'Em City, spreading all sorts of rumours about reasons why, from

Lian Ellen being bored by Si'Em City (likely) to Lian Ellen being mistreated by certain members of the ruling family (nonsense)!

"Now. I believe that the games take place overhead," the priest prattled on, pointing to the web of ropes strung across the domed ceiling. "Extraordinary. Extraordinary. You people are extraordinary. Do people really run upside down?"

He seemed to expect an answer from her. "Not exactly upside down," she said. "Who has been telling you what is going on?"

The priest immediately became apologetic, his eyes and lips drooping dramatically to emphasise his guilt. "Aah. Several people. I'm afraid my English is so poor, I don't always understand what people are telling me."

Why have you come to Si'Empra? Why has the Ülrügh insisted that you should spend the winter here?

"I petitioned the Pope to send a priest," Ülrügh had explained airily to her when he had introduced the priest to her. "It is unfortunate that he is less than competent with communication, but he should be able to teach us sufficient."

Teach us what? Chithra had wondered with alarm. Less than competent or not, the priest seemed to spend an astonishing amount of time with the Ülrügh. She noticed that the few lians the Ülrügh and others had chosen to be close to him were also often drawn into conversations with the priest. Furthermore, she noted that the Ülrügh carefully ensured that she was not part of that coven.

Inwardly she groaned, not feeling optimistic about the outcome of this latest of the Ülrügh's obsessions; she hoped that he would exhibit his usual short attention span for passions that took his fancy.

Ülrügh Redel leant towards her, around the priest. "Chithra," he said. "I have attempted to explain to His Holiness the intricacies of our unique sport, but I am afraid I have failed." Redel gave the priest a winning smile. "Please tell him in his own language."

So, Chithra thought resentfully, this is to be my role tonight: to translate for this man!

Carefully keeping the aggravation from her voice, she said in Spanish. "Indeed our game is intricate." She pointed to ten hanging ropes. "To begin, a team member stands next to a rope – team members alternate at the ropes. When the signal is given, the team members must climb the ropes and reach those discs." She pointed to discs that hung from a hook at the highest point in the centre of the ceiling. "The first person to reach the discs takes possession of one. But in order to score, the team must take the disc to the team's hooks." She pointed to two hooks positioned at opposite ends of the ceiling. "The disc must pass through at least three team members' hands. It can be thrown, but if it falls the team forfeits its chance to score. If the opposite team touches the person with the disc, the disc falls into the possession of the opposite team."

"Good Lord! Extraordinary. Extraordinary! That's very high to be doing such things. What about falling – don't people fall?"

"If a team member falls," Chithra said as dryly as she could, "the opposite team automatically wins the game."

The priest's brow crinkled as he studied the ceiling. "I suppose that's a disincentive to fall, but, nevertheless, it all seems – very dangerous. And, if I may say, rather vigorous."

"There are other penalties. You'll see that the ceiling has many embedded hooks." In the days before contact with the outer world, she wanted to add, there were no hooks, just shaped protrusions in the rock that a rope could be slung over – and the rope might or might not stay fast. "Each player has three ropes attached to their body harness. At least two of the ropes must be attached to separate hooks at any time. A penalty is awarded to the other team if this rule is broken."

The priest continued to look up at the ceiling with puzzled concern.

"It will become clear to you," Chithra assured him. The serving of food had begun. She scanned the platters for delicacies she was particularly fond of. Nearby, she heard Lian Thobias, whom she could always rely on to be as enthusiastic about food as she, chuckle with delight as attendants set before him a platter of goat shanks surrounded by steaming root vegetables. The aroma was enough to make her mouth water.

Amid the clamour, a male voice remarked loudly, "It seems we will eat better than some others in the hall." Disturbed, Chithra swivelled in vain to identify the speaker, and was relieved to see the Ülrügh appeared not to have heard the inflammatory comment.

The forty or so extended families who made up the ruling class of Skyseekers sat at tables set on a large, slightly raised platform in the centre of the grand hall. Also on the platform was a table occupied by the fifty-nine foreigners who would spend the winter in Si'Empra. They had been engaged specifically to teach higher skills, or 'education', as the Ülrügh liked to say, to Si'Emprans. In the past, there had been more such people, but the demand seemed to be less this year – and, in truth, the budget for engaging foreigners had been reduced by the Lianthem.

Radiating from the dais were long tables at which other Si'Emprans sat. From under lowered eyelids, Chithra saw that the platters set on those tables were heaped with varieties of berry bread. Next to each platter, attendants set steaming cauldrons of stew from which people ladled portions into their own bowls. Bottles of grape wine lined the table of those who sat on the dais, and vats of berry wine and water dotted the tables of others.

It will be tasty enough and fill their bellies, Chithra thought. *Whoever made that remark — and I must find out who — could cause trouble! I will find out who it is.*

The noisy hubbub of conversation filled the hall. Only the Ülrügh seemed disengaged from the party. He fed titbits of food to his daughter and made her giggle with an occasional tickle or some other tease. If he acknowledged his surroundings at all, it was to pass a remark to the priest or to glance in the direction of any group that was particularly loud in their revelry. When the platters were almost empty, he set Chrystal on her seat and came to his feet. Almost instantly the room fell silent.

"Winter has begun!" he announced in rich tones that carried to the furthest parts of the hall. "For those of us gathered in our beautiful city of Si'Em, winter is always full of activity. It is a time for us to renew friendships. It is a time for us to learn new ways of living with one another, for discovering new truths, learning new lessons. Friends! Let us make this year one that will mark the beginning of a new era for Si'Empra. This winter we will learn to pray. We will learn to play a different tune."

He might or might not have noticed that the majority of faces closed in puzzlement at his last two statements.

"But!" Redel exclaimed, his voice suddenly buoyant. "It's now time to start schathem!"

He hurdled the table, leapt off the dais and threaded his way among the tables to the back of the hall. An excited cheer erupted. Others – also players of the game – jumped from their seats and hurried to their positions.

"The Red team and the Blue team," Chithra explained, mindful of the task the Ülrügh had given her. "The Ülrügh has the Red team."

"He is to go up there! My word! My word!" The priest sat forward, his face full of childish excitement.

The Chancellor did not bother to hide the pride in her voice. "The Ülrügh is one of the most skilled players Si'Empra has ever produced. His athleticism is second to none." *Except perhaps Lian Ellen.* Chithra closed her eyes at the unbidden thought. She reluctantly acknowledged, as she had several times in the past, that she was jealous of Lian Ellen. Strangely enough, however, she had noticed that the Ülrügh was more affectionate towards her when Lian Ellen was present in the Serai than when she was absent. In fact, the Ülrügh's moods were generally more stable when Lian Ellen was within his vicinity.

Three referees took up position on raised and reclining chairs set at the points of a triangle. The players harnessed up, bracing themselves against the wall. A single gong sounded and they began to haul themselves up, pausing frequently to unfasten one rope to a hook and fasten another to one further up the wall. It was a slow start. When the players were a few metres from each other, some began to work their way towards an opposing team member.

"It is against the rules for two people to use the same hook," Chithra said. She pointed to the Ülrügh, who had climbed the quickest and was not far from the discs. "The Ülrügh will be able to claim a disc, but he will then need to turn to take it to his goal hook. See, there are three Blue players who are moving in towards him. He will need to pass the disc to one of his team members before he is touched."

The Ülrügh was indeed the first to claim a disc. A roar of encouragement sounded from the spectators. He reached out quickly, lifted a third rope dangling from his harness, attached it and swung below the Blue team members, his sudden drop causing the priest to gasp.

"He is only allowed to swing like that if all three ropes are attached," Chithra said. "But note how he swings on his rope below the Blue and passes the disc to one of the Red. Swinging is a useful tactic but it wastes time unless there is another person working with him. See. Now the Ülrügh has to pull himself up his harness ropes and on to the ceiling ones, detach the third rope and reposition the other two so that he can help his team members." *If Ellen had been here, she would have been first to the discs or at least close behind. She would have been ready to clip and unclip his ropes and they would have worked their way over the ceiling as a team – a virtually unbeatable team.*

Another Red player joined the Ülrügh and together they worked their way towards those who now had the disc, clipping and unclipping each other's harnesses. Two members of the Blue team were similarly working their way towards the Red players with the disc.

"The person with the disc must hold it in their hand, which means there is only one hand free for climbing. You can see that it is necessary for another team member to be close by to assist with the harness – ah, they have been touched!"

The referees' gong sounded. The disc changed from the Red to the Blue team, and they scuttled over the ceiling towards their own goal. A Red team member launched herself into the air and managed to touch the foot of a Blue player before dropping into her harness. Again the referees' gong sounded. The Ülrügh snatched the disc and started again for the Red team's goal. Three Red players worked with him, clipping and unclipping his harness. The spectators shouted approval. Two Blue players clipped their ropes to six hooks in the Ülrügh's path, forcing him to detour. Another Blue team member angled in to the detour. The Ülrügh backtracked and passed the disc to one of his team who approached the Red goal from another angle. The Blues repositioned, but too late. The Red team landed the first disc.

The gong sounded and all players clipped three ropes to hooks and dropped into their harnesses, breathing heavily.

"They will rest for five minutes, then they will once again circle the discs, but only halfway to the floor, team members alternating as before."

"Good Lord!" the priest. "It's all very exciting. Not very good for the neck, though – not good at all." Father Augustine rubbed the back of his neck vigorously with his large hands.

Chithra considered letting him suffer neck pain but decided not to be petty. "You will notice that all our seats are fitted with these depressions." She pointed out the scalloped back of the chair. "Rest your head against that. There are cushions available if you need to adjust your height or the back of your chair."

"And what about them?" the priest asked, once he had adjusted his own seat. He nodded towards the people seated on their benches below the dais.

"Oh, they have found ways of coping too. You see that some lie on the floor or swing around on the benches and rest their heads on the table. See how some of them have brought their own cushions for head rests."

The game lasted for half an hour. Only two discs were successfully placed in that time: one for each team. The Ülrügh returned to his seat drenched in sweat and grinning with the pleasure of the game.

In his broken English, Father Augustine began to gush at the Ülrügh's prowess. The Ülrügh waved his hand airily to dismiss the praise. "We are only halfway through," he said. "Let us watch another team while we rest."

Two junior teams played in the intermission – boys and girls barely seven years old yet already strong, nimble and fearless. Rather than playing the whole ceiling, they used only a quarter of the full field.

Intermission over, the adults clambered up the walls again. Even the priest joined in the enthusiastic yelling from the floor as players criss-crossed the ceiling, the disc passing from hand to hand, ropes moving on and off hooks with blinding speed, sudden drops from the ceiling to bypass opposing team members causing spectators an extra thrill. It was soon clear that those who supported the Blue team were pinning their hopes on a boy called Luman, whose nimbleness matched the Ülrügh's, but whose youth and slender body gave him a slight edge. He was Lian Julian's grandson and the Lian did not hold back as he roared encouragement.

In the end, the game was a tie. A second round would be played on another night, and other teams would play as the competition gained momentum. For the rest of the winter the ceiling would rarely be empty of climbers. Either a game would be in progress, players would be honing their skills, or teams would be working out their tactics.

Redel returned to his seat, threw back a full glass of water and lifted his daughter into his arms. "Good people!" he yelled over the racket of the crowd. "Let winter begin!"

He jumped down into a small cleared space and began to swing Chrystal around. A thordilones strummed a cord and one of the stages lit up to reveal an orchestra, which immediately began to play a lively tune. Drums beat out a complicated rhythm and the Ülrügh of Si'Empra danced the first dance of winter. If he felt anger that his half-sister was not there to dance it with him, he did not let it show, nor did it dampen his apparent enthusiasm. No one could dance as he could. In his arms Chrystal squealed and giggled, delighted and fearful all at once.

People pushed tables back to make more room for dancing. Soon the room was full of gyrating bodies and the music became wilder and eased by turn.

Chithra saw Pedro seated at a bench towards the back of the hall. She was loath to rise but even more loath to be in the company of the priest any longer – the man was all smiles and questions!

"Come, Father Augustine," she shouted over the music. "I'd like to introduce you to someone."

The two picked their way to where Pedro was deeply engaged in conversation with others at his table, including some foreign tutors. The conversation stopped abruptly when she approached, and all stood in deference for her.

It was a little quieter away from the music and she did not have to yell to make herself heard. "Pedro. Have you met Father Augustine?"

Pedro bowed politely to the priest, who automatically extended his hand to shake Pedro's, then retracted it quickly when he remembered Si'Emprans did not greet each other in that way, and bowed slightly instead.

"Pedro speaks Spanish," Chithra continued. "He is a principal school tutor. A gifted teacher. In fact, he was responsible for much of the education of our Ülrügh in his later teenage years. Pedro not only speaks Spanish, but also Greek and Latin, if you care to converse with him in those languages." Chithra did not add that she was also fluent in those languages. "Pedro is probably in a better position to answer many of your questions about Si'Empra than I am. I am afraid that I do rather shut myself away in my office." Such false modesty was justified, she believed, in the circumstances.

Pedro glanced at her with his coal black eyes, hiding his surprise at her words so well that she could almost believe he wasn't surprised at all. No doubt he guessed she wanted to offload her burden. Chithra trusted Pedro even less than she trusted Marthin, though every attempt on her part to catch him doing something subversive had come to nothing.

"I am honoured to meet you, Father Augustine," Pedro said.

Chithra was about to leave Pedro to deal with the priest in whichever way he wanted when she caught sight of Redel, looking directly at her.

With a flash of anger she realised that he expected her to stay with the priest. Instead of improving her situation, she had made it worse for herself: she had left good food and wine, a comfortable seat and the amiable company of peers for a hard bench, rough offerings and painful conversation.

CHAPTER 23
Father Augustine, Chocolate Pudding

"So much good, good reading material." Father Augustine wandered along the library's aisle, his long fingers with prominent, yellowish nails stroking the spines of books as he passed. Every now and then he stopped and slid a tome off the shelf to flip it open.

"Ah yes. A good library." Pedro smiled at the priest's enthusiasm. "And now we have so much also on our computers to read." He indicated the monitors lining one section of a wall in the reading lounge.

Father Augustine glanced at the monitors but was clearly not as comfortable with them as with the volumes he was caressing. "This library, it was established when?"

"Some fifty years ago. In the days of Ülrügh Devi's rule. He and the Lianthem grasped the importance of learning as quickly as possible from the foreigners who first landed on our shores."

"Far-sighted. Far-sighted," Father Augustine muttered. He faced Pedro, pushing his reading glasses up on to his broad forehead. "Now. Si'Empra has been occupied for a thousand years, yes?"

"Approximately, as far as we can discern from our legends." Pedro found himself enjoying the priest's company for the opportunity it gave him to practise his Spanish. The conversation at the feast two nights ago had been difficult, even stilted, with Lian Chithra in attendance, but now he found conversation flowed easily; the man had some strange mannerisms but his mind was keen and he was widely read.

This morning Pedro had suddenly been summoned to the Ülrügh's presence and been informed that he was to provide the priest with assistance to render the Bible into the Skyseeker language. The Chancellor had been present as the Ülrügh so commanded. Pedro suspected that Lian Chithra had been the Ülrügh's first choice for the task and that she had suggested him instead.

"But this astonishing progress you have made into modern ways has only occurred in the last eight decades or so?"

"Si'Empra was fortunate," Pedro said.

"Yes. Yes. Lian Chithra tells me. That – ah Lianthem – your Si'Empran ruling council, yes? Wise. Wise. But you weren't colonised like other places. Why? Why?"

Pedro smiled. "Probably our awful weather." More seriously, he continued. "Probably no foreigners perceived we had anything of wealth initially. And when they found our crystal and Cryptal cloth were valuable, it was clear that colonisation would not give them access to those things."

"Astonishing. Truly astonishing. Never heard of Si'Empra, you know. Never heard of this place until our Holy Father – that's the Holy Father the Pope – told me your Ülrügh – he wrote the Holy Father – told me that I might be interested in coming here to answer the Ülrügh's questions about our Faith." The priest plucked at his bottom lip. "Ah. Crystal and cloth. Yes – yes. I have heard of this and your little museum –" he waved in the direction of the library's museum "– I wandered through – displays these valuables. But these are now gone. You no longer produce these. I am not clear why. Is this some art you have lost?"

"Yes." Pedro did not elaborate. If the priest had not been told about Cryptals and Crystalmakers then Pedro thought it wise not to be the one to do so; there was always some danger that he would be overheard or the priest would innocently repeat the information and its source. Pedro always guarded his tongue. He had promised Constance that he would look to Chrystal's safety and the only way he could do so was to stay quiescent in his role in the Serai.

Father Augustine studied Pedro for some time, pulling at his lip. "Hmmm," he rumbled at length. "There is some history here that is of a delicate nature. Each time I ask about it, there is a silence – except the Ülrügh who becomes quite agitated and assures me that evil has had a hand.

"But, let that rest for the time being. Tell me how you and Lian Chithra come to speak such excellent Spanish when most others I meet confine me to attempting speech in English – or, even more horrifying, attempting to understand this impossible language you all speak."

Pedro's smile broadened. Father Augustine was not the first foreigner he had heard complain about the Si'Empran language: the tones and unusual declensions tripped up those who attempted to learn, and were intensely fascinating to visiting linguists. The language had evolved over the years to incorporate some of the melody of the Crystalmaker language, who had, in turn, adopted their tones from the Cryptals.

"I was most fortunate. When I was a child, there was a foreign tutor who was able to give lessons in both English and Spanish. Some of us enjoyed the challenge of learning more than one second language. Some of us have taken Spanish names in that tutor's honour."

"You shared a class with Lian Chithra? But – she has a title and not you?"

"Titles signify membership of the Lianthem – or being family of the Ülrügh. Many lessons, however, were available to all Si'Emprans regardless of family background."

"Ah. You are not a member of the Lianthem – obviously, obviously."

"No. But, especially when I was growing up, most classes were available to all who cared to join them. My parents were goat herders. They had a home near the town of Sinthén, where Si'Empra's leather works are carried out. As I child I spent winters in Si'Em City with an aunt and uncle while my parents overwintered in our home with our goats – they housed the goats in a grotto adjoining our home.

"Does the Lianthem appoint the Ülrügh?"

"Confirms the appointment. Usually an Ülrügh names his or her successor. The Lianthem, in theory, has the power to appoint anyone it so wishes, or dismiss an Ülrügh. It may have happened in our history, I don't know. Generally, an Ülrügh will train his or her successor, just as members of the Lianthem train those they think will succeed them."

"So. It's sort of like an aristocracy. And generally people of Si'Empra are happy with that?

"Yes. Yes they are." The question made Pedro think, though. It did not often occur to him to question the right of the Lianthem to direct the fortunes of Si'Empra. He sometimes believed the Lianthem had lost their way but never thought about challenging their right to rule.

"Hmmm." The priest returned to his wandering among the bookshelves, disappearing into an opposite aisle. Pedro continued his own search for the literature that might help him in the task the Ülrügh and Lian Chithra had set for him.

"What amazes me, though," the priest said, his voice carrying from the other side of the shelves, "is I cannot discern your native religion – I wonder whether your crystal and cloth – I just wonder if that is something to do with it."

Pedro reached up to a high shelf for a copy of a treatise on the Christian Bible and added it to the pile of similar books already on his arm. "You think I should start by translating the Gospel according to St John?"

"Hmm?" Father Augustine's head popped out at the end of Pedro's aisle. He stared quizzically at Pedro for a second. "Yes. Yes." He rounded the corner and returned to Pedro's side, giving his head a single sharp nod so that his reading glasses dropped on to his prominent nose. "That would be very much appreciated. My observation is that Si'Emprans are a gentle people. Lessons of love come out most clearly in St John's Gospel. Of course, in time, it will be necessary to translate the entire Bible."

The priest reached up for his glasses. He used forefinger and thumb – other fingers held stiffly out of the way – to set the glasses more firmly on to the bridge of his nose. He looked over the top of his glasses at Pedro. "I understand that you have been directed away from your duties as a teacher to undertake this task. Will this cause problems in the school?"

Yes, Pedro wanted to say. *We are short of teachers this year – especially teachers who are willing to teach those who cannot pay.* "I will try to continue at least some of my teaching duties," he said.

"Good. I am much obliged to you – delighted to work with such a learned man."

Pedro inclined his head slightly and moved along the rows of shelves towards the librarian to check out his books.

"That cake's done," Müther said.

Richard and Elthán looked up from the board game they were playing. Greçia glanced over her shoulder to the small oven Richard had made for her. "I think it might need a little longer," she said. "It will still be soft in the middle." She bent her head over Müther's foot again, carefully trimming another toenail, and checking for sores and bruises. Müther liked to move independently but the result was frequent injuries.

"You know she doesn't like it too dry," Müther persisted after a short silence.

Greçia and Elthán chuckled. Müther bristled. "I don't care whether she likes it dry or not. I just don't like to listen to you fussing about not making it the way she likes it!" she snapped.

"Oooh, you are so grouchy!" Greçia teased. She pulled a sock over the foot in her lap, and then a shoe. "I'll check the pudding."

An ongoing pleasure for Elthán, whenever she visited Greçia's home, was the opportunity to enjoy the wide variety of dishes Greçia produced. The doctor enjoyed cooking any kind of food and delighted in catering for a crowd, which she often did in winter. At Ellen's suggestion, Elthán had consulted Greçia when drawing up the list of produce Norm Tucker was to procure. "She will be more aware of foods available in foreign lands," Ellen had advised. Greçia had taken the opportunity to include a few luxury items, most being for making a range of sweets Elthán had never dreamt could exist. Although they all enjoyed what Greçia produced, Ellen displayed a shameless appetite for the sweets.

"Does your mouth still hurt, Müther?" Elthán asked, as she studied the board to plan her next move.

"It's fine," Müther muttered. Elthán glanced up in time to see the bulge in Müther's cheek as her tongue explored the gap that, until a few days ago, had held a painful tooth. Müther had objected strenuously to having yet another tooth extracted, but Greçia insisted. There were now four teeth missing in Müther's mouth.

"Ah!" Greçia said, "I've just figured out why you are so grouchy. Your assistant has been ill and you've had to put up with the much poorer quality of service that Richard and I can give you."

"She is not my assistant!"

"Oh come now," Greçia laughed. "You have her at your beck and call every waking hour. Sometimes she goes hoarse reading to you."

"I have never complained about you or Richard–"

"You complain that our English isn't good–"

"I do not!"

"Richard," Greçia appealed. "How often does your mother complain when we try to read all those complicated things to her?"

"I confess that Lian Ellen is a much better reader than I am," Richard said, his tone carefully neutral, though his smile made it obvious that he was enjoying the banter.

"Why, Müther, I've even had you lose your temper with me when I can't pronounce some of the words!" continued Greçia.

"I have not – I only ask for a repetition –"

"Child!" Greçia screeched in imitation of Müther's voice. "You have come across that word now ten times. Why torture me with your deficient memory!"

Elthán laughed. Müther scowled. "Your memory serves you better on some matters than others," she growled. "I cannot remember such a time."

Greçia also laughed. "Ah. Come on. Cheer up. This pudding is not only the way Lian Ellen likes it; it is the way you like it. Now that the tooth isn't there any more, you'll be able to enjoy it even more."

As she talked, Greçia loaded a tray with a mug of hot chocolate, a plate of cheese, dried fruit and flatbread, and a bowl containing a large slice of steaming, self-saucing chocolate pudding.

She handed the tray to Elthán. "Try to persuade Lian Ellen to eat the other food before devouring the pudding."

A strong whiff of goats flooded the room. Müther's nose twitched. "How that boy can tell there's food on the table from where he sits, I do not know," she grumbled.

Phan shuffled into the room, letting the heavy curtain that separated the living area from the goats' winter grotto swing back across the entrance. Phan preferred to spend his days with the goats. His bed and a chair were tucked behind a small enclosure in one corner of the goat pen close to where Rosa had settled herself to hibernate the winter away. Under the light of a naked bulb, he spent his days either lying on the bed flipping through picture books he seemed never to tire of, staring at Rosa, or wandering among the goats and chickens, gabbling to them in his own peculiar language.

But when food was being served, he appeared without needing to be called.

Elthán gave Phan a friendly nod as she made her way to Ellen's room. When she pushed away the curtain to the room's entrance, Ellen looked up from the book she was reading.

"You are looking much better," Elthán said as she placed the tray on the bedside table, shifting aside a battery-powered lamp and glass of water as she did so.

The bedside table and the bed on which Ellen sat – propped up into a corner, with her legs drawn up under the bedcover and a shawl over her shoulders – were the only items of furniture in the tiny room that had previously been Müther's bedroom. The bed was actually a wide shelf at about waist-height, cantilevered off the wall. Although the shelf ran the full width of the room, it had been barely wide or long enough for Müther. Ellen's smaller frame fitted it better; Ellen stored her few personal items under the shelf. Since moving into the room, she had pasted up pictures taken out of the numerous magazines accumulated in Greçia's home: a map of the world, a three-page foldout of a forest with a backdrop of mountains, and pictures of dogs, cats, birds and flowers. There was also one that Elthán particularly liked of a spider web sparkling with dew; Ellen had pasted it near a small air vent so that it shivered from time to time in the flow of air.

"Aah." Ellen eyed the contents of the tray. "This looks lovely. Thank you. I was thinking of getting up to see if I could persuade Greçia to give me some of her excellent food."

"Greçia said I was to encourage you to eat everything else before the pudding," Elthán said, settling on the bed.

Ellen reached for the plate with the flatbread. "I've heard that instruction so often through my life that I have taken to believing people actually mean to say bon appétit."

"Which means?"

"Something like: 'eat with good appetite.'"

"I think Greçia's instruction actually means you should concentrate more on healthy foods rather than picking out the sweet nibbles."

"I shall do as instructed." Ellen shifted the cheese and berries on to the flatbread and rolled the bread into a tight tube.

"Your mother used to despair about your eating habits, you know. Pedro tells me that your love of sweet things motivated you to become a thief."

Ellen took a bite of the roll. In a rather coy but formal tone, she said: "It was most fortuitous that I had the benefit of learning how to steal sweets from a most adept thief when my need to disobey my mother's strict dietary requirements was at its peak."

"Your English teacher?"

"He was a good thief and a good English tutor. I enjoyed his three years of tutorship more than the lessons of many other tutors."

"He was the one who took three virigins with him when he left Si'Empra, wasn't he?"

"Mmm. Virigins were not the only things that he took from the Serai." Ellen lifted the mug of hot chocolate.

Elthán watched her granddaughter carefully sip the thick, hot liquid. She felt a wave of affection for the girl – this most enigmatic of girls. "You know that I was reproached by both Thil and Guild Master Joosthin for letting you loose on the Guild Masters?"

Ellen's eyebrows arched. "They said you let me loose on the Guild Masters?"

"Words to that effect."

"Ah." One shoulder lifted in a dismissive shrug. "They had only themselves to blame," she murmured, taking another bite of the cheese roll.

"I don't think they really knew what to expect," Elthán said.

"Well, they should have done a little more investigation before talking with me then." She examined the end of the roll for a second, and murmured: "The Guild Master of Memory."

Elthán waited for more but Ellen simply continued to eat in silence, interspersing mouthfuls of cheese roll with sips of hot chocolate.

"Thil also asked me how it was that you had a glasaur."

"And what did you tell him?"

"What your mother told me. She said that you often wandered the tunnels under the Serai and once you found an egg."

"Yes. It was funny how I found that egg. It was just sitting there, in the middle of the tunnel like I was meant to find it and pick it up."

"I think the Cryptals meant you to find it."

"So you think Cryptals put it there?"

"Of course the Cryptals put it there. Glasaurs are Cryptal creatures, as you well know. And I think they meant you to find it."

"Me? I mean I love Rosa, but why would the Cryptals want me to have a glasaur? Perhaps they actually meant Redel to find it. Sometimes he used the tunnels too, you know. That would make more sense. Well, it would make sense if they were trying to make friends with Skyseekers because he's the one they should be trying to make friends with. He always thought he should be the one to have a glasaur."

"Did he ever try to own Rosa?"
Ellen nodded.
"She wouldn't of course. Glasaurs bond with the first person they see when they hatch, which just happened to be me."
"But Redel was jealous."
Again Ellen nodded. "It was a bit unpleasant, actually. It got so I pretended I didn't own Rosa. Then, when father died, he tried to kill –" Ellen's voice trailed away and her eyes fastened intently on the end of the cheese roll.
"How?"
"Um – Lian Isoldé stopped him."
"How?"
Ellen took a while to answer, the rise and fall of her chest seeming more constricted. "Well," she said slowly. "I was out of my room and Redel must have come to see me. Rosa was in the garden – she wasn't grown up yet. I heard her screaming and raced to the garden to find out what was wrong. Redel was on top of her, pulling out feathers. I tried to stop him but – he –" Ellen gave a tiny, almost imperceptible shake of her head "– he's stronger than me. And –" again the tiny shake of her head "– and, anyway, Lian Isoldé just appeared in the garden. He's always been a bit scared of her – you know – she does and says odd things – even though she's his grandmother. Anyway, she – she told him in this sort of weird voice that Rosa's death would be his death. Since then he's left her alone. But Rosa's still scared of him." Ellen drew in a deep breath. She lifted her eyes to look into Ellen's, her expression a little too nonchalant to be convincing.

And what else happened in that garden? Elthán wondered.

Ellen placed the last of the cheese roll into her mouth, chewed and swallowed. She glanced at the still-steaming bowl of pudding. "May I now begin on the pudding, do you think?"

"Perhaps you should eat the last of the berries. You've missed some on the plate."

"I'll sprinkle them on the pudding." Ellen picked up the berries one by one and pressed them carefully into the sticky chocolate sauce covering the pudding, licking her fingers when she had finished doing so.

"Guild Master Joosthin tells me that you made a pact with the Cryptals."

Ellen stopped in the act of putting the first spoonful into her mouth.

"Ah." She pulled down a corner of her mouth, giving Elthán a swift, rather guilty look. "Well. Yes. I did say that to the Guild Masters. It seemed like the right thing to say at the time." Her lips closed over the spoon and she sucked the pudding into her mouth.

"So there was no pact?" The information, when Elthán had shared it with other Webcleaners, had radiated a buzz of excited speculation.

"No. No. Of course not. I can't make a pact with Cryptals. I can't understand them. I was a bit astonished the Guild Masters believed me. Mind you, the only truth they seemed to be worried about was whether Rosa existed."

"You have a glib tongue."

"So I've been told – more than once." Ellen stared for a quiet second at the bowl of pudding on her lap. "This time my tongue did nearly land a lot of people in a lot of trouble." She gave a little giggle, as if the memory gave her guilty, childish pleasure.

"From where I stand, you rescued a lot of people with remarkable skill."

"Oh, not really. I was lucky Norm Tucker is such a greedy man and that the Guild Masters ended up having big egos."

"Ego?"

"Oh they didn't want to deal with someone who wasn't as high and mighty as they are. So I made sure I was just as high and mighty as them." Ellen flashed Elthán a grin. "When you're the daughter of an Ülrügh you get to learn how to act high and mighty."

Ellen's tone became more serious. "But I got to wondering, Elthán, do Crystalmakers depend on you entirely for food?"

"The Order commands Webcleaners serve the larger Crystalmaker community in whatever way the community commands."

"The Order? Oh yes – I remember now. We didn't get to learn much about Crystalmakers and Cryptals, you know. Except Pedro and mother used to tell me some things. They said they'd tell me more but –" A small shudder twitched Ellen's shoulders. With the same tiny head shake of dismissal she had made when talking about the incident with Redel, she fixed her attention on the bowl in her hands. Her face clouded and her lips formed into a soft pout. "It's gone!" she muttered. She lifted the mug to her lips and her disappointment deepened. "It's finished." She set the mug on to the tray, and began to carefully scrape up sugary pudding residue from the bowl.

"Ellen, these past few days you have been quite sick with your periods. Greçia tells me that this would not be unusual for you. You are often alone for many weeks. How do you cope?"

The passage of the spoon over the plate faltered.

"I'm fine."

"It wasn't the question I asked–"

"You know, my father would not have been pleased with how I've done things lately. Everything to him was a negotiation. He'd say to me things like: 'How could you have handled it better? How could you have got more from such and such a person? What did that person really want?' He would drive me crazy." She set the pudding bowl on the tray. "But in the end I got to see that getting something was like a game: read what people really want, know what you really want, and find a way to strip out things like your own prejudices that might get in the way of reaching an agreement."

My question is being diverted. Is denial then more tolerable for her? Perhaps it is. Elthán decided not to press for an answer, instead taking up the topic Ellen had offered: "I believe that your father had plans for you to follow in his footsteps."

"Oh! By the BlackŌne's beard! Quite apart from the fact that I couldn't think of anything more utterly tedious, can you imagine what would happen? Si'Empra would rock from one impetuous disaster to another."

"You think Redel is a good Ülrügh?"

"I think that the Lianthem is made up of self-serving individuals who should do their job and see to the proper governance of Si'Empra."

"And Redel?"

"If the Lianthem is unhappy with Redel they should guide him in a different way. At present, it would appear that it suits the Lianthem not to change a system that is currently benefiting them."

"That is quite an insight, Ellen. But Redel – do you bear him no animosity? He has–"

"I think that was the best chocolate pudding I have ever tasted. I hope Greçia can make lots more chocolate pudding. I liked the cheesecake she made, too. She's a really good cake maker. The good part is that she likes people to enjoy her cooking. I'm so glad she added all those ingredients to the list we gave Norm Tucker. Do you think you could persuade her to give me another slice?" Ellen held the pudding bowl out to Elthán, gaze averted.

Elthán shifted herself off the bed, taking the pudding plate. "I'll see what I can do."

Greçia placed another slice of pudding into the bowl, one eyebrow lifted in silent query. Elthán shrugged a little to indicate that she did not want to say anything in front of Müthor and Richard.

"Greçia says that you would be better off having another cheese roll," Elthán lied as she gave Ellen the second helping of pudding and took her seat on the bed again.

"Of course I would be," Ellen said. The uncertainty that had overcome her just minutes before seemed to have vanished. Unabashedly, she picked up a tiny portion of the pudding on her spoon and, with laughing eyes, licked it into her mouth. "I have this vision of turning into a fat jelly-like person, all toothless but with chocolate permanently staining my lips."

"A little more fat on your bones would not go astray."

"Doubtless a winter in Greçia's care will do that. I increasingly find myself scheming of ways to tie myself permanently to her kitchen."

"Well. Staying here might be an option for you. Müther has survived here all these years."

"I hadn't really thought much further than chocolate pudding and cheesecake."

"I would like you to join us for the summer."

"I don't know. I have got into the habit of doing all sorts of things in summer. I have an idea that I might become something like a wandering minstrel – only I'll take care in future not to be meddling one. Maybe in winter this is the best place for me. It would appear that I can make myself useful with Müther, and she teaches me a lot."

"A wandering – minstrel? What is that?"

"Just a storyteller. You know, someone who just wanders around bringing news and stories from place to place. There are some villages around Si'Empra that are just about permanently isolated nowadays, so I'll just visit them and let them know about one another. Sometimes, with a bit of news, they can help one another and that way the Lianthem can't take everything from them. And the children – and even some adults – like stories I make up. It's fun."

"Fun?" Elthán felt that the conversation had become somewhat surreal. "Fun? Is that all you dream of? After what you have been subjected to? After what Constance has been subjected to? Si'Empra is suffering–"

Ellen set her spoon firmly down into the bowl. She fixed Elthán with a glare.

"We are back at this point again, aren't we! I can do nothing about my past except avoid the same circumstances. I got some very good advice once: not to bury myself in things I can do nothing about. So I also choose not to talk about or consider things that are impossible."

"Ellen that is—"

"And so we will talk about other things."

She commands me, Elthán thought. *This child whose ambition is merely to be a minstrel commands me – and expects to be obeyed.* She met Ellen's green-eyed stare, then nodded curtly. "Very well. I have another question you might find less challenging. Why did you mention the Guild Master of Memory earlier?"

"Did I? Oh yes." Ellen relaxed back into her corner. "There is something about her that I don't understand – and neither, I think, do the other Guild Masters. Her reactions – it is almost as if sometimes she reacts to issues that are other than the ones that people around her are dealing with."

"She is, of course, the one who has the best knowledge. Not only is she the Guild Master of Memory – the one entrusted with preserving who we are – she is also the only Guild Master alive today who was Guild Master at The Destruction."

"Mmm. I understand. But I suspect something else is going on in her mind. Anyway, no concern of mine. Can I ask you something?"

"Of course."

"No one speaks of Richard's father. Is there a reason for this?"

"Ah. Mother has always been silent on the subject."

"Do you mind sharing your speculation?"

Elthán shrugged. "Maybe one of Briani's men? When Pedro was asked to move to the Serai to take on a role as tutor, a couple of men came to help him with the move. Greçia had already moved into here, so Pedro had arranged for her to care for Phan and Müther. But Greçia, as you know, goes to her clinic almost every day. One day she returned to find one of the men in the house. He claimed Pedro had asked him to pick up something. A lie, of course; Pedro would never – and did not – do that."

"He assaulted Müther?"

Again Elthán shrugged. "So we think. He might have found her when he broke into the grotto."

"Greçia found Müther with him?"

"No. It took us a few days to find Müther and Phan. They were hiding way up the slope above the grotto. Both were in a distressed state. Müther has only ever told us that Phan rescued her. About what happened before the rescue, she would not say. Nine months later she gave birth to Richard."

"Interesting. Well, whoever the father, Müther has certainly mothered a remarkable son."

"Ah – yes – on that we can agree. And clever – but in a different way to his mother. He has always had a fascination with all things mechanical and electrical. When Pedro lived here, we relied entirely on hot ground water for cooking and oil for lighting. Richard has managed to construct many more appliances.

"You know, Ellen," continued, Elthán. "Those two, Müther and Richard, sometimes I feel they are – how do I say this – they are here with us but only on loan. They really belong – especially Müther – they belong with their own people."

Ellen nodded. "Yes. It is sad. I hope that the Lianthem does sort itself out."

The Lianthem! Elthán sighed inwardly as she gathered the emptied dishes on to the tray. *I have much less faith in the Lianthem than you apparently do, granddaughter.*

CHAPTER 24
Pedro's Room

*I*T WAS LATE INTO the evening when Marthin bid his four pupils a good night. They left the gymnasium, talking excitedly about what they had learnt. Marthin watched them go, his mood the antithesis of theirs, and started slowly toward his rooms.

He did not like the task the Ülrügh had given him: "You are most skilled at weaponry, Marthin. You are to pass on those skills to my adjutants."

In his youth, Marthin had enjoyed his lessons in weaponry. Ülrügh Briani had engaged a huge, muscled, black man from a place called South Africa to teach a number of eager young men the many aspects of physical and violent engagement. Marthin had been mesmerised by the mercenary's stories of battles and wars, of the hard men and women who endured against incredible odds to win victories against evil enemies. Marthin had excelled as much in the lessons on battle strategy as he had in hand-to-hand combat and how to wield a range of weapons. At the time he had not thought anything about his teacher's capacity to speak of killing as if it were a mere technicality; he had not thought about the actual act of killing until he witnessed how cold a person's heart had to be to kill another human. He would never forget the agony that murder – slow murder –

caused another person. He had witnessed the torture inflicted on Lian Grace. It was long ago but sometimes it felt as if he were just returning from that evening at The Shoals. He lived daily with the guilt of his own impotence on that day.

Sometimes he thought that his bond with Mary was the only thing that stopped him from despairing altogether about the shallowness of his existence. He thought that taking on the position as City Steward would shield him from being involved ever again from having to decide on the fate of another human being – except in ways that would help them, such as creating the conditions for the poor to use the Layamlé for shelter in winter.

The Ülrügh's demand that he teach weaponry to the young adjutants was a truly unsavoury burden!

Jon, Lian Chithra's assistant, rounded a corner and hurried toward him. "I've been looking for you. Lian Chithra would like you to unlock Pedro's rooms."

"Oh? And the purpose?"

"I was instructed by Lian Chithra to find out about his progress with translation work. But he won't open the door. She said to find you and that you should investigate where he is."

"He is not at the games?"

"No. No. I just checked. I myself would like to go to the games. The Ülrügh is playing again – and Luman is too."

Marthin nodded. He wanted to go to his own rooms and be with Mary. She had responded well to the latest treatment and, though weak, was good company. But he held the master key and had sole authority to do as Jon asked. "I will find Pedro and – translations you say?"

"Yes. Lian Chithra would like to know about his progress on the translations."

"I assume he will know what she means?"

"Perhaps I should stay with you."

Marthin shrugged. "If you like. But I am capable of delivering a message to her after I speak with Pedro."

"Thank you, Marthin. Most obliged."

Marthin turned off the path to his private rooms and made his way through hallways and upstairs to the Serai and Pedro's door. He knocked, received no answer and used his master key.

The room was empty and dark. Marthin closed the door behind him, switched on a light and looked around: it was a small room containing only a bed, an armchair, a wardrobe, shelving, and a desk and chair. Most of the shelves were crammed with books and folders. An older style computer – monitor pushed to the back of the desk, keyboard almost buried under a sheaf of paper – dominated the desk space; a box-like hard drive whirred softly under the desk. A book lay open on a cleared edge of the desk. Books also lay open on the neatly made, narrow single bed. A printer sat on a shelf just above the computer with a wad of pages in its out tray.

Marthin turned to the faint sound of a radio. The sound came from behind a door next to the wardrobe. He knocked on the door and received no answer. His several master keys did not fit the lock. He considered forcing the door but decided to wait.

IN THE REST IN which Elthán had rescued Ellen some months before, Pedro lay on a wide bench with his legs stretched out before him and his back propped up against a wall. Elthán lay in his arms, her head nestled against his shoulder. As he listened to her talking about Ellen, he rubbed his cheek over the top of her head, enjoying the feel of her soft hair and the warmth of her body against his. He breathed in her Crystalmaker scent, long used to its bitterness and even enjoying it: it was the smell of the love of his life; the smell he longed for as he worked through each day at the Serai and in classrooms, always careful to guard his tongue and his actions.

"She is such a contradiction." Elthán was still agitated even though her conversation with Ellen had been more than a week ago. "What is this nonsense about being a minstrel! Even while she's telling me she wants to be a frivolous storyteller, she's commanding me like she has the authority to do so. She should be turning her mind—"

"My love." Pedro moved Elthán in his arms so he could look into her mauve eyes. He kissed the tightness out of her lips and she responded, her hand coming up to tangle in his short, greying curls.

"My love," he repeated, when she relaxed back into his arms again. "Let Ellen work out for herself what to do with her life. Even as a very small child, Ellen has done what she wants to do. Neither Ülrügh Briani nor Constance could do more than guide her. If you push her, she will push back."

"Pedro! She is in self-denial. She does this thing of talking about something different when she doesn't want to answer a question about herself. It is childish behaviour!"

"She is barely more than a child. For all her apparent confidence and abundant talents, she *is* barely more than a child."

"But *minstrel*, Pedro. What a waste!"

"She visits people in villages and they welcome her. She feels wanted and appreciated. Undoubtedly it is something that gives meaning to her life and she feels safer wandering from village to village than being at the Serai."

"Safe! She goes and visits a village to do this minstrel business and confronts this tax collector. Next thing we know, she's confronting the Guild Masters and getting foreigners involved in our affairs."

Pedro chuckled. "The fact that she says one thing but does another is just evidence that she is behaving like many of her age when they try to give meaning to their lives." More seriously, he said: "Ülrügh Briani, I think, meant to live his dream through Ellen to bring Si'Empra's peoples together again."

"Well that's a dream disappeared."

"Ülrügh Briani was not as clever or as bloody as his father. He made the mistake of alienating Redel while promoting Ellen."

"Redel probably deserved to be disliked by his father."

"You don't mean that," he murmured into her hair. "It is painful for anyone not to have the love and approval of a parent."

"Pedro, you are talking about someone who butchers my people and rapes his sister – not to mention what he did to Müther."

To that Pedro had no response. Pedro held Elthán more closely. He was not a tall man but she was small and he easily fitted his slim frame around hers.

"Anyway, getting back to the topic of Ellen. It would be much easier for everyone if she would be honest about her physical and mental state. For a start, Greçia would find it much easier to doctor her if she would talk about her health problems."

Pedro pressed his lips onto the top of her head. "I would love to be able to hold you in my arms every day and feel your warmth in bed with me every night," he murmured into her ear. "But I know up here," he tapped himself on the temple, "that it is not possible. I cannot live where you live and you cannot live where I do. We make do with stolen moments like these. Inside we both hope there will be a day when we are more together. Perhaps Ellen is also drifting along, doing the best that she can."

"I'm saying that she should let people help her."

"Help her? Here is a girl who the whole of Si'Empra used to idolise. She was athletic, fun and talented. She could charm young and old alike. Her father dies and her world is turned upside down: she develops a debilitating condition that saps at her strength and her brother abuses her. BlackŌne's beard, Elthán! She was on the brink of losing who she is. Give her the space to work it all out and don't push her – everyone wants her to be something, and she is not sure she can be or wants to be anything at all."

Elthán studied him a while, probably wondering at the passion in his tone. Finally, she said: "Perhaps you are right. Perhaps her confusing words and behaviour are a reflection of her inner confusion. But, this past summer I have not asked her to do anything but stay safe, yet I have spent a fair bit of time at her beck and call while she creates dangerous conditions for herself and, may I say, others. She recognises it, too! And she giggles about it, as if it's some game she's narrowly won."

When Pedro, after a pause, did not respond, she continued: "But I do hear what you say and, truth be told, I do hope that she will help us create a better future. I certainly think that the Cryptals have designs on her. I've never seen them attend to another human in the way they do to her – even after The Destruction, they seemed only to herd us into a safe place and then leave us to fend for ourselves. I don't think they are the sort of creatures that practice altruism."

The word 'altruism' rolled around in Pedro's mind.

Altruism. Justice. Equity. Fairness. He thought of the many contented hours he had spent of late with Father Augustine. They had discussed such concepts: long philosophical discussions that exercised the mind with complicated questions and complex answers. Sometimes they had considered the role of hate, greed and lust, but rarely did they recognise the simple fact that, in daily life, altruism, justice, equity, fairness were overlaid by a combination of past disappointments, fear, aspiration, expectation, hope, desire and love.

And Cryptals? They were another issue again. Who knew what social rhythm they lived by.

"Life is a complex weave," Pedro sighed. With another kiss to the top of Elthán's head, he adjusted his position so that she sat up.

"I will make pendle for us to drink and I have brought with me a couple of berry rolls a pupil gave me in lieu of payment for lessons. I will tell you about a priest who is staying with us this winter and who is apparently on a mission – at the insistence of the Ülrügh – to convert us all to some form of Christianity. I'm not exactly sure why the Ülrügh would like us to be Christians, but it appears to be his latest plan to improve the lives of us all. Then I would like you to tell me in detail about Ellen's meeting with the Guild Masters."

He brewed some pendle in a crystal pot and set out glasses and plates on a small table. Elthán took a seat at the table and he sat close to her. She listened with interest to Pedro's account of the priest as she prepared their refreshments, it was clear she did not understand the meaning of Christianity. She finally agreed with Pedro that Redel's engagement of the priest seemed a strange thing.

"He seems like a nice man, anyway," she said, then she told Pedro about Ellen's meeting with the Guild Masters and the landing of provisions by the sailors.

"I have not met this person, Norm Tucker," Elthán said. "But everything I've heard about him makes me suspicious of him. Ellen left Richard in charge of the transactions at the landing. I think she did it because she didn't want to meet the man again, though she said she had other things to do with these villagers that she apparently promised a part of the cargo to."

"If I may venture, my love, I suspect that Ellen was sensitive to the fact that she had managed to arrange such a large shipment when Richard had not. By having Richard manage the landing, she made him a party to the process."

"Ah, I didn't think of that. Do you really think that she thinks of things like that?"

"Depend upon it: she does. But tell me, now that Trebiath is once again occupied, do Webcleaners have a little more freedom in Illiath?"

"No. Illiath is the domain of the Guild of Memory and we remain thralls."

"How goes it with Müther?"

"She misses you. Ellen is showing herself to be adept at many of Müther's most treasured activities – though Müther shows scant appreciation. She is very suspicious of Ellen. I'm not exactly sure why. She tells me that anyone from the line of Devi is touched with madness and she isn't ready to believe that Ellen won't turn out to be mad as well."

Pedro gave a little huff of surprise. "I wonder how she juggles that! There is a strong line of mental instability in her family."

Elthán shrugged. "I don't know. Müther is sometimes unfathomable to me. But, as I said, Müther misses your mind. In spite of her best efforts to encourage Richard into philosophising, he is more interested in tinkering with his machines than taking part in esoteric discussions with his mother, and she never invites Ellen to discuss issues with her."

Pedro had a clear picture in his mind of the cosy room in his old home. He saw Müther, Greçia, Richard, Elthán, Ellen and Phan – and perhaps a Crystalmaker or two – sitting at the long table in the open kitchen area, warm drinks in their hands, treats on a plate in the centre, banter on their lips. In his loneliest hours he wished himself back in that grotto – even given the constant danger he had faced harbouring Müther and Crystalmakers.

As if reading his thoughts, Elthán asked: "Have you ever thought of leaving here and returning to us?"

"Often. But it would not increase the safety of Greçia and I would probably only become another fugitive mouth to feed. Besides, as long as I am at the Serai I can support Katherina and her care of our little granddaughter."

"How is Chrystal? Is she like Ellen?"

"No. Not at all." Pedro's eyes softened as he smiled. "She is much more timid and shy – though wilful at the same time. She has a good set of lungs and can throw exceptional tantrums."

"Poor Katherina! As patient as always, I suppose."

"Katherina adores her. She misses Ellen horribly but attends to Chrystal's every need with all the love she has such a generous amount of."

"And what of Redel and Chrystal?"

Pedro's smile vanished. "He is possessive of Chrystal. He makes me uneasy the way he treats her."

"That man should take a wife!"

"He shows no interest in women. Never has. Even when he married Constance, the word was that he only did it out of pity for her. Nowadays he seems not even to be able to bear touching women. He seems to have even lost interest in the winter games. He turns up every now and then and plays a game, but he's apparently been suffering from headaches."

"He is a headache! Constance only offered herself to him on the condition he left Ellen alone. He didn't keep his end of the bargain," Elthán muttered.

Pedro put his hand over hers. "Let's not talk of Redel. Tell me, instead, how Müther's school is going."

"Good. Good. Ah. Listen to this," she said with a small laugh. "Thil tells me that when he saw Ellen reading and writing he understood why Skyseekers were such terrible people. The Guild Masters – even Guild Master Joosthin – persist in this myth about how corrupting reading and writing is."

Pedro gripped her hand, worry furrowing his brow. "You will be careful, Elthán. Until the Guild Masters change their attitude, the skills and learning the Webcleaners are gaining from Müther is dangerous."

"I just can't see how it can be dangerous."

"Because, as I have explained before, the source of Crystalmaker knowledge from generation to generation, is, at present, in the power of the Guild Masters. By teaching people how to read and write, such knowledge, potentially, becomes available to everyone. Not only might the Guild Masters lose their bases of authority, there is a chance that people will abuse the knowledge."

"They don't hold any knowledge about Webcleaners," she muttered, but she promised Pedro – again, as she had many times before – that the Webcleaners would be careful.

Pedro only dared to stay a couple of hours before saying goodbye. Elthán promised to be in the Rest for some more days and hoped he would be able to visit again. "There are many webs to clean here," she smiled at him. "Webcleaners don't often come to this place."

"Only you," he told her. "And that is enough for me."

He hurried back along the tunnels – past the sealed entrance to the room that had belonged to Constance – to the entrance of his own room. He pressed a depression on the rock wall and heard a soft scrape as a stone slab slipped out of its groove. He pushed one end lightly and it swung smoothly inward, revealing an opening barely half-a-metre square, and letting in sound and light from his bathroom. Quickly, he stripped off his protective overgarments and laid them over a rail near the entrance, crawled through the opening and closed it behind him. It sealed so tightly it was almost impossible to find. It was the same technology used at Greçia's grotto – something the Cryptals knew how to make.

For extra security, he shifted a towel rack over the entrance. He removed his clothes, dropped them into a soapy bucket already prepared with suds, and showered. He washed himself entirely and well. Dogs only needed one molecule of mylin to start barking their warning. He rinsed and re-rinsed his clothes before hanging them up to dry. For good measure he dropped the towel he had just used into a bucket to wash with his next load of clothing.

At last he turned off the radio, unlatched the door and opened it.

He flicked off the bathroom light at the same moment that he saw the light to his bedroom was on and that Marthin sat in the armchair looking at him.

Pedro's face paled as his hand froze on the light switch.

"A long time in the bathroom," Marthin remarked after a laden silence.

"You startled me. I didn't expect someone to be in my room."

"I imagine not. Jon came to find me. Lian Chithra sent him on an errand about translations."

"I must have missed him. I – I was having a shower and washing clothes."

"I noticed; a shower behind a locked door in a bathroom contained in a locked room. This seems like many locks – and one that is unnecessary for a private bathroom."

Pedro made no comment to Marthin's observation.

Marthin pushed himself out of the lounge. "What shall I tell Lian Chithra about translations?"

Pedro took the three steps to his desk, leaving open the bathroom door in case Marthin wanted to look in. He took the pages off the printer's out tray. "I have completed the first part of the translation. Perhaps Lian Chithra would like to read it to comment. I did not find the task an easy one and her proficiency is greater than mine."

Marthin took the pages. "I will relay the message." He turned to leave but paused, one hand on the door handle. "I have waited a long time in this room and I believe that Jon also waited some time for you. Shall I tell the Chancellor that my wait was for you to complete this translation and that you simply did not hear Jon at your door because at the time you were showering?"

He knows. He knows. Chill sweat coursed down Pedro's spine. "As you wish."

Marthin eyed him directly. "Is that the story we shall both tell?"

"It is a good story."

Many hours later, when most of Si'Em City was asleep, Pedro locked himself in the bathroom, quietly slid the slab of stone aside and deposited a note in a small basket under the rail that held the overgarment. He and Elthán used this basket to leave each other messages and gifts. The note read: *My love, it may be some time before I can see you again. This pains me. Stay safe.*

CHAPTER 25
The Telling

THE SUN HAD NOT brightened the sky of Si'Empra for two weeks and would not do so for another two weeks. Outside the Cryptal caves, a blizzard had been raging for days, blowing snow and ice horizontally across the landscape. Inside the caves, insulated from the outer world though they were, the Crystalmakers knew instinctively that midwinter had arrived. They gathered in the Illiath audience chamber to participate in The Telling: the story of their creation.

It began:

> *We crawled from the sea*
> *Into Cryptal arms*
> *They give us our warmth*
> *They give us our light*
> *They give us our homes*
> *They give us our Order*
> *On the plateau we lived*
> *Though through all of Si'Empra*
> *Over rivers and mountains*
> *Through the winds and the rains*
> *On glasaurs we roved*

We made crystal and cloth
From hair of the Cryptal
Fashioned so fine
With dye and with skill
Virigin too
From hair of the Cryptal
With skill
Cryptal faced Cryptal
Others their quarrel
Bloody the battle
Land they divided
Our roots in the clouds
Our lives belowground
From out of the waters
The Skyseekers came
They reaped the land's bounty
Sheltered in caves
Shared what they reaped
For crystal and cloth
Cryptal our lives
Below and above
The Order is all

The beginning section of The Telling was a summary. A vast portion of the many verses of the thirty-four sections of The Telling was told over many days. However, the verses were not chanted in sequence and some were even repeated, though the ceremony always began with the summary verses. Initiates and acolytes from the Guild of Memory led the ritual. Sometimes they used tapestries, displayed only at the time of The Telling, to illustrate their verses. Some verses were chanted or sung only by the initiates or acolytes. Other verses allowed everyone's participation; wind, string and percussion instruments striking up in harmony as people sang and danced.

People came and went throughout The Telling, including Guild Masters and initiates and acolytes from the other Guilds, depending upon the call of other duties. Almost everyone participated at some time, exploring the verses with their interpretations and memories of past discussion. This was the one time of the year when Crystalmakers all gathered together in the one place – including Webcleaners – though the Webcleaners sat apart, shy and awed at being exposed. They watched and listened, sang and danced, but did so quietly and among themselves, as avid as all Crystalmakers to relearn the story of their creation.

On this fifth day of The Telling, Elthán sat among the Webcleaners: cross-legged on a mat on the floor, listening to a verse in the third section:

The Cryptals the guardians
The Order established in six equal parts
The Guilds the division
One to clothe the body
One to create our comfort
One to gladden our hearts
One to remember our words
One to give us light

She sat up straighter and listened with clinical interest to the discussion that began when the initiates finished the chant. She was disappointed to again only hear the usual acclamations by various people about how well the Guilds had performed their duties: "the furnaces of Trebiath are once more operating"; "tapestries are being repaired – oh! the glory of the oldest tapestries".

No one wondered why there were 'six equal parts' but only five Guilds.

Richard had once given Elthán a recording device and she had secretly recorded the verses. With Müther's help she had transcribed them. It had been an interesting exercise. For the first time in her life, she was able to follow the verses in their approximate sequence – though she couldn't be sure that, even after several years of recording, she had managed to record all. Müther had questioned this verse of the third section: "The second-last verse doesn't sound complete – And what are the six?"

"Cryptals, cloth, building, art, memory and crystal," Elthán replied.

Müther had muttered. "Cryptals are not a guild – why would they be one of the six?"

Müther had also wondered why there was an apparent hesitation in the final part of the fourth verse of the summary of the Telling; something that Elthán had not even noticed.

The question had stayed with Elthán – perhaps one of the lesser crafts used to be a guild: making tableware or sewing or preparing food? However, today's discussion clearly indicated that 'the six' was understood in the way she had told Müther: Cryptals being one of the six.

One verse was rarely chanted and, if so, only when most Crystalmakers had tired of The Telling and the audience chamber held relatively few people:

> *The gift of the web*
> *The cleaner renowned*
> *In service of beauty*
> *The Order to serve*

This verse was never discussed by Crystalmakers, even by Webcleaners themselves; its meaning beyond, it would seem, even the Memory Masters. But since Hochhein's creation with web threads, Elthán had begun puzzling over that verse also: could the 'beauty' be web cloth?

Elthán's thoughts were interrupted by the start of a lively song about the making of Trebiath. People jumped to their feet, buoyed because Trebiath was again an inhabited city. A thordilones struck up a chord and flutes joined in. With skips and twirls, figures danced around, singing the verse, repeating it, embellishing it and adding other verse-references to Trebiath. Then, most wondrous of all, the Guild Master of Design joined the dance with his partner, a man as lithe as himself. Others stood aside as the music lilted to a smoother sound and the pair danced the dance of the Making of the Guilds, their graceful bodies bending and flowing as they mimed the wonder of each Guild.

Small hands grasped Elthán's arm.

Elthán turned to find Josie's twisted features close to her shoulder. She smiled to see the bright excitement in the child's eyes. "Mistress," the girl said as loudly as her deformed windpipe would allow. "I am learning the notes of this dance on the thordilones. Müther and the lady with red hair are teaching me."

Elthán smiled, stroking the child's short-cropped hair with affection. "When next you are at the school and I come to visit, you will play it for me. We will all dance to your music and you will make us happy."

Josie nodded enthusiastically, nestling close to Elthán. "Perhaps Müther will sing for us. When she sings, my heart flies."

After the lively dance subsided, the initiates chose to chant from the second section of The Telling:

> *Glasaurs huge*
> *The Cryptals made*
> *Birds In splintering boats*
> *With goat and bird*
> *Skyseekers came*
> *Dark and wild*
> *Rude and crude*
> *With eyes for light*
> *And words that spat*

Of ignorance and fear
Too weak to walk the tunnels
Too strong to be ignored
And we and they did agree
Our land's bounty from their labour
Theirs warm homes in glasaur eyries
And the glasaurs all did vanish
to carry, reap and sow
Berries, seed and reed
Bulbs and root and meat

The verse prompted talk about how another glasaur now stalked above ground. Gossip buzzed around the room. With growing surprise, Elthán noted that some Crystalmakers began casting resentful glances towards the Webcleaners, who reacted by huddling into a tighter group, bewildered by the animosity.

The initiates chanted the beginning of the twenty-first section of The Telling:

The buzz of resentment increased. Every year since The Destruction, this verse raised anger and sorrow. Even from the Webcleaners around her, Elthán heard the mutters of indignation: "We agreed to let Skyseekers live on Si'Empra! They took away the glasaurs! They agreed to provide food for Crystalmakers and Cryptals. That is the agreement!"

In fact The Telling was silent on exactly why the glasaurs ceased to exist. Both Pedro and Müther wondered whether, by the time the large birds died out, Crystalmakers were so divorced from what occurred aboveground that glasaurs had become a myth anyway.

She caught snatches of muttered conversations: "Another glasaur – Webcleaners – doing Skyseeker bidding – stolen – betrayal–"

Elthán blinked, her heart startling into a faster pace as she realised that the sequence of verses being sung while she was in the hall had a pattern: they were cumulatively seeding bad feelings against Webcleaners. She raised her eyes, about to admonish herself for her suspicious mind, only to discover that the Guild Master of Memory was staring at her venomously. *For what?* she wanted to demand. *The Telling clearly declares that glasaurs are Cryptal creatures. We had nothing to do with Rosa's making.*

Elthán glanced at other Guild Masters, noting that the Guild Master of Design was also studying her, but with inquiry in his eyes and no malice. He bent his head slightly to acknowledge her.

Guild Master Joosthin, observed Elthán, was staring at the Guild Master of Memory with slightly more than his habitual scowl.

There is no agreement on the role of Webcleaners in all this, Elthán thought with bleak relief.

Eventually the discussion on glasaurs ran its course and the initiates moved to other subjects, but for the Webcleaners much of the magic of The Telling was lost for the time being. They were silent and unsure, glancing at Elthán for reassurance. She sat still, stroking Josie's hair, feeling her age with a weariness that she did not often succumb to.

Without warning, the floor heaved and roared.

Elthán threw one arm back to brace herself and curled the other protectively around Josie. Crying out in panic, those who were standing, fell; those who were seated on benches – including the Guild Masters – toppled off their seats. Shouts of confusion were drowned as the walls of the chamber flexed like a tapestry unfurling. Every surface shook for minutes that seemed like hours. Crystal sconces fractured; some fell off their housing, plunging the chamber into unfamiliar shadows. A crack tore open in the wall behind the dais and raced into the room, screaming as it rent the earth, dividing the dais in two and causing the Guild Masters to scramble out of the way. Everywhere people tumbled over each other to get away from the opening chasm.

As suddenly as the earthquake had started, it stopped. The break in the floor slammed shut with a boom, showering rock splinters into the air and over everyone in the chamber. For some seconds there was absolute silence as people held their breaths in anticipation. A large sconce behind the dais fell and shattered into thousands of pieces, spilling bright drops of phosphorescent light over the floor.

The WhiteŌne's Song flooded the room, the liquid sound soft and comforting. People began to weep with released tension. When the Song withdrew, people surged to their feet, looking to the Guild Masters for explanation.

The Guild Master of Crystal pushed himself up to standing, holding his hands out for silence.

"The WhiteŌne reveals that the quake is finished. The earth is once more in Cryptal control."

Many pressed him for questions, crowding around him for answers. Where had it started? Had there been destruction of tunnels? Would there be more quakes elsewhere?

"The WhiteŌne assures us that all is now safe. There will be no further tremors this day. Illiath is safe and Trebiath is untouched."

Elthán had not risen from her place on the floor, though she straightened up. The Webcleaners gathered around her; they had not gone to Guild Master Joosthin for information. In soft voices they asked Elthán to translate the WhiteŌne's song for them.

"The quake began in the Central Lands where the mountains are tallest. The Cryptal tunnels there have collapsed," she told them quietly so that only those nearest to her could hear. "Parts of the waterways there have also collapsed and the earth may look different when we view it at winter's end. The tremor we felt was the release of the rock's tension caused by the Cryptals to stop the quake from spreading further through this part of the land. No Crystalmaker was harmed."

Ah. Release of the rock's tension. Crystalmakers understood what that meant: it was how Cryptals controlled the island's volcanic temper. Relieved by what she told them, the Webcleaners eased away, sharing the news with others who had not been close enough to hear.

"Mistress."

Elthán lifted her head, hearing in the voice that the one who spoke was not a Webcleaner.

"Sam!" Surprised to see him, she inspected him quickly. A tic troubled the left side of his face. He looked thin and his hands were tensed into claws that he unconsciously tried to ease out by rubbing the sides of his legs as he bent down towards her. At first she thought he was about to berate her, but there was no obvious threat in his manner.

"Warmth and light, Mistress."

Elthán saw Sam's part sister, Con, standing nearby, clearly ill at ease that he was speaking to a Webcleaner in such an open way.

"Warmth and light, Sam. Are you recovering well?"

"Well enough. Thank you. I am deeply grateful for the help you insisted I should have, even though my family were so rude to you. I remember what you said even though I was not able to understand at the time."

Now Elthán was really surprised. "You are indeed a strong person, Sam."

"Do you meet with your granddaughter?"

"I see her from time to time."

"Mistress, please could you pass on my appreciation for what she did." Sam brought up a tense hand – his movements jerky – to push pale yellow hair out of his eyes. For a second his hand rested on the tic on his face before it dropped to his side again. "She encouraged me, giving me a strength to endure that I have carried with me these past months." Spittle formed at the side of his mouth and began to dribble over his chin. He wiped it away impatiently. "I will be strong again and then, Mistress, I will work with you aboveground."

"Why Sam, I think there are others who might not be so pleased with that idea."

He gave a twisted smile. "I do not know that giving others pleasure is my wish. But tell me, Mistress, can you tell me now what the WhiteŌne sang?"

"The Guild Masters interpret the WhiteŌne for Crystalmakers."

Sam cast a glance in the Guild Masters' direction. "I think you heard more, Mistress. Tell me only if those who were kind to me in my time with the Skyseekers are safe."

"Ah, Sam, that I cannot tell you. The WhiteŌne knows everything belowground but what is aboveground Cryptals must see just as we do. I can, however, tell you that the WhiteŌne sang that the glasaur is safe and I think that will mean that my granddaughter is also safe."

A hand closed over Sam's arm. "We should return to our place." Con acknowledged Elthán with a brief nod.

Sam allowed himself to be led away but he said – quite loudly: "Warmth and light, Mistress Elthán. Thank you for your news and your help."

"All I can hear is a pencil scratching," Müther complained.

At this time of winter, all Crystalmakers abandoned Müther's classes. Even the sick bay was almost empty, with only one Crystalmaker in Greçia's care, his illness nudging him closer to death with every breath. Müther had been showing signs of boredom all afternoon. Richard and Greçia had suggested various activities: reading, a game, taking dictation. Richard had even suggested another lesson on the thordilones. But Müther had rejected all suggestions, professing her desire just to sit with her thoughts, though these thoughts were interrupted by frequent vents of irritability. "If it was less vigorous it might be more bearable. Who is doing it anyway?"

As if you don't know, Ellen thought, steeling herself to be, yet again, the butt of Müther's nagging.

"I will attempt to scratch more quietly," Ellen said.

"Cup of pendle everyone?" Greçia asked.

"Allow me," Richard offered. "Mother, have you finished considering the rest of those lessons you wanted me to write up?"

Characteristically, Müther was not to be diverted. "Lian Ellen, please tell me what you are working on so vigorously."

"Oh, it's just a doodle," Ellen said. She closed the exercise book she had been writing in and put it into a small bag. "If there is pendle, do you think there might be one of those nut biscuits with it?"

Müther pressed on. "Please tell us about your doodle."

"Oh, no. It's not really – I don't write – you know – write things for people – I mean – in Si'Em, well, I used to try my hand with Cheng Yi. He's–" Ellen stopped herself. *I don't have to justify this to Müther!*

Müther, apparently, thought so too: "Such humility does not become you," she scoffed.

From the corner of her eye, Ellen saw Greçia close her eyes, lips pursing into disapproval, and Richard gave his head a small shake. Neither liked the way Müther sometimes treated her.

"I don't know how you can hear anything above the wind that's screaming outside," Greçia said. "Lian Ellen, I think a biscuit would be a good idea – although you've already had three."

"It can't be three biscuits, I'm sure I haven't had a biscuit for a week," Ellen said.

"I am genuinely curious, Lian Ellen. I often hear you scribbling away and I am genuinely curious about what you write."

"Doubtless so you can criticise it," Greçia sighed.

"I will not!" Müther flared indignantly. "Art is not for tearing apart. It is for understanding and, sometimes, that means critique. I have had more than a little critique with what I have produced over the years."

"The difference is, mother," Richard said gently, as he filled a pendle pot with hot artesian water, "you wanted your work to be known and Lian Ellen has just said she does not."

Müther ignored him. "Lian Ellen. I would like to hear what you have written. Please indulge me."

Seeing a flush beginning to creep up Greçia neck and Richard shake his head again, Ellen thought it best to calm the rising emotions and make light of her reluctance. After all, she used to eagerly share all that she wrote, in spite of her father's displeasure at her pursuits as a budding author. Her reluctance now only came when she noticed that blood and bitterness had crept increasingly into her imaginings. These were not stories she wanted to share. "I think if I have at least two biscuits with my pendle I could be persuaded to read a poem."

Two biscuits arrived on a plate.

Ellen glanced at the food, hiding her smile. Müther might be the one pushing for a reading, but she wasn't the only one interested.

Ellen turned to a page of her exercise book that showed a neatly written poem, and cleared her throat.

> *The blue sky beyond my window*
> *Beckons with blind promises*
> *Green trees seduced by the summons*
> *Rustle praise in the breeze*
> *I consider the bounds of infinity*
> *and children in the Square*
> *Their voices spiral upwards*
> *their games the whole world*

I smile at my fancies
And savour the childsong
The blue sky beckons
Only dreams its intent

"Oh! That's lovely," Greçia said. "I would never think of writing anything like that."

Müther sipped at the pendle Richard had poured into her special mug. "The imagery is crafted. But – I am curious. Why did you not read the poem you were working on?"

Richard dropped his head into his hands with a soft moan, but Ellen grinned, wondering how Müther knew.

"Alright," she said. "I will read you that poem – though you will wonder at it because it makes no sense." She flipped through her exercise book until she came to pages that were a mess of crossed out and inserted words. Bits of eraser rubber rolled off the paper as she smoothed the binding open. She tucked her hands under her thighs – in spite of herself, she always became nervous when reciting lines she had created but was unsure about – leant over her book and began to read.

I walked the stone-strewn road,
Dust over the toes
Of my shiny shoes.
Around me the field of green
Glowed
And on it walked the three.
"Who are they?" I asked.
"Oh," my companion replied.
"They are the immortals."
Gabriel, The Whale
And one without a name.
There and known
But forgotten.

THE TELLING

They walked
The Three
To the grand old house.
Their countenance radiant.
In the doorway they paused.
Gabriel said: "There is wrong here!"
To the depths they hastened.
Gabriel's wings swept the air.
Before them
A brook with clear, singing waters
In which the children played.
Among them a man rose
As the three approached.
He ran.
They at his heels.
Pursuit.
On and on.
Not frantic.
Just behind.
A journey.
Gabriel strode strong,
Body noble, face pure.
The Whale effeminate,
Soft and kind.
"Do you remember being born?"
The One Without a Name asked.
"I do," said Gabriel. "A cloud, born in the sky."
"And you, Whale? Do you remember?"
The Whale looked wistful.
Gabriel laughed.
"The Whale is old," he said.
"Birth is no longer a memory."
"I long to be born," said

The One Without a Name
The words murmured with yearning.
Before them the pursued mounted stairs
That receded as he climbed.
And he?
He turned white.
Ethereal.
To disappear on the final step.
They followed.
They knew.
It was an end.
Or a beginning.
To freeze on the final step.
"We are in a picture."
It was The Whale who spoke,
as she gazed out.
Eyes liquid.
Empathetic.
The One Without a Name saw
Before them sat a woman.
A baby at her breast.
Her brown head bent in love.
The child her world.
Otherwise alone.
Lonely.
She turned her face.
Raised her eyes.
She saw
The One.
"When she dies I'll have her name."
The thought was sad.
For birth a death.
My shoes are shiny

Under the dust.
The fields around me verdant.
And this?
This is a dream.

Ellen closed her book and slid it into her bag.

Silence.

She wallowed to try to ease her nervousness, hoping her heartbeat had not sounded in her voice. *Well,* she thought as she picked up a biscuit and dunked it in her pendle, *I knew they'd think it was strange. It is strange. It was just a funny dream I had last night. Sometimes I like to write about my dreams. Maybe one day I will write something about that woman with the child. And maybe I'll write about how sad the one without a name is. I just like to record some of my dreams in poems.*

"How did you come by that poem?" Müther asked at last.

"It was a dream. Like it says –"

Outside the persistent sound of wind was drowned by a deep roar that shook windows and furniture. In the adjoining grotto, Phan, the goats and the chickens began to bawl and screech loudly. The four at the kitchen table held their breath, all movement frozen. Slowly, the roar faded. Before anyone could relax, sound exploded again into the room. Phan hurtled through the doorway, his arms over his head. He looked around wildly then threw himself at Richard clutching hold of him, whimpering pathetically.

Phan was followed by a stampede of goats.

Greçia and Ellen jumped up to herd the goats out of the living area and back into their pens.

"It's only an avalanche, Phan," Richard told the frightened man, patting him placatingly on his broad back. "Come on. We have to get the goats out of here. They will make a mess."

In Si'Em City people were jolted from their beds, objects clattered along the floor and shelves spilled their contents. A chasm opened up in Si'Em Square but no one saw because it lay deep under snow. The same rent snapped through the main lift well of the city, ensuring it would take even more ingenuity to make the lifts work again.

Chithra, deeply immersed in solitary research for her second doctorate – the first had been in the field of jurisprudence and this was in the field of economics and law – overbalanced in her chair, landing heavily on the floor where she could feel the shudder of the earth through her body.

Redel woke groggily from a deep sleep, induced by medication that Lian Pethrie had prescribed for a headache he had been suffering from for several days. "Stress," Lian Pethrie had declared, noting the deep lines circling his eyes. Redel sat up in his shaking bed and stared around his bedroom: the pictures on his walls were swinging from side to side; the ornaments on his shelves were jumping up and down; the computer monitors on his desk rattled against one another.

Rebel bowed his head, accepting that he was being sent yet another message from God. He settled back against his pillow, promising whoever was sending the message that he would deal with it as soon as he woke.

In the Layamlé, the vast, ancient ceiling light sconce cracked in several places before it broke apart, showering shards of crystal down on to the unfortunate people settling down for the night.

In the Central Lands the slope above the Fadil grotto heaved snow and rocks into the valley, blocking entrances to the Fadil grottos and smashing into the villagers' living spaces.

CHAPTER 26
The Oldest Dance

THE COMING OF SPRING had released people, goats and chickens from the confines of the grotto, and Rosa from her hibernation. Blood quickened in everyone's veins as eagerly as the bursts of life over the landscape. Ellen had offered help where she could to sweep away winter and prepare the foundations for the summer harvest. She had even helped to muck out the goats' grotto, shovelling a winter's worth of goat and chicken droppings into wheelbarrows to be emptied into the Chess River ravine.

Now, in a lull in the work, she had wandered away from the grotto and settled on her haunches at the edge of a small plateau overlooking the river ravine.

She fell into deep thought, her brows drawing together as she stared, unseeing, into the frothing waters of the winter melt far below. She was thinking about Phan. Something about him scratched at her intuition and had been doing so since an incident that had occurred one evening this past winter.

She had seen Phan grudgingly follow Greçia into the bathroom and taken her chance to visit the hibernating Rosa – something she did from time to time to escape the closeness of winter living when she knew that Phan was occupied elsewhere.

It did not seem that she had been long with the bird – perhaps she had fallen asleep – when she noticed the outline of a figure crouched in front of her. Alarmed, she groped for the torch she always carried into the grotto and activated it with a few quick pumps. Dark eyes blinked and Ellen drew away with a small cry, for an instant mistaking Phan for Redel. Her initial relief at realising her error was cut short when she saw that Phan had opened the fly of his trousers and was holding his large and distended penis in one hand. He grunted, coming closer to her, gesturing towards his penis and towards her. She drew back, panicked again. Phan tipped his head a little to the side, a small, puzzled frown puckering his brow. More hesitantly, he offered her his penis again, his soft grunts questioning.

"No!" Ellen gasped. "No!" Seeing that the word halted Phan's gestures, she gathered her wits and said firmly. "Put it away, Phan. I don't want it."

Phan's face collapsed into disappointment. Tears gathered in his eyes and he looked at her pleadingly. When she shook her head again, he turned his gaze down and his penis became quite flaccid in his hand.

"Put it away, Phan," she said, trying to speak calmly, past the deafening hammer of her heart. For some reason Phan reminded her so much of Redel that she kept having to blink to get the figure of Phan to crouch before her and not Redel.

Obediently, Phan fumbled his trousers closed. He turned his face, streaked with tears, towards her. His longing was as palpable as her fear. One part of her wanted to comfort him. A stronger part of her wanted to be far away from him.

"Did you have something to eat yet?" she had asked, coming to her feet.

Phan turned his back to her, head hung low, his great shoulders shaking with sobs.

"Shall I get you something?"

He shook his head, shambled over to his bed and lay down. She could hear his sniffles as she made her way back out of the grotto.

Phan had made no further overtures towards her, but she now interpreted his glances in a different way and was cautious about being alone with him.

But something bothered her more than his obvious sexual attraction towards her.

Ellen heard scuffed footsteps and swivelled her head towards the sound.

A rope, set at waist height, followed the path that ran from Greçia's home along the cliff edge to Ellen's plateau. Müther was walking along the path, tracing the sensitive end of the stump of her left arm along the rope to guide herself.

Ellen shuffled back from the edge and watched Müther's progress. On the one hand she hoped the woman would not notice her, on the other hand she felt the need to perform the simple courtesy of identifying her presence.

Still several metres away, Müther stopped abruptly, her face tilted slightly up, nostrils flaring.

"Lian Ellen," she said. "Are you taking the air also?"

"I am," Ellen replied.

"I could smell you. You are never hard to smell. Your scent is a strong mixture of soap and Rosa."

Ellen absorbed this information in silence.

Müther turned her head from side to side. "I assume the beast is nearby."

"Rosa is slightly up the slope to your right. She is demolishing a bush to get at roots she particularly savours."

"And you? What are you doing?"

"I am simply sitting here enjoying the scenery."

Müther's lips tightened briefly and the skin around the scars where her eyes had been crinkled.

Regret? Ellen wondered.

"What do you see?" Müther asked.

"I am sitting on the edge of a slab of black rock that has tipped over and wedged into a scree slope. The slope tumbles all the way into the Chess River's gorge a hundred metres or so below. Snowmelt has filled the gorge with frothy water with a slight tinge of blue. There are also icebergs swirling about in the water. One has wedged into a depression and has little hollows in it. The other side of the gorge is steep and sheer. Every crevice still holds snow, but snow flowers – snowweed flowers – are showing. They are a lime-yellow colour and they are everywhere in the little snow-free pockets on the cliff. On this side, on the scree slope, many plants are in leaf. Most of the snow has gone. Most plants are in flower. Even I can smell the flowers."

"Mostly brimald, pendleweed, jaline, sweensbee, blonalth," Müther said.'I imagine the slope is an astonishing hue of scarlets and pinks, with touches of white."

"Yes. Pale green leaves seem to catch at the shadows under the blossoms. I can just see the end of the suspension bridge to my left. A little while ago I saw Phan, Richard and Greçia finish securing the bridge to make it safe to cross again." Most of the bridge had been dismantled when snowfall began. It isolated Greçia's grotto – and, of course, prevented Greçia from working in Sinthén – but it was a necessary precaution to safeguard the bridge from winter storms and the weight of snow. Besides, it was almost impossible to travel around Si'Empra in winter, bridge or no bridge. "Then I saw Greçia disappear around a bend on the way to Sinthén to her clinic. To my right and in the distance, I can see the dark ridges of the Central Lands. It is a very clear day. I can see the Barrier Cliffs. The top of the cliffs is clear, though it looks like there is a very strong wind blowing up there; the clouds are racing. The cliffs look close enough to touch."

Müther's head moved slightly this way and that while Ellen spoke. Ellen imagined her drawing a picture in her mind.

"You forgot to mention the green orchids near where you sit," Müther said.

Ellen looked around, searching for the tiny, bright green flowers. Now that Müther mentioned it, she could also smell the orchids. "I see them now. They are indeed close by, tucked under a rock and growing on a mossy clump. There are about – maybe six or seven of them, each growing on a long, thin stem."

"I have heard that your eyes are the colour of the orchid flower."

Ellen glanced at the emerald flowers again. "I have heard that also."

Müther smiled tightly. She turned away from the breeze, facing the slope behind the plateau.

"Pedro would bring me here sometimes and we would dance in spring," she said. "He dances well."

Ellen, surprised that Müther would reveal such an intimacy to her, responded: "I, too, have had the pleasure of Pedro's dancing."

"Oh? And what dance would he have done with you?"

Ellen stood up. "If you like, I will dance the dance with you."

Müther hesitated, but, as Ellen had foreseen, curiosity won over reserve.

Ellen guided her off the path to a flat, stone-free patch of grass.

Facing her, Ellen held Müther's arms along the length of her own. Swaying slightly and rhythmically, she whispered the words. "Click, clack, click clack."

Müther's eyebrows snapped up in astonishment.

After a very short hesitation and in a slightly diffident tone, Müther responded: "Click on rock, clack on rock."

Ellen nodded, satisfied that Müther had agreed to the challenge.

This was the oldest dance. Pedro had taught it to her but she had practised it with others also. It was a dance that combined increasingly complex foot movements with word play. Without hands and without sight, Müther was at a great disadvantage. Ellen knew that the older woman would judge her not only on how cleverly she performed the dance, but also on how well she helped her blind partner.

Ellen changed the grip on Müther's arms. In silent understanding, Müther pressed her lower arms over Ellen's to help her with balance; it was an act of total trust.

They came to this arrangement so quickly that the rhythm of their words was not broken.

"Together we'll find the Cryptal crack," Ellen chanted, lifting her feet now in time with the syllables of the words. "Click clack click clack," she repeated, hopping from one foot to the other.

"Click on rock, clack on rock," Müther responded with a stamp hop, stamp hop hop. "Together we'll find the Cryptal crack." Three hops on the right, one to the left, one to the right, hop to the left, two hops to the right, stamp the left.

Müther smiled and took up the beginning of the chant. "Click, clack, click clack." After the third repetition, Ellen changed the beginning of the rhythm. "Crystal creature, crystal creature." The rules were intricate, the soft 'Crys' sound required a side shuffle by the left foot before the right was released for the hop. In the first round Müther could simply still hop from foot to foot as she had before, but in the second repetition she would have to remember the change. Ellen had elected three repetitions to help the memory.

Müther could change her words too, but they had to hold the same basic rhythm; the idea was to increase the ornamentation of the steps while keeping that rhythm. Partners could lead to complexity or back to simplicity.

The two danced on that patch of grass for some time. Müther lost her remaining reserve quickly to the pleasure of movement and rhyme. Several times she burst into laughter when the momentum of steps tangled her legs and stretched her memory.

Ellen's enjoyment was more muted. She could not afford to let her concentration slip. Not only did she find it difficult to coordinate her movements exactly so that Müther could feel and hear her steps, she had to choose the words that Müther would immediately associate with certain steps. That meant recalling all the most popular lines from dances. Now was not the time for Ellen to be clever.

Eventually they released each other, having brought the dance back to its original simplicity.

Müther pushed hair aside from her scarlet, perspiring face. "Pedro taught you that?" she panted.

"Yes." Ellen inspected Müther's face minutely, trying to read her thoughts.

"It is a forbidden dance," Müther said. "It was forbidden by your grandfather because of its close association with Cryptals and Crystalmakers. I cannot imagine it is now again allowed."

"No. Indeed. It is still forbidden. My father did not often beat me, but he caught me practising once and I felt his hand."

"But you continued to dance?"

"Of course. His reaction just made me more curious about the dance. And more sneaky."

"Did he ask who taught you?"

Ellen snorted a laugh. "I told him I'd seen some children dance it in Si'Em Square."

"You lied to you father?"

"I did that from time to time."

Müther inclined her head. "But I can tell that you know the dance better than even Pedro does. There were moves I have never felt him make."

"Many in Si'Empra still dance, and I dance with them."

Müther was silent for some time. "Why?"

"Because I see no sense not to. The dance is part of what defines us."

"Why does what defines us matter to you?"

"How else do we create cohesion and purpose in our society?"

Müther smiled – an enigmatic smile. "You would create cohesion and purpose?"

Oh dear, thought Ellen resignedly. *Here we go again.*

Sure enough, Müther's next question was as Ellen feared: "Will you challenge Redel?"

"No."

"Why not, Lian Ellen?"

Because I don't want to be Ülrügh! Ellen wanted to shout, but there was a deeper reason. "Though the Lianthem now rules weakly, the foundations of our organisation sit with them. There is little support for me in the Lianthem. A challenge against Redel would only harden attitudes against me."

Another enigmatic smile. "Hmm. I see. Tell me – I have heard that Lian Chithra continues to be very powerful in the Lianthem."

"Yes. She is."

"Did she do anything at all when I – disappeared –"

"I was not born yet so I don't know for sure. I am told that after the incident the relationship between my father and Lian Chithra became very icy, though they continued to work with one another as if they had some sort of hold on each other. Perhaps some secret they shared? I don't know."

"Bed secrets," Müther said with a rueful grin. "He bedded Chithra as often as he bedded Thea. They were twins though they looked nothing alike."

Ellen felt a jolt, pieces of a puzzle suddenly becoming clearer.

"What would you do if you were Ülrügh?" Müther continued.

Recalled from her sudden whirl of realisations, Ellen said: "What? Oh Müther, let us not go there."

Müther extended an arm towards Ellen, reaching forward until she found a shoulder. Ellen did not move as the smooth stump travelled to her face, over her lips, up her cheek, resting on an eye and finally over her forehead and into her hair.

"Ahhh," Müther murmured softly, more to herself than Ellen. "I miss my hands. More than my eyes, I miss my hands."

Müther dropped her arm to her side. "My name is Grace," she told Ellen. "Grace."

Reacting to the depth of regret in Müther's tone, Ellen said, "Though I call you Müther, I know you are Lian Grace, the Songbird and a member of the Lianthem whose insight and courage has been so poorly recognised by those who should know better."

Müther – Lian Grace – the Songbird of Si'Empra – said: "Who has taken my place on the Lianthem?"

"No one. My father resisted all attempts to have your place filled and it suits the current Lianthem not to have the full complement of lians."

Müther said softly: "You know, Lian Ellen, for the first time in twenty years, as this winter has drawn closer to its end, I dare to believe that my exile could come to an end. I believe you will be our future Ülrügh."

To Ellen's consternation, Müther slowly dropped to her knees. "And I promise that when that occurs, I will serve you with every fibre of my being."

Dear Reader

Book 2, *Ülrügh, will answer many of the questions you still have; and Book 3, Virigin's Lure, will answer the rest.*

If you have not already subscribed to my mailing list, consider doing so to receive updates.

My website, www.miriamverbeek.com, has lots more information about Si'Empra.

THERE IS NOTHING THAT rewards artists more than if others enjoy their works. I would be delighted if you could provide some feedback.

Since I am a self-published author, your feedback is also important for others. Please let me and others know what you think of this book by writing a comment on either my webpage, www.miriamverbeek.com, Facebook fb.me/verbeekmiriam, twitter @miriamverbeek (#SkyseekerPrincess), and/or completing a feedback request on your ereader.

If you liked my work, please also recommend it to your friends and through your social networks.

Thanks
Miriam

Acknowledgements

I TOLD MY SISTER ABOUT a dream I had once, and how it was somewhat bizarre, about aboveground and belowground people. We laughed about it and our conversation embroidered a little on the concept. My thanks to my sister for that conversation and for her patience in reading the eventual outcome of that interchange. Her comments were encouraging and insightful. Thanks also to my editors, whose meticulous attention to plot and detail have, I hope, been translated accurately by me into this final novel. Also my thanks to my sons, who encouraged me by cheerfully reading drafts and helping me with technical details. Also thanks to my friends, who delight me in speaking of the imaginary characters in this book as if they were real.

Thanks so much to my life partner for giving me the space to write.

About the Author

I'VE LOVED TO CREATE stories for as long as I can remember; characters come tumbling out of my brain and worlds develop around them. I have always wanted to be a writer but, somehow, life got in the way – with writing happening "in between". Not that I regret the eddies of my life. I grew up in a lovely, noisy, active, Dutch/Indonesian-origin migrant family, the second child of eight with a father and mother who knew how to laugh, had a keen interest in not taking anything for granted, and loved to philosophise and read books; they valued education and thoughtfulness. Reflecting now on my childhood, I often wonder why, given that I was often scribbling stories, that my parents didn't encourage me to take up a writing career. I asked my mother about it once (when I was already in my fifties); she said that "It just never occurred to us" – funnily enough, it never occurred to me either. Now, with my children grown up and the space to finally indulge, I've decided to bring my creations to the fore and show them to others.

There are thousands (millions!) of books around. Do we really need more? But there you are – I figure that, like for any creative endeavour, it is not that we "need" more stories or other works of art; but I hope, as any creator does, that the world will be a richer, more enjoyable place with the existence of my creations.

Glossary

Achton	Isolde's husband (Lian)
Adjutants	Redel's special guard
Auchust	Guild Master of Structure
Augustine	Priest
Bachar	Web Cleaner (child) – sings solo
Baltha	City near Si'Em City
Barth	Gunman a in Fadil
Briani	Ellen's father (Ülrügh)
Brimald,	plants on the Chess River ravine
Cecil	Tax Collector (Lian)
Charn River	To the east of the Sith River
Cheng Yi	Miner and seller of gems
Chithra	Chancellor (Lian)
Chris	Web Cleaner (harvester)
Chrystal	Redel's daughter by Constance
Chuck	Charles Janson – US envoy
Cilla	Crystal Maker
Con	A member of Sam's family
Constance	Ellen's mother
Dane	Dominant hothouse owner (Lian)
Devi	Briani's father (ülrügh)

Ellen	Half-sister of Redel
Elthán	Ellen's grandmother
Fadil	Scene of tax collector incident
Ghuy	Headman of Fadil Village
Gigi	Cheng Yi's daughter
Greçia	Doctor at Sinthén
Hawkberry	A plant with a minty smell with a touch of rose
Heinie	Web Cleaner
Hochhein	Maker of web cloth (Web Cleaner)
Illiath	Belowground Crystmaker city
Isoldé	Deranged wife of Achton (Lian)
Jailene	Woman beyond the Barrier Cliffs
Jaline	plant on the Chess River ravine
Jan	German envoy
Jenjen	Web Cleaner (child)
Jess	José's partner
Jon	Chitra's administrative aid
Joosthin	Guild Master of Crystal
José	Sathun's eldest son
Josie	Web Cleaner with scald damage to face (child)
Julian	Owns much property (Lian)
Katherina	Ellen's nursemaid
Lalloon	Sleek beast, the size of a small dog
Lara	Acolyte of the Weavers Guild
Layamlé	Si'Em City's vast, communal chamber,
Lian	Equivalent to 'Lady' or Lord
Lianthem	Equivalent to the ruling council
Lithilian berries	special berries for making a kind of wine
Lonna	Web Cleaner (child)
Luman	Lian Julian's grandson
Moolan	Sathun's grandchild

Müther	Mother of Richard
Northern Lands	Summer dwelling for Richard and Müther
Overshot Gorge	Separates the Si'Em Bluff
Pedro	Ellen's grandfather
Pendleweed	Plants on the Chess River ravine
Pethrie	Crystal Maker
Pethrie	Gynecologist
Pethry	Web Cleaner (child)
Phan	Goatherd living with Greçia
Phiet	Nurse at Grecia's Crystal Maker clinic
Redel	Ülrügh of Si'Empra
Richard	Müther's son
River Orb	East of Thuls Refuge
Rosa	The glasaur
Sam	Captured by Redel (Crystal Maker)
samira	A musical instrument
Sara	Guild Master of Weaving
Sathun	Leader of Thuls Refuge
schathem	Si'Empran traditional climbing game
Serai	Equivalent to 'palace'
Serge	Sam's brother (Crystal Maker)
Shivay	Eurologist (Lian)
Si'Em Bluff	Into which Si'Em City is built
Si'Em City	main city on the island
Si'Empra	name of island
Si'Empra Mayal	Songbird of Si'Empra
Si'Empra Theolel	The Jewel of Si'Empra
Sienne	Refugees from Devi's time (Lian)
Sinthen	linked to Baltha by a road
Sira	Companion of Thanin
Sith Chamber	A huge cave used by the harvesters

Sith Cliffs	North of the Sith River
Sith River	To the west of the Charn River
solnis	Hunting animal
Sonia	Crystal Maker
Stephan	French envoy
Sweensbee	Plants on the Chess River ravine
Tham	Nurse at Grecia's Crystal Maker clinic
Thanin	Web Cleaner (deputy to Elthan)
Tharnie	Guild Master of Design
Tharyl	In charge of Crystal Maker food storage
The Barrier Cliffs	Separates the The Others
The Lost City	On top of the Barrier Cliffs
The Shoals	Skyseeker rubbish dump
Thea	Briani's first wife (Lian)
Theon	Refugees from Devi's time (Lian)
Theresa	Sathun oldest daughter
Thil	Illiath Gate Master
Thimon	Web Cleaner (harvester)
Thobias	Engineer (Lian)
Thordilones	A musical instrument
Thrake	Orthopedic surgeon
Thren	Joosthin's friend and Overcome
Thull	Son of Theon
Thyrol	Web Cleaner
Trebiath	Belowground Crystmaker city
WhiteŌne	Source of Song
Whyphoon	Elthan's teacher (Master)
Zarl	Acolyte to Joosthin

Made in the USA
Middletown, DE
25 September 2018